BL   S

Mart   Brien was educated at the Oratory School and Hertford Coll   Oxford. He was travel editor of British *Vogue* in the 1970s and   ritten for a number of international publications. After twen   years on the road Marseilles remains one of his favourite desti   ns. He is the author of five previous crime novels – *Jacquot and   aterman, Jacquot and the Angel, Jacquot and the Master, Jacq   the Fifteen* and *Confession.*

MARTIN O'BRIEN

BLOOD COUNTS

arrow books

This paperback edition published by Arrow Books 2011

10 9 8 7 6 5 4 3 2 1

First published in Great Britain in 2010 by Preface Publishing
20 Vauxhall Bridge Road
London SW1V 2SA

An imprint of The Random House Group Limited

www.randomhouse.co.uk

Addresses for companies within The Random House Group Limited
can be found at www.randomhouse.co.uk

The Random House Group Limited Reg. No. 954009

A CIP catalogue record for this book is available from the British Library

ISBN 978 1 84809 059 0

Typeset in Times by Palimpsest Book Production Limited,
Falkirk, Stirlingshire

Printed and bound in Great Britain by CPI Bookmarque Ltd, Croydon, CR0 4TD

For Susan and Simon,
my other editors
at 20 BWD

1998

There were seven entry wounds – four in one body, three in the other – but only two of these wounds had been fatal.

The first of the killing shots was effected by a 9x19mm Parabellum cartridge fired from a police Beretta 92G at a range of no more than ten metres. Milliseconds after leaving the muzzle of the Beretta it broke through the skull of Taddeus Manichella two centimetres above the right eyebrow, mashing a path through the soft tissue of the frontal lobe and exiting four centimetres behind and below the left ear.

The second killing shot was another 9x19mm Parabellum bullet, also fired from a police Beretta 92G at a similar range, entering Tomas Manichella's chest four centimetres to the left of the mid-sternal line, shredding the muscled anterior wall of the heart, cutting down through the lungs and lodging in the lower spine.

During the police pathologist's autopsy which followed the shoot-out in the Roucas Blanc district of Marseilles only two bullets were retrieved from the brothers' bodies, leaving a total of twelve entry and exit wounds. None of these wounds was treated except for the massive cranial damage to the back of Taddeus Manichella's head where a wedge of gauze dressing was applied and bandaged into place to contain the splintered remains of the skull and to prevent any further leakage.

After three weeks in police custody, the refrigerated bodies of the twin brothers were shipped on an overnight SNCM ferry from Marseilles to their home in Corsica. For ease of transport the thick, black and zippered plastic bags containing their bodies had been put into two deal coffins. On arrival in Ajaccio, after passengers had disembarked from the vehicle ramp and companionways, the cargo hold was opened and the coffins discreetly transported to a dockside warehouse. It was there, in the late-afternoon, that two women, the twins' sisters, took possession of the caskets, driving them back to the family farm in the village of Tassafaduca, high in the hills above Corte.

As is the custom in such remote and isolated settlements the first thing the women did was to open the caskets, unzip the bags and lay out the bodies on trestle tables in the kitchen. They did this alone, that first night, after the children had been settled in the roof space of the old family home and their elderly parents seen off to bed. By the light of a low-wattage ceiling light and a scattering of home-made candles, the two women washed their brothers' bodies and plugged their wounds with a thick poultice of honey, chestnut flour, macerated myrtle leaves and crushed arbutus berries.

Wounds washed with love, plugged with hatred.

They worked in silence, one sister to one brother, their fingers soon red and aching with cold, the putrefying stink of the bodies barely disguised by the smoky tallow scent of the candles and the sweet perfumes of the honey and herbs. When the two bodies had been properly prepared and dressed in clean clothes they were returned to their caskets with red coral charms clasped in their hands, and the night-time shadows of the old farmhouse were filled with a light tap-tap-tapping as the lids were secured for the final time.

At eleven o'clock the following morning the caskets were taken from the family home and carried in slow and sombre procession through the steep tilting streets of Tassafaduca to the church of Sant' Anselmo. There, with family and villagers crowding into the icy nave, prayers were said and blessings given before the brothers were delivered to the village's small hillside cemetery, their caskets lowered into a single shallow pit, jerking and tipping on their ropes, rough wooden edges scraping against the stony sides of the grave until they lay five feet down, one beside the other, heads pointing north.

It had taken two days to dig this pit with spade and pick-axe, three of the twins' cousins volunteering for the task. Another month and the two coffins would have been left in a barn for the winter, or a fire would have been lit and kept alight long enough to soften the ground for digging. But the snow had not yet come, just a dusting on the distant peaks of Monte Cinto in the west and on Pica Tassa to the north. In its place, that bleak winter morning, came a chill, shawling drizzle that silvered the mourners' best black homburgs, stiff black suits and woollen headscarves, all hands gloved or pocketed against a sharp little breeze that whipped through the chestnut trees and snatched at the brown tufted grass.

On these hillsides Taddeus and Tomas had played as boys, and as young men they had learnt to hunt here – boar and partridge and quail – before the summons came to leave the island and serve their master. At twenty they had gone, and more than twenty years later they had come home for good, attended now by a silent, jostling crowd of mourners. At their head was the twins' nodding father, borne along in his favourite chair by four burly nephews and set beside the single grave, with their shawled, whiskered stub of a mother at his side, shuffling rosary beads through crooked fingers. Then came their two sisters, their five uncles, assorted cousins and family friends, and the elders of the village of Tassafaduca, its slate walls and steeply pitched roofs crowding together on the slope below the cemetery.

No tear was spilled. No flower was laid. Just pale faces framed in black, and dark, dulled eyes cast down towards the hard ground. They had done this before, all of them gathered there. In these distant hills they knew death, just as they knew life, and neither held any surprise for them. It was the way things were. Life and death. Just that. And as the single, hollow bell of Sant' Anselmo tolled through the valley of Tassafaduca, taken up by the nearby campanile *of Cabrillio and Borredonico and Scarpetta, and the first shovelful of earth and stone drummed over the wooden lids of the twins' coffins, the mourners turned their backs on the grave and made their way home.*

But it wasn't over.

And the brothers Taddeus and Tomas Manichella were not forgotten.

Part One

1

1999

IT WAS A SPRING WEDDING. A country wedding. A twenty
minute drive from Cavaillon, on the northern slopes of the Grand
Luberon, in a meadow as green as Eden, under a milky sapphire
sky. And most of the guests, Jacquot could tell at a glance, were
country people. The suits the men wore gave the game away, either
too tight – not yet old or worn enough to justify a fresh purchase –
or a size too large, as though room had been left for growth, or its
owner had shrunk with age. Collar tips were turned up, shirt cuffs
buttoned and frayed, ties loud and wide, faces nut brown, stiff hair
brushed flat. Their smiles and gusts of laughter were as broad and
as big as the land, and their voices rang out in a jolly *patois*.

As for the women, Jacquot decided, their outfits were gay and
colourful and festive but had about them a sense of 'best'. They
looked like the kinds of dresses that had served as long and as
well as their men's suits, bought from a catalogue, or a market somewhere, or years earlier from fashionable boutiques in Cavaillon or
Apt, or cut from patterns on kitchen tables. Taken from creaking
armoires, hung up in the shade to air out any mustiness, maybe dry-
cleaned for the occasion, they were worn with an easy, comfortable
familiarity.

The only items of dress that appeared to cause any real discomfort, however, were shoes, men and women's both. Brightly polished

7

and sensibly heeled they may have been, but Jacquot could sense their pinching grip, their stiff ungiving edges, the way their owners swayed between the tables set beneath the trees, the way they stood chatting in groups, lifting a foot like a horse lifts a hoof, just to ease the weight off biting leather. And when they started to dance on the large squares of ply pegged out on a stretch of level ground, not a few of the women kicked off the offending items. Harder for the men – stooping to untie all those laces.

It was late afternoon now and the rain that had threatened had failed to show, the sun still bright and warm as it slipped down through the branches, dappling the cloth on Jacquot's table – thick white damask, crumpled now, ringed and stained with spilled wine, spotted with grease from the hog-roast sandwiches they'd all fetched themselves from the firepit. It was, he decided, tipping back the last of his coffee and glancing at his watch, just about time to call it quits and head home. It had been a long day.

They had arrived at the church in St-Florent at eleven that morning – Jacquot in linen suit and loafers, Claudine in a matching light blue jacket and sleeveless dress that he hadn't seen before. She looked long and lean in the outfit, the jacket high off the waist, the dress's satin sheen sharpening slim hips, firm breasts and flat stomach; tanned legs in blue court shoes, long neck sliced with a single string of pearls, dark hair caught up and combed into a tight little chignon. They'd sat at the back of the church, by the stone font, because they weren't really family enough to claim anywhere nearer to the altar. The invitation from *famille* Blanchard had been sent to Claudine in recognition of the help she'd given the bride's younger sister preparing her art-work portfolio for admission to Aix's École des Beaux Arts. When their daughter was subsequently awarded a place, Blanchard *Père et Mère* were convinced that Claudine, who sometimes lectured at the school, must have pulled some strings with the admissions board, rather than believe in their daughter's talent. And so, the invitation.

As for Jacquot, he recognised some of the faces from town, men and women both, knew one or two of the names, had once sorted

8

out a quarrel between two of them over a boundary wall, for which both parties – now reconciled – gave him bone-crushing hand-shakes and mighty slaps on the back. And though he didn't realise it at first, when bride and groom came down the aisle arm in arm at the end of the service, he knew the groom too. Or rather, it turned out, the groom knew him, or knew of him.

Standing in line at the firepit, the young man had come over to Jacquot and introduced himself.

'Noël Gilbert, Chief Inspector. Police Nationale, Marseilles. I saw you at Roucas Blanc last year. The Cabrille place.'

'Daniel. The name's Daniel,' he replied, shaking the offered hand, taking in the sharply cut black hair, spiky on the neck and above the ears, the red cheeks, the tiny shaving nick on the point of the chin. He didn't recognise the lad, but he remembered the Cabrille place in Roucas Blanc, the shoot-out he'd missed by a matter of minutes, the blood on the garage walls, on the floor, the sharp scent of cordite and the tell-tale faecal stink of a stomach wound.

'You were there? With Peluze?'

The younger man nodded, letting go of Jacquot's hand.

'If it weren't for Chief Inspector Peluze I wouldn't be here now. Pulled me down behind an old Porsche when the bullets started flying. What a noise in that garage. First time under fire and, well, I suppose I was frightened. I didn't know what to do.' He shrugged, spread his hands in a there-you-are gesture.

'You'd be lying if you'd said any different. We all would. And it doesn't change. Don't let anyone tell you otherwise. A gun's always a gun. And a bullet may be small . . .'

'She's clear, you know? Off the hook.'

Jacquot frowned, took another step closer to the firepit, the smell of roasting pork thick and succulent, carried on a smoky breeze.

'The Cabrille woman?'

'Mademoiselle Virginie Cabrille. All charges dropped.'

'You're kidding?'

Gilbert shook his head.

'Nothing. Free to walk.'

9

Jacquot was stunned by the news. Kidnap, attempted murder, murder . . . It couldn't be.

'But we found the Lafour girl on her boat . . . And Chief Inspector Gastal dead in her basement. And the two *gorilles* . . .'

'She had a lawyer down from Paris. Slippery as a peeled grape, he was. He wouldn't let us pin a thing on her. No charges filed.'

Jacquot noted that 'us' – the police as family, the team. He had a feeling this young man might go far.

'So you're not in Marseilles these days?' the groom asked.

'Cavaillon,' replied Jacquot. 'They put me out to graze.'

Gilbert took this in, nodded, cast around for his new wife. They both spotted her at the same time, a dozen tables away, surrounded by a gaggle of great-aunts and grandmothers, a tall, big-boned country girl in an off-the-shoulder gown that showed a generous swell and plunge of cleavage. In church the shoulders, and cleavage, had been concealed, her hair piled high beneath the veil; now the veil was gone and the hair was loose, a bundle of black curls tumbling over bare white shoulders. She had a lovely smile, thought Jacquot, and twinkling mischievous eyes. Gilbert had chosen well.

'You'd better go and rescue your wife,' said Jacquot, stepping up to the serving tables now, first in line at last, and holding out his two plates. Fat wedges of pork were carved off the haunch and dropped onto them, along with blistered belts of crackling, thick slices of buttered bread and a healthy sprinkle of rock salt on the side. 'Never a good idea to let the old ones give the young ones too much advice.'

'I think you might be right. So . . . if you'll excuse me, Chief Insp—'

'Daniel. At weddings I'm Daniel, remember?'

'Okay, okay. Thanks . . . Daniel.' He held out a hand, forgetting Jacquot's loaded plates. For a moment Gilbert wasn't sure what to do, a pat on the arm or back just a little too familiar with a senior officer, even at a wedding, even if said senior officer had told him, twice now, to use his christian name. Instead, he'd raised his hand – somewhere between a wave and a salute – and hurried off.

10

'You're dreaming.' It was Claudine, her shadow falling across the table, her hand sliding over Jacquot's shoulder. 'Whoosh,' she continued, pulling out a chair. 'That old farmer sure knows how to rock and roll. Had me in quite a spin.' She guided a stray wisp of hair back into the loosening chignon with long, delicate fingers, slipped off her shoes and laid her legs over Jacquot's knees. 'And you sitting here, a million miles away.'

'I was thinking . . .'

'Don't tell me if it's work . . . It's been too nice a day,' she replied, reaching across for the disposable camera left on each table. She wound on the film, pointed it at Jacquot and pressed the button.

'*En effet*, I was thinking,' he said, 'that maybe it's time I took you home . . .' He dropped a hand to her leg and let his fingers trail up her bare brown shin, rubbing her knee with his thumb when he reached that far, knuckles idling at the hem of her dress.

She gave him a long, cool look.

'I can tell when you're lying, Daniel Jacquot. And it won't work, you hear?'

'What? It's the truth.'

'And you want to leave? Just as things are hotting up?' She glanced back at the dance floor. The DJ's amplified but strangely muffled voice spread between the tables and out across the pasture. The sun had slipped behind the hills now but already there were lit candles on tables and lanterns in the branches. They darkened the sky, brought the night closer.

'You were the one who said she was tired.'

And it was true. At breakfast Claudine had complained of a poor night's sleep, the second or third in a row, and had sighed deeply at the thought of a long country wedding.

'That was earlier. Now I'm not.'

Jacquot shook his head and chuckled.

Claudine straightened her back.

'So? I've changed my mind. I'm a woman, I'm allowed. That's what we do, didn't you know? Just to keep you men on your toes. Talking of which . . .'

'Three dances – two fast, one slow,' he told her. 'The slow one to get you in the mood.'

'Three fast, two slow. I need priming.' She leant foward and ran her fingertips across his cheek.

'It's not fair. You're younger than me.'

'You want it the other way round, you should have settled on someone else, someone older, someone closer to your own age, *hein*? In their sixties, or maybe even their seventies; with one of those frames to help them get around.'

'You drive a hard bargain, Madame.'

His fingers flicked at the hem of Claudine's dress.

She brushed them away as she might a settling fly and raised her chin in that way she had – as though trying to see over his head. Haughty as hell. God, how he loved her when she did that.

Through the trees the first bluesy, bursting rhythms of a Jackie Wilson number blasted from the speakers. Both of them knew the song. A favourite. 'Higher and Higher'.

'Okay,' he said, shifting her legs from his lap and pulling her to her feet. 'You win.'

'That's right,' she replied, gripping his arm as she bent to pull on her shoes. 'And don't you ever forget it, Daniel Jacquot. *Allons-y.* We dance.'

2

IT WAS SHORTLY AFTER FOUR the following morning when the call came through. Claudine groaned as Jacquot reached out for the phone.

'*Oui?*'

'Boss, *c'est moi.*' It was Jean Brunet, his assistant.

Recognising the voice, Jacquot eased himself up on an elbow and peered at the bedside clock radio.

'Jean, what . . . ?'

'I know it's early, I know it's Sunday, but you'd better come. Le Mas Bleu, on the Maubec road. There's a body.'

Jacquot pressed his fingers into the corner of his eyes, rubbed his face, tried to wake himself up. A 'body' usually meant murder. Not an accident, not a suicide, but murder.

'Where on the Maubec road?'

'The new place. With the avenue of cypresses. Believe me, you can't miss it.'

Despite his assistant's confidence, Jacquot did miss it. Half-an-hour later, as the sky began to lighten over the Luberon heights, its wooded slopes looming ahead of him, Jacquot turned through Coustellet and started along the back lanes to Maubec. At the Maubec–Robion crossroads he looked left and right and took the former, giving it two kilometres before he decided he'd

13

made the wrong choice and turned back for Robion. A kilometre or so past the crossroads he saw the first sign – *Le Mas Bleu, à droite 100 mètres* – and a minute later he did as requested, turning between spotlit stone gateposts into a gravelled drive leading between six pairs of tapering cypress trees. At the end of the drive was another pillared gateway, smaller but no less grand, and beyond it Le Mas Bleu. Even with the sky lightening fast, its stone façade was spotlit, six lights spilling upwards between blue shuttered windows and either side of a double front door studded with blackened nail heads.

As he pulled up in the forecourt, he spotted Brunet lounging against the side of his squad car, chatting with a couple of uniformed *képis*. His assistant was a little shorter than his companions, lithe and lean in leather blouson, jeans and trainers, with a sharp, angular face below a thin crop of dark hair. In his spare time Brunet cycled with a local club – road-racing, hill-climbing and time trials – and the exercise showed in his wiry, muscled frame. Even when he was relaxing – leaning against the squad car as he was doing now, or sitting in a chair, or standing at a bar – there was always something coiled and dynamic about him, as though he was waiting for a flag to drop, or a starter's gun to fire. He was in his mid-thirties, single, and when work and training allowed as enthusiastic in his pursuit of women as he was in his cycling. His reputation in both areas of endeavour, Jacquot knew, was well-established and well-deserved.

Cutting short his conversation with the *képis*, Brunet hurried over.

'Welcome to Le Mas Bleu, Monsieur,' he said with a small bow, as though Jacquot were an arriving guest and he the manager.

Over Brunet's shoulder, Jacquot took in the sculpted olive trees either side of the front door and the blue-glazed pots of shooting lavender on each step. He'd heard of the place but never been here. Open just a couple of months, he seemed to recall. An old farmhouse and attached barn transformed into a bijoux little hostelry, beds covered in Provençal quilts and old stone walls

14

left bare, Jacquot suspected. He wondered what the food was like.

'So. You say we have a body?'

'Murder,' said Brunet, as they crossed the forecourt together. 'Woman, mid-twenties, a single gunshot wound. Husband swears he was asleep, didn't hear a thing.' Brunet looked doubtful. 'He's putting on a good show, mind you . . . the wide-eyed, stunned look. One of ours, too. Marseilles PD. Name of Gilbert. You want to have a word?'

Jacquot stopped in his tracks.

'Gilbert? Noël Gilbert?'

Brunet gave him a look. 'You know him?'

'He was married yesterday. I was at the wedding,' Jacquot explained, and they started forward again, a little faster this time, up the front steps and into the entrance hall. It was just as he'd expected: bare stone walls, terracotta pantiles for sconces, kelim rugs on polished wood floors, and a fine old fireplace exploding with stiff-stemmed, purple-tipped gladioli in more blue-glazed vases.

'That's what he told us,' said Brunet. 'That he'd just got married. But so far we don't even know the wife's name. Can't get anything else out of him. According to the hotel owner, a Monsieur Valbois, the room was reserved by Gilbert for one night only, and paid for on his credit card.'

'This Valbois, he knew it was a honeymoon booking?'

'Apparently Gilbert told him. Said he wanted the best room, but only gave a Marseilles address when he made the reservation. Didn't say anything about the bride . . . her name, where she lived, where the wedding was. Just said they'd be arriving late. I got in touch with Marseilles PD but so far they haven't been able to give us much more than his personnel file details. Parents dead. Lives alone in the family home. A couple of commendations. Future looks bright.'

'Where is he?' asked Jacquot.

'Valbois let us use one of his spare rooms. That's him, now.'

Across the hall a man in sleeveless cardigan, check shirt, cotton trousers and tasselled loafers came down the stone stairs and headed in their direction.

'He's by himself? Gilbert?' asked Jacquot, acknowledging Valbois with a brief nod, but keeping his attention on Brunet.

His assistant shook his head.

'There's a *képi* with him. In the room. And one outside.'

Jacquot nodded, then turned to the owner, gave him a short smile, shook his hand. A weak, damp handshake; long, tapered fingers and lacquered nails, Jacquot noted.

'Monsieur Valbois, I believe?'

'Clément Valbois. *Oui, c'est moi.*' The man looked to be in his early forties, slim and delicate, his narrow face pale with shock. 'But this is all so dreadful,' he said, hands pressed to his cheeks.

'Monsieur Valbois, I'm Chief Inspector Jacquot. From Cavaillon. Please . . .' He took the man's elbow and directed him to a pair of armchairs set either side of a painted longcase clock. A sunflower decorated the face of its circular pendulum and a low oily tick sounded from its chained mechanism. 'So, what can you tell me, Monsieur?' Jacquot asked, as they settled in their seats.

Perching on the edge of his chair, Valbois dropped his hands to his lap and leant forward.

'They arrived late, just after eleven, and went straight to their room.'

'You were here when they arrived?'

'My partner, Gunnar, he was here to welcome them. A bottle of champagne had already been sent up to their suite.'

'Gunnar . . . ?'

'Larsson. Gunnar Larsson.'

'And he is where, exactly?'

'In Aix. He left at midnight, when I took over.'

'Aix?'

'A party he just didn't want to miss.'

'So he doesn't know?'

Valbois shook his head.

'I didn't want to spoil his fun. He's been working so hard . . . '

'And when will Monsieur Larsson return?'

'Later this morning. For lunchtime. He'll be horrified.'

Jacquot nodded.

'Did he say anything to you about Monsieur and Madame Gilbert? Anything he might have noticed? Anything . . . strange?'

'Nothing. It was late. They were tired. He showed them up to their room and he left them.'

'So the first you knew about this was when Monsieur Gilbert called you? When he found the body?'

'He didn't call, Chief Inspector, he screamed. It was just after three. Everyone was woken. A terrible, terrible noise. Just this high-pitched screaming wail. I heard it down here.'

'You are full, Monsieur?'

'Just three other rooms, thank goodness.'

'So . . . six other guests?' Jacquot guessed.

'That's correct, Chief Inspector.'

'And when you heard this scream, you went to his room?'

'When I reached his floor he came running down the corridor towards me.' Valbois drew a breath. 'Completely naked. Screaming, *"Ma femme, ma femme. Elle est morte. Elle est morte."*'

'You went into their room?'

'I had no choice. He caught me, by my arm. Pulled me there. Back to their room. Persille. All the rooms are named after herbs. Persille is the largest, has the best view, and fully en suite . . .'

'So you have seen the body?'

Another deep breath. Valbois held it as though his life depended on it, and then let it out in whispered bursts.

'*Oui*, Chief Inspector. I saw her. As though she were sleeping. And the pillow red. Just a deep, deep scarlet. *Affreux, pauvre chérie* . . .'

'Was there any blood on Monsieur Gilbert?'

'Everywhere.'

'All over? Body? Hands? Face?'

Valbois gave it some thought.

17

'Just down one side – where he had slept beside her? Where the blood . . . I suppose, where it . . . pooled.'

Jacquot took this in.

'Monsieur, thank you. Now I would like to see the room, if you please.'

3

PERSILLE OCCUPIED MOST OF THE top floor, apart from a wide corridor running the length of the roof space with four windows overlooking a cobbled courtyard and fountain below. A gendarme stood at the room's fabric covered double doors. Jacquot stepped past him with a nod, Brunet followed and the owner, Valbois, came up behind, not sure whether to follow them in or wait outside with the *képi*.

Inside the room, Jacquot paused and looked around. Like the rest of the house, the walls were bare mortared stone and the floorboards a worn oak strip, a dozen or more beams branching from walls and floors to support a gently pitching tiled roof. The summer before, this would have been a dark old attic filled with a generation's worth of tat. Now it smelled of perfumed candles or possibly bath oils – warm and close up here in the head of the house – the lighting delivered not through dusty, broken panes and low-watt bulbs but by means of concealed up-lighters hidden among the tied beams above their heads, beams softly coloured with what looked like a green limewash. These same soft shades of green were repeated in overstuffed upholstery, a scatter of rugs, pleated blinds on three mansard windows and, at the end of the room, raised on a low dais, the drapes hanging around a four-poster bed and its quilted cover, half-spilled across the edge of the mattress and dais step. It wasn't to Jacquot's taste – too staged and deliberate – but he could see that it would look good in a brochure, or to illustrate a magazine article.

Quietly, slowly, looking from side to side – two new suitcases open on a pair of stools, clothes dropped on the floor and draped over the back of an armchair, an empty bottle of champagne, its label floating in the melted ice water – Jacquot made his way towards the dais and bed at the end of the room.

The girl was lying on her back, head on the pillow, haloed by dark curls, lips parted and kiss-smeared with lipstick, one mascara-ed eye open – a cold disinterested blue – the other a scorched blackened pit between eyebrow and cheekbone. Not a spot of blood on her face. That was all on the pillow behind her head, just the one side of it where the blood had spilled from a hole that Jacquot knew would be the size of a saucer, shards of bone and wads of tissue blasted into the goose down.

He tried to remember her name – Inès? No. Ilena? No. Irèna? No. Isabella . . . Isabelle. Yes, that was it. Isabelle Blanchard. Izzy. Someone had called her Izzy.

Jacquot's eyes dropped from her face to her body, oddly flat-chested now, the weight of her breasts sliding to her sides, nipples drawn out of shape as though the torso had been stretched or deflated. The quilt had been tossed aside but a crumpled top sheet still covered her legs and belly. One arm lay across it, noticeably hairy, the other thrown back over the pillow. It was how she had fallen asleep, possibly in the glow of their lovemaking, sprawled and satisfied. And that's how she'd stayed, after the gun had been fired and blown her brains out. A splinter of light from the bedside light glanced off her finger. She was still wearing her wedding ring.

Jacquot followed the spread of blood from the pillow into the centre of the bed where it had soaked down into the mattress where Gilbert had been lying. The impression of his body was still there, curved and hollowed, and there was a sudden and sure certainty in Jacquot's mind that Noël Gilbert had not killed his wife. Hadn't touched her. Just woken to a warm stickiness on his skin, reached for the bedside light. Then looked down between them. With waking, light-squinting eyes. Taking it in. Trying to shake off sleep and make sense of it.

The blood, the stillness, that dark, mascara-ed hole . . .

A cold dread, a mounting disbelief.

Trying to blink the image away, rub it from his eyes.

But the picture didn't change, didn't go away.

Jacquot breathed deeply through his nose, stayed still, trying to get a sense and measure of what had happened here.

Who would want to kill her? A country girl.

And why in the eye?

Why not between the eyes? In the head? In the heart? All of them deadly shots.

Was there significance there in that single killing shot to the eye?

Something the eye had seen?

And why not the husband too?

Why had he been spared?

And why hadn't he woken up?

Little wonder that Brunet was doubtful.

Jacquot knew how his assistant would read it: Gilbert, a young city boy forced into a marriage he didn't want; suddenly, for some as yet unknown reason, driven to despair on his wedding night; a fit of madness, *un moment de folie*, *un crime passionel* . . . But it was worth remembering that Brunet was a single man, older than Gilbert, with a formidable reputation for bedding, and moving on from, a significant number of women. Brunet was a tomcat . . . but maybe Gilbert wasn't.

Jacquot took another long breath in through his nose, let it out, then frowned and sniffed again – shorter, double sniffs. Something hung in the air, beneath the scented candles. Not the warm, crumpled scent of lovers' sheets, nor the cold ashy note of cordite. Something sharp and astringent . . . something that shouldn't have been there.

He went to Gilbert's side of the bed and, reaching out a hand to the stone wall, he bent down to the pillow, sniffed again. Something cold. Metallic. Chemical. A hospital smell.

He turned away from the bed. Brunet was sitting in one of the

21

chairs, waiting for him to complete his preliminary search, knowing his boss wouldn't appreciate any interruption. Behind him Monsieur Valbois had strayed past the door, hands clutched in front of him, almost stooping, like a room service waiter asking if there was anything more he could do . . .

'Murder weapon?' asked Jacquot.

Brunet shook his head.

Jacquot looked past him, at Valbois.

'Did any of your guests hear a shot?'

'No . . . nothing. Just the scream,' replied Valbois.

'The bathroom?'

'Through there, Monsieur,' he replied, pointing to a door in the corner of the room, half hidden behind a fine Coromandel screen. Jacquot stepped past it and leant into the bathroom. White marble tiling, double vanity, a pair of mirrors framed with tiny lightbulbs, like an actor's dressing-room mirror. Towels on the floor, a puddle of water by the shower, toiletries on the vanity. And beneath the vanity more tiling to conceal the plumbing, just a small hatch for access.

Could they have showered before making love? wondered Jacquot. It seemed unlikely – the opened bottle of champagne, the clothes cast off on the floor. Or had Gilbert gone there afterwards, as his new wife slept?

Pushing himself off the door frame Jacquot turned and crossed the room, Brunet getting to his feet, Valbois standing aside. Outside the room, Jacquot pointed down the corridor.

'What's down there?'

'Just a linen room, Chief Inspector. Each floor has one.'

Jacquot strolled down to it, glancing out of the corridor windows as he passed. A small sign read *'Privé'*. He tried the handle, the door opened and a warm smell of freshly laundered linen coiled snugly out of the darkness.

'There's a light on the left,' said Valbois. 'On a string. Just pull it.'

Jacquot did as instructed and the room lit up, revealing floor-to-ceiling duckboard shelving laden with towels and sheets and pillowcases and quilt covers, and all the paraphernalia of housekeeping: boxes of soap, shampoos, tissue paper, loo roll. He stepped in, made his way between the shelves until he reached a small open space with an ironing board leaning against a wall. The Gilberts' bathroom wall. And there, beside the legs of the ironing board, was another small hatch. He moved the ironing board aside, squatted down, ran a finger across the rough wooden architraving fitted around the access panel. He looked closer. A tiny snag of blue, caught on its splintery edge.

Jacquot got to his feet, gave a last look round the room, came out into the corridor, pulled the light switch and closed the door behind him.

'So,' he said, smiling at Valbois and Brunet. 'Let's have a word with Monsieur Gilbert.'

4

NOËL GILBERT WAS SITTING IN a buttoned leather chair in front of a stone fireplace, its blackened basket filled with pine cones. He wore a towelling dressing gown and was hunched forward, elbows on knees, forehead resting in his hands. He gave no indication that he had heard Jacquot and Brunet come in, or Valbois and the gendarme being dismissed, or the door closing, or Jacquot taking a seat in the armchair opposite him.

'Noël, it's Daniel. Daniel Jacquot. We met . . . yesterday. From Marseilles.'

There was no response. Jacquot hadn't really expected any. Instead he leant back in the chair and crossed his legs. He was in no hurry. His colleague, Brunet, might believe that Gilbert had killed his wife, for want of some other more convincing explanation, but Jacquot was now even more certain that he hadn't. The set of his shoulders, the trapped collar of his dressing gown, the snot-filled, muffled breaths. He might not yet know why the man's wife had been killed, or who had killed her, but Jacquot knew that it wasn't Gilbert who had held the gun to her eye and pulled the trigger.

Because this was a professional hit.

Almost an execution.

With a silencer, had to be. Otherwise there was no way Gilbert could have stayed asleep.

But why this young, bouncy, just-wed country maid?

A jealous lover? Not with a silencer.

So was it, perhaps, mistaken identity?

Had the killer been after a different target and gone to the wrong room?

Who else was staying at Le Mas Bleu? The other guests. Six of them, Valbois had confirmed.

Someone famous? Maybe political? Some underworld, gangland payback?

Their names, addresses, contact numbers . . . he'd have Brunet . . .

'I didn't do it.' When Gilbert finally spoke it was in a thick, phlegmy rasp, muffled by his hands.

Jacquot waited a beat, noting the open right sleeve of his dressing gown and a long smear of browning blood.

'I know that,' he replied, softly.

Sitting to one side, on the edge of a pretty chintz-covered day bed, Brunet frowned.

'You want a drink? A cigarette?'

Gilbert raised his head, cheeks and forehead creased and red where his fingers and the balls of his hands had been pressed against them. The red fading to an ivory white.

'I want my wife back, is what I want.' His voice was thick, uncertain. He cleared his throat. 'I want this not to be real. I want to wake up in a minute and for everything to be . . .'

He gave Jacquot a pitiful look, then glanced at Brunet.

'But a cigarette . . . That would be good. I gave up, for Izzy.'

Jacquot reached into his pocket, pulled out a crumpled pack of Gitanes and lit two, passing one to Gilbert.

'No filter. I'm sorry.'

Gilbert tipped back his head and inhaled deeply, then sank forward, elbows on knees again, cigarette dangling from his fingers, head lowered. He blew out the smoke in a long grey stream down between his towel-clad knees.

'It's a mistake,' he said, looking up. 'Who would do this? Why?'

'And you didn't hear a thing?'

Gilbert shook his head and his shoulders tensed, as though the sudden movement hurt. He closed his eyes, red and raw and wet, tightly, as though to relieve some unseen pressure. Then, with the hand that was holding the cigarette, he pressed hard against his forehead.

'You got a headache?' asked Jacquot, leaning forward, breathing in through his nose as though searching for some elusive scent.

'A blinder.'

'You drink much yesterday? Last night? The champagne . . .'

'Enough, but not to feel like this.'

Jacquot considered this.

'Do you remember anything?'

'Nothing. We left the party around eleven, got here maybe twenty minutes later. Saw the manager, and went straight up to our room. Drank the champagne . . . partied a bit . . . you know . . .' Gilbert took a breath, tried to blink away tears, tapped ash amongst the pine cones. Jacquot remembered the clothes on the sofa and floor. 'And now this,' Gilbert continued. 'I just . . . I can't . . .' He pursed his lips, looked helpless, lost.

And then something seemed to dawn on him, and his shoulders slumped.

'Do they know? Her parents? I didn't call . . . What's the time?'

'No one knew who to call. Who to get in touch with. All they had were the reservation details: your name, credit card and home phone number.'

'What can I say? How do I tell them?' There was a pleading in his voice, in his eyes. What to do? How to do it?

'We can do that – if you want? It may be better that way.'

There was a knock at the door.

It was Valbois.

'The doctor has arrived,' he said in a whisper, as though not wishing to raise his voice, disturb anyone. 'Can he see . . . ?' Valbois caught Gilbert's eye. 'Is it okay for him . . . ?'

'Tell him to go ahead,' replied Jacquot. 'He knows the score. I'll be there in a minute.'

26

The door closed. There was the sound of muted conversation in the hallway. Then silence. Jacquot let it stretch out.

'It will hurt for a long time,' he said at last, tossing his cigarette beneath the basket of cones. 'I cannot pretend to you it will be any other way. You know that, too, Noël. But you will survive. You will get through this.'

He got to his feet and reached out a hand, laid it on Gilbert's shoulder. There was a muffled sob and a nod of the head, pink scalp showing through the black brush-cut.

And on that scalp, caught in the bristly hair, something that shouldn't have been there. Like a small twisted tack, thin, knotted.

'*Attend*,' said Jacquot, reaching for it, plucking it from the side of Gilbert's head. The boy didn't move.

Jacquot lifted what he'd found to the light and examined it.

A tiny wizened sprig of vine.

5

'HE DID IT. THERE'S NO other possible, credible explanation.'

Jacquot winced as though he'd bitten down on an olive pit.

'*Non, non, non,*' he said, shaking his head.

He and Brunet were sitting at a table in Le Mas Bleu's empty dining room: the same burnished wood floors, the same kelims, the same bare stone walls, a grand stone mantle over a hearth spiky with last year's lavender. There were seven other tables ranged around the room, each laid with golden Provençal print cloths, the chairs tall ladderbacks with rushwork seats. String-tied napkins lay at each place like scrolled messages from some ancient kingdom, the china was a weighty faience, and in the centre of each table was a blue glass bowl scattered with assorted nuts and kernels and dried poppy-seed heads. Everything exactly so. The way Valbois liked to take his breakfast, Jacquot supposed. But it was all a little too perfect, too . . . restricting for him. The only things that made him feel at home were the scents of freshly baked bread and percolating coffee, both of which had been served to them by Valbois himself. It was a little after six and a low Sunday sunlight slanted across their table. Outside, a wide, stone-flagged terrace led down to a lawn edged with gravel paths and a border of flaking eucalyptus and lime. Beyond the trees, the slopes of the Luberon lay pooled with dawn shadows.

'The silencer. The gun. He could have got hold of both, no trouble.' Brunet was playing with the string that had secured his napkin, twisting it around his thumb, tugging on it.

'So where are they now?' asked Jacquot. 'You searched the room.'

'He could have popped her, left the room, gone to the garden, buried it somewhere. Maybe to pick up later. He's a cop. He'll know what we'll do. He'll make sure we don't find it.'

'And why would he kill a woman he's only just married?'

Jacquot broke off some *petit pain*, smeared it with butter and cherry preserve and popped it in his mouth. It was still warm. Just delicious. But it cost a small fortune. He'd seen the printed menu card. Eighty francs for breakfast! Bread and conserves, juice and coffee. For eighty francs in town, he'd have enough for a couple of Auzet's plum croissants, his favourite *oeufs brouillés* at Le Sept, and a large café-Calva at Centenaire to kick-start his day. And change.

'Maybe there's a policy,' Brunet was saying. 'Insurance? Some kind of pay-out we don't yet know about. Or maybe, you know, she told him something he didn't want to hear. Other lovers. Suddenly she wasn't what he thought she was. Or maybe there was a quarrel. Maybe he couldn't get it up and she laughed . . . took the piss . . . and he loses the plot . . .'

Jacquot smiled. Exactly what he'd imagined Brunet would come up with.

'And he comes prepared? With a gun and silencer? On his wedding night? Just in case . . .'

'Like I say, he wouldn't have had any trouble . . .'

'And then he drugs himself?'

Brunet frowned.

'Drugs himself? There's drugs now?'

'His headache. The smell on him. On his pillow. The reason he didn't hear anything. Whoever shot his wife, put him out first.'

Brunet turned down his mouth, considering this new piece of information.

'Could be,' he said, at last. 'Then again, maybe he set it all up. Shoots her, loses the gun, makes it look like someone drugged him

'. . . I mean, I'm just going through the motions here. See where the *crottes* land. Like, why didn't they tap him too? Why leave him?'

Jacquot grinned, reached for the faience coffee jug, filled their blue-glazed cups.

'Well, we'll know soon enough. I've asked the boys to check that linen room and hatch, and test the pillow, swab Gilbert for corresponding traces, and powder burns too. It's not easy cleaning yourself up.' For a brief moment, he recalled the towels on the wet bathroom floor, the used shower, but a second later he dismissed them. They had nothing to do with it – he was sure. 'In the meantime,' he said, pushing himself away from the table, 'there's a call we need to make. But first . . .'

They left Le Mas Bleu in two cars, Jacquot leading the way. At the bottom of the drive he turned right rather than left – the direction of the Blanchards' farm – and headed towards Robion. Behind him, Brunet flashed his lights as though to say 'wrong way', but Jacquot just gave a wave through the window and carried on, making a second right a few hundred metres further on, down an old farm track rutted with lumpy stone and dawn-damp earth. Fifty metres in, he braked, left the engine running and started to walk, looking at the track and then peering over a low stone wall at the distant pantiled roof of Le Mas Bleu.

By the time Brunet caught up with him, Jacquot was pushing the toe of his boot through the grass at the side of the track.

'This is where the killer parked,' he said, pointing at a parallel set of furrows in the grass, a broken stand of gold irises and a ridge of turned dirt.

'And that,' he continued, nodding down the line of vines, stretching across two fields in a diagonal line towards a distant line of cypresses, 'is how he, or she, made their approach.'

6

AT A LITTLE AFTER EIGHT o'clock that Sunday morning, with the sun already starting to put out some warmth, Jacquot and Brunet pulled up in front of the Blanchard's farmhouse. Both men were silent. They knew what was coming. And both men had done this same call enough times to know that it never got any easier.

'Looks deserted,' said Brunet, coming over to Jacquot's car and leaning down by the open window. The house rose three floors above them, the top windows shuttered. Their green paint was peeling, the wooden panels warped with age and weather, and one or two slats not quite as they should be – just as the shutters at Le Mas Bleu would once have been. On the left of the house was a barn with closed doors and on the right an open-sided building housing a tractor, assorted farm machinery, some wrapped bales, and two cars – both Renaults, an estate and a four-wheel drive flat-bed. Beyond it, Jacquot could make out the first of the trees in the orchard, lanterns still hanging in the branches.

'They had a late night,' he replied, pushing open the car door and climbing out. He'd just swung it shut when Monsieur Blanchard appeared from between the barn and farmhouse. Jacquot recognised him from the day before – short, broad-shouldered, big-bellied, with rosy unshaven cheeks and a thick head of grey hair that now stood high and proud and ruffled from his bed. From which, it was clear, he hadn't long ago risen. He might have been wearing trousers and boots but his flies were open, his bootlaces untied and there was a dressing gown over his singlet. He was carrying a pail filled with eggs and there was straw caught on the sleeves of his gown. When he saw Jacquot and Brunet coming in his direction, he put down the pail, brushed away the straw and tied the cord of his dressing gown.

'Messieurs?' he called.

'Monsieur Blanchard. It's me . . . Daniel Jacquot. I was here yesterday, at the wedding, with Claudine?'

'Ah, Madame Eddé. Claudine. *Mais bien sûr. Quelle jolie femme. Bouf!*' Blanchard peered at his visitor from under grey wiry eyebrows. Jacquot smelt wine on the man's breath and the warmth of the chicken house on his robe. 'And you, Daniel. Of course.' They shook hands. 'What a day, heh? *Pouf*, it will take me a week to recover. Maybe a month. At my age . . .'

Blanchard's eyes then turned to Brunet – whom he didn't recognise and was almost certain hadn't been at the marriage of his eldest daughter the day before – and he jutted his head forward as though the better to focus on Jacquot's assistant.

'My colleague, Jean Brunet,' said Jacquot.

'Colleague?' Blanchard frowned.

'I'm afraid we're here on a police matter.'

Jacquot could see that not for a second did it strike Blanchard that the 'police matter' might be of any significance or concern to him.

'Someone run off the road last night?' he asked, squaring his shoulders before giving the matter some consideration. 'There were enough here who might have done. No one hurt, I hope?' He gave them a big smile, reached down for the pail and picked it up. 'Come on in. Eggs are fresh and coffee's on . . .' He moved past them. 'So who was it? Who's made a fool of themselves? Don't tell me . . . Ricard. Pissed as a stoat he was, and his wife not much better. Never could hold her drink, could Madame Ricard. Stumbled out of here . . . what? Must have been near three when the disco finished.'

In the kitchen, stone-floored, high-ceilinged and with lace-curtained

windows set either side of the back door, Monsieur Blanchard swung
the pail of eggs onto the table and went to the range, lifted a bubbling
coffee percolator.

'Take a seat, Messieurs. You want some coffee?' He filled his
own mug and waved the pot at them.

Jacquot and Brunet shook their heads.

Blanchard came back to the table, pulled out a chair.

'*Dieu*, what a night! One down and three to go. Daughters . . .
I'll be a poor man when they're all wed.'

Jacquot gave a tight smile, as if to agree that that would very
likely be the case, and Brunet nodded.

It was Brunet who got the ball rolling.

'It's about your daughter that we're here,' he began, maybe
sensing that Jacquot, as a guest at the previous day's wedding,
might be holding back, not wanting to start. He glanced at his boss
before continuing, but Jacquot shook his head. He could do this.
He was just waiting for the right moment. When Blanchard's eyes
settled on him, Jacquot knew the moment had come.

'And which of the little minxes is it this time? Don't tell me . . .
Justine. I've asked her mother a million times . . .'

'It's Izzy, Monsieur Blanchard, and I'm afraid I have some bad
news. Is your wife up?'

'Izzy? But she just got married. She's on honeymoon.' He glanced
at the kitchen clock, its big hollow tick filling the room. A real
Provençal farm clock, not the painted pretender put up in Le Mas
Bleu. 'Should be getting the train any time for Paris, the two of
them. Back in a week . . .'

This was how long it took for the phrase 'bad news' to filter
through to Blanchard. Of all his daughters, Izzy was the one now
removed from his care, no longer his responsibility, out in the
world with her new husband. When it did finally get through to
him – a visit from the police and the suggestion of bad news – a
tight little frown played across his features, as though there had
to be some kind of mistake.

'Liiiii-se-ette,' he called out for his wife, as though she was the one who should be there to take responsibility for her girls, and deal with whatever they might have got up to.

'I'm here, I'm here, what's all the fuss about?' came a voice from the hallway, and into the kitchen came Madame Blanchard, wrapping the ties of a housecoat around her waist. She was as stout as her husband, but her hair was neat, brushed, pinned back, a pair of button-like black eyes flicking between the three men in her kitchen.

Both Brunet and Jacquot got to their feet and stayed standing as Jacquot informed mother and father in a soft and sorrowful voice that their eldest daughter, Isabelle Blanchard, now Gilbert, had been found dead in her bed at Le Mas Bleu.

Madame Blanchard dropped the ties from her fingers and stared across the kitchen table at Jacquot as though he was speaking in a foreign language and she hadn't been able properly to understand what it was that he had said.

'But she just got married,' said Blanchard *Père*, as though that somehow made the announcement of her death invalid, unlikely. How could anyone die the day after their wedding?

'What happened? Where is she?' asked Madame Blanchard, reaching for a chair and letting herself down onto it. Of the two, she seemed the more alert.

'Dead, you say?' asked her husband, now shaking his head as though that simply wasn't possible. She'd be back in a week. After her honeymoon in Paris. There was room for no other possibility.

'She was found earlier this morning,' continued Jacquot. 'By her husband, Monsieur Noël Gilbert. She had been shot.'

'Shot?' gasped the old man. 'Shot, you say? How? Why? Who?'

'Please, please tell us this is all some horrible joke,' said Madame Blanchard, clearly hoping it might be just that. Just a joke. Just some dreadful mistake.

'I regret, Madame, this is no joke. She died in her sleep. We are still trying to establish . . .'

'And Noël?' asked Madame Blanchard. 'Where is he? Why isn't he here? Has he been shot too?'

34

'Your son-in-law has been taken to the hospital in Cavaillon. He was in some considerable shock.'

'But what was he doing?' demanded Blanchard. 'Is he to blame? Is he the one who did this?'

Jacquot shook his head.

'At this time, it seems highly unlikely that Monsieur Gilbert had anything to do with his wife's death . . .'

'But where was he? How did he let something like this happen?' demanded Blanchard, slapping the top of the table with the palm of his hand. 'He's her husband, for the love of God!' As a kind of defence mechanism, Jacquot knew, the old man was now focusing his attention on the poor performance of his son-in-law as husband and protector and provider, rather than facing directly the issue of his daughter's death.

There was no such artifice or deflection from Madame Blanchard.

'Someone . . . killed Izzy? She's been murdered?'

There was a movement behind Madame Blanchard. Jacquot looked over her shoulder. There, standing at the kitchen door, in the shadows by the old farm dresser, listening to this exchange, were three young girls, Izzy's sisters – twelve, sixteen and the nineteen-year-old whom Claudine had coached for the École des Beaux Arts. Jacquot wondered how long they had been there. Long enough, it seemed. A scream pealed out of the oldest girl as the church bell in St-Florent started calling the faithful to Mass.

7

'I JUST CAN'T BELIEVE IT,' said Claudine, shuffling an omelette onto Jacquot's plate.

It was Sunday night, about the same time that he and Claudine had returned from the wedding the previous day. Jacquot had come back an hour earlier after a long day at headquarters, had showered, put on clean jeans, shirt and a pullover, and slipped his bare feet into a ragged pair of espadrilles. He was hungry and tired when he took his seat at the kitchen table, but pleased to be home.

'Yesterday,' Claudine continued, 'we were at her wedding . . . today, *pouf*, she is gone. It's another world. Just . . . *incroyable*.'

Having emptied the skillet she took it back to the range and returned to the kitchen table with a small bowl of tomato salad that she placed beside Jacquot's plate, found him a serving spoon from the table drawer, then pulled out a chair and dropped onto it. She hadn't cooked anything for herself. Instead, she played with a glass of Apremont, her favourite Savoyard wine, swirling it round, staring into its sparkling depths as though she might find some answer there. She looked pale with shock, her eyes dulled with sadness.

'You should eat something,' said Jacquot, helping himself to some of the tomatoes.

Claudine shook her head.

'I couldn't. I just couldn't.'

Jacquot glanced at her across the table. He had known she would be upset, but had been surprised to find her quite so unsettled, so saddened. Normally Jacquot's work was a subject for limited conversation only, but this evening – probably because it was all so close – she had wanted to talk.

Claudine had known about the killing long before he got home. By mid-morning word was out, and telephones were ringing from Cavaillon to Apt and beyond. When Jacquot called to say he wouldn't be back for lunch there was no resigned sigh, just a catch of breath and, 'How could they? How could someone do something like that? A young woman, on her wedding night.'

He had calmed her, soothed her, told her that he loved her, and would be home for supper. He would call again. He would let her know what time . . .

'So what have you heard?' asked Jacquot, slicing into his omelette, its golden skin speckled with the green sorrel that grew in wild profusion on the side of the road leading to their millhouse. As he took his first bite, he reflected that it was always interesting comparing local gossip with the established facts of an investigation – the few that there were at this early stage. It also gave him an opportunity to listen, not talk, and to concentrate on his first real meal of the day. The warm, damp *croque monsieur* at lunchtime from the canteen at Cavaillon police headquarters really did not count.

'I knew there had to be something pretty serious for you to be up and out so early,' Claudine began. 'After you'd gone I lay in bed and felt guilty about making you dance so much. You must have been exhausted?'

Jacquot's mouth was full. He waved his fork hand. *Pas du tout*. Not at all.

Claudine put down her glass and slid her fingers along its stem.

'It was Madame Tapis who called and told me the news. After that, the phone never really stopped.'

Jacquot swallowed, reached for his wine.

'And what did Madame Tapis have to say?'

Madame Tapis ran the *pharmacie* in Coustellet just a few

kilometres from Le Mas Bleu, and anyone who had their prescription passed over her counter was part of the *groupe,* to be brought up to speed on any or all newsworthy items that came her way. In her white sneakers and tight white pharmacist's overall she was a whispering almanac of local information and gossip – from birth to death with marriage, adultery and divorce in between. If no prescription needed to be filled and the details couldn't be personally passed on over the counter of her cramped premises on place Dubert, then Madame Tapis would pick up her phone and start dialling. Once the old dame had something to pass on, it was as good as taking an advertisement in the paper – only a great deal swifter and more effective.

'Apparently, some time in the night, Izzy was murdered,' said Claudine. 'Shot. In her bed. And Noël asleep beside her.'

Jacquot took another mouthful of his omelette and nodded.

'That's about right,' he said, scooping up a forkful of the accompanying tomato salad.

'And?'

'And what?' he replied, dabbing away a dribble of vinaigrette from the side of his mouth.

'Well, there must be more. I mean, how come Noël didn't wake up? And how come he wasn't murdered too? And anyway, who would want to kill poor Izzy?'

'Madame Tapis didn't have a theory?'

'There is a feeling . . .' Claudine paused, played with her glass.

'A feeling?'

'A sense that, maybe, Noël . . . got drunk. Was drunk. Lost his temper, maybe . . .'

Once again she paused and looked embarrassed, as though it somehow wasn't right that she should think such a thing, let alone pass it on, share it.

Jacquot finished his omelette and pushed his plate away, wiping his mouth with his napkin, throwing it down and reaching for his wine.

The movement seemed to snap Claudine back to the kitchen

table. And somehow lighten the moment. She gave him a stern look.

'The sink is behind you, Monsieur. There is a dish-washer, but it is not me.'

With a slow grin Jacquot did as he was told. On his way back to the table he put his hands on Claudine's shoulders and leant down to place a kiss on her neck.

'Noël Gilbert did not lose his temper,' he whispered in her ear. 'And he was not drunk.'

'Then how . . . ?'

'That is what we will find out. In the meantime, I regret to say that Noël Gilbert has been transferred to Aix General Hospital after slitting his wrists in a bathroom at Cavaillon Hospital. But I didn't tell you that . . .'

Claudine might have been one of Madame Tapis' *bande* at the pharmacie, but Jacquot had long ago learnt that she could be trusted with a secret. She may listen to the rumour mill, and often pass on what she had heard, but she would never contribute to it. Much to Madame Tapis' irritation, Jacquot suspected, knowing as she did that Claudine lived with a *flic*.

Claudine was aghast at this news, hands flying to her cheeks.

'*Bon Dieu!* That is terrible . . . Is he okay?'

Jacquot spread his hands. He didn't know. He had only heard about the incident after getting back to headquarters from the Blanchard's farm. All he could do was repeat the latest bulletin he'd received from Aix General just an hour or so before leaving headquarters. that Noël's condition was now stable, despite an enormous loss of blood.

'He was in a private room, with an officer outside the door. Somehow he'd got hold of a pair of scissors, asked to be taken to a bathroom and then locked himself in. By the time they broke down the door he'd slit both wrists. And when you do it down the length of the arm, as he had done, rather than across . . .' Jacquot demonstrated what he meant '. . . well, it's clear he really did intend to kill himself. Another few minutes . . .' Jacquot shrugged. 'What we need to establish is whether that action was the result of remorse and guilt or because he was devastated by what had happened to the woman he loved.'

'So what do you think?' asked Claudine.

'What? Innocent or guilty?'

She nodded.

'When I saw him this morning, I believed he was innocent. Immediately. He was shocked – I mean, really shocked; couldn't have acted it. Just so raw, so . . . helpless. Searching for someone to explain to him what had happened, and what it all meant.' Jacquot shook his head, remembering the lad's desolation. 'And I believe it still. Even more convinced. And he was drugged, of course. Did I mention that? Which is the other reason I believe he's innocent. Jean thinks that all this could have been engineered, arranged, set up by Noël – for whatever reason – but I don't think so.' Jacquot reached for his cigarettes and lit up. He offered the pack to Claudine, but she shook her head.

'What do you mean drugged? An injection? What?'

'There was a strange smell on his pillow, and in his hair. Chemical. As though someone had come up behind him and put something over his nose and mouth . . . so he didn't know what was going on. Which could, of course, give us a lead: what chemical? How easy is it to get hold of? Who would have access to it? It's the way we start . . .'

'Narrowing down the game,' said Claudine, breaking in. 'I know, you've told me.' She gave him a sad smile. She didn't want him to misunderstand, to feel she was putting him down. 'But what I want to know is why anyone would want to kill poor Izzy?'

Jacquot reached for an ashtray, put it beside him and tapped his cigarette against its edge.

'Well, there you have me. I simply can't explain it. No motive that I can see. Either emotional or financial. She wasn't wealthy. There was no insurance policy we've been able to find. No jilted lovers, on either side. She was just a country girl, on her wedding night, with her new husband.'

40

'Maybe the killer was after someone else. Maybe it's a case of mistaken identity.'

'According to the owner of Le Mas Bleu, there were no last-minute room changes, which could have proved significant. The suite had been booked weeks ago by Noël – and what he booked he got. The best room in the house. As for the other guests – six of them, three couples – well, there's no one you'd put down as a possible assassination target. A couple of ramblers in their sixties starting out on a Luberon hike, an English travel writer and his girlfriend, and a retired couple from Belgium who are hunting through Provence for a house in the sun. Brunet has interviewed each of them, taken statements, addresses and personal details. There was nothing they could tell him. And nothing that aroused his suspicions.'

A silence settled between them and Jacquot watched through his cigarette smoke as Claudine considered all that she had learnt. A gentle frown had stitched itself across her forehead, her dark eyebrows were angled, her warm brown eyes staring into her glass. She wore no make up, her skin lightly tanned but not dark enough to hide the scatter of freckles across the bridge of her nose. That would come later, he knew, at the end of summer. As for her long black hair she had tied it in a knot, secured by a small paintbrush, and the black polo neck sweater she wore gave her a sad, sombre look. She reminded him a little of Juliette Greco, made him think of smoky Paris jazz clubs and Beat Poets.

At times like this – sad, silent, contemplative – Claudine had the look of a woman who knew the world, knew how the world worked and was resigned to it. She had, too, the look of a woman who knew her men as well as she knew the world, a woman with a past – self-assured, bold, mysterious – a woman who had taken many lovers.

But Jacquot knew better. She'd been married twice, with not much time between to play the field. Her first husband had died in a car crash and left her with a daughter, Midou, currently working in Guadeloupe for Sous-Marine-Ecologique. As for husband number two, he had been caught in the marital bed (now the guest room) with one of Claudine's best friends, and promptly been let go. As Jacquot looked at her, he decided he had never been happier with a woman than he was with her, thanking all his lucky stars for the twists and turns of fate that had brought them together.

They had first met at an art gallery in Marseilles. He had missed the opening night, Claudine's first ever exhibition, and visiting a few days later, had mistaken her for a gallery assistant rather than the artist herself. It was almost a year before they met again, at Hôtel Le Grand Monastère in Luissac where she was helping to run a painting party and he was investigating the disappearance of one of the guests. One evening he had played piano for her, croaked a few lyrics, and been utterly unmanned – the look of her, the presence, that sharp, jibing little tongue, the haughty toss of her head, the jutting chin, that slow secret smile that slid across her mouth and crinkled her eyes. He had kissed her for the first time in the hotel reception area but it had been another two months before they became lovers. A year later he'd surrendered his small attic apartment in Cavaillon and for the last three years they had lived together in Claudine's millhouse on the road to Apt. Taking a last drag on his cigarette, Jacquot folded it into the ashtray, then tipped back his head and blew out a column of smoke.

Three years. Just a magical time.

'Sometimes I wonder how you bear it,' said Claudine at last, breaking the silence. 'The horror you see, the dreadful things you have to do.'

'I bear it as a doctor or a nurse bears it. Bad things happen.' Jacquot waved his hand as though it was of no importance; just a fact of life. 'But it helps to come home to a place like this, and to a woman like you.'

She reached a hand across the table.

Jacquot leant forward to take it.

'Just promise me you'll always come back?'

'Just so long as you promise me you'll always be here when I do?'

Claudine held his eye. He knew she was thinking of a suitable retort. He was right.

'So long as you continue to behave, and watch your manners, and do the washing up.' Then she paused, thought of something else, and her face hardened. 'And find whichever bastard it was who killed Izzy Blanchard.'

8

THE BLANCHARDS' WEDDING PHOTOS ARRIVED on Jacquot's desk first thing Wednesday morning. They came in six cellophane envelopes, along with the pathologist's report and initial forensic findings.

Since the pathology report provided little to go on beyond confirmation of death by gunshot, approximate time of death, height, weight, age, gender and colouring of victim, and since the initial forensic findings offered nothing more than a single 9x19mm Parabellum slug retrieved from the Gilberts' mattress, a few strands of blue wool from the access hatch in Le Mas Bleu's linen room, and more than seventy separate sets of fingerprints (hotels – and poor housekeeping – made such dreadful scenes-of-crime, reflected Jacquot), it was the arrival of these wedding photos that quickened his interest.

He had noticed the disposable cameras in a basket in the Blanchards' kitchen when he and Brunet had visited the parents to break the news of their daughter's death, and remembered them from the dining tables set out in the meadow the day before. At a decent and respectful hour on Monday morning he had sent Brunet back to the farmhouse to request a full list of wedding guests – those who had attended and those who had not – and to ask also if he could take away the table cameras so that their film could be developed in order to help with the investigation. According to

Brunet, Madame Blanchard had a list of names and addresses in a kitchen drawer and seemed only too happy to surrender the cameras – looking at them as if she couldn't quite work out what they were, or their significance, and only too happy when she finally realised what they were to be rid of them.

Putting aside the dossiers from Pathology and Forensics, Jacquot reached for the first of the cellophane wraps, opened it and counted the film wallets it contained. Six of them, with up to twenty photos in each. In all, approximately seven hundred pictures to check through.

Every face to be identified.

Every person interviewed.

Every name crossed off the list.

Until there were none left.

Police work. Building the wall, stone by stone. It had to be done.

And maybe someone, along the way, would provide them with a lead, or another avenue of investigation would open up the search and redirect their efforts.

By six o'clock that evening, on a trestle table in the squad room, a little over seven hundred colour photos had been sorted into three main groups: close-ups (including bride and groom), group shots (usually *à table*), and general views of the reception – the Blanchards' farmhouse, the meadow, the queues at the hog-roast, the dancing – with anything up to thirty people in frame: back views, side views, in focus and out of focus, taken in daylight, and at night, using the flash. Among them was a photo of Jacquot leaning back in his chair with a pair of bare legs in his lap and a mischievous look on his face. There was also a stack of black-and-white contact sheets which the official wedding photographer had brought in the previous evening. Each of these images would be numbered, pored over with a magnifying glass, and frequently blown up for ease of identification.

In the absence of anything else to go on, it was the only place to start: a pile of photographs which, in the days that followed, as the investigating team visited and interviewed the people in the photos or taken from the Blanchards' invitation list, steadily increased in size as more prints were produced by wedding guests with their own cameras, all carried back to police headquarters in Cavaillon for checking and cross-referencing – snaps taken at the church, during the procession through St-Florent to the farmhouse, and at the reception that followed – until every single person captured on film had been accounted for.

It took a little over two weeks.

Until only three photos remained.

9

'THERE, THERE, AND . . . THERE.'

Once by one, Brunet laid the three photographs on Jacquot's desk. Each of them was a 15×18cm enlargement in grainy black and white, the office lights shining off their glossy surfaces: the bride and groom making their way out of Église St-Florent amid a rain of rice; walking down the main street at the head of the wedding procession; and a wide-angle shot taken at the gates to the Blanchards' farm.

Jacquot picked up the first photo and peered at a red-circled head at the back of a crowd of villagers gathered on a bank of grass outside the church. The figure seemed somehow isolated, alone, standing apart from the main action yet observing it all the same. But even enlarged the person was too far away to make out any expression or even the most basic features.

Man or woman? Old or young? Impossible to say.

The second photo was of St-Florent's main street, no more than a village road with a *boulangerie* and small bar-café amid the cluster of houses, no cars visible as Noël and Izzy, hand in hand, headed towards the family farmhouse with their friends and family following. And there was another red ring, a face in the crowd watching the procession. Wearing what looked like a scarf or hat. Or maybe it was just a shadow.

'The same person? What do you think?' asked Jacquot.

'These two photos, maybe,' replied Brunet, leaning over Jacquot's shoulder to point. 'But the last picture's a little clearer.'

This time the circled head and shoulders were closer, a little more in focus. Standing by the gates to the farm as the procession flowed through. Clearly not invited to the hog-roast reception.

Jacquot looked at the first two pictures again. A definite similarity. Possibly a hat or scarf covering the head. The same person.

'Looks like just one person, doesn't it?' asked Brunet with a sly smile.

'That's what it looks like, but now you're going to tell me differently.'

'Pick up the first picture, at the church, and the last picture, at the farm, and look at them together, side by side.'

Jacquot did as instructed, angling the photos so the light didn't flash off their surfaces, obscure the image.

'There, you see? In the first picture, in the churchyard, the figure is either holding up a hand to shade their eyes or wearing a hat or scarf. And there, just below, between the two people in front, you can just see what looks like a belt buckle.'

Jacquot peered at the image, and nodded.

'But here, at the farmhouse gates, what appears to be the same person, also shading their eyes against the sun, is wearing trousers but with no buckle. And it also looks as if there's a difference in height. Compared with the people around them. One tall, one short.'

'So two different people . . .'

'Could be three . . .'

'And no one recognises them, no one remembers them, the people standing beside them?'

Brunet shook his head.

'Nobody we've spoken to.'

'They could be tourists, just passing through St-Florent when the wedding happens? People do that . . . they stop and watch, join in.'

'Of course, that is possible . . .' Brunet let his words trail off.

'But you don't think so?'

'No, I don't, Boss. There's something . . . just something not right about them. It's as if they're scouting things out, stalking the newly-weds.'

'And you're the one who thought that Gilbert had done it all by himself, set it all up?'

'Back then, I did, yes, you're right. But then I looked at this report from Forensics that just came in from Aix.' With a flourish Brunet produced a file from behind his back, laid it on top of the photos and flicked it open. 'The pillowcase from Le Mas Bleu, and Gilbert's hair samples. According to our chemical friends down the road, there are traces of Dyethelaspurane still present in the cotton, and in the hair fibres. You were lucky to spot it. It has a swift evaporation rate when exposed to air, creates like a wave of . . .'

'So they just dripped it onto his pillow. They didn't even need to touch him?'

'That's how it looks.'

'Tell me more about Dyethelaspurane.'

'Soon as I got something to tell you, Boss.'

10

AT ABOUT THE SAME TIME that Brunet was showing Jacquot the three photos at police headquarters in Cavaillon, Madame Minette Peluze was parking her car outside her home in Marseilles' tenth arrondissement, a few streets away from Boulevard de la Chapelle. On the seat beside and behind her were half a dozen carrier bags from the local *supermarché*, *charcuterie* and *poissonnerie*, her husband's suit in a plastic wrap from the dry cleaner's, and in the boot of the car a large cardboard box containing a dozen bottles of Bellet red and white – an expensive treat but her husband's favourite. She would leave the wine for Claude to bring in, she decided; too heavy for a woman of her years to manage. She'd have him fetch it in when he got home from police headquarters.

Struggling up the steps to their house, Madame Peluze dropped the bags on the porch, searched for her key, unlocked the front door and pushed it open. Stooping down, she picked up her shopping and cleaning and stepped inside, kicking the door closed behind her. In the kitchen she hung her husband's suit on a hook on the back of the door and set about unpacking the bags: sweets for the grandchildren, the makings of a cake, a box of cake candles, a six-pack of Orangina, and packets of crisps and crackers and biscuits for the following day's birthday party – *le petit* Nicolas, five years old.

After hiding away these goodies, Madame Peluze set about unpacking her other bags – olive oil, potatoes and a pot of *tapenade*; bread, butter and cheese; and, finally, a now sodden paper-wrapped parcel of monkfish and snapper, shrimps, squid and a rustling net of mussels, for a *Marmite du Pêcheur*. This fishermen's stew was another favourite of her husband's and would be the centrepiece of an anniversary *dîner à deux* served in her trusty old Staub casserole dish that very evening. Claude had promised to be home early, had made arrangements for one of the boys at headquarters on rue de l'Evêché to cover for him the following day. With the weekend upon them, if the gods blessed them, then she and her husband would have a whole four days together. Please, she prayed under her breath, don't let anyone murder anyone else for the next few days.

With her shopping unpacked and put away, Minette Peluze looked at the clock on the kitchen wall and decided that a little 'something' would be suitable reward for her morning's exertions. She poured herself a small Pineau des Charentes on the rocks, lit a cigarette and sat back in a kitchen chair. Life, she thought, sipping the ice-cold apéritif and taking in a deep drag of the filtered Cool *menthe*, was good. And if Claude kept his promise and put in for retirement at the end of the summer, it would be better still. He was too old for it now; it needed a younger man, and he knew it. She took another sip of her Pineau and the chill sweetness puckered her cheeks. Another six months and he'd be free to hand in his badge and gun and be done with it all. Thirty years in the service; it was enough, surely?

A second Pineau followed the first, with a second cigarette to accompany it. She went to the window above the sink and latched it open. She and her husband had given up cigarettes nearly a year before, but they each smoked privately, secretly, without the other knowing. So as not to offer temptation. It was a compelling theory. If he knows I'm smoking, thought Minette to herself, he'll want to smoke – and vice versa – so they both smoked on their own, when the other wasn't around. But no amount of cooking, Minette knew, would cover the smell of tobacco. Claude would spot it at once – and immediately be tempted to light one up himself. She couldn't have that on her conscience. With the grandchildren round so often, well, it really wouldn't do. Her daughter Laura – and her son-in-law, in particular – would not be pleased. They might limit the number of times the grandchildren visited, might even refuse to let them stay over. And Minette couldn't bear the thought of losing those kids. Little Nicolas, little Natalie.

Maybe it was the shopping, maybe it was the two Pineaux, but Minette felt a comfortable drowsiness settle on her as the clock struck two. She was ahead of herself, she decided; she could take a nap and still have everything under control by the time Claude returned home. Twenty minutes – half an hour would do it – with her feet up on the sofa. A cat nap.

And that was what Minette Peluze did, opening the windows in the *salon* to pull the shutters closed so that the early afternoon sunshine slanted down in cool stripes onto the tiled floor, before settling herself on the sofa, making sure her new hairdo didn't get too pressed out of shape.

Somewhere a fly buzzed but she couldn't be bothered to find it. The house creaked. A car drove past. A dog barked.

Closing her eyes, she thought of her grandchildren, and that big hulking husband of hers beaming when he saw what was for supper. That look in his eye, cast in her direction. She knew what that look meant and the prospect warmed her.

Maybe she slept, she couldn't say. All she knew was that she was suddenly awake, her eyes wide open and a cushion pressing down against her face. She tried to twist and turn away from it, but the cushion and the hands that held it stayed in place, following her every movement. Her first thought, as she tried to straighten herself against the springs of the sofa and sit up, was that Claude was back earlier than expected, and kidding about. In which case this was no joke. He'd frightened her. And spoiled her hair. And she could feel her heart thumping.

But she suddenly knew that it wasn't Claude. As well as the

52

hands on the cushion, someone now jumped astride her lower legs, hands locking her knees. There were two people here.

She arched her hips, then lashed out with her arms and fists, flailing for something to fight against, finally finding the arms of whoever it was holding the cushion. They were long and strong, but bare and thin, and she knew they belonged to a woman. She latched on to them, a hand on each forearm, trying to tug them away, so she could breathe. But the arms were locked tight and couldn't be moved. So then she scratched them with her nails, pinched the skin, tried to reach for the head that must be there somewhere above her.

But she could find nothing, nothing more to grab hold of, and her breath, she suddenly realised, was nearly gone from all this panicking exertion. She needed to breathe, she needed to draw breath, but the inability to do so made her panic even more and she started screaming into the cushion, screaming and screaming until there was no breath left in her lungs and no new breath to take in, nothing to suck through the cushion, a tightness now settling on her chest and a muffling blackness creeping into her head.

No more breath, no more breath, the tightness now easing, the blackness now softening into a deeper, darker blackness, her body beginning to tire and cease its useless resistance.

She was going to die.

She was dying.

She simply couldn't believe it.

11

'HE IS NOT A WELL man,' said the senior nurse as she led Jacquot down a lino-covered corridor at the Institut Briand. She talked as she walked, glancing back over her shoulder, the lino tiles, shiny and sticky, squeaking beneath her rubber-soled trainers. 'Such a terrible thing to happen.' Her voice was soft and caring still, but her expression was hard and grim and unsurprised. She had seen too much.

Jacquot nodded his agreement, taking it all in: a high corniced ceiling with neon strip lights, bars on the corridor windows, no pictures or furnishings, the doors on his right set with metal plates around the locks and sliding grilles at head-height. The air here was cool and still and smelt of polish.

'Just through here,' said the nurse, as they approached a set of double doors. She reached for the bunch of keys chained to her belt, rummaged through them and by the time they got to the doors, she had the right one in her hand and was fitting it into the lock. 'He probably won't look at you, and he may not say anything. Don't be surprised. It's the way he is, I'm afraid. *Le pauvre.*' As far as the nurse was concerned, this had all the makings of a wasted journey for the policeman from Cavaillon.

The Institut Briand was between Carpentras and Courthézon, a thirty kilometre drive from Cavaillon, in flat farmland south of the

Montmirail cliffs. Jacquot had taken the autoroute, keeping to the inside lane except when slower-moving lorries forced him to overtake. The morning was bright and sharp and there was no hurry, his speed calculated to keep the draft from his open windows to a minimum, the sound of passing traffic muffled by a tape of classic favourites that had started with Brazilian jazz as he left Cavaillon and settled into banjo-plucking bluegrass as he turned off the autoroute, flashed his badge at the *Péage* toll and followed the signs for the Institut.

It was the second week of May, the verges of the road were dry and dusty, and the cherry trees were in bloom – white, cream and pink squares scattered across the landscape. It was, Jacquot decided, a good time to be alive – a judgement hastily revised as he swung through the Institut Briand's brick-pillared gates and, at the end of a cherry-lined drive, saw the Gothic brick façade: black bricks and red bricks, laid straight, herringboned, or patterned in square and diamond shapes. Put up at the end of the nineteenth century by a farmer who'd done well from his plums and apricots but had no eye for architecture, the building seemed narrower than it should be and its tall windows, corner turrets and steeply pitched slate roof gave it an odd perspective – as if it had been squeezed by giant hands. It was a brooding, unnerving structure. As Jacquot drew closer, a single cloud slid in front of the sun and a shadow raced down the drive towards him.

Since Aix General Hospital was not equipped for the long-term psychiatric care that his physician considered appropriate, Noël Gilbert had been transferred to the Briand a couple of weeks earlier and, according to the nurse who had greeted Jacquot at reception and was showing him the way, he wasn't likely to be leaving the institute any time soon. As well as being deemed a continuing suicide risk, Gilbert had suffered a sudden and severe breakdown, literally shutting himself down for hours at a time – eyes wide, mouth open, hunched forward. There was no response, no apparent awareness of anything around him, the nurse told Jacquot. As she babbled on, he wondered about patient confidentiality, finally deciding that, as a *flic*, he was probably considered comparable to the staff and consequently in the loop.

'There he is,' said the nurse, pushing open the doors and pointing across a small courtyard, more a large lightwell than a garden, a square of gravel framed by concrete paths. Sitting on a bench directly opposite the door, with another nurse close by, was Noël Gilbert, legs out in front of him, head back, staring at the small patch of blue sky four floors above him. He wore what looked like loose, striped pyjamas and a pair of rope-soled espadrilles.

'Thank you,' said Jacquot. 'You've been most helpful.'

'*De rien* – it's nothing,' said the nurse. 'When you want to leave, my colleague will let you out.' Stepping back she closed the doors and Jacquot heard the double click of the lock.

There were no other patients in the courtyard and he wondered whether Noël had been brought here for the meeting rather than have it conducted in his cell – for that was surely what all those locked doors had been that he had passed in the corridor. With a brief nod to the second nurse, answered with a quick glance and tight smile before she returned to her crossword puzzle, Jacquot headed for the bench and sat down beside Gilbert.

'Hello, Noël. Remember me? Daniel Jacquot. From Cavaillon.'

He hadn't expected any response and he didn't get any.

Gilbert didn't move. Not a blink, not a murmur. No sign even of breath being drawn. Not a single movement. He could have been a shop-window dummy propped beside Jacquot on the bench. He was pale and gaunt and looked several kilos lighter than the last time Jacquot had seen him, back in that empty guest room at Le Mas Bleu.

Noting the bandaged forearms, Jacquot crossed his legs and made himself comfortable, in no hurry, playing much the same game as he'd played that Sunday morning at the hotel. He looked up at the tiny square of sky, just like Gilbert, and let his gaze wander down the brick walls, counting the windows, the diamond patterns, catching every now and then a passing shape or shadow beyond the glass. A pigeon clattered into the lightwell, circled the courtyard looking for a perch, then thought better of it and made a hasty retreat.

'Pigeon breasts. Delicious,' said Jacquot, softly. 'Cold. From the fridge. With hot mashed potatoes.' He didn't expect an answer; he didn't get one. More minutes passed in a strange, almost companionable, silence.

Finally, Jacquot reached into his pocket and pulled out a pack of cigarettes. He held them up for the nurse to see. She nodded; he could smoke if he wished. He lit up, left the packet and lighter between him and Gilbert, and started to smoke.

He was half way through his cigarette when Gilbert shifted on the bench, worked his neck as though it was stiff from looking at the sky, and drew in his legs.

'Can I have one?' he asked. His voice sounded cracked, dry.

'Help yourself.'

Over on her chair, the nurse heard Gilbert's voice and looked up from her crossword.

Jacquot didn't turn, kept his eyes fixed on the far wall, but he knew that the other man was looking at him. He was right.

'I know you, don't I?'

Jacquot nodded. He heard the cigarette packet being shaken and the rasp of his lighter. There was an indrawing of smoke and a low, halting exhalation.

'I remember now. You were kind. Thank you.'

Jacquot said nothing, tapped some ash from his cigarette.

They smoked on in silence for a few minutes more.

'They think I'm going to kill myself.'

'You try it once, that's what they do. Reckon you're going to do it again.'

'Sometimes I want to. Early in the morning is the worst, when I wake up. And remember.'

Jacquot nodded, dropped his cigarette onto the path and ground it out with his shoe.

'Early morning's always bad. That's what happens when you lose someone.'

'Other people feel like this?'

'Sometimes not as bad. Sometimes worse. It depends.'

Gilbert took a last drag of his cigarette and flicked the stub on to the gravel where it let off a coil of smoke, then died.

'Why are you here? Why do you want to see me?'

'I want you to look at some photos.'

'Identify someone?'

'Well, that would be very useful. If you can.'

'Show me,' said Gilbert, sitting straighter, turning towards him.

Jacquot straightened up too, reached into his pocket. As he did so he noticed that the nurse had put down her newspaper and was watching them.

'Just three pictures,' he said, sliding the photos from an envelope. Before he could offer them, Gilbert had taken them from him. They were the photos taken at the church, in the street and going through the gates to the Blanchards' farm, but without the red circles.

Gilbert shuffled through them, held them together like a hand of cards. Then, one by one, he lifted them up, turned them to the light, and scrutinised them.

'See anyone in particular?' asked Jacquot.

Gilbert nodded. 'These two,' he said, holding the cards together again, pointing with a finger.

Jacquot smiled. 'Those two, okay. And two, you say? Not three?'

Gilbert looked at the images a little longer.

'I think it was just the two of them.'

'So, can you identify them? Do you know them?'

Gilbert shook his head.

'Men or women?'

Another shake of the head.

And then, 'Are they the ones?' Gilbert didn't have to add – *who killed Izzy*.

'Right now, all we want to know is who they are,' replied Jacquot. 'If anyone recognises them. So we can cross them off our list.'

'I don't know who they are, but I do remember them. Seeing them there.'

'Any reason?'

Gilbert nodded, sighed.

'They were the only people I saw that day who didn't smile.'

12

NAMES WOULD HAVE BEEN GOOD, a solid identification, even a confirmation as to gender – male or female. But the fact that Noël Gilbert had picked out from the crowds the two unidentified people that they had narrowed it down to, that he remembered them, for not smiling, for not being caught up like everybody else in the joy and happiness and celebration of a country wedding, meant that the trip to the Institut Briand had not been entirely wasted. But as he headed south, back to Cavaillon, what Jacquot couldn't get over was what had happened when he'd said goodbye to Gilbert and tried to leave.

The young man had seized his hands and squeezed them tight, pinning him to the bench.

'Take me with you,' he'd pleaded, his face just centimetres from Jacquot's, tears flooding into his eyes. 'I'm fine. I won't do it again. I'm fine, I promise you.'

Minutes earlier he'd seemed so normal – smoking, talking, looking at the photos. Remembering. Yet suddenly he seemed gripped by a kind of manic desperation.

'She'll look after me . . . Izzy. She'll make sure I'm okay, you'll see.'

'Time for the nice Monsieur to go,' the nurse had said, after hurrying over, trying to loosen Gilbert's grip on Jacquot. When she finally managed it, his body slumped. His arms and hands went loose, but the nurse still held on to them.

'I think you'd better leave now,' she'd told Jacquot. 'I've called for someone to show you out.' And she'd nodded to the door across the yard.

Forty minutes later, parking in the basement at Cavaillon police headquarters, Jacquot still hadn't quite been able to shake off the feelings of shock and sadness. They were right to have sent Gilbert to Briand. There was no way they could let him go from there. Not yet. As he reached the squad room and passed through to his office, Jacquot wondered just how much time it would take before they could. Swinging off his jacket, he hung it on the back of his chair and sat himself down. He was lighting a cigarette when the phone started ringing.

'*Oui*, Jacquot.'

'Daniel, it's Al.' The gravelly voice was unmistakable. Al Grenier, the old timer from Marseilles, the longest serving officer at police headquarters on rue de l'Evêché and the only man on the squad who'd never called Jacquot 'Boss', back in the days when he had worked Homicide.

'*Eh bien*, my old friend . . .' began Jacquot, a smile digging into his cheeks. It was a long time since they'd spoken.

'I'm afraid your old friend has some bad news for you,' interrupted Grenier. His tone was business-like, controlled.

An immediate chill settled over Jacquot and the smile was wiped away as he sat up at his desk, heart suddenly beating fast. 'Who?' he asked. Bad news from Grenier could only mean someone down, one of the boys in the Homicide squad killed or seriously hurt.

'None of the boys. It's Claude's wife . . . Minette.'

The news hit Jacquot like a bunched fist to the solar plexus, the breath driven from his body.

Minette? Minette Peluze? It couldn't be.

In an instant he could see her. Round cheeks, hands on wide hips, a ringing laugh that would wake a sleeping elephant. And then, up

61

close: her sweet, enchanting smile; her naughty, twinkly eyes; her bubbly wit and humour; the way she rock 'n' rolled – no one like her on the dance floor – and Claude, her husband, looking as though he was marking time, tapping his feet, swinging his hips, spinning her round. Jacquot could see it all in a flash. Of all the wives on the squad, of all the girlfriends, lovers, partners, occasionals, there was no one like Claude's wife Minette. Over the years she had played mother-hen to any number of young detectives starting out on rue de l'Evêché, and there wasn't a man on the squad who would hear a word said against her. If police headquarters had a resident saint it was Minette Peluze.

As Jacquot remembered all this, a deep sadness settled over him, a griping emptiness that settled into his belly.

A heart attack, that's what it would be. Just too much fizz, too much brio, for that mighty heart of hers to sustain.

Or a car crash. She was, after all, the world's worst driver.

Or maybe a stroke. Out of the blue. No warning.

In her kitchen, Jacquot hoped. That would be the best place. With its country range, and herbs tied in bunches and hung from the ceiling beams, with its scrubbed oak table and its stacked shelves of Kilner jars – containing everything from star anise to webbed mace, vanilla pods to cumin. The conserves and confits. No one cooked like Minette. Everyone on the squad treasured an invitation to dine with the Peluze family. Her *gigots* and *carrés*, her *boulettes* and *beignets*, her *soupes* and *salades*, lasagnes and moussakas and *gratins* . . . it was a happy man who came into *Maison* Peluze to find Minette in an apron, her kitchen warm and steamy and filled with appetising aromas. Jacquot remembered the last time he'd seen her, the previous winter coming to the kitchen table with that cast-iron Staub casserole of hers held high and steaming, filled with her legendary *pot-au-feu*. On a chill winter's eve, after a long day chasing bad guys, there was nothing like it.

And now she was gone. And Claude, Jacquot knew, would be devastated. The ex-legionnaire and loyal sidekick would have gone down hard. Never a birthday went by, or Christmas or an anniversary, without that tough old man racking his brains for something new to give his wife, to excite and thrill her.

'How?' asked Jacquot, grateful that Al had given him some time to take in the news.

'At first, it looked like she'd had a stroke or a heart attack. Lying on the sofa, a load of shopping in the kitchen – their anniversary, for God's sake – and Claude with the whole weekend off.'

'Who found her?'

'Her daughter called by with the grandchildren . . . You can imagine. The kids thought Nana was asleep.'

Jacquot paused. He hadn't been listening properly. There was something he'd only just registered.

'You said "At first".'

'That's right, Daniel. Someone killed her. Smothered she was, though she was left to look like she'd nodded off. She'd taken out her dentures, set them on a side-table. Like she was just taking a nap. It wasn't till the ambulance people got there that they noticed the broken blood vessels in her eyes. Then there was the bruising round her knees, and traces of blood and skin tissue under her nails. Probably from the person holding the cushion. Two assailants by the look of it – maybe more – but nothing stolen. Like it was her they were after.'

'How's Claude?'

Al grunted.

'You need me to tell you?'

'I guess not.'

'There's a funeral, day after tomorrow. Eleven o'clock. La Bouilladisse, out past Aubagne. It's where she grew up. A family crypt even. I thought you'd want to know.'

'I'll be there.'

'You and everyone else.'

13

AL GRENIER WASN'T WRONG. THEY were all there – family, friends, local dignitaries. Black suits and civic sashes and Légion buttonholes, even dress uniforms for the heads of the Police Nationale and Gendarmerie. And not a black armband in sight; for Minette Peluze there could be no such informality. And every man jack from the squad on rue de l'Evêché was there. They must have closed up headquarters, Jacquot thought to himself; there couldn't have been many left behind.

A funeral service had been held earlier that morning, for family only, at Église St-Croix in La Bouilladisse, but the interment in the town's old cemetery was open to all. The cemetery was smaller than Marseilles' St-Pierre, a long rectanglar plot of land on the crown of a wooded hill above the town, and by the time Jacquot arrived, actually caught behind the cortège as it wound its way up the hill from the church, most of the *allée* and gravelled path around the Martine family crypt was tight with mourners, a wide, spilling pool of black against the glaring limestone. By the time he'd joined the crowd, having parked some distance down the road from the cemetery gates, the casket had been taken from the hearse by pallbearers and was being blessed by a curé dressed in brilliant white lace surplice and purple stole. Over the heads and shoulders of the mourners, nodding to familiar faces turned in his direction, and with the advantage of his place on the slope, Jacquot was able to see the flick of holy water and the sign of the cross from the curé as the pallbearers prepared to carry the casket into the crypt.

As they moved forward Jacquot caught sight of Claude Peluze, standing with his daughter and grandchildren and son-in-law. Jacquot was too far away to make him out in any detail, even with the slope in his favour, but the lowered head and sagging shoulders of his old friend told Jacquot all he needed to know.

It was exactly then that he noticed something else, a movement away from the crowd of mourners, beyond the Martine crypt, higher up the hill near the cemetery gates. Two figures dressed in black. In trousers and coats, by the look of it. Two men? A man and a woman? Two women? It was difficult to tell from this distance. All he could say for sure was that they looked like mourners, visiting a family grave. But then one of them raised an arm and shielded his or her eyes against the sun, clearly looking in their direction. Hardly surprising given the crowd gathered around the crypt, spilling across the *allée*, quite a size for a small cemetery in a small sleeper suburb of Marseilles.

But there was something in the way the figure moved. Bold, direct, curious. Shielding eyes. Watching.

And with the shock of sudden recall, Jacquot had it. The photos back in Cavaillon. The two unidentified figures at the Blanchard wedding.

In the churchyard.

In the street.

At the Blanchards' gates.

But it was a ridiculous idea – to imagine that the same two possible suspects from the Blanchard wedding might also be here in La Bouilladisse. It was a cemetery, for goodness sake, open to anyone to visit a family grave, to pay their respects. That's all they were, a couple of mourners momentarily distracted by the sight of the crowd down the slope – nothing more. He shook away the troubling thought; so unlikely, so . . . ridiculous. Yet he kept his eyes on them, darting between them and Minette's casket as it was manhandled into the shadowed interior of the family crypt. And as the casket disappeared, the two distant figures turned and went back up the path, as though their visit was at an end and they were headed home.

For a moment Jacquot didn't know what to do: whether to stay where he was or go after them, get a closer look at them, maybe ask for their names, see what car they drove. What any policeman would think of doing; following up, on the off-chance.

But it was ridiculous. Quite ridiculous.

There was no possible reason to suppose . . .

Yet even if he'd decided to do it, there was no time now. The pallbearers re-emerged from the crypt and the gates were closed with a jarring clang, the family turned to their limousine and the crowd of mourners began to disperse, making their way to their own cars. As the black-clad pool spread out, thinned, it didn't take long for the boys from rue de l'Evêché to gather round Jacquot: Al Grenier, who'd made the call, Luc Dutoit, Etienne Laganne, Charlie Serre, and the stutterer Pierre Chevin. Hands were clasped, backs slapped, but the greetings were quiet, the smiles quick and strained.

'You coming to the house?' asked Laganne, pulling a cigarette pack from his pocket, shuffling some out, offering them round. All except Al Grenier, who didn't smoke, helped themselves, snapped lighters and settled into a loose circle. With a frown Laganne regarded the empty packet, crumpled it and was about to chuck it away when he remembered where he was, balling it up and slipping it back into his pocket instead.

'It's at their daughter Laura's house,' said Charlie Serre, Laganne's partner. 'Up in the hills above Roquevaire. On the way back to the autoroute.'

'She's done all Minnie's recipes,' added Laganne, as though that was all the excuse they needed. 'Apparently it was stipulated in the will. "When they come and get me I want feasting. I want everyone to have one last taste. And remember." Something like that.'

'So w-w-w-we'll be eating w-w-w-well,' said Pierre Chevin, running a finger between his tanned jowls and stiff white collar.

'If anyone's got an appetite,' replied Al.

14

IT WAS ANOTHER LONG WALK for Minette's farewell luncheon. By the time Jacquot and the boys arrived at the daughter's house on the slopes above Roquevaire there was nowhere to park within two blocks of the *impasse* where the family lived.

'It's a no-smoking house,' warned Al, as they made their way up the drive past a swimming pool and tennis court. 'The son-in-law's particular about that.'

'*Merde*,' said Laganne, who'd stopped en route to buy a fresh pack.

'Don't worry,' said Charlie Serre as they trooped through the open front door. 'You can't smoke inside, but there's a terrace out back which the husband doesn't mind people using. I remember Claude telling me.'

'What does he do?' asked Jacquot, taking in the wide sweep of the front hall and staircase, the paintings, the rugs, and the clean, lean, steel furnishings. For the daughter of a Marseilles *flic*, Laura had certainly done well for herself. There was never any doubt that she was a chip off the old block but, as most of the boys had told Claude over the years, she was a lot better-looking than her old dad.

'Surgeon. Down at Témoine,' replied Laganne. 'Probably seen enough lungs to know it's not a good idea.'

As they stepped from the hallway into the main *salon*, it looked as though most of those who had attended the funeral service and interment had also come back to the house. Set on two levels, the distant terrace clearly visible through a far wall of glass, the *salon* was packed with a shifting tide of black against the terracotta floors, the low murmur of voices not quite animated enough to lend the gathering any sense of frivolity or ease. But Jacquot judged that this mood would not last long. As well as stipulating that all her classic dishes should be served for her send-off, Minette Peluze had clearly made similar arrangements with regard to drinks. She knew who her guests would be, she knew what they drank. And she'd made damn sure it was on tap. Winding through the crowd were a corps of waistcoated waiters bearing trays of whisky, Pernod, wine and champagne. As the squad came into the *salon*, one of these waiters approached them and his tray emptied rapidly.

'Never understood champagne at a funeral,' said Charlie Serre. 'Whisky's much more like it,' he added, nodding approvingly at the measure and tipping back his glass. 'More melancholic . . . more appropriate.'

'And j-j-j-just the kind of shot you'd get from M-M-M-Minette herself,' remarked Chevin, adding a dash of water to his Pernod, returning the carafe to the tray and nodding his thanks to the waiter. 'And I think we owe it to our hostess to make this a m-m-m-memorable occasion. F-F-F-Festive even.'

'Now you know why they've got the bubbly,' said Laganne. 'She means us to have a party.'

But first there was the duty call, the careful approach to the widower, extending their sympathies and condolences. As he drew closer, Jacquot was stunned to see how much his old friend had aged, how much weight he'd shed. It was maybe six months since they'd last met, up at the Cabrille place on Roucas Blanc where Peluze had run the job. Back then he'd been his usual big-shouldered, lumbering self. Now he was half the size. When he shook Peluze's hand and hugged him, Jacquot could feel the bones. A couple of weeks since Minette had died and he'd aged a decade.

'It's good to see you, Daniel, and good of you to come. Minette always had a soft spot for you. Can't think why.' Claude and Jacquot gripped each other's shoulders and Claude smiled sadly, big brown eyes cast down. So much to say, but no need. Best left unspoken. Just a few nods were enough and then, from behind, a hand taking Claude's arm, turning him. He was needed elsewhere. More well-wishers. More condolences.

'I'll catch you later,' he said, nodding to the terrace and mimicking a smoke with two discreetly raised fingers.

'I'll be there,' said Jacquot and released his friend.

Thirty minutes later, leaning against the balustrade, shaded by a copse of oak and pine and overlooked by the slopes of the St-Baume Massif, Jacquot was watching Minette's grandchildren play on a swing when he felt a tap on his shoulder. It was Claude, fixing a smile on his face as Jacquot turned to greet him.

'Don't do the sympathy thing or I swear I'll knock your teeth out,' were the first words he said.

'I haven't eaten yet, so I won't risk it,' replied Jacquot.

'Good. Because you'd be missing something. Believe it or not, Laura's a better cook than her mother. I wouldn't have said that if the old girl were standing next to me, mind . . . but there you are.'

The smile faltered, so Jacquot took up the slack.

'I heard the basics. Who's handling the case?'

'Guimpier at the office,' replied Claude, nodding towards the tall stooping figure of Yves Guimpier, head of operations on rue de l'Evêché. 'And then there's Luc and Al on the street . . . the rest working back-up. Couldn't be in better hands.'

'Any suspects? Leads?' asked Jacquot, lighting a cigarette.

'Nothing. Not a thing. The house was clean. No sign of a break-in, or a burglary interrupted, or a struggle . . . them being caught on the property when she arrived home and panicking. Everything neat as a pin, just the way she liked it.' As he spoke Claude seemed to relax, the springs unwinding, talking police talk – detail, speculation, conjecture – the familiar team language that skated over any personal involvement. 'Not that anyone needed to break in,' he continued. 'The silly moo left the key in the front door. She did it all the time. I was always telling her . . .' He took a breath, held it in. 'Whoever it was – probably a pair of passing chancers – all they had to do was see the key in the lock, and take a look.'

'And then?'

'She was having one of her naps. Wakes up, catches them in the act and they panic. Put her down on the sofa, because that's where she is. Do it with a cushion, because they're not tooled up. Then scarper quick. Chancers, like I say.'

'And not take anything? Her purse? Jewellery?'

Claude shook his head and reached for Jacquot's cigarette. He took a quick drag, handed it back.

'The place was clean. Nothing missing that I could see.'

Jacquot frowned.

'Seems odd, that's all.'

'Like I said, they must have panicked, is all. Being surprised, being seen. Someone able to identify them.'

'And it had to be two? A pair of them?'

'Two or more. One on her legs, one for her arms, maybe another with the cushion – who knows?'

'But nothing stolen, you said?'

'Look, I know what you're thinking . . . The other possibility. Not just passing chancers, but someone watching the house, waiting for her.'

'Like you say it's a possibility.'

'Who knows, Daniel? I've made a lot of enemies. You too. All of us.'

'So you'll be checking your arrests, grudges . . .'

'Prison releases . . . *oui, bien sûr*. All that.'

'But nothing yet?'

Claude shook his head, took a swig of his whisky.

'When the boys I've put away come out from Baumettes, all they want to do is keep a low profile in case I come calling. In a blue moon they might think to take a shot at me – but that's a blue moon. Maybe just a couple of times since I started. As for the wife . . . believe me, they're not going to try something with the wife.'

71

'So what's your theory?'

'Right now, I can't put any of it together. You know how it is at the start. More questions than a quiz show, and not a single answer. But these things grow, gain momentum. Something will turn up. Someone will make a mistake. And then we'll have them, eh?' He might have been talking about an up-coming grudge match between Marseilles' home football team, Olympique, and long-time rivals Paris St-Germain at the Stade Vélodrome. He cleared his throat. 'You been having some fun too, I hear?'

'What's that?'

'The Gilbert boy. Police Nationale. Soon as they heard he was in the slot for his wife's murder, the boys over on Garibaldi went ape.' Rue Garibaldi was the Marseilles headquarters of the Police Nationale, and PN boys stuck together.

'He was never in the slot,' said Jacquot, tapping out his cigarette in a Coke can that someone had set up as an ashtray. 'Clean as a whistle.'

'They heard he was in the slammer.'

'Of sorts. A psychiatric hospital. Under observation. He slit his wrists.'

'Jesus Christ . . .' Claude shook his head, as though, finally, he couldn't make sense of the world.

'I saw him at the wedding. He introduced himself. Nice kid.'

'Got it all in front of him, they say. Marked out. And now this.' Claude looked away, down at his grandchildren. Jacquot could see the man start to weaken again.

'He told me Virginie Cabrille got out. Walked,' said Jacquot, keeping the conversation moving along. 'I couldn't believe it.'

Claude grunted.

'You and the rest of us. She brought in some snappy Paris lawyer and just . . . brazened it out.'

'But the Lafour girl? The kidnap? The woman didn't have a leg to stand on.'

'She blamed the brothers . . . the Manichella boys. Said they did it all themselves. That she had no idea what they were up to. Said she was as shocked as anyone when she found out. They'd worked for her father, she said – in the grounds, odd jobs, chauffeurs – and the annexe came with the job. Same with the skipper on her yacht – Milić. The boat might've been owned by the Cabrilles, but she claimed she had no idea he was holding the girl. If she'd only known . . . blah, blah, blah. And, of course, there was nothing to tie her in. When some bright spark dug up phone records and pointed out that a call had been made to the yacht on a Cabrille landline, her lawyer promptly informed the Magistrates' office that no such call had been made by his client, that the number was registered to the brothers' service apartment and not the main house or lodge.'

'Wasn't there a note – a ransom demand?'

'Couldn't stick it to her. Paper, pen, envelope – could have come from anywhere. Hand delivered by a messenger no one's been able to track down.'

'What about Gastal? What she did to him in that basement of hers. And blood all over her.'

'Consensual sex. According to Mademoiselle, that's the way he liked it and she'd simply obliged. Apparently it wasn't the first time he'd visited. As for the blood, well that was just part of their playtime. And, of course, he had a dodgy heart.'

'I didn't know that.'

'Nor did Gastal. But they brought in some Professor of Cardiology from the Institute of Cardiac whatevers who testified that the man could have dropped dead at any time, eating and drinking the way he did. No exercise, unless he had his clothes off. And as if that wasn't enough, they also hauled in some high-class hooker from Lyon to say he'd paid her for the same kind of treatment while he was stationed there with the DGSE, and that she had obliged. Until, she said, his *préférences exotiques* became just a little too *exotique* for her tastes. And that was it, my friend. Out on bail within thirty-six hours, then home custody for a couple of weeks while her lawyer shot down every argument we came up with. No case to answer. *Tout fini.*'

73

Jacquot thought back to that November night, standing in the grounds of the Cabrille estate, a slow drizzle drifting in from the sea, watching with Peluze as she was led away in handcuffs.

'What was it she said? That night, remember? We were standing near the garage. She came over, gave you a look and said . . .'

'"I win". Yeah, I remember. And turns out she was right.'

Back in the *salon*, the blade of a knife was tapped against a glass and a voice was raised:

'*Mesdames, Messieurs, à table, s'il vous plaît. À table, à table, s'il vous plaît.*'

'You hungry?' asked Claude.

'Couldn't eat a thing.'

'Me neither. So let's join the queue before everything goes.'

15

THE BOYS FROM THE SQUAD were among the last to leave Laura's house, and they took Claude with them, back into Marseilles, telling his daughter he'd be fine, they'd look after him. They were lying, of course, and as Jacquot made his way carefully home to Cavaillon the following morning – aching neck, tight squinting eyes, a dozen sharp clamps screwed into his skull – he wondered if Claude was feeling the same, and how the rest of them were coping on rue de l'Evêché. None of them, surely, could have escaped the night's activities unscathed. Minette Peluze would have been proud of them.

As far as Jacquot could remember the evening had begun at Bon Mou, a members' club off rue Paradis, with more beers and whiskies, and from there they had moved to Le Vieux, a restaurant down on the port run by an ex-con who owed some favours. Jacquot couldn't remember reaching for his wallet once, and hadn't seen anyone else do it either, until they stumbled out of Le Vieux and he'd spotted Laganne pass their waitress a green Curie – a five-hundred franc note. Just to say thanks, for putting up with their bad behaviour – nothing more than that.

Afterwards, with the smell of the sea in their nostrils and a bellyful of food to soak up the booze, they'd settled at Paragon, a squad favourite, beyond the Joliette quay. They'd taken a corner table in the back room, squeezing round it, and at some stage in the proceedings, for reasons he couldn't now recall, Jacquot had mentioned the couple he'd spotted at the cemetery, and how, for a moment, he'd considered checking them out. Something to do with always being on the beat, never being able to leave off being a cop.

Why? Charlie Serre had asked. What about them?

And Jacquot had told him about the investigation in Cavaillon – the murder of Gilbert's wife, the wedding pictures, more than three hundred people identified and all, save two, accounted for. Two people. In black. One tall, one short. Just like the ones at Minette's funeral.

'Men or women?' asked Serre.

Jacquot shook his head. 'We can't be sure.'

'Then maybe you should have,' suggested Serre with a twinkle in his eye. 'Checked 'em out, I mean.'

'Why's that?'

'Where did you say you saw them again?'

'Just inside the front gate, top path, at the edge of the trees.'

Serre had taken a moment to work out the exact position. 'Well, I'll tell you one thing for free,' he'd said. 'They wouldn't have been there to visit their old dad.'

'How come?'

'How come?' Serre began to chuckle. 'Because up there, it's a plague pit – that's how come. A common grave. A few hundred people buried there, back in seventeen hundred and something. No names, just a small plaque. But, hey, maybe the pair of 'em were tourists, historians, lovers looking for a bit of privacy amongst the crypts. And then two hundred of us pile in . . . you know what I'm saying?'

And as Jacquot turned off the autoroute and rattled over the reedy, gravelled bed of the Durance into the dusty, glaring outskirts of Cavaillon – which made him squint even harder – he wished now that he had checked them out. Were they two women, two men, or a man and a woman? He'd never know now. Nor would

76

he know how they might have reacted, as they saw him approach. Would they have made a run for it? Or would they have stayed to answer his questions, provide plausible reasons for their presence there? A couple of history scholars, like Serre had said, checking out the plague pit. Or tourists. Or lovers – however unlikely. Five minutes, that's all it would have taken. Nobody would have missed him. But he hadn't, and though he could see no reasonable cause to have done it, he was still irritated with himself.

He should have.

He should have gone. Should have taken a closer look.

And he certainly would have done if he'd known it was a plague pit up there, and they couldn't have been visiting family graves. Standing in a perfect position to watch Minette's funeral, shading their eyes against the sun the better to see. Just like the two at the Blanchard wedding all those weeks before.

But were they the same people? It seemed so unlikely.

And what could possibly link the two events?

The wedding of a country girl to a Marseilles *flic*, and the funeral of the middle-aged wife of a Homicide officer on rue de l'Evêché.

Two cops, that's all. A gendarme and a Chief Inspector. And their murdered wives . . .

But two murders so different in style.

One, an expertly executed shooting; the other a clumsy smothering.

One clearly planned; the other most likely a burglary gone horribly wrong.

It was way out there . . .

But still . . .

16

AFTER BUYING HIMSELF A BLISTER pack of Ibuprofen at the *pharmacie* on Cours Bournissac and washing down a couple of pills with a sweet cappuccino and Calva at Fin de Siècle on Place du Clos, Jacquot headed for police headquarters and his corner office overlooking the railed lawn of Église St-Jean.

Brunet was waiting for him, followed him into his office, and laid down a file on the desk. If he noticed Jacquot's pained, squinting expression he gave no sign of it.

'All you need to know about Dyethelaspurane. Or rather, where you can get hold of it.'

'Which is?' asked Jacquot, pulling off his black jacket and tie from the day before. Across the road a flight of pigeons took off with a rattle of wings from the slatted belfry of the church.

'Pretty much everywhere there's a hospital pharmacy. You need a prescription and most supplies are directed in-house – for surgical procedures, sedation. What you can't do is buy it over the counter.'

'So we're looking at someone who maybe works in hospitals . . .'

'Or knows someone who does.'

What Jacquot had been hoping for was a tighter, more limited source for the drug, something easier to follow through – just a few hospitals, a few outlets. But it wasn't to be.

'Worth following up?' asked Brunet.

'Let's just flag it for now – maybe revisit down the road if Forensics identify the same drug at another crime scene. And maybe check back the last twelve months . . . see if there's anything on file.'

'There's something else,' said Brunet, a dismissive wave of the hand, as though whatever he had to say really was of no importance, and he couldn't think why he'd bothered to bring it up.

Jacquot knew that wouldn't be the case. His assistant loved keeping the best for last. When Brunet didn't say anything, Jacquot had to press him.

'*Eh bien*,' began Brunet, perching on the edge of his boss's desk. 'We have a maybe identification. From the photos.'

'Who? Where? When?'

'A friend of one of the uniform boys, Gaston Lapierre. He manages the Total garage on Avenue de Verdun. Coming into town from the autoroute, you drive right past it. No good for servicing, of course, now that Gaston's boss has run down the workshop,' added Brunet, for a little bit of local colour, 'but the gas is cheaper than Briol's place.'

'*Oui, oui*, thank you,' said Jacquot. 'But what did he see? And when?'

'A man and a woman. In a VW. A Beetle, he thinks. Dark colour: black, blue, green . . . he can't quite recall. Filled the tank late afternoon, a few days before the Gilbert wedding in St-Florent. At first glance, from behind the till, he thought the driver was a man wearing trousers and a trucker's cap – but when he came in to pay, Gaston realised it was a woman.'

'She pay card or cash?'

Brunet spread his hands, regretfully. 'Cash, what else?'

'Registration?'

A shrug this time from Brunet.

'Young or old?'

'Mid to late thirties, Gaston reckoned.'

'And the passenger?'

'He didn't get a good look, but reckoned it was the husband.

Tall, thinnish, a little older, wearing what looked like a leather jacket. Said the one who paid was wearing jeans tucked into black boots, and a blue jumper. Well-built girl, he said. Which means she had tits on her.'

A blue jumper. Jacquot remembered the threads taken from the service hatch at Le Mas Bleu, snagged on the rough wood.

Blue threads. Maybe, maybe . . .

'I get the picture. Anything else. Voice? Accent?'

'Two words was all she said. "M'sieur" when she went in to pay, and "Merci" when she took her change and left. The only reason he remembered her was the boobs.'

'And they were coming into town, or leaving?'

'Gaston thinks they were heading out, but he couldn't say for certain.'

Jacquot gave this some thought.

'So a few days before the wedding, if it's them, they're either heading for the autoroute or they've just come off it, which suggests they don't live locally.'

'If it's them.'

'Any luck with hotels, *pensions*, *chambres d'hôtes . . . ?*'

'Nothing between Cavaillon and Apt and a dozen kilometres north and south – Cadenet, Lourmarin, Pertuis and up to Gordes, Roussillon. But like you said, maybe they came further. Drove in for the day and then hit the autoroute back home.'

In other words, Jacquot realised, there was no point pursuing that particular avenue. The further they went from Cavaillon, the more places they'd have to screen. It wasn't worth the effort right now – not on such a slim chance, and with such limited resources. Of course, if he'd followed the plague pit 'mourners' at Minette Peluze's funeral, he might have got to see what they drove. If it had been a VW, then they'd have had something to go on.

If only, if only.

Instead . . .

17

MORE THAN A MONTH AFTER Noël Gilbert had woken to find his new wife dead in bed beside him, the police investigation into her murder had got no further than two suspects, a man and a woman, in their thirties, maybe forties, driving a black or dark blue or green VW, last seen at a Cavaillon garage a few days before the murder, possibly the same two people in the three pictures taken at the church in St-Florent, in the procession down its main street, and outside the gates of the Blanchards' farmhouse. And possibly the same couple that Jacquot had taken for 'mourners' at the cemetery in La Bouilladisse.

Possibly. Nothing more certain than that.

As far as he and his team had been able to ascertain, their two suspects had not been guests at the church ceremony, or at the reception and hog roast that followed, and no one they had interviewed remembered seeing them with the exception of Noël Gilbert and the *garagiste* Gaston Lapierre. As for the murder weapon, a 9mm automatic with silencer, police had searched the grounds of Le Mas Bleu, swept the storm culverts either side of the Maubec–Robion road, and retraced the killers' route through the vineyards, but found nothing.

'What about the car?' asked Guy Fourcade, Cavaillon's examining prosecutor, who had called Jacquot in to review an investigation that was rapidly grinding to a halt. The two men were sitting in Fourcade's office in the Magistrates' building, a set of three french windows behind his desk overlooking place Lombard in the old town. One of the windows was latched open, the leaves on the plane trees outside shifting gently in an afternoon breeze. It was not a meeting that Jacquot had been looking forward to. When investigations stalled, it was Fourcade's job to get them started again, or know the reason why.

Fourcade was in his late forties, still fresh-faced with bright enquiring eyes and a tidy crop of short black hair, and though he projected an air of easy camaraderie – all on the same team, kind of thing – Jacquot wasn't taken in. After their first few encounters he had mentioned it to Claudine: the frosty edge to Fourcade, that thin, covering smile.

She had told him all he needed to know. 'He played rugby to club level, but unlike you he never made it any further. And he was not a happy man when I had to make it clear to him a few years back that I was not interested in taking him to my bed. Oh, and the hair is not his own.'

Three very good reasons, Jacquot supposed, but still no excuse.

'According to the garage-man, Lapierre, it wasn't anything special,' replied Jacquot. 'A Beetle, he thinks. Dusty, dirty. Done some travelling, he said.'

'So not a rental then? Privately owned?'

'That's how it looks,' said Jacquot. 'But without a registration number . . .' He spread his hands. He didn't have to say anything more. Both men knew that Volkswagen Beetles might not have been the most popular car in France, but there were enough of them around to make tracing one an almost impossible undertaking. And, as Brunet had speculated, it didn't even need to be French. It could as easily have been registered in Germany, or the Netherlands, or Switzerland. Indeed anywhere in mainland Europe.

The two men fell silent, Fourcade with his elbows on his desk, twisting a pencil between his fingers, Jacquot sitting back in his chair, legs crossed.

'So what's next, Daniel?'

'We have an alert out for any incident involving our likely suspects, a man and a woman in their thirties, early forties, driving a dark-coloured VW, and on the drug used on Gilbert. Right now, there's nothing more we can do – until something else happens, something we can tie into the Gilbert murder.'

'You don't believe this is a stand-alone?'

Jacquot could tell from his tone that Fourcade thought it was.

'There's just no reason for it, Maître. A country girl? New husband put out for the count while she gets a bullet in the eye? And the killer uses a silencer? We've been through Gilbert's background and there's nothing of note, nothing to explain it. There's something else going on here; we've only got a part of the story. It's just . . . we need something else to go on. And we haven't got it yet.'

'Well, let's hope you get it soon,' said Fourcade, his voice sharpening a little, his eyes narrowing. 'People aren't happy, Daniel. The Blanchards are well-known around here, and popular. There are going to be some awkward questions coming my way very soon and I'll need some answers. Just as soon as you can supply them, *s'il te plaît.*'

And then the smile was switched back on, a friendly hand resting lightly on Jacquot's arm as Fourcade walked him to the door and bid him *adieu*.

Outside on place Lombard, Jacquot lit up a cigarette and wondered again about the 'mourners' at the cemetery in La Bouilladisse. For some reason he couldn't shift them from his memory, still cross with himself for not checking them out. If only to eliminate them from the enquiry.

18

IT WASN'T JUST GUY FOURCADE, the town's examining magistrate, who was asking questions. That same evening, back at the millhouse, Claudine went over the same ground.

'It's been weeks,' she said, as she settled at the table that Jacquot had laid on the terrace. The sun had slipped behind the hillside at the back of the millhouse, but the evening shadows creeping down from the woods that surrounded the property were still warm and smelled of resin. Salad was tossed, wine poured, and the *carré d'agneau* he had grilled on the fire-pit divided between them.

'I just can't believe that nothing's happened,' she continued. 'I know you're doing everything you can, but it's just so . . . unfair. That no one has been brought to book for it.'

Jacquot glanced across at her as she sliced through her cutlet, took a small mouthful then sat back from the table. She looked drawn and tired, and he could see how the investigation's lack of progress, lack of leads, lack of everything, had started to wear her down. She was too close to it, he realised. She knew the victim, knew the family, their farm just a few kilometres away. And the killing of a young woman, on her wedding night, with a new husband in her bed and the future all ahead of them, had been particularly cruel.

'Think of a car,' said Jacquot. 'With a full tank and an empty road ahead of it. That's what a police investigation is like. At first it's full speed ahead, but then the tank starts to empty and other things get in the way. Diversions, distractions, wrong turnings. What's needed is more fuel, something to keep that car rolling along. And right now, it seems, we're a long way from any filling station.'

Claudine reached for her wine, swirling it in the glass, staring into its depths.

'You need another murder, don't you? That's the filling station, isn't it?'

'I'm afraid it is. Another scene-of-crime. That's what we need. Wherever it happens. Just so long as we hear about it, make the right connections.' He picked up a curved bone with his fingers and stripped away the remaining meat with his teeth.

'You don't think this is local then, someone living around here?'

He shook his head, swallowed, wiped his lips with a napkin.

'I don't think so,' he began. 'The silencer . . . leaving the scene so clean. It's just too professional. Too carefully thought out. What really worries me is that, for some reason we don't yet know, the murder really was a case of mistaken identity. If that's what it was, then we're pretty much wasting our time, and I'm sorry to say that I doubt we'll ever get to the bottom of it.'

'That poor, poor girl. Everything to live for.' Claudine pushed away her meat, barely touched, and turned instead to her salad, scooping up some leaves.

'And her poor, poor husband, Noël.'

'Is it true what I heard?' she asked.

'Madame Tapis?'

Claudine nodded.

'Apparently . . .' she began.

'. . . He's been transferred to a psychiatric unit? Once again your Madame Tapis is correct. The Institut Briand near Courthézon. He recovered from the first suicide attempt, but there's real fear that he might try again.' Jacquot fell silent, remembered his visit. The pleading, the desperation, the biting grip of his fingers, the tears, and, most disturbing, that haunting belief that Izzy was still alive, that she hadn't been shot, that she would help him, she would look after him, care for him.

Somewhere in the woods, an owl hooted. For a while they sat in silence, listening to the sounds of the night – the slowing buzz of insects, a crackle and tumble of burnt logs in the fire-pit.

With a long sigh, Claudine pushed herself away from the table.

'I'm off to bed. You coming?'

'Maybe a last glass . . .'

She made to gather up the dishes.

'Leave them. I'll do it,' said Jacquot.

She nodded, smiled, came over to kiss him. He could smell a light flowery scent he didn't recognise.

'Nice perfume.'

'Eau de toilette. Not so expensive. I've been wearing it a week. Some *flic* you are.'

She stood up and turned to go. If he had hoped to ease her sadness over supper, he knew he hadn't quite managed it. She still looked tired, he thought, and she seemed somehow relieved that the perfume had not sparked too much interest, that she would have the bed to herself for a little while yet.

'You okay?' he asked, letting her fingers trail through his.

'Gloria Gaynor . . .' she replied. It was a game of theirs. The name of a singer, and the title of a song.

'"I will survive . . ."'

'You got it.'

Later, the table cleared, the fire-pit left to glow in the dark and die, Jacquot went through to the salon, poured himself a small cognac and turned on the television.

Let her rest, he thought, plumping up the sofa cushions. A good night's sleep would do her the world of good.

19

THE TIMBER MERCHANT DELACROIX ET Fils was based in Marseilles, in the west of the city, close to the freight yards of Le Canet, and just six blocks back from the wharves of Arenc and Mirabe. The Delacroix had run this yard for more than a century, a family of jobbing carpenters who'd started out in the repair and refitting of fishing boats, barges and sailing ships and ended up timber merchants as well as expert woodworkers. Not only did they now buy the wood – importing hard woods mostly, shipped to the wharves by suppliers in South America, West Africa and the Far East – they also worked it into whatever form or shape the city's construction bosses wanted. Anything from simple architraving to bed-frames, from garden gates to windows, doors, flooring, and, in recent years, decking and the skeleton frames for conservatories. Coffins, too. Anything needing wood.

Delacroix et Fils employed more than a hundred men, the workforce accommodated in four wings around a central yard, or in the receiving sheds at the docks. Raw timber was brought off the ships, stacked, sorted and trimmed in the company's dock warehouse before being transferred to the main yard where the sawyers and carpenters set to work on whatever orders the firm had received. It was a prosperous, if noisy business – everywhere the whining scream of spinning steel: table saws, jig saws, trimmers; the tappety-tap of the

joiners in their leather aprons, and the machine-gun spitting and snapping of the rivetters and staplers; the industrial clatter of the yards
and dock warehouse all overlaid with the raw, red resinous scent of
split and bleeding wood.

Most of the workforce stayed at Delacroix their working life,
down on the wharves or up in the yard, in some cases four generations of the same family employed by the company. It was that
kind of place. And the best of those workers – those with the
eye and the talent, who were prepared to take on, at the same
wage, a five-year apprenticeship – became cabinet-makers,
Delacroix cabinet-makers. For more than a century, these skilled
artisans had supplied Marseilles' most prestigious addresses: the
shelving and counters for the Parfumerie Pagnon and Nouvelles
Galeries on Canebière; the table booths at Restaurant Basso on
the Quai des Belges; the banisters and panelling for the old Hôtel
Splendide; even the ticket-booths and stage flooring at the old
Grand Théâtre.

It was a fine tradition, and at the end of his apprenticeship twenty-
six-year-old Antoine Berri was ready to put on the soft leather
apron and move to the first floor studios where Delacroix's cabinet-
makers – the Cabbies – worked their bespoke magic. But before
Antoine could do that, there was one final test: to design and make
something, in his own time and out of hours but with full access
to Delacroix tools and machinery, to showcase the skills he'd
acquired. Antoine's maquette, his calling card for the Cabbies, was
a matching pair of bedside tables in sandalwood and ebony. It had
taken him a month to design them, a further month to select from
Delacroix offcuts the woods and grain patterns he wanted, and the
last three months to cut and fit – not a nail or a screw used – the
constituent parts of the two tables. Eight finely tapered legs,
perfectly matched marquetry tops in satinwood and ebony, bowed
cupboard doors no larger than a handkerchief, and two sets of oval-
fronted drawers, wood runnels waxed and chalk-dusted until they
slid as easily as a powdered hand from a silk glove. In another
month he'd be finished, the tables ready for waxing and polishing

and finishing before presentation to, and judgement by, those Delacroix cabinet makers who had gone before him.

At a little after six o'clock one Saturday evening in late May, with the last of the sun streaming in gold squares through the dusty workshop windows, Antoine was working on his tables' back panelling. This should have been the easiest part of the job – the bevelled panelling out of sight against a wall – but Antoine knew the Cabbies, and knew that that would be the first place they looked. Make the back as good as the front, and you couldn't go wrong. But it was the devil to carry off: sighting down a pencil line no thicker than a cotton thread, and feeding the panel of splinter-happy sandal-ply to the blade of a ten-inch table saw with teeth no bigger than, but just as sharp as, a kitten's.

So great was his concentration setting up the next crucial incision, so tight and muffling the ear protectors, that Antoine heard not a sound on the sawdust floor behind him. Nothing until a wrap of cloth came round the side of his head, brushed his cheek and was clamped over his mouth and nose.

Pushing himself away from the work table, his first instinct was to turn himself round, to face his attackers – probably some of the lads from the first floor come in that Saturday evening to give him grief. But the grip on his mouth and nose held, and his breath became suddenly sweet, a strange scent in his nostrils, a little like the fine varnish he used – which was why he suspected his workmates – until the power of it seemed to take the blood and muscle from his legs and arms, and drained away any desire to resist.

Instead he felt himself buckle and fall, felt himself caught, lifted . . .

A sleeve rolled up . . .

And that was it.

20

JACQUOT DROVE INTO CAVAILLON POLICE headquarters, dropped down to the basement car park and found a space. It was a Thursday lunchtime, the last in May, and he'd spent the morning walking through a belt of woods on the heights above Apt. A farmer there had lost his dog, a truffle hound, and all the man could think of was who to blame, who to point the finger at. The dog had been stolen or, more likely, killed, he'd told Jacquot, by one of his competitors, of whom there were many, though none so talented as he, nor so lucky with their own hound. A dog that earned him a healthy income each year – though he was wary of putting a figure to it. Which was how the complaint had filtered through to the squad room in Cavaillon. With little to do in terms of the ongoing Gilbert investigation, Jacquot had taken the call and paid the visit.

Two hundred thousand francs a year, the farmer had finally whispered, as they trudged through the wood: a light cover of holm oak that let in the early summer sun, low branches scraping their shoulders, the leaf litter rustling with every step. Eight years old and the mutt had paid his bed and board a thousand times over, the farmer confided as Jacquot paused on the slope to light a cigarette, wondering how much farther they'd have to walk. It wasn't the first time a complaint like this had been made, and it wouldn't be the last, reflected Jacquot, taking a grateful pull on his cigarette. Every year some truffle hound went missing and the owner called it in.

Killy, the dog was called, after the skier. A spaniel. 'Ran smooth as a torpedo through calm seas,' the farmer said. 'Never took his snout more than a couple of centimetres off the ground. Knew a truffle like a car knows a Stop sign. And never greedy. *Non, non, non.* Not like those fat old pigs up in the Périgord. Snuffle up the tubers before you can get a hand to them, with the bulk and temperament to keep you out of the picture. My old Killy'd just sit there and point and watch you scuff up the earth with your hands till you found it. Just so long as you had a biscuit in your pocket, Killy was happy.'

They'd found Killy thirty minutes after Jacquot's cigarette break, curled up at the base of an old pine that looked as though it had only the slimmest of holds on the earth, a web of sinewy roots rising up out of the ground they clung to as though hating the touch of dead leaves. The dog looked as though it was asleep, nose tucked into hindquarters, tail tidily curled. It was the nose that gave the game away. Two bright-red, pin-prick puncture marks. Bitten by a snake, its money-making snout too close to the ground.

On other occasions when Jacquot had helped locate valuable truffle hounds, the grateful owners had pressed a nugget of the tuber into his hand, as thanks. This time, however, when Jacquot pointed out the tell-tale snake bite, the farmer just turned on his heel and stomped off without another word. It was difficult to say whether he was angry that his dog was dead, or that his competitors could not now be brought to account. Whichever it was, Jacquot was left to find his own way back to his car.

Back in his office, nursing a coffee and wondering how he was going to spend the rest of his day, he saw Brunet striding across the squad room.

'How was Duplessis?' he asked, pulling out a chair and swinging it round so his legs straddled it, arms hanging over the back.

'Disagreeable,' replied Jacquot, looking at the file dangling from his assistant's hands.

'Never happy, that one. Grumpy as all hell.'

'You could have mentioned that.'

Brunet spread his hands in an I-suppose-I-could-have-done way that directed Jacquot's attention to the file he was carrying.

'What have you got there? More lost truffle hounds?'

'Something you'll like, Boss.'

Jacquot waited a beat. When no response was forthcoming, Brunet apparently more concerned about some loose stitching on his jacket, he said, 'Tell me before I die of old age.'

Still working the loose thread, Brunet said, 'Berri. Antoine. Twenty-six. Single. Lives down in L'Estaque. Your part of the world.'

'And?'

'Works at Delacroix et Fils. Maybe you know it?'

Jacquot nodded. Anyone who lived in Marseilles had heard of Delacroix et Fils. For a short while in the late-fifties his own mother had worked for the company, sketching designs for their catalogues and producing art work for their advertising posters. She had taken him there once. He remembered the sharp smell of wood and the ear-splitting screech of saws.

'And?' he asked.

'Lost an arm to a table saw. Saturday evening. Bled to death before anyone found him.'

Jacquot winced. Not a good way to go.

'And our interest in the case?'

Brunet shrugged.

'Just thought you ought to know.'

'And why, particularly?' Sometimes, with Brunet, it was like drawing blood from a stone.

'Ah, because before he lost his arm, Monsieur Berri was drugged.'

Jacquot sat up at that.

'Dyethelaspurane?'

Brunet flicked through the file in his hand. Found what he was looking for.

'*Le même,*' he said. The same.

21

BERNIE MUZON, ONE OF THE squad from rue de l'Evêché, was waiting for Jacquot outside the Delacroix works entrance. Jacquot had called him from Cavaillon. Set it up. As he pulled into the kerb, Muzon recognised Jacquot and levered himself out of his car. He wasn't as tall as Jacquot, but he was still a big man, well-muscled and broad in the shoulder, with a grin to match, brown hair thick and curled, eyes blue and jaw coated in a rough five-o'clock shadow. As usual he was dressed in blue jeans, black T-shirt and scuffed trainers. He reached back into his car and pulled out a blue linen jacket, slipped it on. He was straightening the sleeves as Jacquot came over.

'Sorry about the wait,' said Jacquot, noting the deep tan.

'It's nothing. *De rien*. Better here than a desk at headquarters,' said Muzon, shaking Jacquot's hand.

Jacquot smiled. No change there, then. Muzon was a ferret, a real door-knocker, the kind of cop who loved getting behind the wheel of a car, and going after someone. Loved sizing up some new face, and framing the questions right. Getting to the bottom of something. Anything but sit at his desk. Muzon was a man who liked being out on the streets.

'Hear you guys had quite a time at Minette's?'

Jacquot admitted that they had.

'I'm sorry I missed it. She was a grand lady.'

Both men knew why he hadn't been contacted, told about her death. He'd been on holiday with his wife and kids, two weeks in the French Caribbean that they'd been saving for. If someone had told him about Minette's murder, Bernie Muzon would have been back there for her funeral in La Bouilladisse and hot on the trail of whoever had killed her, leaving the wife and kids on the beach, the holiday ruined.

'So what's the interest here?' asked Muzon, as they headed for the Delacroix Reception, a few metres along the pavement from the arched and cobbled works entrance.

'The report said this Antoine Berri was drugged, prior to the . . . amputation. Dyethelaspurane?'

'That's what the pathologist said. Trouble is, this Dyethy-stuff . . .' Muzon always hated having to pronounce difficult drug names '. . . is widely available. Not over the counter, of course, but easy to get hold of if you know how. Either at source – the factory in Switzerland – or from a hospital pharmacy. There's around twelve thousand of those, by the way, if you were thinking of checking. But why the interest?'

'We had the same drug crop up in another investigation.'

Muzon frowned as he pushed open the Reception door, held it for Jacquot.

'That should have been flagged. It should have come up.'

Jacquot sighed, a regretful spread of the hands, a sly smile.

'Sometimes the big cities don't work as fast as the provinces.'

After signing in at Reception, Muzon sending out another sly smile of his own at the pretty blonde receptionist, the two men pushed through another door, walked down a corridor lined with portraits and sepia pictures of past Delacroix family members and stepped into the main yard. Stacked eight metres high with islands of tarped timber, it was wide enough for a pair of trucks to turn without touching, cobbled, and set round on all sides with brick warehouses. In the centre of each warehouse wall was a massive loading gate from which came the searing screech of saws and the scent of split timber, the only things Jacquot could remember from his long-ago trip here with his mother.

'It's over there,' said Muzon, steering Jacquot to the nearest door – much smaller than the others, in a corner of the courtyard. Once inside, the screeching of heavy guage saws gave way to the quieter buzzing hum of smaller gauge equipment.

The room was about thirty metres long and roofed in slanting corrugated sheets, its stone floor carpeted with sawdust, strewn with offcuts and furnished with a dozen workbenches and saw tables set along the walls. Half of these tables were in use, carpenters bent over their work, glancing up at Jacquot and Muzon, but the first of the work stations just inside the door had been sealed off with a line of police tape, its yellow and blue chevrons looped around workbench and saw table.

It was five days since the killing but there were bloodstains everywhere. The spinning blade, fed by the rushing pulse of Berri's sliced artery, had seen to that, spattering blood across the saw-hood and engine housing, over the shiny metallic surface of the saw table itself, and in a spraying arc up the nearest wall, across three dusty window panes and onto the ceiling. As Jacquot bent under the tape, he could also see that the blood had dripped down into the sawdust, a dried scarlet stalactite still hanging from the bottom half of the blade beneath the saw table.

'Kid was working on his first piece, finishing it off for the judging,' Muzon explained. 'The apprentice thing, you know? Working late, like he'd done before, but being Saturday night he was the only person in this part of the works. He was found by one of the security guards. Apparently the saw was making an odd noise – juddering, the guy said, catching – so he came over to take a look.'

'No chance of an accident?'

Muzon stood aside while Jacquot inspected the work station.

'Not a chance,' he replied.

'The arm and hand were taped down?'

'That's right. Industrial duct tape. Common brand. Whoever did it set that saw there in gear, started it up and fed the lad down to the blade. Like a piece of timber.'

'What's your bet? Killer or killers?'

'You ask me, I'd say two perps, possibly more. Berri was a big guy to put down, even with the drug. And as dead weight, big and heavy to haul up onto the table. I'll tell you one thing for sure . . . whoever it was must have been covered in blood.' Muzon nodded to the stains on the walls and windows.

'Maybe they came in overalls, like the workforce,' said Jacquot. 'Just stripped them off after the killing and dumped them.'

'If they did, they didn't dump 'em around here. Nothing's been found in a four-block radius.'

'Many people about, that time of night? On a Saturday?' Jacquot scuffed the toe of his shoe through the flattened sawdust, stained a dark brown from the spilt blood and sticking to the stone beneath.

'Security, like I said. Three of them in all. And a couple of the trimmers across the yard doing overtime. That's it.'

'Anyone see anything? A man and a woman, say? Or maybe an old VW Beetle, dark colour, parked out front?'

Muzon shook his head.

'Nothing like that. Everything as normal for time and place.'

'To get in here they'd have had to come the way we did?'

'Nope. Reception's closed on a Saturday, so they'd have come in through the works entrance near where we parked.'

'So they knew their way around? They didn't have to ask for directions?'

'Maybe they scouted the place out. Easy enough to do. Maybe someone visiting the showroom and company museum,' said Muzon. 'There's regular guided tours – school trips, tourists, customers, that kind of thing.'

'Any motive? Someone didn't like this Berri guy? He owed money? Dealt drugs? Slept with someone's wife, daughter?'

'That would help, but no. Nothing. The kid was popular, told a good story, worked hard. Had talent, too. No girlfriend, but straight.'

'And someone saws off his arm,' murmured Jacquot. 'It doesn't make sense.'

After a final look round, the two men stepped back into the sunshine and started across the yard, passing down a line of tattooed timber, heading for the street where they'd parked.

'Of course, Police Nationale are all over it,' said Muzon. 'And all over us, too, to get it sorted.'

'Why's that?' asked Jacquot. 'Straight homicide surely?'

'Antoine Berri had a brother. A twin, Jean.'

'So?'

'He's one of ours. A *képi*. Works on rue Garibaldi. The PN.'

Jacquot stopped dead in his tracks.

'His brother's a *flic*?'

Muzon nodded.

'That's right. Just like you and me.'

22

AFTER PARTING COMPANY WITH BERNIE MUZON, Jacquot did not return immediately to Cavaillon. There was something he had to do first, something he'd been meaning to do for some time, yet somehow had never got round to. The trip down to Marseilles for Minette Peluze's funeral might have been hijacked by the squad, but his visit to Delacroix provided him with a second chance, another opportunity to do what he'd been planning. And, if he was lucky, he'd maybe kill two birds with one stone.

Jacquot saw her a hundred metres off, halfway down rue Francis, coming out of Fleurs des Quais, the flower shop where she worked. She didn't see him and he didn't wave or call out her name. All he did when she turned away from him and headed off in the same direction was quicken his pace. He would catch her up.

The woman he was following, in a pretty print dress, with a bag over her shoulder and a spring in her step, was called Marie-Ange Buhl and twice the previous year the two of them had worked together on cases that he'd been involved in. It had started the summer before in the Luberon where Jacquot was investigating the murder of a German family living in Provence. With her help he had uncovered a secret that had turned the investigation upside down. By chance they had met again just a few months later when Jacquot had been working undercover in Marseilles, searching for the missing schoolgirl, Elodie Lafour, and once again her help had proved invaluable, the 'help' in question being her special gift or an ability to 'sense', to 'feel' something. Of course he'd been as sceptical as the next man when she'd first tried to explain it to him, these special powers she had, but he had seen enough by now to know that she was no fraud, that there really was something 'special' about her.

But it was more than just a professional relationship; there had always been much more to it than that.

Special powers aside, Marie-Ange Buhl was one of the most beautiful women Jacquot had ever set eyes on. Slim, tall, effortlessly elegant, with a bob of shiny black hair, smooth, lightly tanned skin, and a smile to melt the heart. From the moment he first met her, in a hot-house orchidarium outside the village of St Bédard, he had been unmanned, enchanted, and gently, irresistibly seduced. Maybe not in the way he might have wanted, or at least sometimes thought about, but in a close and confidential manner all the same. Close enough for her to be dangerous, close enough for her to work her way into his dreams and imagination. He was old enough to be her father, felt his age every time he looked at her, yet it never stopped him being aware of her, aware of her beauty, her singleness, her possible availability. For there had always been a sense that his feelings, his imaginings, might not necessarily have been unfounded, that they might even have been reciprocated. There had been moments, moments when . . .

But recently, he suspected, that singleness, that availability – the possibility of something happening – had been compromised. Those 'moments' had passed. Which had made him feel a little safer, but at the same time a little sadder too.

The last time he had seen her, the previous November, they'd been at the Témoine Hospital in Marseilles, at the bedside of Léo Chabran, a skipper with the Gendarmerie Maritime. Chabran had been involved with the pair of them in a firefight in the Golfe du Lion, during which action he'd been seriously wounded, and airlifted to the hospital with bullet wounds in his arm and shoulder. In the months that followed, it was Chabran, Jacquot was certain, who had come between them. It hadn't been difficult to see. From the moment he and Marie-Ange had met Chabran in the wheelhouse of his coastguard cutter, Jacquot would have been blind not to see the flush in her cheeks when Chabran looked at her, the tiny smiles she gave him in return, the covert glances she cast in his direction as he brought the cutter in on its target; the way she responded to his command, his authority. In such charged surroundings it was really no surprise that Marie-Ange's interest in him should have been aroused. And as Jacquot stood at the man's hospital bedside the day after the firefight, it soon became clear that Chabran was equally taken by Marie-Ange.

Which, Jacquot recalled, had made him feel a little uncomfortable, as though he was intruding, that he shouldn't stay long. Which he hadn't. It had also made him feel a little . . . jealous.

With promises to stay in touch, Jacquot had taken his leave of Chabran, and Marie-Ange had seen him down to the hospital entrance. Jacquot recalled how they'd stood in the lift with two porters and an empty trolley between them, the four of them held in an uneasy silence until the lift doors opened on the ground floor. It was there, in the hustle and bustle of the hospital entrance that they had said their goodbyes. Jacquot had offered his hand, not sure what else to do, but Marie-Ange had leant forward and given him a kiss, disconcertingly close to his mouth. There had, he remembered, been something weighted about that parting – as if there were things that needed to be said. Things that he should say. But then he'd thought of Claudine and their life together, thought of the man lying two floors above them, and in the end he had said nothing. The last Jacquot saw of Marie-Ange she was standing with her back to him in front of the elevators, waiting for a lift to take her back to Chabran's bedside. As he watched the doors open, and then close on her, he'd known he had done the right thing. Holding back. Either he'd have made a fool of himself, or worse, far worse, he'd have made a fool of Claudine. But that didn't mean it didn't hurt. It did. And he'd felt an unexpected press of sadness as he drove away from the hospital.

And now there she was, Marie-Ange Buhl, just a few steps ahead of him, close enough for him to smell the scent of flowers on her, as she came to a halt on the corner of La Canebière, waiting for the lights to change so she could cross the road.

He drew close, reached out a hand . . .

'Marie-Ange,' he said, touching her shoulder.

23

THE SUN WAS BEHIND HIM as she turned, swiftly, as though taken by surprise, and she lifted her hand to shade her eyes, to see who it was.

He gave her a smile – a big easy smile. Despite any discomfort or uncertainty he might have been feeling, he knew he was pleased to see her and that there was nothing he could do to hide that delight.

'Daniel. *C'est toi!*' she cried, and flung her arms round his neck and hugged him to her, there on the corner of rue Francis and Canebière, as the lights changed, the traffic stopped and lunchtime crowds swarmed past them. Her body was warm and young and close against his, and he felt an unexpected burst of longing. 'But . . . but what are you doing here?' she asked, releasing him, but catching hold of his hands and swinging them between them. 'How come . . . ?' It was clear she was as pleased to see him as he was delighted to see her, but he wondered how he would have managed if the roles had been reversed, if she had come up on him, tapped him on the shoulder. It didn't bear thinking about, and he was pleased that he'd had a chance to compose himself.

'It's lunchtime,' he said. 'I was hungry.'

It had been a joke between them that no case in which he was involved could be properly investigated without stopping for lunch.

And on cue she let out a peal of laughter, rocking back on her feet, putting a hand across her mouth. The first time Jacquot had heard that laugh, in the hot-house in St Bédard, it had sent a shiver through him, the most beautiful laugh he'd ever known. He'd been child-ishly pleased that it was something he had said that had made it happen.

'So you just happened to be here, looking for somewhere, or you came to invite me to lunch?' Marie-Ange gave him a shrewd, amused look. 'In which case, Chief Inspector, I do believe you must have followed me from the shop. That's right, isn't it? You've been following me.'

Strangely flustered Jacquot replied, 'You're right, you're right. I was coming to invite you to lunch. I was on my way to the shop when I saw you come out. But you were a good way off, and it's taken me till here to catch up.'

She gave him another long look and he felt as if she could see right through him, right into his heart. It was as unnerving and disconcerting as it ever was with Marie-Ange Buhl.

'Then you're in luck, Chief Inspector. I am free for lunch. And a long lunch too, *si tu veux*. It's my half-day and I have nothing planned.'

With the time to spare – he'd expected a rushed lunch break meal somewhere close to the shop – Jacquot reached past her and flagged down a cab.

'I know just the place,' he said.

Twenty minutes later, on the far side of the Vieux Port, after excited greetings and smothering hugs from Madame Jules, propri-etress of Chez Jules et Jules, Jacquot and Marie-Ange took the last of six small tables squeezed into line in a dead-end passageway off place Gombert. In less than a minute napkins had been brought, a basket of bread, a bowl of olives, glass tumblers and a pitcher of Provencal rosé, Madame Jules bustling out from a door at the end of the passageway with everything in a single armful, cutlery in her apron pocket. Behind her, in the house's shadowy interior, her husband, Jules, worked a shelf of bottles and a simple open grill. When he caught Jacquot's eye, he waved a griddle fork and shouted out another greeting.

'Do you know the owner of every restaurant in Marseilles?' asked Marie-Ange.

'Only the good ones,' Jacquot replied, more composed now. 'The rest are in jail.'

And so it went, light talk to begin.

'I meant to call,' he said. 'See how you were. But . . .' he shrugged. 'You know how it is?'

'But you're here now. That's the important thing. And it's good to see you. Like old times.'

'St Bédard. The docks.'

'*Exacte*. So, Monsieur Restaurant Marseilles,' she said, looking around for a menu, a blackboard, 'what do you recommend?'

'Absolutely nothing. We leave it all to Jules and Jules . . . whatever Madame found in the market and however her husband's cooked it.'

They didn't wait long to find out: a dish of grilled red peppers cut into seared strips, doused in olive oil and studded with sea salt; a jellied terrine of octopus, its curling tentacles braised with a wine cork, Jacquot explained, to keep the flesh soft; and a trio of thumb-sized chicken *boudins* in a speckled tarragon sauce.

It was over the *boudins*, branded from the griddle, that Jacquot mentioned Léo Chabran's name for the first time.

'Do you ever see him? Do you keep in touch?'

'This is just delicious,' said Marie-Ange, dropping her eyes to her plate and making a business of scooping up the *boudins'* buttery sauce with a piece of bread.

Jacquot knew a curved ball when he saw it and knew what it meant, and for a moment he wasn't quite sure how he felt about it. Having it confirmed that this woman, sitting with him here at Chez Jules et Jules, this woman who had so occupied his own thoughts, should have taken a lover. For that, clearly, was what she had done.

When she finally looked up from her plate, a little flustered, unsure how to respond, he managed a smile.

'I wouldn't have been much of a detective if I hadn't seen that one coming.'

Marie-Ange blushed, lowered her eyes again.

'It's . . . Well . . .' She took a breath, glanced up at Jacquot. 'You're right. We are . . . seeing each other.'

'I'm pleased,' he said, which wasn't altogether true. 'That's good,' he continued, needing to convince himself as much as put Marie-Ange at ease, nodding at the prospect of it. 'He seemed to me a very good man.'

As he spoke, Jacquot watched her expression – a mixture of relief, embarrassment and, possibly, sadness. It made him feel just a little better about it, this loss of her to someone else, to know that she *had* had feelings for him, and that in another life things might have worked out differently.

'How is he? The wounds, I mean.'

Marie-Ange blushed again. Just like Claudine, he thought to himself. Sassy on the surface, but soft on the inside.

But not that soft.

'Everything in working order,' she countered.

Touché.

'Is he back at work?'

She nodded.

'The service gave him two months' leave. When he was released from Témoine he moved back to his apartment in Toulon. I took some time off to look after him there, and . . . that's when . . . you know . . .' She gave a shrug, a nervous smile, pushed away her plate. 'But you're not here to find out about my love life, are you? There's something else on your mind.'

And she was right. There was something else on his mind. The second bird he had come here to kill. If anyone could help with the Gilbert murder, it was Marie-Ange with her special gift, that second sight. As Madame Jules cleared their plates with a '*trés bien, trés bien*' that they had done the meal justice, he slid a hand into his jacket pocket and pulled out the three photos he'd shown to Gilbert, handed them to Marie-Ange.

Like Gilbert she shuffled through them quickly, then examined /
each one more slowly. There were maybe twenty people in each
of the photos, but she didn't hesitate.

'These two,' she said, pointing out the same figures as Gilbert,
the same blurred faces that Brunet had circled in red. 'There is
something not right about them.'

'What exactly? Can you tell?'

She started to shake her head, still looking at the photos. 'It's
just a feeling. They are not nice. They shouldn't be there.'

'So two men? Or a man and a woman, or . . . ?'

'Ah, *non*, *non*. *C'est deux femmes*. Two women.'

'You're sure?'

'*Mais c'est clair*, *non*?'

'Not immediately.'

'Well, I'm telling you now. Two women. For certain. What have
they done?'

'You don't know?'

She glanced at him, sternly.

'I'm sorry. I didn't mean . . .' He grinned, held up his hands.

She handed back the photos.

'Sometimes I can tell more. But with those . . .' she gestured at
the photos as Jacquot slipped them back into his pocket, 'with
those, it's just a feeling that they are not good people to know. I
would say that they are dangerous. Very dangerous. *En effet*, I
would say . . .' She closed her eyes, opened them a moment later.
'I would say you should be very careful of them, Daniel. And catch
them as quickly as you can. Whatever it is that they have done.
And before they do anything else.'

And that was how it was left, as Madame Jules returned to their
table with a platter of cheese and a dish of apple slices soaked in
Calvados.

After their lunch together, out on place Gombert, Jacquot hailed
a cab and held open the door for her.

She reached up and kissed him on both cheeks.

'I won't leave it so long next time,' he said.

'You had better not.'

And that was it. She slid into the back seat, he closed the door, and the cab swung away from the kerb.

Through the rear window, a raised hand, a look, a smile.

Which he returned.

And then she was gone.

24

AFTER HIS LUNCH WITH MARIE-ANGE, Jacquot headed back to Cavaillon, taking the littoral flyover past the Joliette quays, skirting L'Estaque and climbing into the hills above the city. By the time he'd swept through the road tunnel and out into open country he'd managed to put Marie-Ange and Léo out of his mind, and settled down to consider what she had told him over lunch.

About the photos.

Two women. Their suspects were two women.

Not two men, not a woman and a man. But two women.

And if that's what Marie-Ange said, if that's what she had got from the photos, then it was good enough for him. The fact that she'd also sensed danger from the blurred images, sensed a threat from them . . . well, that really did tie it all in.

But that was as far as it went. He might have had a clearer bead on Izzy Blanchard's possible killers thanks to Marie-Ange's insight, but what did Izzy and Antoine Berri have in common? Because there sure as hell had to be something, if only because of the anaesthetic Dyethelaspurane. In the Blanchard case it had been used to put down Noël Gilbert before his wife was shot, and at the Delacroix workshop to incapacitate Antoine Berri before his arm was sliced off. Two deaths in two months where Dyethelaspurane had been used as an incapacitating agent when, according to Bernie Muzon, there'd been no other recorded cases of the drug ever being used in criminal activity. Either it was a mighty coincidence, two different sets of killers getting their hands on the same drug at pretty much the same time, or whoever killed Izzy had also killed Berri.

But what was the link between them?

What was the motive?

All he could say for sure was that the husband of the first victim, Noël Gilbert, and the brother of the second victim, Jean Berri, had been cops. Both of them stationed at the Police Nationale headquarters on rue Garibaldi.

Winding up his window, Jacquot reached for his cigarettes, lit one up, then re-opened the window, just enough to suck away the smoke and for tipping out the ash. Drawing in the first lungful he went through everything else they knew about the victims, looking for anything significant.

Both victims much the same age. Within a couple of years of each other.

One just married, the other about to finish his apprenticeship at Delacroix et Fils. As Muzon had said, that Delacroix apprenticeship was a big thing. After five years on the same salary, you got a raise, joined the team. Like a marriage, there was a sense of new beginnings, everything up for grabs. Only for those new beginnings to be taken away at the last moment.

But that's where the similarities ended, and the stories diverged.

One victim a woman, one victim a man. So no likely sexual context – a serial obsession being played out, a rape gone wrong, infidelity, jealousy, rivalry.

Both victims murdered in different places – eighty kilometres apart – in the Luberon and Marseilles.

And murdered at different times of day – early morning and late evening – in bed and at work.

And in different ways:

A silenced gun and a bullet in the brain – cool, clean, professional.

A spinning table saw – violent, messy and amateur.

If the killers were the same, how come the style was so different?

Finding the link, making the jump . . .

Connections, connections, connections.

It was always the same, thought Jacquot, as he came off the autoroute and crossed the bridge into the dusty, sun-glaring outskirts of Cavaillon. Maybe he'd call Marie-Ange, ask for her help. Take her to the Gilberts' room at Le Mas Blanc, to the Delacroix workshop. Maybe she'd pick something up, 'sense' something. Right then, he needed anything he could get.

The phone was ringing when he got back to his office. He hurried to pick it up if only to stop the clamour.

It was Claude Peluze. After using just a couple of weeks of his compassionate leave, the old cop was back on the beat   kept clear of Minette's murder investigation but otherwise back with the squad.

'I was just speaking to Bernie,' he continued. 'He said there might be a link between the Berri killing at Delacroix and your case up there in the Luberon. Some drug or other?'

'That's right. Dyethelaspurane. It's a strong anaesthetic. Gilbert was put down with it before they shot his wife, and so was Berri's brother before they dropped the saw across his arm.'

'They?'

'Possibly two women. That's all I've got at the moment.'

'Well, here's something else for you, something which Bernie didn't know,' said Peluze. 'Jean Berri and Noël Gilbert were two of the cops with me at Roucas Blanc when we paid a call on Virginie Cabrille. In fact they were the ones who took down her *gorilles* in the garage shoot-out.'

Jacquot's heart leapt.

'You're kidding me? That's . . .'

'I know. It makes you wonder.'

'But you were there too,' said Jacquot, without thinking, instantly regretting it.

'And look what happened to me,' Claude fired back, as though he'd already thought it through and was expecting the response. 'Which brings something else to mind,' he continued. 'If you add Minette into the mix.'

110

'And what's that?' asked Jacquot.

'You read the Bible, you'd know. *Exodus*. Old Testament. Gilbert's wife shot in the eye. Minette they take out her dentures, remember? And now this hand thing . . .'

Jacquot grunted – that was a long shot, he thought. Claude, back at work but obviously still broken up with grief, sounded like he was letting his imagination run away with him.

'And that's not all,' said Claude in a quieter, less Messianic tone. 'If I remember rightly, it wasn't just me and Gilbert and Berri involved. You were there, too. You were a part of it. *En effet*, you pretty much ran the whole show. Brought it all down.'

25

SO CLAUDE'S THEORY WAS THIS: someone had killed the nearest and dearest of three police officers who had been involved in the same operation, a shoot-out in Roucas Blanc eight months earlier. And for whatever reason – maybe out of religious conviction or simply to taunt the police – the killers, these two women, were following the old Biblical formula. Eye for eye, tooth for tooth.

Revenge, Claude had told him. Plain and simple. Someone getting their own back. On anyone who'd something to do with that shoot-out at Roucas Blanc.

And whoever they were, the killers were still out there.

As far as Jacquot could see, there were only two possible lines of enquiry.

They were looking at someone close to the two *gorilles* who'd been shot – the Manichella brothers.

Or Virginie Cabrille, for whatever reason.

As in all the most perplexing cases, Jacquot decided, Claude's theory was either a long shot, a very long shot that really should be discounted . . . Or it was right on the money.

And long shots – even the longest of long shots like this one – sometimes paid off.

Putting down the phone to Claude, Jacquot remembered that

night at Roucas Blanc when the two brothers had been shot and their bodies were being bagged. He'd been standing beside Claude at exactly the moment when Virginie Cabrille was brought down from the house.

His friend was right. Jacquot had been there. And she had seen him.

And if what Claude had said about the eye, the hand and the teeth was right, then he'd better watch out. Or rather he'd better watch out for Claudine. The thought sent a shiver through Jacquot.

'You okay, Boss?' It was Brunet, leaning round the door.

'Me. Yes, of course I'm fine. Why shouldn't I be?' and he waved his assistant in.

'So how was Marseilles?' asked Brunet, grabbing himself a chair – sitting in it properly this time, crossing his legs, leaning an elbow over the chairback.

'The killings are different. The way they're done. Absolutely no similarity in method and execution. A silenced bullet through the eye, here; a table saw and a hand, there. The murders weeks apart, in different places. If it weren't for the Dyethelaspurane, I wouldn't start to credit it. Just not a goer. But there's something else,' he continued, and ran Brunet through what he'd just heard from Claude, about Noël Gilbert and Jean Berri both working for the Police Nationale, and both of them being at the shoot-out in Roucas Blanc. The two *flics* who'd fired the killing shots, putting an end to the Manichella brothers.

Brunet whistled.

'That's pretty persuasive, Boss. I mean, that's definitely worth taking seriously. Someone out for revenge . . .'

Jacquot nodded.

'Which is why I want you to get all you can on Tomas and Taddeus Manichella, and I mean families and loved ones as much as any police record. Anyone who might bear a grudge as a result of their deaths, and be prepared to play it.'

'What about that woman – Virginie Cabrille?'

'Top of my list.'

113

Brunet swung off the chair and headed for the door where he paused and turned, a thoughtful expression on his face.

'Weren't *you* at the shoot-out, Boss?'

That evening, back at the millhouse, Claudine had friends for supper – an English couple called Cayford who had a holiday home near Goult, and two artist friends Gilles and Natalie. After supper, when their guests had gone and Claudine had cried off a last drink on the terrace, pleading tiredness and seeking her bed, Jacquot cleared up the dishes, stacked the machine, then picked up a torch and went outside. He walked around the millhouse, front, sides and back, then stepped out onto the lawns, sweeping the torch beam across the damp grass as though looking for footprints, flashing it through the bushes and trees that bordered the gardens, sending shadows darting away.

But there was nothing, and as he locked up the house he chuckled to himself.

Upstairs, in the darkness, he slid softly into bed and turned to Claudine.

She was almost asleep.

'Did I tell you?' she murmured. 'Midou's coming to stay.'

26

MIDOU BÉCARD, CLAUDINE'S DAUGHTER FROM her first marriage, arrived at Marignane airport a week later from Guadeloupe in the French West Indies. Jacquot had supposed that Claudine would do the pick-up alone, but he'd supposed wrong.

'You'll have to take the morning off,' she told him the day before her daughter's arrival. 'Midou will be most upset if you're not there to meet her too.'

Jacquot was surprised, and touched.

'Midou upset? Doesn't sound like the Midou I know.'

'Then you don't know much, Monsieur *Flic*,' Claudine had replied, and left it at that. There was no argument. He would be there, or else.

Since taking up with Midou's mother, and moving into the mill-house three years earlier, Jacquot had come as close to having a family as he could ever remember. Midou might not have been his daughter, but in a short space of time, on her occasional visits home, he had come to . . . well, if not quite love her as a father, then to enjoy her company and be proud of her. That she was so like her mother made it easier, of course; the independence, the wilfulness, the speaking her mind. She might have been just a year or two into her twenties but Midou Bécard knew how to dole it out if she felt in the mood.

'Ah-ha, Daniel, so you got rid of the 'tail at last.'

That was the first thing she said to him, after bounding out of the arrivals hall at Marignane airport, hugging and kissing her mother and then turning to him with an equally warm embrace. Even after the overnight flight from Pointe-à-Pitre and her connecting flight from Paris, Jacquot could still smell the sea on her.

'I've had it woven into a place mat for you to take home,' he replied, releasing her from his hug. Slim and sinuous, with wide, dark eyes she was like the fishes she studied, he'd often thought. But more beautiful than any fish, and more mouthy. Her mother through and through. And after her time in the tropics her skin glowed like warm honey, her short brownish hair bleached at its flyaway tips from the sun.

'It suits you, though. You look younger,' she said. 'Better watch out, Maman. Or someone'll snatch him, and he'll be off.'

'Midou, what a thing to say!' laughed Claudine, as they left the arrivals hall and headed for the car park, the two women arm in arm, Jacquot bringing up the rear with Midou's cases.

They were crossing the car park, Midou and Claudine just a few steps ahead, coming out from between a row of cars, when there was a sudden rush of air as a large black 4x4 with shaded windows shot past them, close enough to snatch away their breath. None of them had heard or seen its approach and none of them had expected any car to be travelling quite so fast in an airport car park. There was no time to do anything, except stand there, the three of them, and watch the car – a Toyota Landcruiser – head for the exit, wheels squealing over the hot tarmac. Coming round behind them, on the Arrivals access road, the driver, a young man, leant out of the window and gave them the finger.

As he packed away Midou's cases in the back of their own car, it struck Jacquot that if the Toyota had been a VW with two women in the front seat, the result might have been a little more significant than just a close shave.

It also made him realise just how easy it would be to target Claudine and, now that Midou was here, her daughter too.

27

A RIBCAGE OF SCAFFOLDING HAD been set around the Cabrille mansion in Roucas Blanc, a rustling skin of blue tarpaulin stretched across it to conceal its stuccoed walls. The driveway was filled with builders' vans and rubbish skips, pallets of wrapped stone tiling, cinched lengths of new timber, and pyramids of sand, cement and gravel which stood beside a pair of bright orange cement mixers. A large generator chugged away on the front lawn, and a snarl of black cabling snaked out from it towards the house. In the morning sunshine the air smelt of hot sand, diesel and warm wood.

As Jacquot and Muzon climbed the steps to the front door, grit and fallen plaster crunched beneath their feet and water dripped from above. Passing into the gap between the tarpaulin and the walls was like stepping into a giant blue tent filled with the sounds of drills and hammers and scrapers, and the shouts from a workforce climbing like a troop of monkeys through the scaffolding above.

'This'll cost,' said Muzon, as they stepped through the gap and into the entrance hall. Though quieter and drier here, there was no less a sense of scurrying activity as workers in yellow hard-hats, boots and *bleus*, with the holstered tools of their trades slung like gunbelts around their waists, went about their work, the sounds of their voices and labour echoing in the open space.

'I hear she can afford it,' replied Jacquot, pleased at last to be doing something.

After his unsettling conversation with Claude Peluze, Jacquot had been forced to wait for this meeting with Virginie Cabrille. When he'd phoned to set a date, he had been informed that Mademoiselle Cabrille was in the Seychelles, that she had been away for a month and wouldn't be home for another ten days. It gave her a sure-fire alibi for the Berri killing, but it didn't necessarily mean she wasn't involved in some way or other.

'Help you?' came a voice from behind them.

Jacquot and Muzon turned. The man was dressed in working clothes – boots, blue dungarees, a yellow hat and a reflective green waiscoat – but there was hardly a smudge of dirt on him. The foreman or site manager, Jacquot decided.

Muzon flashed his badge.

'We're here to see Mademoiselle Cabrille.'

'Down the hall there. Second door on the left last time I saw her. And watch yourselves. She's not happy.'

Muzon and Jacquot exchanged a look, thanked the man, and followed his directions. Not that these were altogether necessary. As they made their way down the hall, a woman's voice cut sharply through the rattle of hammers and the scream of drills.

'They stay as they are, in the manner stipulated and as agreed months ago with your superiors. *Compris*?'

When Jacquot and Muzon entered the room, Virginie Cabrille was standing by a window with her back to them, her hands on her hips. She was wearing heeled boots and a blue Levi shirt untucked over white jeans. She was already a tall woman, but the boots gave her an added few centimetres which she was using to add menace to her message, towering over a much smaller figure, a middle-aged man in a tightly buttoned jacket, collar and tie. He carried a clipboard and wore a hard-hat that looked to be a size too small. Someone from the city council, Jacquot guessed. He had that look about him. Not much chin, an icebreaker of a nose and sloping shoulders. The hands gripping the clipboard were small and delicate and his brown leather shoes neatly laced.

'The property is protected, Mademoiselle,' the man replied, trying to sound reasonable, but determined not to give ground. 'There are some things that cannot be changed, and what you have done with these windows goes far beyond . . .'

'It goes far beyond nothing, Monsieur. And the job is done. You are simply wasting my time. Speak to Niot in Planning. He gave me his assurance . . .'

Pausing in the doorway, Muzon gave a little cough. Virginie Cabrille spun round, as if here was someone else daring to spoil her day, and gave them a brisk once-over.

The last time Jacquot had seen her she'd been wearing light blue Capri slacks, a dark blue twin-set and penny loafers. She had also been covered in blood – her sleeves, trousers, throat and cheeks. This time she looked a great deal more presentable, though no less defiant: short black glossy hair with a straight parting, a long, patrician nose and small slanting eyes as hard and as black as door-nails. Her face and arms and the unbuttoned front of her shirt showed a deep tan.

'And you are?' she asked.

'Chief Inspector Muzon, Mademoiselle, and my colleague Chief Inspector Jacquot,' said Muzon. 'An appointment was made.'

The hard look softened and a patient smile stitched itself across her lips.

'*Mais bien sûr . . .*' She came forward, shook their hands, a strong, confident grip, then she turned back to the man from the council. 'Speak to Niot. And sort it out,' she told him. The last four words were spoken in short, sharp jabs, and in capital letters – And. Sort. It. Out. – so there could be no confusion, no mistake. With a nervous bob in her direction and a passing grateful nod to Jacquot and Muzon for saving him any further tongue-lashing, the man scuttled past them.

'Tedious, tedious, tedious,' she sighed. 'Such petty little rules.'

'Planning permission can be a minefield,' agreed Muzon, looking around. Even in its current distressed state – bare plaster, dusty

119

floorboards, and a high ceiling where cracks had opened wide enough to show a criss-crossing of lathes – it was a beautifully appointed room, a classic Empire *salon*. Through a set of open french windows and a gap in the blue tarpaulin, the distant sea glittered like diamonds spilled around the rocky shores of the Frioul islands. 'Especially in a house like this.'

'Times change, Chief Inspector. What suits one age does not necessarily suit another, *n'est-ce-pas*? And if it hadn't been for my father, this wonderful old house would have been left to rot years ago. *Pouf!* Fallen down. Lost for ever. One minute no one cares about houses like this – happy to let them go. The next you can't hang a picture without some job's worth *fonctionnaire* taking measurements. Like that weaselly little bureaucrat, telling me that these new windows are seven centimetres too wide. Seven centimetres.' She held up a little finger. 'When the plans – and measurements – were approved months ago.' She dropped her hand. 'But I am sure you are not here to hear about my problems with the town council?' she said, eyes moving to Jacquot. A frown settled across her brow. 'Your face seems very familiar, Chief Inspector . . .'

'Jacquot,' he replied, supplying the name.

'Jacquot? Jacquot? Have we met before, Chief Inspector . . .'

'Yes, we have, very briefly.'

She appeared to give it some thought, as if trying to place the when and the where, though Jacquot suspected she remembered quite clearly, knew exactly who he was.

'I'm so sorry, I can't quite . . .'

'At your garage, Mademoiselle. In November.'

The frown was replaced by a smile, a wide smile of recognition, as though she was completely unperturbed by remembering the circumstances surrounding that first encounter.

'Ah, now I have you. Of course. Such a terrible night. *Mais, alors* . . .' She spread her hands. 'What can I say?' She gave them both a forgiving smile. 'Mistakes can be made, I suppose.'

There was a knock on the door behind them. The foreman, taking off his hard-hat, asked if she could spare a moment, he needed to talk to her. Virginie Cabrille excused herself and went over to him. It was clear he wanted to get his men into the room to start work. She came back to them.

'It appears my site manager is keen to get on in here. Perhaps we should adjourn somewhere a little more . . . private.'

28

WITH A SIGN THAT THEY should follow her, Virginie Cabrille led Jacquot and Muzon through the french windows, stepped between the sheets of blue tarpaulin and led them out onto a wide stone-flagged terrace.

'There, that's better,' she said, breathing deeply. 'Away from all that plaster and dust.' There wasn't a speck on her, but she brushed down the front of her blue denim shirt, leaning forward to dust off her trousers. It was impossible not to see the swell of her cleavage and the loose sway of her breasts.

She looked up quickly and smiled, as if catching them out.

'So, Chief Inspectors,' she said, leaning against the balustrade. Behind her a distant container ship passed beyond the Marseilles roads and out into the open ocean. 'What can I do for you this time?'

With a nod from Muzon, Jacquot started in.

'I wanted to ask about the two men employed by you who . . .'

'Employed by my father,' Virginie Cabrille quickly corrected him. 'Taddeus and Tomas Manichella. They were brothers, and they worked for my father, not for me.' It was a swift rebuke, a clear warning that he should get his facts straight, that she was not to be taken lightly. But she accompanied the reprimand with a pleasant smile.

'But they were still resident . . .'

'They lived on the property, that is correct. But after my father died, I gave them notice. Three months to move out of the garage annexe. Like a lot of things to do with my father, there was change needed. And it wasn't just a matter of interior decoration,' she added, waving at the house behind them. 'I make no apology for my father, Messieurs. He was old school, set in his ways. And those ways were not necessarily . . . what one might expect or admire in a parent. Now that he is gone, things are very different.' Again, the bright accommodating smile, flashed from Jacquot to Muzon and back to Jacquot.

'I believe the Manichella brothers were with the Cabrille family for some years . . .' he persisted.

'For as long as I can remember.'

'So surely it must have been difficult to let them go?'

'Yes, it was. But these things happen. And my father had made generous provision for them in his will. It was not as if they were being cast out into the street. I believe they were thinking of returning to Corsica, buying some land there. They were Corsican, you know.'

Jacquot did know. He had read the file which Brunet had put together. Born in Tassafaduca, in the highlands beyond Corte. A wild and distant place. Mother and father still living, two sisters, uncles and aunts, cousins and nephews by the score. He'd already put in a request for the island's authorities to check out the family, a visit from the local gendarmerie to make sure they were all accounted for.

'Can you think of any reason why Taddeus and Tomas Manichella should have reacted so violently that night, when the police came calling?'

Virginie Cabrille smiled.

'No, I can't. Although my attorney discovered that the first policemen to enter the premises were in plain clothes, did not knock or show credentials.'

'I am sure they would have made themselves known, shouted out "Police",' said Muzon.

'Perhaps they did. Who can say? We only have your word for it.'

123

Another glittering smile. 'Maybe Taddeus and Tomas would have a different perspective, a different version of events.'

'Did you know that they carried guns? Guns which, by the way, were not registered with the authorities?' This from Jacquot.

'No, I did not. I never saw any guns . . . ever. Although, as I said earlier, my father was often in a position where protection would certainly have been a consideration.'

'And why might that have been?' asked Jacquot, knowing full well that Arsène Cabrille, Virginie's father, had been one of the city's most notorious gangland leaders, unlikely to go anywhere without a couple of heavies like the Manichella boys to watch his back.

'He was an old man, Chief Inspector. And wealthy. And in a city like Marseilles those two qualities might easily have been taken for . . . let's say, vulnerability. But with Taddeus and Tomas to keep him company . . . well, such a thing ceased to be a possibility. They had been in the army, I believe. They knew a thing or two. Maybe those guns were from their army days?'

Jacquot nodded, took this in.

'And can you think of any reason why someone would want to avenge their deaths?'

Virginie Cabrille frowned.

'I'm afraid I don't follow.'

'The two policemen, who *were* in uniform, who fired the killing shots, have since been . . . targeted.'

'Targeted?'

'The wife of one was murdered, on her wedding night. The twin brother of the second policeman was also murdered.'

Virginie Cabrille gasped.

'But that is awful. How shocking.'

'Indeed, Mademoiselle.'

'Could it be coincidence?' she suggested, pulling a packet of cigarettes from her pocket and a hefty gold lighter.

'Possibly, possibly. Two such deaths, so far apart in time, in place, in method, might indeed be construed as coincidence, or been missed altogether. But there was a third death. The wife of the officer in charge of the operation.'

'So now it's three deaths that appear to be related to the action carried out here in November?' She lit her cigarette, pocketed the lighter and took a deep drag.

'That's correct.'

'And you think I might know something about it?' A light breeze snatched the smoke from her lips as she exhaled.

'As I said, maybe you can think of a reason why someone would want revenge.'

'Well, I am afraid I can't help you there, Chief Inspector. Taddeus and Tomas weren't married, they had no children, and what family they have is in Corsica.'

'Where blood counts, Mademoiselle. An island known for vendetta, for revenge. For the settling of scores.'

'So I have heard, Chief Inspector.' Her expression started to harden. 'In which case, I suggest you take yourself to Corsica and make enquiries there. Rather than come here and waste my time.' She glanced at her watch. 'As you will know, I have provided your department with every possible assistance in their investigations, at a great deal of personal inconvenience, and there, I'm afraid, it must end.'

And then her expression softened again and she settled a look on Jacquot. She frowned, tipped her head from side to side, as though sizing him up. And then, a sudden flash of recognition.

'Now I have you! Now I have you . . . I knew I had seen your face somewhere, and not just that horrible night last November. Daniel Jacquot . . . that's the name, isn't it?'

'That's right. It is.'

'And not from around here either. A little off your patch if I'm not mistaken?'

'How do you mean?' Jacquot was beginning to feel uncomfortable, as though the balance of power was shifting. Beside him Muzon coughed lightly, cleared his throat.

'I mean, Chief Inspector, that Marseilles is not your usual

stamping ground. I'm right, aren't I? I knew I'd seen you before. You're up country, aren't you?'

'The Luberon, Cavaillon.'

'That's right. The Luberon. And how's your wife?'

'My wife?'

Virginie put a hand to her mouth, as though she'd said something indiscreet, but her look was playful, eyes twinkling with amusement.

'So sorry. Of course, yes, your partner. She's an artist, isn't she?'

Jacquot felt his blood run cold. She was taunting him. How did she know all this?

'How do you . . . ?'

'Aix. Aix-en-Provence. At the Galerie Gavan. I saw your picture, the two of you together . . . an exhibition in Aix, wasn't it? Natalie someone. She does those enormous abstracts. She was standing with the two of you. It was in *Sud*, the party pages. I saw it.'

She was right. There had been a photograph – Natalie and Claudine and he drinking champagne in front of one of Natalie's paintings. And the names in the caption beneath – Natalie Benoît, with Claudine Eddé and Daniel Jacquot from Cavaillon. But how could she have assumed that Claudine and he were married or even partners? Unless she'd checked.

'But now, *vraiment*, if you don't mind, I really must get on.'

'Just a couple more questions,' Jacquot managed, keeping his voice steady.

She cocked her head.

'Your whereabouts at the time of the murders.' He counted off the dates for the three murders.

'For what purpose?'

'Simply to eliminate you from our enquiries, Mademoiselle. Nothing more than that.'

'Then you'll have to contact my secretary. She keeps my diary. She'll know. Although I can tell you that the last date you mentioned, the end of May, I was out of the country.'

Jacquot nodded, seemed to consider this.

'Was there anything else, Chief Inspector?'

'Just a small thing. I believe the Cabrille family manages a number of clinics. The Druot Clinics. There's one here in Marseilles, another in Lyons . . .'

Virginie Cabrille started to shake her head. 'There is a clinic here, and in Lyons, and others, but they are not "managed" by the family. Nor are they owned by the family. *En effet*, the clinics are administered by a board of trustees, funded by the family.'

'And at these clinics, would the drug Dyethelaspurane be used?'

'I am a businesswoman, Chief Inspector, not a chemist nor a doctor. I have no idea what drugs are used at the clinics. Why should I?' She flicked her cigarette over the balustrade. 'So, if there's nothing else, Messieurs?'

'For the moment . . .' began Jacquot.

'Good,' she cut in, reaching forward to shake their hands. 'Then if you'll excuse me, I have a million things to do.'

Part Two

29

IT WAS LÉO CHABRAN'S USUAL morning run. Out of the kitchen of his uncle's home, across the gravelled stable yard, past the walled garden and on to the drive. Eight pairs of flaking plane trees, more than a century old, rising out of grassy banks, a green tunnel arching over his head. Cool, shifting shadows at this early hour. At the front gate he turned right, out on to the country road and into the sun for the first time, feeling its warmth settle on his neck and shoulders, heading down the slope towards the village of Cruis, crossing the bridge over the dried-out watercourse but turning off into the woods before he reached the first houses.

Whenever he stayed with his uncle, Léo always followed the same route, at the same time every morning, a little before eight o'clock. Twenty kilometres, start to finish, the first three kilometres an easy downhill trot until he turned into the trees where the road gave way to a pine needle path and the land began to rise. It wasn't a steep path, but it was long and winding and narrow, and the treacherous surface of slippery pine needles always slowed his pace and made each footfall count. Soon he would be a hundred metres above the family home, be able to glimpse its pantiled roofs through the trees, following the rise and fall of the ridgeline before dropping down the slope for the final push. The final kilometres. Back on the road. Downhill again. Then up the drive, heart pumping. No sound save the pounding tread of his running shoes and the drawing of breath through nose and gritted teeth. By the time he reached the stable yard his uncle would be up and he'd be able to smell the coffee.

But that was still a long way off. Leaning into the slope, coated in a sheen of sweat, Léo glanced at his watch. Forty minutes since turning off the road. Not quite halfway, yet despite the distance covered and the incline of the slope his breathing was controlled, the stiffness in arm and shoulder had eased, and the burning sensation in the muscles above his knees had passed. It had been a good run so far and he felt a burst of exhilaration. Soon he'd be home, smell that coffee.

In the meantime, dodging past a wall of limestone that jutted into the path, with the pine needles sponging beneath his feet and the new morning scent of resin sharp and clear, Léo took his mind off thoughts of the track and let it wander to the woman he'd left sleeping in his bed. The new woman in his life. Marie-Ange Buhl. They had met the previous November, late one night in the port of L'Estaque. One minute he'd been leaning over his chart table, in the wheelhouse of the coastguard cutter he commanded, the next she was there, reaching forward to shake his hand. One of the most beautiful girls he had ever seen – a cap of black hair, eyes the colour of caramel, slim and elegant, a lovely, yet hesitant smile as she shook his hand. Enough to take the breath away. Which had surprised Léo. He was no slouch when it came to women, but this one . . . this one was different. He knew it immediately.

A policewoman had been his first thought, coming aboard with that man Jacquot, the police inspector. The two of them chasing after a missing girl. His cutter, the *P.60*, at their disposal according to the fax message he'd received prior to their appearance from the Préfét Maritime in Toulon. Which was how he had come to pick up two bullets in his left arm and shoulder in the action that followed. Yet when he woke in hospital the following day, there she was, asleep in his bedside chair, so he had time to focus on her, remember her, remember what had happened until the moment the firing started. And note once again how beautiful she was.

At first he had been certain that the girl, Marie-Ange, and the policeman, Jacquot, were lovers. There had seemed something so tight and close between them. It was only later, while he recovered from his wounds in hospital, that she let him know that this was not so, that Daniel Jacquot was not a lover, and that she was not a policewoman, but a *fleuriste*, a flower-shop girl. There in Marseilles. For the life of him Léo couldn't think of a better job for her. Just perfect. The scent of the flowers on her hair when she leant over to straighten his pillows, the golden smears of pollen on her sleeves, the way she arranged the blooms she brought him – every day – fingers dancing over the stems. Standing back to say, '*Voilà, regardes, comme elles sont belles*,' brightening his drab hospital room not just with flowers but with funny cards and silly little toys that she bought on her way to the hospital and that made him laugh. Like the jack-in-a-box with the pirate eyepatch, and the plastic submarine for his bath. He had them still.

He'd spent ten days in hospital while his wounds were treated, and she'd visited every day. And when the time came for his hospital discharge, with two months' disability leave in which to recover before recall to active duty in the new year, she'd helped him move back to his apartment in Toulon, seen him settled and comfortable, sleeping on the sofa the first night, but coming to his bed the second.

And that's how it had been ever since. Those first weeks together in Toulon; Christmas spent at Cruis with his uncle, who'd taken to his latest 'companion' with extraordinary enthusiasm – as though he knew something that Léo didn't; the next few months interrupted by nothing more onerous than three-day patrols with four days off, and numerous weekend visits to Cruis.

But now it was his last weekend before full recall, a new command and a senior posting at La Rochelle. He would be away longer, their time together shorter. He had to act, today. He had to do now what he had always imagined he'd be able to put off until some distant time. That time, he now realised, was here.

Which was why, as he levelled out on to a wider stretch of

pathway just below the ridgeline, he'd decided that this evening, in just a few more hours, before dinner, he was going to walk Marie-Ange down the drive and, under the plane trees where the men of his family traditionally proposed to their women, offer her the ring and promise her his love, and . . .

The shock was immediate. The ground seemed to give beneath the ball of his left foot. A hard, springing sensation. A screech of metal and something swift and sharp clamping and biting his leg, pitching him forward, bringing him down with a thump, the air driven from his lungs, then sucked back in to be expelled in a piercing shriek as a wave of burning, bursting, agonised pain shot up his leg.

If his mind had been on the track he might have seen it – an odd, unlikely-looking ridge of pine needles and holm oak leaves spread across the path. Something not quite right about it. But his mind hadn't been on the track, and he hadn't really registered it, and before he could do anything about it, his foot slammed down in the middle of it.

Before he blacked out Léo Chabran saw a length of shiny new steel chain leading to the nearest tree trunk, and looked back over his shoulder to see the wicked overlapping jaws of a rusted hunter's trap clamped around his leg, a few centimetres beneath his knee. There was blood oozing thick and fast from the torn flesh, and the leg looked oddly misshapen as though the toe of his trainer was not quite sitting straight, pointing off into an altogether impossible direction. That's when he saw the bone tent-poling the skin on the inside of his calf-muscle, and heard soft laughter and gentle clapping.

For a moment he believed that help was at hand. Someone come from nowhere to spring the trap off his leg, call an ambulance, care for him and comfort him until the emergency services arrived.

Then he saw their faces, and he knew he was mistaken.

30

MARIE-ANGE BUHL SMILED AS she dressed. She had beaten him
to it, waking before him, reaching out a hand, bringing him to her
with a gentle touch and softly whispered entreaties. She looked at the
bed, at the still warm marks of their bodies impressed upon it, the
lace-edged linen sheet twisted into a knot, and the folded quilt slipping like a slope of snow to the floor.

This morning she'd made Léo late for his run.

Downstairs in the kitchen, Marie-Ange made herself a pot of
coffee, stacked a tray with warm slices of brioche, butter and a pot
of conserve, and went through to the morning room, her favourite
room in the house save their bedroom. It was perfectly fit for its
purpose, this room, facing east across a silvered landscape of olives
towards the slopes of the Lure hills. It was stone-flagged, low-
ceilinged and heavily beamed, which might have given it a chill,
shadowy feel if not for the early-morning sunshine that poured into
it, the furnishings deep and soft and welcoming in an old-fashioned
chintzy English way, and the table by the french windows which
she used for her breakfast wide enough to take her tray, and a book
or newspaper if she ever tired of the view. Not that that was ever
really an option.

Setting to with an appetite, she looked across the lawns towards
the lower rougher slopes where twenty hectares of olive trees

135

stretched away from the house, and from between their ancient twisted limbs she spotted the old man, Léo's uncle Davide, step into the sun. He wore his customary cream cotton work trousers, and a blue denim shirt that showed up the deep mahogany of his chest and face, shadowed now beneath the brim of a battered sun hat that Marie-Ange knew had belonged to his wife and that covered a wild thatch of white hair. Every morning, before breakfast, he wandered through those trees of his, testing the fruit, checking the leaves, the bark, thinking whatever thoughts he had in those quiet early times. If he'd been younger, Marie-Ange had decided, he'd probably have joined Léo on his run.

But Davide Chabran wasn't young. He was in his eighties, slowing down physically if still filled with brio and wit and affection. The first time Marie-Ange had met the Comte de Chabran, it was as if she had known him for ever. She found him sweet and engaging, kind and caring, and he took to her with an equal enthusiasm. It wasn't always Léo who stayed up with the old man, listening to his stories of another world, of war and command, music and parties and lovers, and it hadn't taken long for Marie-Ange to feel a real warmth and genuine regard for him.

Now, half-way across the lawn, he looked up and spotted her in the window, took off his hat and waved it, a long sweeping wave that spoke of great distances. She waved back and, pushing herself away from the breakfast table, she went through to the kitchen, brewed some fresh coffee and brought it to the table just as Davide tramped across the terrace, dusting his hat against his trouser leg, kicking off his trainers and slipping his feet into the heel-flattened Moroccan slippers he'd left by the french windows.

'Is he gone?' asked the old man, sitting down at the table.

'Just. He was late this morning.'

'Nothing could surprise me less,' he said, and with a small smile he held out his cup while Marie-Ange poured.

It happened as she put down the cafetière. A sudden dryness in the mouth, a shutting out and lessening of the sounds around her – the old man's chatter about the olives, the ticking of a clock – until all she could hear was the thumping of her heart, and a muffling of volume as though she had just plunged her fingers into her ears. These were sensations with which she was familiar, the start of one of her 'moments', a special kind of intuition that tuned her in, somehow, to the past or the present. She had had these 'moments' since she was a young girl; sometimes they were triggered by something she saw or heard, but most often they came without warning. Whatever the cause, she had learnt to pay close attention to whatever thoughts were stirred, to what she saw or what she heard – distant actions, dimly perceived, or low, barely audible whisperings. It was how she had come to know Jacquot, writing him anonymous letters when she saw in a newspaper the photo of a young man whom he had arrested for murder. He had the wrong man, she had written, and when her letters failed to change things, had come and found him. That he had responded in the way he did – accepting her 'insight' and putting her recommendations into play – was one of the reasons why she had started to feel so strongly about him. The kind of man he was. So unlike a policeman. So easy to fall for.

If not for Léo . . .

Now, as the silence deepened around her, Marie-Ange felt an overwhelming sense of threat. Chilled to the bone, she felt goose bumps race over her skin, even with the morning sun slanting over her. She was no longer having coffee with the old man, she was out in the hills, on a woodland path, and she could hear the rhythmic beat of Léo's breath and footfall, drawing closer and louder as he laboured up the slope. But she couldn't see him. Just hear that panting breath.

But that wasn't all. She was suddenly aware of a presence in the woods, in the trees and undergrowth either side of the path he followed. Something cold and dangerous and malevolent.

Shadows moving, settling, hunching down, waiting . . .

With a groan, Marie-Ange pushed herself out of her chair and without a word hurried from the room, ran along the echoing passageway and crossed the stone-flagged hall. Snatching up her car keys, she leapt down the front steps and threw open the door of her old 2CV. The engine caught on the second turn and a moment later she was racing down the drive, screeching through the gates and out into the road without pause.

How far ahead was he?

Could she get to him in time?

Before he reached that curve in the path, where the shadows waited.

Abandoning the car past the bridge she scrambled up the slope, following his route, the sweat soon popping from her pores, running down her back. Up and up she went, stumbling, panting with the effort, pausing to draw breath and shout out his name. 'Léo! Léo! Where are you? Wait for me. Wait for me!' Then on again.

She knew she was too late before she saw him. Felt a drenching chill of dread as she came round that last bend just below the ridge-line, where the path narrowed and tightened into a sharp right-hand turn . . . the section of path that she had 'seen' in the morning room.

And there he was, her Léo, sprawled on the ground up ahead, his left leg caught in the metal jaws of some monstrous kind of trap, his wrists bound, a strip of duct tape plastered across his mouth.

She flung herself down, leant over him, tugged aside the tape as he opened his eyes, recognised her. A rictus of a smile creased his lips, before pain and doubt and fear slid across his features and snatched it away.

'Who did this?' she cried. 'What's happened to you . . . ?' She started to tug off her scarf, to tie a tourniquet, to stop the bleeding.

'There's someone here,' he whispered. 'Someone . . . in the trees.'

As if on cue, Marie-Ange heard the swish of a branch from behind her and spun round. Two figures had stepped out from the cover of the trees, one from either side of the path, one close, one a little further back.

A man and a woman.

A skirt and trousers.

But then Marie-Ange saw she was mistaken. Not a man and a woman, but two women. The one in trousers, farther back, looked

138

taller and older; her companion was younger, shorter and, by the look of it, carrying something behind her back.

'We need help,' said Marie-Ange, knowing instantly that there was no help to be found here, not from these two women. She had seen them before, just a distant blurred image, but she recognised them immediately from the photos that Daniel Jacquot had shown her at Chez Jules et Jules in Marseilles. They'd seemed dangerous to her then, put a chill in her blood, but now they looked even more menacing. She scrambled to her feet, put herself between the women and Léo, an instinctive defence.

But it made no difference. The woman closest to her brought a hand from behind her back, and Marie-Ange saw the gun.

Beside her, she heard Léo grunt and try to get to his feet, to do something, to protect her. But there was nothing he could do, and Marie-Ange stood rooted to the spot, her gaze fastened on the gun as the woman raised it and levelled it at her chest.

There was a curiously blank expression on the woman's face.

Cold, clinical, unmoved.

An executioner's face.

And Marie-Ange knew with a deep and numbing certainty that this unknown woman, on a bright summer morning, on this sun-spilled hillside above Cruis, was going to pull the trigger.

And that there was nothing she could do about it.

That she would die.

Just seconds left to live; the time it takes to squeeze a trigger.

Marie-Ange didn't hear a thing, didn't feel any pain, just the thumping impact of a 9x19mm Parabellum bullet which lifted her clear off her feet and sent her spinning backwards.

31

'SO ARE YOU GOING TO grow it again, or not?' asked Midou. She sat back from the kitchen table with a twinkle in her eye and reached for Jacquot's cigarettes, tapped one out, lit it. She loved teasing him almost as much as she enjoyed shocking her mother. The smoking was a new development and though there wasn't much her mother could do about it – she smoked herself, after a fashion – Claudine had still not quite got used to seeing her daughter with a cigarette.

Jacquot ran a hand across his scalp. He knew what Midou was talking about. A few months after that visit to a barber's shop in Paris – where he'd had pretty much the whole damn lot taken off – his hair was starting to thicken again, and lengthen. Not yet long enough for a ponytail but definitely heading in that direction; already long enough to show the start of a wave off the roughly central parting, to cover his ears and curl over his jacket collar. Black hair, Corsican hair, that showed up his tan and sage green eyes. When he slept now, there was no prickling stubble pressing against his head from the pillow, no itch on his scalp.

Jacquot shrugged.

'Maybe. It depends on your mother.'

'I like it as it is now. It suits you. It suits your age. But the pony-tail . . .' Claudine grinned '. . . the ponytail was good, too. It was the first thing I noticed. The ponytail and your eyes.'

He had had the ponytail for years, from his earliest rugby days, and after playing in the blue shirt with the gold *coq* on his chest, scoring the winning try against *Les Rosbifs* at Twickenham in his one and only appearance in the national side, Jacquot had become known for it, been recognised on account of it. Not that he wore it in that style to be recognised. He wore it that way because he was used to it, liked the feel of it. And, of course, he'd been younger.

'Perhaps I should grow a beard or moustache,' he said.

'No,' cried Midou. '*Jamais*!'

'Absolutely not,' said Claudine, suddenly looking stern, as though he might be serious.

Jacquot grinned at her, started to chuckle. As if . . .

She picked up her napkin and flung it at him.

It was a Sunday afternoon at the millhouse and the three of them had just finished lunch, taken at the kitchen table. It was too hot to sit outside, all the doors and windows jammed open to catch a breeze. A lunch cooked by Midou with no help from her mother or Jacquot beyond making sure her glass of wine was kept filled. She had announced this service – the cooking of this Sunday lunch – midway through the week.

'I'm going to cook something called Ayam Batutu,' she had told them. 'It's this chicken coated in spices and steamed in banana leaves. There's a little Indonesian place in Pointe-à-Pitre where they cook it – just fabulous! You'll love it.'

And so, for two days, Midou and Claudine had toured every market and specialist shop from Apt to Aix to Avignon in a search for the right ingredients. And every time the two of them set off on one of their jaunts in Claudine's rattle-bag Renault with its temperamental dashboard gearstick, Jacquot whispered a prayer for them, making the little Sign of the Cross that his own mother had taught him, to keep them from harm.

The thought that Claudine or Midou might be names on a killer's list simply because they were his nearest and dearest – their deaths guaranteed to cause the real target, himself, the most extreme grief

141

– had begun to hit home: Noël Gilbert losing his new bride; Peluze losing his wife; that cop Berri losing his twin brother. Another murder would surely confirm it, whoever else was on that list. But there was already this growing sense of a pattern to the killings, and the more Jacquot thought about it the more anxious he became.

At least now, as Claudine rose to clear the table and Midou reached over to pour him a fresh glass of wine, they wouldn't be tramping around the countryside together, shopping for exotic ingredients and presenting an easy target. Claudine had some paintings to finish for an autumn exhibition at Gilles' gallery in Aix, and Midou had some research notes to type up for her doctorate. For the next few days, they would be where he could keep an eye on them.

'Can you eat a ripe camembert after Ayam Batutu?' asked Jacquot.

'If anyone can, it's probably you,' replied Midou. 'And why not? We drank red wine with it. Back on the island it's usually beer.'

Jacquot got to his feet and crossed to the cellar door, careful to lower his head as he stepped through it, and went down the stairs. Claudine, who normally liked her cheese but had recently complained of its ripening smell in her kitchen, now made him keep it where they stored their wine. It was an imposition that Jacquot had gently railed against, but somehow the smell of his cheeses seemed to complement the surroundings: the hard-packed earth floor of the cellar, its coolness, the low-wattage light, the tick and wheeze of the old deep-freeze. Jacquot was coming back up the wooden steps, closing the door behind him, when the phone started to ring.

Claudine reached for it.

'*Oui*? *Allo*?'

Jacquot prayed for it to be a friend. A social call. But when he heard the words, '*Ne quittez pas, il arrive maintenant*', he knew his prayer hadn't been answered.

He laid the cheese on the table and took the phone from Claudine. He put his hand over the mouthpiece and raised his eyebrows at her.

'A man. An old man by the sound of it,' she said. 'I didn't catch the name.'

Jacquot raised crossed fingers, leant over to kiss her cheek, then turned his attention to the caller.

'*Oui, c'est moi*, Daniel Jacquot.'

'Monsieur Jacquot. Please excuse me for calling you at home on a Sunday.'

Claudine had been right. The voice was old. And weary. But at least it wasn't Brunet. He wasn't being called in for something. His Sunday with Claudine and Midou was safe. More wine with the cheese. Then coffee, a stroll in the garden and a snooze on the sofa.

'It's not a problem. How can I help, Monsieur . . . ?'

'Chabran. My name is Davide Chabran. From Cruis, near Forcalquier. I believe you know my nephew, Léo?'

At the table mother and daughter whispered together, both of them hoping that this call would not mean Jacquot's hurried departure from the dining table. They had had a grand lunch, they were having fun, the rest of the afternoon and evening stretched ahead of them – it would be such a shame if it were to finish now.

But one glance was all it took for them to know that something was wrong, to see the look on Jacquot's face. He seemed to slump at the phone and the colour drained from his cheeks. He reached for the pad and pencil that Claudine kept nearby and wrote something down, scribbling away. Then he listened for a moment longer.

'I am very grateful for your call,' he said at last, his voice struggling to contain both shock and emotion, and with a whispered '*adieu*' he settled the receiver onto its cradle.

'What is it?' asked Claudine. She knew it was bad news.

'Someone I know . . . two people, in fact.' Jacquot took a deep breath and sat down, somehow managed a smile. 'I'm afraid it's not good.'

32

THE FIRST THING JACQUOT DID that Monday morning was call up a crime report from the investigating team in Forcalquier. The relevant papers were faxed through and Brunet brought them in as soon as they arrived.

'Anything I should know? Anything I can do?' he asked. He'd clearly taken a look at the documents before handing them over to Jacquot.

'Let me read through this, and then we'll talk.'

Brunet nodded and swung out of the office.

It didn't take Jacquot long to take it in, the murders of Léo Christian Chabran, nephew of the gentleman he had spoken to on the phone the previous afternoon, and Mademoiselle Marie-Ange Buhl, from Metz, where her father, Jacquot remembered her once telling him, managed the railway marshalling yards.

The first reports he read comprised the various statements taken after the discovery of the bodies – from the two hikers who had found them, and from a duty officer at the local gendarmerie in Cruis where their discovery had been reported – and an initial scene-of-crime report from the Forcalquier police.

The hikers had found the bodies on a wooded path more than a kilometre from the road. Jacquot read their signed statements, taken down in small capital letters by the reporting officer in Forcalquier:

'They looked like they were, you know, in the act, the woman on top of him,' one of the hikers had said. 'For a minute or so, it felt like we were intruding. We nearly turned back. But then we realised they weren't moving.'

Within an hour, the hikers had reported their discovery and returned with the local gendarme from Cruis, the nearest settlement. His report indicated two bodies found at approximately 2.47 p.m. The woman was in her late twenties or early thirties, he'd guessed: dark hair, jeans, trainers, and a white T-shirt heavily bloodied from a bullet wound in her back – actually the exit wound. The man she was sprawled across the gendarme had recognised immediately, a local, Léo Chabran, dressed in running shorts, trainers and a blue T-shirt. He lay on his back, the lower half of his left leg caught in a hunter's trap.

These initial observations were added to by the scene-of-crime team from Forcalquier. No sign of a struggle, beyond the male victim squirming around on the layer of pine needles on the path, presumably in an attempt to free his leg from the trap; no sign of any cartridge cases; and no sign of any ambush spot – flattened grass, cigarette ends, sweet papers, footprints – in the surrounding area. In the investigating officer's opinion, a double homicide committed by a person or persons unknown. Enquiries were on-going.

The pathology report didn't take the investigation much further. The male victim's lower left leg had been caught in a large mammal spring-trap, the points of its teeth clamping tight either side of the leg, just a few centimetres below the knee. As well as excessive muscle and ligament trauma, the popliteal artery had been ruptured and the victim's leg broken in two places – both fibula and tibula. Since the breaks were splintered rather than clean, it was the pathologist's opinion that the break had been caused not, primarily, by the snapping teeth of the trap, but by the subsequent fall forwards putting pressure on the weakened, possibly cracked, bones. In conclusion the pathologist judged that the victim had died from his injuries due to trauma shock and extensive blood loss. As an addendum, he also noted that the victim's wrists had been tightly bound and that glue residue had been found around the mouth, suggesting that some kind of restraint had been used, and that adhesive tape had been used to keep the victim silent, maybe to stop him screaming from pain or crying out for help, though neither cord nor tape had been found at the scene.

As for the woman, she had suffered a fatal frontal gunshot to the heart. The bullet had smashed through the third thoracic rib, pulped most of the right side of her aorta and severed one of the pulmonary arteries, nicked her right lung and exited a few centimetres above the right hip. But it wasn't the only killing shot. The victim had also taken a second bullet to the forehead, fired at close range, close enough for the muzzle blast from the gun to leave powder marks on the skin.

The inference, Jacquot knew, was clear. Whoever had shot her in the chest had followed through with a second, closer shot to the head, just to make sure. Though no bullets or cartridge cases had been found, both wounds were consistent with the kind of damage caused by a 9x19mm Parabellum.

According to the pathologist's report, time of death was estimated at between ten and midday, for both victims. Given the male victim's injuries and consequent blood loss, the pathologist reckoned the first attack – the ambush with the trap – had taken place maybe an hour prior to the woman's death. It was difficult to be certain, but in the pathologist's opinion they had both died as near simultaneously as dammit.

The final two pages contained personal information for the two victims. Age, sex, last known address, employment details, next of kin. Everything reduced to that.

Jacquot put down the file, dismayed by what he had read. Here were the details he had not learnt the day before from Léo Chabran's uncle – who had found Jacquot's name in his nephew's address book and was simply calling to pass on the bad news. On the phone it had been hard enough to take it all in, to comprehend that they were gone, without pressing for more information. Now he knew.

And what registered – with a cold and dread certainty – was the likely reason for their deaths: their closeness to the Manichella killings. Even though they had never been at the house in Roucas Blanc both Marie-Ange and Léo had contributed to the shoot-out simply by their involvement in the Lafour case.

Just like Noël Gilbert, Jean Berri and Claude Peluze.

And then there was the manner of their deaths.

A near-severed lower leg.

'Foot for foot'.

And a bullet to the heart; a bullet in the forehead.

'Wound for wound'.

Jacquot had read the reports on the shoot-out at Roucas Blanc, knew how the Manichella brothers had died. The only thing he couldn't remember was which brother was shot in the head, and which one in the heart.

But there was now no doubt in his mind that this double murder confirmed the pattern of killings suggested by Claude Peluze. Right now that long shot was beginning to look a great deal more credible

Which meant that all that was left was 'burning for burning' and 'stripe for stripe'. That's what it stipulated in the Bible. *Exodus*, 21:23. He had checked – just out of interest. 'An eye for an eye, tooth for tooth, hand for hand, foot for foot, burning for burning, wound for wound, stripe for stripe.'

Which meant two more murders to go.

It also confirmed that he, too, would almost certainly be a target.

Or rather, someone near and dear to him.

'So, Boss?' It was Brunet. Standing in the doorway. Knowing that something was up.

Jacquot snapped to.

'Get us a car. We're taking a drive.'

33

IT WAS A FAST ROAD from Cavaillon to Céreste. Under the railway line, out through the melon fields and on to the D900, past the *impasse* that led up to Claudine's millhouse. Forty minutes after leaving headquarters they were through Céreste and heading up towards Forcalquier.

Brunet was driving.

'Done some time trials along this stretch,' he said, looking at the road with a cyclist's eye. 'It looks like it's an easy ride,' he continued, 'but the surface is shit. Nasty camber, ragged edges, and those little bits of gravel spit off a bike's back wheel like you wouldn't believe. Traction's just a bugger too. And on a stretch like this, going up, through the bends, you need some grip.'

Jacquot gave a little grunt, acknowledging Brunet's attempt to lighten his mood, distract him. After he'd run his assistant through the deaths of Marie-Ange and Léo, tying in their murders with the action at Roucas Blanc and the deaths of Izzy Gilbert, Antoine Berri and Minette Peluze, Jacquot had dutifully answered a couple of questions but had soon fallen silent, staring through the window as the distant wooded slopes of the Luberon slid by.

It was warm and sunny and the trees either side of the road flicked past with hypnotic regularity. Despite the pleasing rush of dusty country air through his open window, and a fleet of bright white clouds moored bow to stern above the Grand Luberon, white sails full, stretching away into the distance, Jacquot felt badly undone by the murders in Cruis. What had happened to Noël Gilbert's new wife, and to Jean Berri's talented carpenter twin, he'd been able to accommodate, as he had, just about, the news of Minette Peluze's death. As a cop, Jacquot knew how important it was to establish some kind of distance from the deaths, to call up a certain emotional detachment so that he could operate professionally – with an open mind. But with the murders in Cruis, it was easier said than done.

Just a few weeks earlier he and Marie-Ange had sat across a table from each other at Chez Jules et Jules. He remembered that warm, close hug he'd received on rue Francis when he tapped her on the shoulder, the kiss she had given him when they parted on place Gombert, that final glance and smile and wave from the back seat of a taxi, and everything in between: the flowery scent of her, the sound of her voice, her crystalline laugh; the way she looped her hair behind her ear, the light, delicate way she wiped her lips with her napkin, the way she held a cigarette – at the tips of her fingers as though unused to smoking but prepared to give it a try; the way she sipped her wine, sliced her terrine, and wadded her bread to wipe through the boudin's sauce. He remembered the hothouse where they first met, and the flower shop in St Bédard where she worked, and how she'd just disappeared when the case had closed. He remembered, too, his surprise and delight at meeting her again, just a few months later in Marseilles, her old bouncing, jouncing, groaning 2CV, her tiny apartment with its peeling pink plaster walls, and her soft rose-scented bed where she had tended to his wounds . . .

And now . . . now she was gone. Absolutely gone. He would never, ever see her again.

Yet not once, not even when he'd shown her the photos at Chez Jules et Jules, had he thought to warn her what was going on, that she might also be a possible target. And nor had he followed up their lunch, calling her to arrange visits to Le Mas Blanc and the

Delacroix workshop. That failure, he now realised, could have cost her her life, and he felt the guilt wring his heart as they drove into Forcalquier and found a space in the gendarmerie car park.

'*Voilà*,' said Brunet, turning off the engine. 'Forcalquier. Cleanest, clearest air in La Belle F.'

34

'IT IS A TRAGEDY. EVERYONE is . . . shocked. No one can really believe it.'

Ballarde, the investigating officer in Forcalquier who'd been called in after the bodies of Léo and Marie-Ange had been found, was a small man with rimless spectacles, a healthy paunch pressing against his shirt buttons, and thinning brown hair. He wore grey Sta-prest trousers and brown suede shoes, and a grey jacket a shade darker than the trousers hung from the back of his chair. He took a deep breath, let it out in a sigh and shook his head.

'The Chabran family is well known?' asked Jacquot, looking down on the market square from Ballarde's second-floor office. The Monday market was in full swing, the *place* crowded with stalls, a chequerboard of coloured awnings that seemed to shiver as much from a light breeze as the hustle and bustle in the walkways between them.

'Well known and well loved. For generations,' replied Ballarde.

'And Davide Chabran?'

Ballarde spread his hands.

'The Comte? Where do I start? Eighty-six years old. A naval officer until Toulon in 1942, a fearless *résistant* for the duration, much-decorated for his exploits after the war. His wife died years ago, but he never remarried. Has no children. The estate will pass to Léo . . . Would have done.'

'So what will happen now?' asked Brunet, sitting on a plastic sofa below a wine map of France, each of the principal regions highlighted in different colours.

Ballarde started to shake his head.

'There is another nephew. A few years younger than Léo. He lives in Australia. Not a Chabran. The name is Hugonnet. At least it's French.'

'And Léo's father and mother?' asked Jacquot.

'Killed in an air-crash. Early seventies. Léo Chabran must have been about thirteen or fourteen years old. The parents were going on holiday. To Sicily. On the flight from Rome to Palermo, the plane flew into a mountain.'

'And Léo had lived with his uncle ever since?' asked Jacquot, noticing that Ballarde's desk was not only piled with teetering, spilling files but made of metal – an old-style office desk, the kind a junior civil servant might be given. Strong, utilitarian. When Jacquot had arrived in Cavaillon, the same kind of desk had occupied his new office. By the first lunchtime he had had the item removed and gone into town in search of a suitable replacement.

'That's correct,' replied Ballarde. 'The family had a house near Manosque. Monsieur le Comte sold the property and moved the boy into the château.'

'Tell me about the trap,' said Jacquot. 'Are they still used hereabouts?'

'Snares, maybe; and sometimes small gin-traps. But nothing as large as the one we found. A real monster. Weighed in at around eighteen kilos . . . big enough to bring down a bear. Whoever put it there must have known what they were doing. And they'd have needed clamps to set those springs.'

'In the report you said it was American.'

'An American manufacturer, that's correct. Cornelius Truscott, Traps and Supplies, Oregon. Stamped in full on the foot-pad. But it was old – a real antique – and the firm is long gone. We checked.'

'So there's no way of finding out where it might have come from?'

Ballarde shook his head.

152

'It could have been in someone's attic or cellar. Maybe even an antique shop. You know, something to hang on the wall. I have one of my men checking, but I'm not hopeful.'

Jacquot nodded, breathed in the sharp scent of lavender from the stalls in the *place*.

'Léo Chabran worked for the Gendarmerie Maritime, as I'm sure you know. Based in Toulon. Did he spend a lot of time here, with his uncle?'

'A regular visitor. At least once a month. And always here for the olive harvest. The estate has maybe twenty hectares planted. They make their own oil. Huile d'Olive Maison Chabran. It is very good. You can buy it in the market.' Ballarde tipped his head towards the open window, indicating the market stalls below.

'And when Léo Chabran visited, did he always go for a run? And if so, did he always follow the same route?'

'According to his uncle, he never missed a morning's run. And always used the route he was found on. It's roughly circular, around twenty kilometres in all, from the house towards the village, then up through the woods to the top of the ridge, and back down again. It would be a tough run, I'll tell you that.'

'And the Chabran house is near Cruis, I believe,' said Jacquot, turning away from the window, leaning against the sill.

'The château, yes. A few kilometres beyond the village, on the road to La Bane. There is a set of gates, with stone anchors set on the pillars. The family has a long tradition of serving in the Navy.'

Jacquot took this in. So Léo was following in his family's footsteps, albeit with the Gendarmerie Maritime rather than the fleet.

'But if you wanted to see Monsieur le Comte,' Ballarde continued, 'I am afraid he is not at home.'

'But I spoke to him just yesterday,' said Jacquot, puzzled.

'Then you would have spoken to him in Metz. He left on Friday, after Léo's burial, to attend the young lady's funeral. According to his housekeeper, he is not expected back until Thursday or Friday.'

153

35

HEADING OUT OF FORCALQUIER ON the road to Cruis, Jacquot tried to shift from his mind the words that Ballarde had used.

'. . . *the young lady's funeral.*'

He'd never thought as far as a funeral. Somehow it sounded even more final than the news of Marie-Ange's death. Her funeral. A funeral that had taken place just the day before, according to Ballarde, while he was eating Ayam Batutu at the millhouse with Claudine and Midou. And he hadn't known about it. When Davide Chabran called, the old man had said nothing about it – just going through his nephew's address book and calling up people he didn't know to pass on the terrible news. Going through the motions.

If he'd known about the funeral earlier, Jacquot now wondered, would he have gone? The distance involved, the time it would have taken, a long way to go for . . . for a woman he'd known no longer than a year, for no more than three or four weeks in total – their time together in St Bédard and Marseilles. It was not, after all, as if she had been an old friend whom he had known for years – a family member, an old friend, a lover. To travel to Metz to attend her funeral might have seemed . . . excessive. *De trop*, a little over the top.

And yet, and yet . . . She was a woman who, even in their brief time together, had stolen into his heart, touched something deep inside him. And whose loss had rocked him to the core.

Of course, he would have gone. Of course, he would have been there, at the end. Just like Davide Chabran, an old man in his eighties, who *had* made the journey to Metz, to attend her funeral, to pay his respects, an old man who probably hadn't known Marie-Ange any longer or better than Jacquot had.

Yes, he would have gone, and he would have mourned her deeply. Just as he did now. And he regretted that he hadn't known, that he hadn't gone.

Regrets, he thought, such useless but such damning things.

When, some fifteen minutes later, they reached the Chabran property with its closed wrought-iron gates, pillars and stone anchors, Jacquot had Brunet slow down. At the end of an avenue of plane trees, the sweeping front steps of an ancient château could just be made out, the rest of the building, set on rising ground, lost behind a screen of gnarled branches and shifting leaves.

'Must be quite a place,' said Brunet, as they moved on, heading towards the bridge and village, following Ballarde's directions.

They found the track a hundred metres after the bridge, on the left, just as Ballarde had told them. Parking a few metres further on, where the road widened a little, the two men set out along the path through a mix of pine, holm oak and stray, twisted olive trees, surrounded by the drilling hum of insects, the liquid chirping of birds and the raw resinous scent of pine. At first the path was level, a dusty leaf-litter track wide enough for them to walk comfortably side by side, but soon it began to narrow and steepen. Maybe it was all that cycling, but Brunet quickly drew ahead, leaving Jacquot to climb on alone. All those cigarettes, all those long lunches were starting to tell, he decided, but then he comforted himself with the thought that Brunet was a good ten years younger.

It wasn't long before his assistant was out of sight, no sign of him save for the occasional flash of his white shirt up ahead in the

155

trees, and the distant crack of a trodden branch. It was growing warmer, too, the sun slanting down the hillside, streaming through the trees, dappling the path. Jacquot slid off his jacket, slung it over his shoulder, and climbed on, aware of his heartbeat and the closeness of his shirt. And as he climbed he thought of Léo Chabran jogging up this path, the catch of his breath, the weight of his steps, the physical demands of running over this sliding cover of fallen pine needles. In the wheelhouse of that coastguard cutter, Jacquot had noted the man's build, the lithe, easy way he moved. Now he knew why.

Jacquot had just started thinking about stopping for a moment to draw breath when he saw up ahead that the path levelled out, running parallel to the ridge but still some distance below it. He would stop there, he thought to himself, before climbing on, and this he did, congratulating himself that he had come so far without actually opening his mouth and gasping for breath. Since there was no view to speak of, the valley concealed by the woods, he contented himself with his immediate surroundings, a wider section of path – almost a clearing – with trees on one side and a rising slope of bare rock on the other. Leaning back against a slab of limestone, he tuned in to the hum of insects and watched a lizard skitter across the pine needles, clamber onto a rock and scuttle away.

Two weeks before, on a fine sunny morning such as this, Léo Chabran and Marie-Ange had come this way. And before them, along this same path, their killers had come too, lugging that eighteen kilo trap along with them. If the killers really were the two women in the Gilbert photos, then they'd have to be pretty tough and determined to carry off something like this, Jacquot decided. Just to make a point. So many other, easier ways to have killed Léo Chabran, and still remove his foot.

What they had done, thought Jacquot, was nothing less than a grandstanding performance. A bold, dramatic act. Long rehearsed and well directed, the two women watching his movements, familiarising themselves with his routine, the play of his day in Toulon, Marseilles and here, until they'd identified this path through the woods, the route of his morning run, as the most suitable place of execution. To cause his lover, Marie-Ange, the greatest possible grief and pain.

Jacquot wondered how many times they had come here, to check out the path, maybe concealing themselves amongst the trees to watch Léo jog past. To watch his footfall. The way he ran. To place the trap in exactly the right place. Many times, he guessed. Until they were sure.

Yet Marie-Ange had died too. At about the same time as Léo, according to the pathologist; but some considerable time after the trap had been sprung.

Which meant . . .

Which meant she had come looking for him.

Something the killers could never have anticipated.

Marie Ange just turning up like that, coming up quietly on this pine-needle path while the killers watched the life blood drain out of Léo.

Or maybe she'd called out his name, and they had heard her coming?

Or maybe they'd met her on the path, going back down to their car after Léo had died?

Whichever it was, she would have seen their faces, been able to give the police a description.

She had to die as well. No alternative.

It was then, as Jacquot reached for his cigarettes, going through it all, that he realised something else. If Marie-Ange had never been meant to die, hadn't been a part of their hit, then the bullets in her heart and her head were not the 'wounds for wounds' he had at first assumed. Never had been. And it was out of synch, too, he now realised. After 'foot for foot' came 'burn for burn', not 'wound for wound'.

Which meant that there were still *three* more killings to come.

'Boss? You down there?' It was Brunet's voice, somewhere up ahead.

'Taking a leak,' replied Jacquot, pushing himself off the rock, trying to keep a grip on these thoughts. '*J'arrive, j'arrive*. I'm coming.'

Five minutes later, he caught up with Brunet. His assistant was squatting down beside a tall slab of rock that jutted out from the undergrowth, causing the path to veer to the left before curving back to the right. There was still a twist of blue-and-white scene-of-crime tape knotted to an overhanging branch.

It was, Jacquot decided, the perfect place to conceal a trap. The path here, forced between a stand of trees on one side and a steep slope on the other, was narrower and more deeply grooved than Jacquot had seen so far, covered with a thick surface dressing of pine needles and holm oak leaves. You could almost see where a jogger's foot would fall as he rounded that bend, the layer of pine needles deep enough here to conceal a trap whose open jaws – nearly a metre across – were almost the width of the path.

'Right there,' said Brunet. 'That's where they laid it. And I reckon that's where they hid themselves.' He pointed to a bank of trees where the slope downhill wasn't so steep, maybe twenty metres back from the bend with enough ground cover to hide in. Jacquot walked over to it, stepped across a length of fallen timber, and squatted down. He glanced back over his shoulder at the path – a clear view between the trees, a perfect observation post. He looked back at the nest they must have lain in – roots, pine needles – no different from any other square metre of the wood. They had left no sign.

'What now, Boss?'

Jacquot came out of the trees and clambered back onto the path. He looked around. He would remember this place. The place where Marie-Ange had died. For a moment, a very odd moment, he felt very close to her. As though she were standing right beside him, pushing back that loop of black hair, tilting her head the way she

158

did – and those dark, velvet eyes of hers settling on him, seeing everything.

'Lunch,' he replied.

And as he said the word, he shivered.

36

THE FOLLOWING FRIDAY EVENING, OVER a salad and steak supper at the millhouse with Claudine and Midou, after a slow and unrewarding week in which memories of Marie-Ange, bidden and unbidden, had filled his thoughts, Jacquot suggested a trip to Forcalquier for the following day. He had someone he had to see in a nearby village, he told them, and maybe they would like to accompany him?

The proposal was greeted with enthusiasm. There was an artist's supplies shop in the town that Claudine had heard about, and Midou wanted to buy some jeans. After a week spent holed up at home, mother and daughter were keen to get out of the house.

So, early Saturday morning, the three of them set off, agreeing to meet up later for lunch.

After dropping them in the market place, Jacquot followed the road that he and Brunet had taken earlier that week, out of town to Lurs and from there to Cruis. This time the gates of the château were open and Jacquot turned in and drove up between the peeling plane trees. He could have phoned Davide Chabran who, according to Ballarde, had returned home the previous day, to ask his questions but he wanted to meet the eighty-six year old man who had travelled to Metz for the funeral of his nephew's girlfriend. Of course, since the pair of them had been murdered together, it would have been a simple courtesy to attend both funerals. But Jacquot was equally certain that Marie-Ange must have made an impression on the old man, and he wanted to know more.

Coming out of the trees into a gravelled forecourt, the honeyed limestone walls of the château finally revealed themselves – three floors up to its overhanging pantiled roof, eight windows per floor, with a high round tower at one end. The stone of this tower was patched and flaky with age, its windows smaller and narrower, rustling green ivy reaching up to the tower's waist as though to support it, tracing itself around the first two of the four ascending windows.

Jacquot parked in the shade and climbed the steps to the front door, but before ringing the bell he turned to take in the view of the Lure hills to one side and a sweep of silvery-green olive groves to the other. It would be a wonderful place to wake up in the morning, thought Jacquot, to stand at a bedroom window and take in such a grand prospect.

'*Oui*, Monsieur?' The voice took him by surprise and he started. He hadn't yet rung the bell but someone had seen his arrival, presumably the little old lady who stood before him – a wide pleated apron, small waistcoat-like jerkin, chubby arms and what sounded like wood sabots as she led him into the hall, cool, almost chill, after the summer sunshine.

'If you would wait a moment, I shall see if Monsieur le Comte is available.'

As she waddled away – clack-clunk, clack-clunk over the stone floor – Jacquot caught another sound, soft, familiar, in some distant part of the house, a piano, long plaintive notes, played at a haunting tempo. He recognised it instantly. 'Summertime'. *Porgy and Bess*. George Gershwin.

And then, just as quickly, he heard a door open and the volume increase, then die away. It hadn't been a radio or a record as Jacquot had at first assumed, but someone actually playing. A moment later the old lady was back.

'If you go on down there, you'll find him in the music room,' she told Jacquot briskly, and with that she marched off – clack-clunk, clack-clunk – to some other part of the house.

He did as he was told and as he crossed the hall the piano started up again, somewhere ahead, at the end of a vaulted stone corridor. More Gershwin. Just two or three tuning notes before the Comte, who was surely the one playing, settled into that trilling unmistakable two-finger intro to *Rhapsody in Blue*, piano substituting for clarinet. The accelerating lightness of *Rhapsody* after the longeurs of 'Summertime' had a celebratory ring, as though the player were in some way pleased by the interruption. The other way round, he would clearly not have been.

'The devil to play, Chief Inspector, but jolly good exercise for aged fingers like mine,' said Davide Chabran, turning on his piano stool as Jacquot entered the room. A trim, straight-backed figure, the Comte de Chabran pushed himself up and stumped over to greet his guest. He was brown as a nut, taut and wiry as salted rope, with a wave of white hair rising off his scalp, his eyebrows magnificently curled and his eyes a sharp, seafaring blue. He was wearing slippers so there was no sound on the stone floor, but his voice was given a certain resonance by the vaulted ceiling. 'When I can't do that intro, I'll know I'm on the way out.'

They shook hands, a surprisingly firm grip from an old man, and Jacquot apologised for turning up unannounced. Chabran shrugged the apology away; it wasn't needed. And in that single movement, hands raised as high as his head, the Comte reminded Jacquot of his old friend and protector, Jean-Pierre Salette, the retired harbour master in Marseilles. The pair of them would have hit it off in an instant – from different social circles, certainly, but two of a kind.

'Do you like Gershwin?' asked Chabran, taking Jacquot's elbow and showing him to a chair on the other side of the piano. Before he could answer, Chabran continued. 'Died aged thirty-eight, did you know that? Gershwin. Same as Léo. I heard him play once, at a party in Paris. I'd just left the Conservatoire. Not good enough to make a career of it, I'm afraid, so I was on my way to La

162

Rochelle . . . naval college, you know. Like the rest of the family. Very good looking young man was Gershwin. Like me, he had no children. Never married either, though I did.' Chabran settled himself on the piano stool, crossed his legs, laid his hands in his lap, the thumb of his left stroking the fingernails of his right. 'His brother Ira was there too, at the party,' continued the old man, as though describing an event he had attended just the night before. 'Not as handsome, mind, but very smart.' Chabran tapped his temple. 'To write lyrics like his, he had to be, I suppose.'

Then, suddenly, he was back on track, finally answering Jacquot's question with a sparkle of amusement in his pale eyes.

'But no, please don't worry. At my age, any interruption is a good thing. There aren't enough people around these days. There ought to be more visiting, don't you think?' Then he stopped abruptly. 'But there you are. That's the world we live in. So what can I do for you? How can I help, Chief Inspector? It is Chief Inspector, isn't it? Audrette's a little deaf, I'm afraid. It's about Léo, isn't it? And that lovely Marie-Ange. Nearly three weeks now and I simply cannot come to terms with it.'

'I am very sorry for your loss, Monsieur. I didn't know your nephew well, but he was a remarkable fellow.'

'He was that, he was that indeed,' agreed Chabran, working his lips, tightening his jaw to keep back tears that Jacquot could see were very close. 'So, where did you meet? How? When? Tell me. I must admit I was not familiar with your name when I saw it in Léo's address book.'

Jacquot did as he was asked, and ran the old man through the action in the Golfe du Lion the previous November. He made much of Léo's role in the endeavour: the way he'd skippered his cutter and commanded his crew; the way he'd led from the front; his professionalism and good manners, then his calm under fire, explaining how he had been shot, and how he had stoically endured the pain of the wounds until he could be properly treated.

These recollections brought a beam of pleasure to the old man's face and he nodded along, clapping his hands with delight when

163

Jacquot told him about the dash of Calva in the wheelhouse coffee, and Léo leaping aboard the ship they'd been stalking.

'Yes, that's Léo. Following in the family footsteps. *La vie de l'océan. La vie des vagues.* I had always hoped for a flag commission, a ship of the line, but there you are. And you've got him in one. *En effet*, you speak of him as though you had known him much longer?'

Jacquot shook his head.

'Just that one night – a few hours – and only a few minutes the following day, in the hospital. We promised to stay in touch . . . and I'm sure we would have . . . but we never did.'

Chabran waved away the note of regret in Jacquot's voice.

'*Mais, bien sûr*, of course you would. It's just that when we're young, time has a nasty habit of tripping us up. There seems so much of it, and then . . . but I'm babbling. And you have questions to ask, I'm sure. So please, do ask them.' Chabran spread his hands in a go-ahead way, eyes fixed firmly on Jacquot. 'I am at your disposal, Chief Inspector.'

'I understand that Léo was a frequent visitor here?'

'*Mais, oui*. It was his home. It would have been strange if he had not been.'

'But given his work commitments, he still came back regularly?'

'Whenever he could make it. At least once a month. And always for the olive harvest.'

'And when he visited, he always went for a run?'

'That's right. Always in the morning, before it got too hot.'

Jacquot remembered his own climb earlier in the week, how the sun beat down through the trees and blasted off the rock.

'Did he have a favourite route?'

'Always the same. Down the drive, towards the village and up through the woods, along the ridge and back down to the road. About twenty kilometres all in. Pretty tough. Last time I tried it, I was in my fifties. Never again. Marie-Ange ran with him a few times, but she told him it was far too tough for her and she'd stick with her yoga.'

164

Yoga? Jacquot was taken by surprise. He hadn't known that Marie-Ange practised yoga. He felt a wince of regret; he hadn't really known her at all. Yet this old man . . .

Through the open door of the music room came the rising and unmistakeable clack-clunk step of Audrette heading in their direction. Chabran consulted his watch.

'Midday. *Exacte*. *Et voilà*,' said Chabran, looking to the door.

With a stern face Audrette made her entrance carrying a small silver tray with two glasses of milky pastis and a jug of iced water.

'Messieurs,' she said, placing the tray on the open lid of the piano. She poured the water for them, handed them their glasses and then withdrew with more clack-clunking.

'Our father, Léo's grandfather, used to drink Martinis. Imagine, a Frenchman! And he was very strict about them. The preparation, the measures . . . had to be just right. He would pour in the gin, then take up a bottle of vermouth, just loosen the cap above the cocktail shaker, *et voilà* . . .'

'He sounds quite a man.'

'Oh, he was. And, you know, as Léo grew older, so many times I could see my father in him.'

Jacquot smiled. Lifted his glass.

'To Léo,' he said.

'And Marie-Ange,' added Chabran with a tight little smile.

The two men sipped their drinks. The pastis was ice cold and the aniseed taste was strong, puckering the insides of Jacquot's cheeks.

'You went to her funeral, I believe. In Metz.'

'That's correct. In fact, I called you and some other friends of Léo's from my hotel room, though I didn't know you were a Chief Inspector back then. I had just come back from her funeral, and it seemed a good time. Something for me to do. A duty. And being a Sunday, as I said . . . somehow appropriate. Also it was two weeks or more since their murders. I was more able to break the news to his friends without breaking down myself.'

'It was good of you to let me know. And kind also to attend the funeral.'

'But it was Marie-Ange. How could I not have done?'

Jacquot smiled. He remembered the galvanising effect she'd had on men – all those old codgers in St Bédard almost beside themselves when she took over the Chaberts' flower shop for the duration of their son's trial. And even as level-headed and practised a womaniser as Salette, the old Marseilles harbour master who'd worked the trawlers with his father and always kept an eye open for Jacquot . . . even he had been undone by her.

'She was a remarkable young lady,' he said, setting his drink on his knee, feeling the iced glass through his jeans.

'She was indeed. Quite remarkable,' Chabran replied, holding Jacquot's eye a moment longer than he needed to. 'So you knew Mademoiselle Buhl as well?'

Jacquot admitted that he did, that they had met the previous summer.

'Tell me, Monsieur, did Marie-Ange spend a lot of time here, with Léo?'

'The first time she came, Léo had just been discharged from hospital. They stayed a couple of days, and then returned to the city.' Chabran said it as if he couldn't remember the city's name, or which city even. 'But it was plain to see that there were . . . feelings between them. Strong feelings. After that they came up whenever they could, as her job allowed, and after Christmas they were here almost every weekend. Which was extra work for poor Audrette. But a delight for me.'

'How so?' asked Jacquot, already knowing the answer, but wanting to hear it from him. To fill in any gaps.

Chabran smiled a far-away smile.

'I may be an old man, Chief Inspector, but my eyes are still sharp and my memory still fresh.' He took another sip of his pastis, smacked his lips. 'By then, you see, I had begun to realise that this was a serious liaison, *une vraie affaire de coeur*. That Léo had met someone . . . significant. In his time, my nephew brought a number of girlfriends here. I actively encouraged it. There is nothing like a pretty woman in a house like this to bring it to life. But, as I say,

166

Marie-Ange was different. And so was Léo. *En effet*, Chief Inspector, they were going to marry. He told me just the day before he died. He hadn't asked her, just wanted to know what I thought.'

Jacquot felt a ripple of regret and sadness. Had Marie-Ange known that? Had Léo actually got round to asking her? Before his run?

'And what was that, if you don't mind my asking? What did you think?' asked Jacquot.

'As I said, I couldn't have been more delighted. Marie-Ange, ah, she was . . .' Chabran cast around for the right word.

'*Formidable*?'

'*Oui*, that's it. *C'est ça, exacte. Une fille formidable.*'

For a moment there was silence as both men remembered the woman who had come so unexpectedly into their lives, and so captivated them.

Chabran broke the silence.

'What I can't understand is why? Why could this have happened? To Léo . . . to Marie-Ange. And so far, nothing to explain it. The last time I spoke to the police in Forcalquier, after getting home from Metz, they still had nothing to report. No new developments.'

Jacquot spread his hands, unwilling to tell the old man what he believed. Instead, he asked, 'Would it be too difficult for you to tell me what happened on the morning of their murders?'

'Difficult, yes. But not impossible,' the old man replied, straightening his back. 'Not if it helps bring to justice whoever did this dreadful thing.' He took a breath, looked out of the window. 'It was breakfast-time, maybe eight-thirty. I'd been down to the olives and come back to the house. Marie-Ange had made me coffee, brought it through to the morning room, just along the passageway there, and we were sitting in the sunshine. I was telling her about the olives, how it looked like it was going to be a good harvest and that she should come up for it – with or without Léo. And then, *alors*, the strangest thing. The colour just . . . drained from her face. Suddenly, just like that. At first I thought, *Bon Dieu*,

167

she's having a heart attack. I mean, she was grey. And when I asked if she was okay, it was as if she didn't hear me. Or even see me.'

Jacquot nodded, knowing now that what he had guessed in the woods had been right, that she had 'sensed' something, had 'felt' the danger that her lover was in, and gone looking for him. If she hadn't, she'd still be alive.

Chabran caught the look.

'She knew things, didn't she? There was something . . . She knew something had happened.'

'That's what it sounds like. You see, Marie-Ange had this . . . she had this . . . gift. Like a kind of psychic thing. She seemed able to tap into things. The past, the present. It's how we came to know each other, how our paths crossed in the first place.' Jacquot took a sip of his drink. 'But do carry on. What happened next?'

Chabran took a breath, turned his head to gaze out of the window.

'She stood up, almost shaking, said she had to go, something like that, and was gone. I heard her hurry down the passageway, across the hall, and the front door slam. That was it. I never saw her again.' He fell silent a moment, looked down at his drink. 'I still hear those footsteps, you know?'

Somewhere in the house a clock chimed the hour. Jacquot looked at his watch, finished the last of his drink, got to his feet.

'*Eh bien*, Monsieur. It was kind of you to see me. And thank you for your time. And, once again, I am so sorry . . .' He turned, put his empty glass on the tray.

'Stay for lunch, why don't you?' said the old man, getting to his feet, finishing off his own drink. 'Audrette always has enough . . .'

'I regret, I cannot. I am meeting a friend in Forcalquier.' He looked at his watch again. 'Twenty minutes ago. She will not be happy.'

Chabran covered his disappointment with a brave smile that wavered at the edges, either at having had to revisit something so ghastly or at the prospect of another lonely meal.

'Then you had better hurry, *cher* Monsieur, and hope the waiters are good-looking enough to keep her entertained, but not too good-looking, eh? Which restaurant, might I ask?'

Jacquot told him.

'An excellent choice,' said Chabran, nodding his head. 'The best in town, if you ask me. Have the trout if it's on the menu. Madame knows not to mess it around. And please, remember, whenever you are close, do call in. It would be good to see you again.'

'I shall do that, Monsieur. Thank you.'

37

'TELL ME WHAT'S WRONG.'

Claudine laid down her paintbrush, one of a set she'd bought in the Forcalquier supplies shop, and took the mug of coffee that Jacquot had brought through from the kitchen. It was Sunday morning and she had started early in her studio – working on one of the largest canvases she'd attempted, a giant watermelon hacked open, spilling juice and seeds, with a peacock stepping past it, all deep reds and greens.

She pulled out a stool and settled herself on it, legs crossed, one heel clipped over the runner, holding the mug between her hands and sipping carefully.

'You were in such a low mood at lunch yesterday, and you drank far too much. Even Midou noticed.'

'Was I? Yes, I suppose I was,' he began, thinking of his talk with Davide Chabran, remembering the sadness he'd felt as he drove back to Forcalquier for lunch – for the old man, so lost now and lonely in that empty house; and for Marie-Ange and Léo too. Such a loss, such a waste.

'It's to do with those friends of yours who died, isn't it?'

Jacquot nodded, leant back against her mixing table, folded his arms. When Claudine had asked about them the previous Sunday, he had told her that they were colleagues, that they had worked on some cases together, and provided no further information. But things were different now. Since he was certain that the murders of Izzy Gilbert, Antoine Berri, Minette, Léo and Marie-Ange were linked, had been carried out by the same people, with a high probability that the motive was revenge for the killing of the Manichella brothers – either Virginie Cabrille on her own account, using some unknown muscle, or members of the Manichella family (they were Corsican, after all), or a third possibility as yet unknown – it was increasingly clear that his own name would be on the killers' list. And that Claudine and Midou, as his nearest and dearest, were now at risk. He had worked undercover on the Lafour case, been a part of the action in the Golfe du Lion, and had stood beside Claude Peluze at the house in Roucas Blanc when Virginie Cabrille was led way in handcuffs. Since the deaths of Léo and Marie-Ange, this had preyed on his mind – the 'low mood' that Claudine was talking about – leaving him silent and uncommunicative, given to prowling round the grounds at odd times, checking that all the doors were locked at night, always keeping an eye open for a dark-coloured VW and on the look-out for anyone watching the property, anxious whenever Claudine and Midou went anywhere without him.

Catching Claudine's eyes fixed on him over the rim of her coffee mug, Jacquot realised the time had come to explain himself, to let her and Midou know what was going on. And this he did, quietly, soberly, holding up a finger when Claudine tried to interrupt, until he had finished outlining his case – the murders, the links, and the biblical allusions which so clearly pointed at revenge as the motive. It would be interesting to see if, with all the information to hand, she came to the same conclusion. That she and Midou were at risk.

'So these new murders, these are your "filling stations"?'

He smiled at the reference, remembering what he had told her after Gilbert's death, and nodded.

'So how long is it between the murders?' she asked.

'About a month, give or take. Time for them to set things up properly. Although they've had since the shoot-out last November to plan it all.'

'And you're suggesting there's a possibility they may strike here? At us? Midou and me?'

'A strong likelihood, in my professional opinion,' corrected Jacquot. 'And not just here, in the house. Anywhere.'

'Well, you're not sending us off somewhere, on our own, to be out of danger, I can tell you that. We are staying put.'

Jacquot smiled. He had certainly thought about sending them away, somewhere safe, maybe as far away as Midou's home in the French West Indies. But where was safe? Where was out of reach for such professional, single-minded killers with revenge in their hearts? The answer, he'd concluded, was nowhere. So he'd already decided that Claudine and her daughter were better off staying here, at the mill-house, around Cavaillon, where he could keep an eye on them, life as normal. And he would have argued his case vigorously if Claudine had suggested otherwise. But, of course, she hadn't.

'I kind of feel safer in my own backyard,' she continued. 'If you know what I mean? Doing the things I normally do. Routine. Of course, it would be better if Midou hadn't decided to come and stay, but there we are. We can look out for each other.'

And with that she put down the coffee mug, pushed off her stool and picked up her paintbrush and palette.

'But right now you are wasting my time. And yours. Haven't you got lunch to cook? Out with you. Out. Out.'

38

GEORGES ROCHET, JACQUOT'S BOSS AT Cavaillon police headquarters, was standing at his office window with a pair of binoculars clamped to his eyes when Jacquot knocked and entered. Rochet didn't lower the glasses, or turn to greet his visitor.

'Beautiful, beautiful creature,' he murmured. 'Just . . . beautiful. *Il n'y a pas de plus belle.*'

But Rochet was not talking about a woman, and his binoculars were not aimed at the street. Instead he was focussing on a moving speck in a patch of sky above the Sainte-Jacques ridge.

'Peregrine falcon – mistress of the skies,' continued Rochet. 'Faster than the male . . . fastest creature on earth. Or rather, above it.'

A tall, gentle man for whom Jacquot had a high regard, Rochet was a widower who loved the opera, good food and birds in pretty much equal measure, timing his holidays for the annual migration at Falsterbö in Sweden, or a twitching trip to some other reserve. He also liked smoking a pipe, a selection of which were held in a rack on his desk, and his office smelt warmly of tobacco.

'I always think raptors look a little scruffy,' he continued. 'But not the peregrine. This one looks like she's just stepped out of Colette's on place Lombard. Every feather in place, sleek and beautiful.'

He lowered the glasses, turned and settled his sharp grey eyes on Jacquot.

'So, Daniel, how's everything going? What can you tell me that I can pass on to that Fourcade of ours? To keep him off our backs. He really is most persistent.'

Taking the chair that Rochet indicated, Jacquot brought his boss up to speed: the two unidentified women at the wedding in St-Florent; the VW Beetle they might be driving, if the *garagiste* Lapierre's identification of a man and a woman amounted to anything; and the links they'd established between the Gilbert case and the other murders.

While he spoke, Rochet, a particular man, wound the binocular straps around the bridge of the glasses, slipped them into their worn leather carrying case and settled behind his desk.

'The attacks are well-planned and well executed,' Jacquot continued. 'Getting in to Le Mas Bleu, knowing the name of the Gilberts' suite and getting out, job done, leaving not a single trace . . . well, that's some act. Same with Berri – knowing the lay-out of the Delacroix yard, knowing about the kid's apprentice piece, how he worked on a Saturday evening. That kind of thing takes time to put together. Minette Peluze as well, following her, waiting for their moment, then striking. And watching Léo Chabran. Taking him out on one of his morning runs.'

'And you say the likely motive is revenge for this action in Roucas Blanc last November?'

Jacquot nodded.

'That's how it looks. The brothers who were shot – Tomas and Taddeus Manichella – worked for Arsène Cabrille, and at the time of the operation, following Cabrille's death, they were still working for his daughter, Virginie. Or, at least, living on her property.'

'You have interviewed her?'

'Yes I have. A real piece of work. She maintains that she had terminated their contract and given them notice, which makes it sound as if she's hardly going to start looking for ways to revenge their deaths . . .'

'If she's telling the truth?'

Jacquot smiled, and nodded.

174

'Which is why Bernie Muzon in Marseilles has been keeping an eye on her. Her phones have been tapped, her movements covered, but so far there's nothing to link her to the murders. She's alibied-up. I had Brunet check. On holiday in Ibiza when Gilbert's wife was murdered, in Paris when Minette Peluze was killed, in the Seychelles when Berri died, and on a flight back from a business meeting in Zurich for the killings in Cruis – Léo Chabran and Marie-Ange Buhl. Of course, this doesn't mean she isn't directing the action, but it's pretty near impossible to make anything stick.'

'What about the brothers' family? They're Corsican, right? A long tradition over there of an eye for an eye.' Rochet gave Jacquot a skewed look; he knew that Jacquot was half-Corsican himself.

'We've had the local boys quietly check out the family. Everything as it should be. Every family member accounted for. And no movements off the island.'

'So is it over? Are they done, whoever they are, these two women in the VW? Or do you think they're going to strike again?'

'Oh, they'll strike again. Or try. It's just a matter of who next, and when, and where. And getting there in time to stop it.'

'Apart from you, who else was involved in this Lafour case? Who else might be on their list?'

Jacquot spread his hands.

'I can't think of anyone. No major players.'

Rochet reached for a pipe, slid out a desk drawer for his tobacco and after tapping the pipe against the edge of his desk started loading the bowl.

'And have you mentioned all this to Claudine?' he said at last, tamping down the tobacco and setting it alight.

Jacquot said he had and told Rochet just how Claudine had responded.

Rochet gave a wry smile, letting the smoke slide from between his lips.

'Exactly what I would have expected of her. An exceptional woman, Daniel. So you're going to use her as bait. And she knows it. To try and lure the killers in?'

'The sooner we can catch them, the sooner all this ends.'

'So what shall I tell our Monsieur Fourcade?'

'Tell him there's a bigger picture. That the Blanchard murder is just a part of something else that's going on. That . . . for now . . . we must wait.'

Rochet nodded. Sucked on his pipe.

'Oh, he'll like that. He really will.'

39

SOLANGE BONNEFOY LAY CURLED AND warm in her bed and listened to her lover move around the darkened room. In a few more moments he would be dressed, ready to leave, and he would come to the bed, lean over and kiss her. He would not tarry. Maybe he would whisper something if he suspected she was awake. If he thought her still asleep, the brush of his lips on her cheek or forehead would suffice.

She had felt him leave her bed an hour before and had opened an eye to see the green digital read-out of her bedside radio flicking to 5.02. Two or three minutes either side of five in the morning and Hervé Montclos, curator of the Balon Gallery in Marseilles, woke without any sound from an alarm and left their bed. Only when he stayed at her apartment on a Friday or Saturday night would the following mornings begin in a different manner.

As she lay there, listening to the fall of the shower – always put on first to cover the sound of the lavatory flush – Solange marvelled at the good fortune that had brought this man into her life. She had met him just six months earlier, at a Christmas dinner party held at a friend's house. Of all the guests – most of them fellow lawyers and their wives – Hervé was the only one she hadn't recognised, and as such, she well knew, the man who had been brought to the table to partner her and balance the numbers. As a single woman of a certain age, never married, Solange was used to such arrangements, accepted them with good grace, though always felt a particular elation when her better, closer friends didn't bother with such a caring, considerate, if clumsy, convention.

Sure enough, within five minutes of her arrival, she was steered towards the man and gently introduced. She was struck first by his eyes which bunched up in a web of wrinkles when he smiled, warm and brown, filled with a bright and sharp intelligence, but also shadowed by a deep sadness. He had just arrived in Marseilles, he told her, from Montpellier, to take over as curator of the Balon Gallery on rue Grignan. Though he had lived so close to Marseilles, he was ashamed to admit that he had never before visited the city.

'And do you like what you have found?' she had asked.

'Now I do,' he'd replied, more gallantly than flirtatiously she had mistakenly decided.

Hervé Montclos, she later discovered, was also Visiting Professor of Antiquities at Aix University, a fellow of the Académie Française, and the author of more than a dozen scholarly works on the history of Abyssinian sculpture. He was fifty-nine, recently widowed and the father of three daughters all of whom had now flown the coop. Finding himself alone in the sprawling family home outside Montpellier, he had, six months earlier, resigned his position at the city's celebrated Fabre Museum, sold the house and accepted the curatorship of the Balon.

It was in the Balon Gallery just a few days after that Christmas dinner party, giving Solange a private, after-hours tour of the exhibits, that he had kissed her for the first time, pressing her gently against an Aksumite stone plaque. On the lips, softly; his hand placed just a centimetre or two below the rise of her right breast. She had experienced a certain breathlessness at this unexpected move, which had been interrupted, sadly, by the arrival of a security guard. Two days later they were lovers.

There was no doubt in Solange Bonnefoy's mind that Hervé was the most important man in her life. The most important man ever. There had never been anyone like him. Not that she had a particularly wide range of experience on which to base such a judgement. There had in fact been few other men in her life, few men to share her bed. She was too tall, she knew; too awkward in her skin to be a natural lover; too intelligent to suffer fools; and, increasingly, too set in her own ways. She also felt a clumsiness in intimacy – always had – as though her tall, gangling frame was somehow not suitably equipped for the delicate manoeuvrings of love-making. Height, shape, intelligence, and now age had determined the course of her love life.

Until now. Until Hervé.

'Are you awake?' she heard him whisper.

'Dreaming,' she whispered back.

She felt him lean down, one hand gently pushing back her hair, lips brushing her cheek.

'I'll call you later. Dinner?'

'Miramar. My treat,' he replied.

'Shall I meet you there?'

'I'll pick you up at the office.'

Another light kiss, the warm fresh smell of him.

And then he was gone.

The apartment door closing.

With a sigh, now that she was alone, Solange swung herself from their bed and padded through to the bathroom. The room was warm from him, the mirror frosted with condensation, but otherwise there was no sign that the bathroom had been used before her. Everything in its place – no towel on the floor, no rumpled shower mat, no bristles in the sink, the lavatory seat lowered, everything gleaming, untouched. What a find, she thought, wiping a hand through the condensation and smiling at herself.

Taking a gown from the back of the bathroom door she went through to the kitchen and put on some coffee. Three floors below she heard his footsteps clatter down the steps of her apartment building and start up the road to where he had parked his car the night before. She leant forward over the sink, found the right angle and watched him stride away. Slim, tall, a long loping pace, briefcase swinging, one hand holding down his hat against an early morning breeze coming off the harbour. A moment later he was out of sight, and a moment after that she heard his car door slam shut with a hefty clunk. If she stayed where she was, she'd see him drive past. Just one more look. To keep her going till this evening and their dinner at Miramar.

But there was no 'one more look'.

He did not drive past.

And nor would there be any dinner that night at Miramar.

40

CAFÉ-BAR VERNIX, ON THE corner of boulevard Georges Durand and place Méribel, opened early for the army of office cleaners who, from around four o'clock every morning, Monday to Friday, streamed out of the various government buildings that occupied much of the length of Durand. Made up of hard, blank-faced walls, darkened by the shadows of a double line of plane trees down the centre of the boulevard, the offices behind these walls controlled everything in the city from building permits to road works, from education to health, birth certificates to death certificates. And being government offices they were cleaned every night of the week – floors polished, bins emptied, desks wiped, phones swabbed.

Café-Bar Vernix was a popular haunt for these workers, as much for its coffees and *chocolats chauds* as its generous tots of cognac and Calva, for those who needed a little something to rev them up after their shift or to help put them to sleep when they got home and the sun came up. For the café's proprietor and his three waiting staff, this was the start of a busy day that didn't really ease up till early evening. Once the office cleaners had departed, the office workers – *les fonctionnaires* – arrived, calling in for their morning *lattes* and *espressos* and returning at lunchtime for their *omelettes frites, spaghettis* and *salades,* all this to a busy soundtrack of clattering plates, shouted orders and the hiss and sputter of the Gaggia, set on the bar like some alien spacecraft issuing orders.

It was here, at a little before five in the morning, that two women found themselves stools in a corner between bar and window and ordered *chocolats chauds* and warm croissants just delivered from the *boulangerie* next door – which didn't open for another hour but took advantage of the café's custom by off-loading a couple of early trays. Like so many of the women who worked as office cleaners and passed through Café-Bar Vernix, these two had scarves on their heads, wore overalls and trainers, and had official-looking name tags pinned to their chests. And as they sipped their drinks and dunked their croissants, they kept an eye on rue Carème which started on the other side of place Méribel, a gentle slope of nineteenth-century townhouses, four floors high, each façade three windows wide in the classic Marseilles fashion. Once these houses had been the homes of wealthy traders from the docks and go-downs of the Vieux Port and La Joliette, but now, with only one or two exceptions, they had been turned into upper-end apartments, the highest with a view across the rooftops to the old port and Fort St-Jean.

It was in one of these apartments that Madame Bonnefoy, one of Marseilles' most seasoned and respected examining magistrates, lay in her bed and listened to her lover in the bathroom, getting dressed in the dark of her bedroom. The new man in her life.

For the last four nights the two women drinking their *chocolats* in Café-Bar Vernix had followed Monsieur Hervé Montclos from the gallery where he worked to his home in Prado with its underground residents' car park. Which wasn't what they wanted, not at all what they were after. The two women who followed him wanted something far more dramatic, something far more visible and telling than a basement parking lot. What they were waiting for was the road outside Madame Bonnefoy's apartment, where her lover parked when he came calling, so she could see what happened to him.

So she would know.

And that's what Hervé Montclos had done the previous evening, coming back late from a reception at the Gallery Balon and parking no more than fifty metres uphill from the lawyer's apartment. With one of the women keeping watch, it had taken but a matter of moments for the other to break into his white Audi estate, connect the wires to the ignition, and fix the small supply of 7-weight Plexi-Lye-40 to the base of the steering column.

Now the two women sat in Café-Bar Vernix and waited, until the older one spotted movement up the slope. From this distance they could see it was a man but until he stopped at the white Audi, they could not be certain it was him.

When he did so, they knew.

And with curious eyes they watched him unlock the driver's door and slide in.

The blast – a black and orange ball of roiling smoke and fire – sounded from this distance like a dull *whumph*, but the force of the explosion was enough to make Café-Bar Vernix's window shudder and the reflections in it quiver and shake. Moments later came a second blast as the Audi's petrol tank blew and a breeze from the harbour pushed a billowing cloud of black smoke down the street towards the café. It was out of this cloud that twisted pieces of bodywork now rained down onto the street – a crumpled door, a section of the back seat, the hood and hatchback – rattling over the cobbles and pavement and setting off a dozen car alarms.

There was a hungry crackling of flames, and a stunned silence among the booths and at the bar as every head turned to the window. And then a monstrous clanging sound echoed down the street as the Audi's front axle, its wheels ablaze, crashed down and began a slow flaming descent of the slope, coming to an abrupt halt against the small fountain in the middle of place Méribel.

'*Numéro cinq,*' said the smaller of the two women.

'Ssshhh!' said the other, holding up a finger, as the café's proprietor, staff and patrons crowded past them and out onto the pavement.

The two women followed, pausing for a moment to watch the flames and smoke billowing from the blackened husk of the car, its axle lodged against the fountain and the sweet smell of baking from the *boulangerie* wiped away by the harsh stench of petrol and burnt rubber.

In the minutes that followed lights flicked on in every building, and the pavements around the *place* quickly filled with people, woken by the blast, coming out in dressing gowns to see what had happened. In such a crowd, with everyone's attention focused on rue Carème, it was a simple matter for the two women to slide away unnoticed, just a couple of office workers heading home after a long night shift.

As they came to the corner of Boulevard Clemenceau the first sirens started up.

'What a way to start the day,' said the taller of the two women.

'Quite a wake-up call,' replied her companion.

41

IF THE KILLERS WERE WATCHING the millhouse, Jacquot knew how important it was to keep to the same routine. If they sensed for a moment that he knew what was going on, what was being planned, then there was a risk they'd put together something else that might be harder to spot or defend against. Things had to stay the same, so that he could draw the killers into the open, flush them out. Right now he had the advantage of knowing what they didn't know he knew. He was ready, on the alert. All he had to do was go through the motions, as though nothing had changed: leaving for the office in the morning, coming home for lunch now and then, as was his custom, or meeting up with Claudine and Midou in town, and always leaving for home at the same time – early – each evening.

In case one of the killers was watching the house, and another watching police headquarters in Cavaillon – which is how he would have played it – Jacquot held to this pattern as strictly as he could, but had precautions in place. He had equipped the millhouse phone line with an automatic alarm call to police headquarters. If there was anything wrong, all the girls had to do was press zero, whichever phone they were closest to – bedroom, kitchen, salon, bathroom. They didn't even need to lift the receiver. Of course the killers could cut the lines, but it was still an option . . .

As a further defence, Jacquot had also taken possession, at a nod from Rochet, of two police-issue Berettas for Claudine and Midou and, after lowering the kitchen blinds one night, he had shown the two women how to use them. He was relieved that neither of them had put up any argument, nor winced or shivered when he told them that the chest was a wiser and an easier target than head or limbs, and whether the shot was high or low or wide the chances were that a 9x19mm Parabellum fired in this area would put down your assailant every time. They'd listened to him carefully and they did what he told them – how to hold the gun with two hands, how to work the safety with their thumbs, and how to aim on the straight rather than bother with the sights. The only problem was where to keep the guns. Since there were no children in the house, they could afford to be a little more daring, but for one reason or another each location was found wanting. Finally they agreed on the salad drawer in the fridge and in the downstairs cloakroom, the two of them promising Jacquot that they'd take one of these guns with them whenever they left the house. And never travel alone.

'But we are not going to miss the concert because of all this,' insisted Claudine. 'Just so long as that's agreed right now, right here?' In two weeks Cavaillon was playing host to George Benson, one of Claudine's favourite musicians, for a one-off outdoor concert between dates in Juan-Les-Pins and Nice, the gig arranged in memory of the father of one of his supporting group who had been born in the Luberon, all ticket receipts to go to a local charity. 'If I don't hear George Benson sing "Breezin'" live, those killers of yours will be a soft option, because your life, Chief Inspector Daniel Jacquot, will not be worth living.'

'Agreed,' said Jacquot, as keen to see Mr Benson as Claudine was. As Cavaillon's highest-ranking police officer under Georges Rochet – who would more likely prefer an evening's opera in Orange – there was every chance that Daniel might even get to meet the big man. He'd been joking for weeks that if Claudine behaved herself, he might see if he could arrange an introduction. And, frankly, the risks of attending the concert were minimal. They'd be as safe in a crowd as they were in the millhouse, and he'd be with them the whole time.

One morning, a week after his talk with Rochet, Jacquot was driving into town from the millhouse, keeping an eye out for dark-coloured VW Beetles, when he heard a radio report about an explosion in Marseilles. It had only happened a few hours earlier and there were few details as yet beyond the fact that it appeared to be a car-bomb in a residential street in Endoume and that only one fatality had been reported.

This news item made him remember, in an instant, another bomb in Marseilles, an anarchist bomb tossed from a passing car, the bomb that had killed his mother, and fourteen other people, and changed his life for ever. And with his eyes fixed on the road ahead Jacquot saw again the red print dress she was wearing that last morning of her life, the way its square-cut top framed the red coral necklace his father had given her – to keep her safe – and the canvas bag she carried with painting dungarees and plimsolls packed away inside, the heels of her favourite red shoes clicking on the pavement as they walked together down the slope of Le Panier into town, the kiss on both cheeks when they parted at the school gates.

He'd watched until she was out of sight.

And he never saw her again.

Later, he passed the shop where she'd been working, painting a backdrop for one of its window displays, a sheet of wood nailed into place where the glass had blown inwards and cut her down. Strange, he thought, how his mother and Claudine were both artists.

More than forty years later, that final memory of his mother was still piercingly sharp – that particular shade of red in her skirt, the brown skin of her arms, the smell of her hair when she kissed him – just as sharp as the last memory he had of his father, Vincent, lost at sea just months before his mother's death. A cheery salute from the stern of his trawler, that lopsided grin of his and a long sharp whistle between his fingers that set the seagulls aloft.

As the morning wore on, little more information about the explosion in Marseilles was forthcoming beyond the fact that the victim

187

was called Hervé Montclos, recently appointed curator at the Balon Gallery on rue Grignan. So far the police were at a loss to explain why a museum curator's car should have been targeted, and were appealing for witnesses – anyone who might have seen anything suspicious in the hours leading up to the explosion. It was a residential street. Had somebody been seen loitering around Montclos' car?

It wasn't until that evening when Jacquot was back at the millhouse, watching the TV news that he suddenly spotted a familiar face in the report on that morning's explosion: Solange Bonnefoy, one of the city's most renowned examining magistrates. She was being escorted by gendarmes into Police Nationale headquarters on Garibaldi. At first he assumed she had been brought in to direct the investigation. But he was wrong. According to the news reporter, Hervé Montclos and Solange Bonnefoy had lived together. At approximately 5.55 that morning he had left her apartment, walked to his car, unlocked it and climbed in. As he switched on the engine, the car had exploded.

Jacquot's blood went cold and a shiver stole across his shoulders.

Solange Bonnefoy.

Who had asked Jacquot to track down her kidnapped niece, Elodie Lafour.

Who had sanctioned the raid on Roucas Blanc.

And who had pursued Virginie Cabrille so unrelentingly in the days after her arrest.

Another name that Jacquot hadn't considered as a target, another name he had never thought to link to the current investigation.

42

THE FOLLOWING MORNING, IN HIS office at police head-quarters, Jacquot put a call through to Solange Bonnefoy's chambers on Cours Pierre Puget in Marseilles. He had her home number but felt that, in the circumstances, her office would be the best place to call; less intrusive, it would give her space until she decided to do something about it. As he'd expected Madame Bonnefoy was not at her desk, but would he care to leave his name or a message? he was asked.

'Just say Daniel called,' Jacquot told her assistant. That's all he needed to say. So that she knew he was there if she needed him, if she needed to talk.

He hadn't expected a prompt reply and he didn't get one. It was two days before Solange Bonnefoy phoned him back.

'It was good of you to call, Daniel.'

There was no need for her to say who it was. When he heard her voice, he shooed Brunet from his office, and closed the door to the squad room.

'I am so very sorry, Solange. You must be . . .'

'Devastated? Or strong? Which camp are you in, Daniel? So far callers are falling into one or other category.' He heard her try a chuckle, but she couldn't quite carry it off.

Jacquot smiled. 'The devastated camp.'

'And you're right. That's what I am. Completely and utterly. And I really don't want to hear that "strong" rubbish. I'll leave being strong for some other time. Right now I'm just plain . . . devastated.'

Jacquot waited a beat before he continued, heard her blow her nose on the other end of the line. 'I didn't know you . . .'

The nose was wiped, the tissue wadded into her sleeve. He had seen her do it so many times – most effectively in her prosecutor's robes in court – that he could see it now, as though she were there in his office, or he in her chambers.

'We kept it quiet,' she replied, her voice thickening. 'And it was early days. And there were his children to consider. Blah, blah . . . You know how it is.'

There was a long, weary pause, broken by fresh sniffs. The nose was blown again. It didn't take much for Jacquot to add to the tissue and sleeve image her long face drawn and puffy, her grand prow of a nose reddened by the attention, and her grey hair usually so wavy and bouyant now likely lank and lifeless.

The killers had done what they had set out to do, thought Jacquot. They had taken one life and ruined another.

A true, horrible and bitter revenge.

'You know what? The thing I regret the most?' she said at last.

'*Dis-moi*,' replied Jacquot, with a soft, slow kindness.

'That morning, the last time I saw him, I pretended to be . . . not quite awake. Just mumbled something about dinner. So when he left, all I got was just the sense of his lips against my cheek.' She sighed. 'If only I hadn't pretended sleep . . . if only I'd let him know, he would have kissed me properly, with love. The right kind of kiss for a last kiss, don't you think?'

Jacquot let her think about that for a moment. There was no need for words from him and he pictured her at the end of the line, remembering that lost moment.

And then she was back, with another grim little chuckle.

'You know, what I can't get over is the irony of it,' she continued. 'Here am I, a symbol of law and order and justice, and where do I live? Just a few doors down from one of the city's most notorious *parrains*. Can you believe that? Some gangland boss with more blood on his hands than wrinkles. Apparently he keeps a mistress there. That's what the police have told me, and according to them that's how come my man was blown to bits. Mistaken identity. A gallery curator and a gangland boss. Would you credit it? And I've just found out they drive different cars. How could it be mistaken identity? Tell me that.'

'It isn't,' said Jacquot.

There was a silence at the end of the line as Solange Bonnefoy absorbed those tight, short words. And their message.

'I'm sorry to say it was very much deliberate,' he continued.

Finally, she spoke. 'What are you saying, Daniel? What do you know?' Her words were icily direct, unwavering. It was the way she sometimes spoke in court, or in her chambers when the two of them were reviewing evidence – a warning that she should not be toyed with.

'Maybe we should meet,' said Jacquot.

'Where and when?'

43

'IT'S THE SIXTH MURDER OF its kind, all of them linked, in the last four months. Someone's got a list of names, and yours was on it.'

Jacquot and Solange Bonnefoy were sitting under a trellis twined with honeysuckle in the back garden of a small family-run brasserie in the centre of St-Calme. It was two days after their phone call and their lunch had given Solange an opportunity to get out of town, get some fresh air. It also meant that Jacquot hadn't needed to stray too far from Cavaillon. As for the lunch – a starter, *plat du jour*, dessert, coffee, at 200 francs *tout compris* – both of them had professed a lack of appetite when they greeted each other in the bar but when the food arrived had found themselves tucking in with an unexpected gusto.

'So why didn't they blow *me* up?' asked Solange, spearing a grilled artichoke heart from their dish of *hors d'oeuvres*.

'That's the point,' Jacquot explained. 'To make it harder. To make the revenge sweeter, stronger.'

'Daniel, are you talking about someone trying to settle a score? There'd be a queue round the block. I gave up worrying about that my first year in practice. It just doesn't happen. And remember what Juvenal said: "Revenge is the pleasure of a tiny mind", and tiny minds don't think up things like this.'

She popped the heart into her mouth and chewed, rolling reddened eyes at the taste.

'You know who told me that line, by the way?' she continued.

Jacquot shook his head, went for a thin slice of country sausage.

'Mademoiselle Virginie Cabrille, while I was trying to tie her in with that blackmail letter she swore she never sent to my esteemed brother-in-law. "Revenge is the pleasure of a tiny mind", she told me. "And mine, Madame Bonnefoy, is not a tiny mind." How do you like that?' Solange pushed away her plate and reached for her glass.

Jacquot could see that for this short moment Solange had left her sorrow behind, that she was enjoying herself, and he let her go on.

'I checked it later. She'd got it wrong. Or maybe she'd got it right – and just wanted me to know. You know what the whole quote is? Something like . . . "It's always a tiny mind that takes pleasure in revenge. You can deduce it without further evidence than this, that no one delights more in revenge than a woman." What about that? Of course a man wrote it, but still . . .' And then Solange paused, thought about what she'd just said. 'Are you telling me that all this has something to do with Virginie Cabrille? The shoot-out in Roucas Blanc?'

Jacquot waited for their table to be cleared and the main course – a simply grilled *loup* with buttery sauce and nuggety new potatoes – to be served. 'Given the victims, that's the only case it can be tied in with,' he said, after the waitress had wished them both *bon appétit* and left them to it. 'But I have not a shred of evidence beyond the circumstantial. Not the kind of evidence, you can be sure, that I would feel comfortable presenting in your chambers, or in a court of law. In fact,' he continued, starting in on his sea bass, dipping it into the sauce, 'everything points to her *not* being involved. Categorically not involved, never less than a hundred kilometres from any crime scene. We've bugged her phone lines, we've got her under surveillance twenty-four / seven. But there's nothing we can pin on her. And all the time she's behaving as though she's trying to put distance between herself and her father, like *he* may have been one of the city's most lethal godfathers but *she* has no intention of following in his footsteps. According to the boys on rue de l'Evêché, she's sold off his merchant fleet and used the money to fund three more medical facilities – paediatric clinics in Paris, Lyons and Grenoble; and one insider said she's cut ties with the other families, surrendering some of her father's interests into their care. For a price, I'm sure. It's like she means to go straight. Everything she's done since she was released from the tender care of State authorities last November has been whiter than white.'

'Have you met her?'

Jacquot said that he had, the first time at the house in Roucas Blanc on the night of the raid, and just a few weeks ago in Marseilles.

'What did you think of her?'

'Cold,' replied Jacquot. 'A young, attractive woman,' he continued, 'but . . . cold, isolated. As though her heart has been lead-lined, insulated from any kind of feeling.'

'Oh, she has feelings, all right,' said Solange, peeling the skin from her fish and slicing into it. 'They're just not the right kind. The word I would use is malicious. Cold, as you said, but conniving and cruel too. And absolutely heartless. *Dis-moi*, Daniel, you think she could have brought someone in? Contracted out the killings?'

Jacquot shrugged. 'The brothers' family in Corsica seemed the obvious place to start. Revenge . . . an eye for an eye . . . it's a national sport over there. But we've checked. The whole family's where it should be. Aged parents, a couple of daughters, one married with kids, the other not, some cousins and nephews too young to carry off anything like this . . . As for bringing people in, well, old man Cabrille probably had a pretty useful phone book for this kind of work. But again, there's nothing we've been able to find.'

'So who are the other victims?'

Jacquot went through the list, from the Blanchard bride to Antoine Berri, Minette Peluze, and the two most recent victims at Cruis, Léo and Marie-Ange.

'Buhl? Marie-Ange Buhl. The girl I met?'

'The same,' replied Jacquot. 'Léo Chabran was her lover. They were going to get married.'

Solange looked deeply shocked. 'I can't believe it. She was so beautiful, so young, so . . .' She narrowed her eyes on Jacquot. 'I have to say, Daniel, that when I met her I suspected there might have been something between you. The two of you seemed very close.'

It wasn't a question, but Jacquot felt an answer was due. 'No, there was nothing. And she was very young, as you once observed. Too young for the likes of me.' He gave her a smile which he managed to hold. 'But it doesn't make it any easier.'

Once again their plates were cleared and peach *crèmes brûlées* served to them in tiny copper dishes.

'Forensics? Ballistics? Witnesses? Rumours?' asked Solange, tapping through the crust of her dessert and scooping out the cream. 'Do you have anything?'

Jacquot shook his head. 'Every scene-of-crime is clean. I mean, professionally clean. No fingerprints, footprints, tyreprints, no cartridges to retrieve, no shell casings. The only thing they've left at the scene is an animal trap, the smell of this Dyethelaspurane they've used in two of the murders, some threads of clothing and a tiny sprig of vine. And all we have to go on is a dark-coloured VW and two women – who may or may not be involved. But if the pattern continues, as it has so far – eye, tooth, hand, foot – what we're left with now is wound for wound, stripe for stripe.'

'You forgot burning,' Solange remarked, digging the last of the crust from the side of her dish.

'No I didn't,' he replied. 'I just didn't mention it.'

'You'd have made a good lawyer, and an even better prosecutor, Daniel.'

'I didn't like the costume.'

She chuckled, a little tearfully. 'So what now? Where to from here?'

Jacquot shrugged. 'The next on the list. So far they've kept it in order, so it's wound for wound. Then stripe for stripe. A whipping? A flaying?'

'A bruising? A battering?'

'The problem is I can only think of one other name involved in the Lafour case who hasn't yet been hit.'

'I was just coming to that,' said Solange, giving him an anxious look. 'What does Claudine think?'

'She's not thrilled. But she understands what this is all about. And that there's not much else we can do. A forced hand.'

'You're presumably taking precautions?'

'In every possible way,' Jacquot assured her. 'There's a direct-link home-alarm wired through to headquarters, there are two handguns in the house – Claudine's daughter is staying with us at the moment, just to complicate things – and while I sit here with you, three armed *képis* from the local police are playing gardeners, front, sides and back of the house.'

Solange finished her *crème brûlée*, laid down her spoon and settled a hard, uncompromising look on Jacquot. 'So it could be both of them. Wound and stripe. You had thought of that, I suppose?'

Jacquot nodded. 'It's a possibility, yes.'

'You could have sent them away.'

'Better they stay where they are so I can keep an eye on them,' he replied.

'And use them as bait.'

'Can you think of any other way?'

Solange Bonnefoy shook her head, then lifted her empty glass. 'But if you thought about getting me a refill, I might just come up with something.'

44

AS THE DAYS PASSED, JACQUOT grew increasingly jumpy. A slammed car door in the street, an exhaust backfiring, a horn blaring were enough to have him tense, start to reach for his gun – a gun he usually left in his desk drawer but now buckled diligently to his belt.

As well as jumpy, Jacquot had also begun to get angry. This slow-burn anger had started up, almost without him knowing it, when he'd read through the pathologist's report on Marie-Ange – the way the killer had fired that second shot to her head, to make sure she was dead. Point blank, the tip of the silencer just a centimetre or two from her skin, close enough for the muzzle flash to burn. There was something so cold and callous and ruthless about it, something so careless and merciless, and it was that single unnecessary action that had lit the fuse deep inside him. Now that flickering spark of anger had grown into a red-hot flame that made him screw up his eyes and set his teeth tight in his jaw, made him clench his fists and want to scream with rage – and not just because these shadowy killers had gunned down a young woman he had known, respected and . . . felt strongly for, but because those same killers were now threatening his own family, intent on killing them – in whatever manner they'd decided on – just to cause him pain.

Both Claudine and Midou, however, seemed far more at ease.

They might have limited their trips to town – only doing so at planned times and along planned routes that could be covertly supervised – but in all other respects they followed an easy daily routine which, to someone watching, would have appeared quite normal. When Jacquot left for Cavaillon after breakfast, Claudine went to her studio at the back of the millhouse, while Midou sat in the kitchen working on her thesis. With the door between studio and kitchen left open they carried on an occasional, easy conversation – always aware of each other: the swish of a paintbrush being rinsed, the turn of a page, the tap of a keyboard, a cough, the scrape of a chair. And after lunch, at the kitchen table or under the vine on the terrace, the two women would take it in turns to have a siesta, one after another – a forty minute nap on the sofa while the other one stayed awake and kept watch. All the ground floor doors locked.

As the days passed, Jacquot also felt increasingly convinced that he, Claudine and Midou really were being watched. Without any kind of evidence to support this belief, he was suddenly certain of it. He could even pinpoint the moment he first felt it: getting out of his car in the police headquarters' outdoor car park and walking across the gravelled yard to the front steps of the building. In the space of that thirty-metre walk, it was as though he could feel eyes burning into him, and in as casual and relaxed a way as he could manage, he'd glanced around him, as though someone had called his name, or he'd heard something, or something had caught his attention. Of course, there'd been nothing to see, just the church of St-Jean, the usual flock of pigeons taking off from its slatted wood belfry, a passing car, a woman pushing a pram. That was all. But as he went in through the front doors and strode over to the lifts, he was as certain of the sensation of being watched as if someone had actually tapped him on the shoulder.

There had been no giveaways then, and none since, either at headquarters, in town, or out at the millhouse – no distant wink of sunlight off the lenses of binoculars, no rustling in the undergrowth, no suspicious shadows, no tangible sense of being followed. But still he couldn't shake off the feeling, a sixth sense that someone was there, close by, watching and waiting.

It wasn't a pleasant feeling either.

Nor was it pleasant being so powerless.

Doing nothing – not being *able* to do anything.

It was even worse than the waiting.

At first it had felt like time was on his side, that the three- to four-week gap between murders during which, Jacquot supposed, the killers stalked their prey and planned their attack, gave him equal time and space to prepare.

But prepare for what?

The trouble was, he had no idea when an attack might take place, where it might come from, or how it might be effected. Which meant that instead of having time to prepare, all he had was time to fill. And while he waited there was never a moment when the words 'wound for wound' and 'stripe for stripe' didn't scream through his head.

It didn't take long for the strain of this hanging around, this waiting for something to happen, to make itself felt. For Claudine and Midou, too. The frequently repeated wish, usually brought up at the breakfast table or over supper, and certainly thought about in the hours between, that whatever was going to happen, would it damn well happen soon. In short, the waiting was unbearable.

It was for this reason that Jacquot decided to act, to follow up something that had been on his mind. Niggling away at him.

After clearing the assignment with Rochet, he called Brunet into his office.

'I have a little job for you,' Jacquot began.

Brunet looked suspicious.

Jacquot played it just as Brunet would have played it – stretching it out. It was a small pleasure but he enjoyed it.

'Thought you might like it.'

Brunet said nothing, just raised an eyebrow. Jacquot wondered if he knew he was being played.

'Maybe take your bike,' he continued, recalling that drive the

199

two of them had taken to Forcalquier and Brunet complaining about the road surface. 'Challenging stuff up in those hills. Good practice for your time trials. And exercise too. Your legs'll be aching after a couple of kilometres.' Jacquot chuckled.

'You want me to go cycling?'

'Yes, I do.'

'And where do you have in mind?'

Jacquot gave it some thought.

'Corsica.'

45

IT DIDN'T TAKE LONG FOR Brunet to report back.

'It's the sisters,' he said, phoning in the news just three days after his departure for Corsica. 'The Manichella sisters.'

Jacquot felt the sudden, warm pleasure of a hunch paying off. He knew those Corsican hills, and he knew how the local gendarmerie could be. Either money had changed hands or they'd been hoodwinked. They hate us over there, he'd told Brunet the day his assistant left; don't believe a word they tell you. Find out for yourself.

And that's what Brunet had done, riding his bike through Borredonico and Scarpetta and up into Tassafaduca, just as Jacquot had recommended, stopping at the small *pension* on its sloping main street to stay for the night. It hadn't taken him long to cosy up to the inn-keeper's daughter and find out all he needed to know.

'Apparently the Manichellas make the best honey in the region, so I dropped in unannounced to buy some. The old man's a little weak in the head, and the old woman's not far behind him, but it's the two sisters who live either side of the farm who run the place and do the work. The elder one's married, with a couple of kids, but her husband's in clink; the younger sister's single. And there's no sign of them.'

'Out at work?'

'The farm's the work – a few goats, the hives, some maize, chestnuts. But right now everything's being looked after by two other women, cousins probably, who are just about old enough to play the part. If the local boys didn't know the family set-up, they could easily have been fooled.'

'And how exactly do you know that? That the women are cousins?' asked Jacquot.

'Because when I was leaving with my honey, I heard one of the kids ask her aunt – *tatine* – when her *maman* was coming home.'

Jacquot smiled. He wondered if the child had received a hiding for that slip.

'We'll need photographs,' he said.

'Already done. From the local paper in Corte. Last year Miel Manichella won an award at an agricultural show. Photos were taken at the prize-giving. And there they are, the two sisters side by side. Nothing like the cousins.'

'Where are you now?'

'Ajaccio.'

'When are you back?'

'Got a flight booked first thing tomorrow morning.'

'Can you fax the pictures over?'

'Check the machine in the squad room. They should be there already. I sent them twenty minutes ago.'

'Good job. Thanks, Jean.'

'There's something else,' said Brunet. 'Could be a coincidence, maybe not, who knows?'

'And that is?'

'On the way up to Tassafaduca there's a small settlement I rode through called Cabrillio. It reminded me of that woman, Virginie Cabrille? Just outside the village there's this big old castello, so I called in and asked for directions. The owners are Italian, and had just moved in. Turns out they bought the place a couple of months ago, from . . . guess who?'

'You're joking?'

'*Exacte*. Virginie Cabrille. Apparently her father was born there, the old family home. Seems that once upon a time they were pretty big in these parts.'

Thanking Brunet again, Jacquot put down the phone and, wondering at the coincidence, went through to the squad room. Just as Brunet had promised, there they were, four ink-smudged black-and-white photos and a photocopy of the accompanying newspaper story lying in the tray. He flicked through the images, two head-and-shoulder shots, and two full-length photos of the sisters receiving their prize. On the newspaper report a caption for one of the pictures read: *Mme Marita Albertacce and Mlle Marina Manichella receive their prize*. The fax machine and photo-copying may have darkened the pictures but the faces were easily identifiable.

The two women were dressed in summer frocks, floral prints that pressed against their bodies in what must have been a pretty stiff breeze. As well as wearing similar frocks both women were dark-haired, but that was where any similarity ended. One, the elder by the look of her, had a gaunt, drawn face, lined by such fatigue and disappointment that the smile looked more like a tight grimace. She kept her hands thrust down into the pockets of a cardigan, and her shoulders stiffly around her ears, as though trying to ward off a chill. Her sister, a head or more shorter, was far prettier, her smile one of genuine delight, taking the prize with both hands. She seemed, even in those breezy conditions, to radiate warmth. The two sisters looked as though they had come from different worlds, different social spheres   the one pretty and privileged, the other plain and deprived.

But what really irked Jacquot was the fact that they had identi-fied these women as possible, if not probable, killers so late in the day. If the Corsican gendarmerie had been more efficient, or less corrupt, he might have had these pictures a great deal sooner and been able to do something with them.

But better late than never, he decided, and he had a sheaf of

203

copies run off. He had no intention of putting them out for public consumption – in local papers, or pinned to gendarmerie notice-boards throughout the region – but he told his officers to fax copies to all the hotels and *pensions* they had visited to see if anyone, this late, might recognise the two women.

46

THE FIRST CONFIRMATION CAME THROUGH the following morning, from the owners of a *pension* on the Manosque–Forcalquier road, no more than a dozen or so kilometres from the woods where Léo and Marie-Ange had been murdered.

'They stayed two nights,' said Madame Archant when Jacquot called at her house later that morning, at the end of a dusty track on the slopes above Manosque. At some point in its past it had been a small farmhouse, now much extended to provide four guest rooms on the first floor, all en suite Madame Archant was at pains to point out, as though Jacquot were planning to stay or writing a report for a tourist guide. There was a small dining room, with a terrace, across the hallway for guests, but the kitchen, she told him, showing him to a chair beside an empty blackened fireplace, was the family's room. She was a pretty woman in her early forties, Jacquot guessed, with brown hair caught in a bun and a stout little body bound by an apron, her wide hips pressing against the kitchen table as she worked on a parcel of dough, glancing through the window at her husband and son sawing wood over a trestle.

There was something pointed about her show of exertion, Jacquot thought to himself, the way she set into the dough, as though she was angry about something, something to do with the two women who had come here to stay. It was clear she hadn't taken much of a liking to them, but Jacquot decided to approach the subject slowly.

'Last month, you said?'

'That's right. In the old stable. Two bedrooms. Self-contained. Like a *gîte*.' The words came out staccato as she vigorously folded and worked the dough.

'And did they say what they were doing here?'

'Just passing through. Lovely country. A driving holiday, they said.'

'And they paid cash?'

'Had to. No cards here.'

'And how did they spend their days?'

'Out first thing. Back in the evening. Didn't see much of them.'

'They had a car?'

'Black it was. Or maybe dark blue. German, I think. One of those Beetles.' The dough was dealt with, floured in her hands, its top criss-crossed with a kitchen knife and then laid on a tray. The first of a batch. Madame hauled out another fistful from a bowl and slammed it down on the table, sprinkled flour over it and set to work, pushing in the heels of her hands, grinding down with her knuckles.

'Registration?' he asked, hopefully.

'Didn't look. No reason,' she replied.

'Old or new?'

'Not new. Looked like it had done some travelling.'

'Any dents, scratches, stickers?'

Madame Archant shook her head.

'They have much baggage?'

'One case. Between them. There was probably more. In the car,' said Madame, huffing and puffing over her dough.

'What makes you think there was more in the car?'

'I saw it, didn't I? In the back seat. Bags. Like carrier-bags. Stuffed down behind the front seats. Messy, it was. Maps for their driving holiday, food wrappers. Blankets too, and a couple of pillows. Like they might have camped in it.'

Jacquot nodded to himself; camping out certainly seemed an option.

Madame glanced across the table at him.

'So? What have they done? Bank robbers? Murderers? What are you after them for?'

'To help with an investigation,' replied Jacquot.

Madame grunted, laid a second *boule* on the tray, sliced its top and reached for more dough. There was, Jacquot felt, a sense of disappointment in that grunt, either because she wasn't likely to get more information, or because her two lady guests weren't in the kind of trouble she felt they deserved.

'*Dites-moi.* Did you know they were sisters?'

'Sisters?' Madame said the word as though it didn't come anywhere close to describing the two women who'd stayed in her house. 'If you say so, but . . .'

'But?'

'They were so different. The way they looked, the way they behaved . . .'

Jacquot took this in, seemed to consider it. Then, getting up from his chair, he gave a small stretch, as though working his back, and leant against the mantle. 'If you don't mind my saying, Madame Archant, I get the feeling you didn't much care for them, the two ladies.'

Madame let her breath hiss through her teeth, as much from her rolling and pounding as from obvious disapproval. Jacquot was right; he'd touched a nerve. He looked out of the window. Her husband was bent over his trestle, sawing steadily, elbow and shoulder powering up and down. His shirt was off and he was clearly a tough, well built man a little younger than Jacquot. The branch he was sawing was quickly despatched and another reached for. The son, eighteen or nineteen, a good-looking lad with a tanned face, equally strong frame and mop of brown hair, helped him position the new wood on the trestle, then set about stacking what had already been sawed.

Had the husband done something he shouldn't have? wondered Jacquot.

But he was wrong. It wasn't the husband, it was the son.

'She should have known better,' began Madame Archant, stiff with indignation. 'The younger one, that is. It's just not the way to behave. Took advantage, she did. My age, too, or thereabouts. Old enough to be his mother.'

'She was . . . friendly with your son?'

'Friendly! I'll say. Jean caught them at it. In the barn. The second night! They were booked for three nights. But that was it. Gave them notice at breakfast.'

'How did they react?'

'The younger one, she couldn't give a damn. Just gave a simpering little smile.'

'And her sister?'

'Not amused. Face set like stone.'

'And you don't know where they were heading?'

'No idea. And good riddance.'

'Would you mind if I spoke to your son?'

'Not much point,' said Madame, wiping her hands after the last *boule*, picking up the tray and heading for the oven. 'Deaf and dumb, he is. Now you know. Just took advantage, she did.'

Back on the road, heading back to Cavaillon, Jacquot felt a strange elation, and knew that it had not been an entirely wasted trip. He might not have acquired much hard information – really nothing more than confirmation of what they'd already established – but he knew there was more to it than that. The sudden proximity to the killers that Madame Archant had provided him with was cause for excitement. He had met someone who knew them, who had seen them, who had had them staying in their house. And through Madame's unguarded, possibly pointed, comments he had also established a sense of their characters, the kind of women they were. He felt he was beginning to get to know these Manichella sisters – Marita, the elder, and Marina. The way they looked. The way they behaved. So much more than he'd got from the photos. And the differences between them:

The elder – cool, sensible, focused. Probably the one in charge.

And the younger one – flighty, nervy, ruled by her emotions, careless of the impression she made.

They were polar opposites – two competely different characters.

And he was getting closer to them now. He was on their trail. And that pleased him.

But it wasn't over.

When he got back to headquarters, there was Brunet fresh from his cycling holiday in Corsica, tanned and glowing, with a look on his face that Jacquot recognised.

'Another confirmation,' he said, when Jacquot strode into the squad room.

'When? Where?'

'April.'

'And . . . ?'

'Le Mas Bleu.'

47

GUNNAR LARSSON WAS TALKING TO three guests in the hall of Le Mas Bleu when Jacquot and Brunet came up the hotel's front steps and through the front door. When he spotted them, Larsson made his excuses and came over to greet them. He was as tall as Jacquot but half the size – cadaverous was the word that sprang to mind when Jacquot shook his hand. Just the merest flick and he could easily have swung the man over his shoulder, like a bag of brittle kindling. But for all his thinness, his skeletal frame and skull-like features, his voice was a deep unexpected growl that sounded like someone else was speaking.

With the pleasantries over, coffee offered and declined, Larsson showed them through to the *salon*, where Jacquot got down to business.

'My assistant tells me you recognised the photos we sent you. The two women.'

'Of course. From our opening party. The beginning of April. It was Clément who recognised them.'

'They were invited?' For a moment Jacquot imagined their names on a guest list beside a contact number. But he knew that was unlikely. He was right.

'At the time we assumed so. But there were so many people here . . . it was mayhem.'

'So you didn't know them?'

'We sent out three hundred invitations, Chief Inspector. Most of those went to friends, but others were sent to magazines, newspaper editors. So that we could pull in some publicity. You know the sort of thing . . . A number of journalists – whom we didn't necessarily recognise – turned up and introduced themselves. These two women were with them. One had a notebook, the other had a camera. We just assumed . . .'

'So you actually met them? Talked to them?'

Gunnar smiled uncertainly. '*En effet*, I showed them around the hotel. There was a group of them – wanting a quick peek at the rooms. So, of course, I laid on a little tour. We had no guests staying, it was easy.'

'And who did they say they worked for? Did they have a business card?'

Gunnar looked uncomfortable, as though he had somehow contributed to the tragedy through his carelessness.

'I really don't remember. It was just, you know . . . the camera, the notebook; like any other journalists. Maybe they said the name of a magazine or newspaper, but I cannot recall. We were simply being good hosts. In our business, at an opening, you don't want to appear unfriendly, especially to journalists.'

'So how come you remember these two particularly? Was it something they said? Or did?'

Gunnar hesitated, gave a low chuckling little laugh, as though what he was about to say might sound rather silly.

'I remember . . . I remember they had dirty fingernails. It was the first thing Clément said, the following day. "Did you see their fingernails?" And I told him I had. We couldn't believe it. I mean, when you write for *Sud*, or *Boutique*, or *Vogue*, or *Elle* or the other big titles, you don't have dirty fingernails. Not Lifestyle writers. It just doesn't happen. And their hands. Big, strong hands . . . real workers' hands, country hands . . .' Gunnar started to shake his head. 'There was just something about them. Not quite right. But you don't think about it at the time. You have guests, it is a party.

211

And there is also a job to do. Promoting the hotel . . . So many people to talk to, Clément and I. And the staff to keep on their toes . . . the food, the wine.' He sighed.

'On this tour of the hotel, did either of the women ask any questions? Take any notes?'

Gunnar shook his head.

'I'm sorry, Chief Inspector. When we saw the photos last night, we recognised them immediately. And remembered the fingernails. But that is all.'

'Please don't worry, Monsieur. You have been very helpful.' Jacquot got to his feet. 'One last thing. Did the woman with the camera take a lot of pictures?'

Gunnar gave it some thought.

'Yes, she did. Which, come to think of it, is also strange. She was just taking snaps – nothing you could really publish to accompany a magazine or newspaper story. Like the camera was a toy, something to play with. And not what you would call a professional's camera.'

'Did any of the other journalists have cameras?'

'No, they didn't. They're the ones who write the story – a glass in one hand, a note-book or tape recorder in the other. The photographer usually comes later. Or they ask for a press pack which comes with a selection of transparencies.'

'Do you remember if she photographed anything in particular?'

'*Poufff*. Just strange things – doorhandles, windows, the floor. Sometimes it was like she was doing it for fun, to tease or annoy us. Her colleague wasn't pleased either. Gave her a look, if I remember.'

On the way back to the office, Jacquot and Brunet played it between them.

'So they find out where the Gilberts are spending their first night at least a month before the wedding. How do they do that?' asked Brunet.

'If they hung around Madame Tapis' *pharmacie* in Coustellet they'd have found out soon enough,' said Jacquot. 'Local gossip, something overheard in a local bar or café while they're checking Gilbert out – easily done.'

Up ahead the first of the town's traffic lights swung into view across the road. It was red and Brunet started to slow, timing his approach so he wouldn't have to stop.

'So they start the stalk back in Marseilles, looking for options, and follow him up here,' said Brunet. 'Find out about Izzy Blanchard, the wedding, the reception . . .'

'And decide this is as good a place as any. For what they have in mind. Remember, too, there are no parents, no one else close to him. Just Noël.'

The light turned green and Brunet increased his speed.

'And now they're back.'

And now they're back, thought Jacquot.

Somewhere out there, among the shadows, biding their time.

48

DIRTY FINGERNAILS. JACQUOT LOVED THAT. In most investigations it would be a scar or a squint, a gold tooth perhaps, or a tattoo. But dirty fingernails was a first. And women with dirty fingernails. He could imagine a man with dirty fingernails. But somehow not a woman.

And how fitting that Clément Valbois and his lover Gunnar Larsson should notice such a thing.

He was thinking this, on his way back home that evening, when something in his wing-mirror caught his eye. What looked like a car, a dark rounded hump, a few hundred metres back, occasionally sliding into the mirror's line of sight but otherwise all but hidden, backlit by the fiery furnace of a setting sun that had cloaked the countryside in a thick cover of reds and golds. He glanced in his rear-view mirror, but there was even less definition there – the Renault's back windscreen covered in a fine dust that seemed to absorb the setting sun and colour out anything behind it. But his curiosity was aroused, his eyes now flicking from the road ahead to his left-hand wing-mirror, keeping track of the vehicle behind him.

Slowly, without drawing attention to the move, Jacquot steered away from the centre of the road and drew closer to the verge. Checking his wing-mirror again, he could now clearly see that the car was keeping pace with him, in no hurry to overtake. On a road such as this, between Cavaillon and Apt, at this time in the evening when people were eager for their homes, it was rare not to have a car race past a dawdler. But his new position, closer now to the edge of the road, with a wider view in his wing-mirror, brought him little satisfaction. The other vehicle was still too far back for him to make out model or colour or who was driving.

Again without making it too obvious, Jacquot let his speed drop by a few kilometres an hour. But still the car behind him did not appear to draw any closer, as though matching his gradual decrease in speed.

By now his curiosity and attention were firmly fixed on the car behind him, and he wondered for how long it had been trailing him, if indeed that was what it was doing. As the road slipped by he thought back over his route from police headquarters – just the usual flow of traffic for a Thursday evening, nothing remarkable, thinning as town gave way to country, pavements to dry, dusty verges – but he couldn't recall noticing it, coming up behind him, following the same route. Already there were a number of turn-ings the driver could have taken but had not, the car still holding its course and speed and distance behind him. For a moment Jacquot regretted he was driving his own car. If he'd been in a squad car, he'd simply have switched on the lights and waved the driver down.

By now he was approaching the left-hand turn for the mill-house. But rather than indicate and slow for the turning he kept up his speed and carried on, towards Apt and Céreste. He knew what he was going to do. On the next section of straight road, he was going to pull over and switch on his emergency lights. The driver behind would either carry on past him in a swirl of golden dust, or pull up ahead to see if help was needed. If the car just drove past, he would start off again and follow it, find out where it was going, and maybe who was driving. The prospect of a dark-coloured VW and two women in the front seats was almost too much to wish for.

But the driver behind did neither. As Jacquot pulled in and

switched on his emergency lights, the car behind swung suddenly to the right and disappeared down a narrow track. Jacquot swore softly and, checking the road both ways for oncoming traffic, pulled out in a squealing U-turn that set him on the lane back to town.

Up ahead, on the left now, he could see a plume of dust between the vines that braided the hillsides hereabouts, and as he passed the turning he caught a flash of brakelights in the swirling golden cloud. Jacquot knew that lane. It was unsurfaced, a farmer's track used to access the fields, but it came out at St-Beyelle and joined the old country route between Cavaillon and Brieuc. Keeping his speed low, he headed on for the next turning – another, better route, narrow but surfaced, that also led to St-Beyelle. If he managed his speed, he was almost certain he would meet up with the car at the Brieuc–Cavaillon crossroads. And if the car *was* a Volkswagen, or was driven by two women, he would stop them or give chase, get a registration number if nothing else.

What he didn't want to do, however, was draw too much attention to himself, to alert them – if they really were the Manichella sisters – and then lose them. Once again he regretted being in his old Renault, with no radio to call for assistance. Out here he was on his own, with just his wits and his service Beretta in the glove compartment for company.

Keeping an eye on the other car, still concealed behind the vines but betrayed by its pluming trail of golden dust, Jacquot indicated left and took the turning, just a couple of kilometres now before his road intersected with the track and the old Brieuc road, and the two cars came together.

But when he reached the crossroads, his view only fleetingly interrupted on the way there by the odd farmhouse and villa and rise of land, there was no sign of any traffic coming through St-Beyelle – no lights, no dust. And no sound of a car either. Coming to a stop in front of St-Beyelle's small stone chapel he switched off the ignition and wound down the window. Not a sound. Just the warm tick of his engine, the springs in his seat and a soft evening pulse of cicadas.

He sat there for a couple of minutes, waiting. But no car appeared. Since there were no turnings off the track that he could remember, save gateways into fields of maize and vine and melon, and since there was no way the other driver could have crossed ahead of him, it was clear the car must have pulled in somewhere the other side of the village while Jacquot's view had been obstructed.

Because the driver had finally arrived home after a hard day at the office?

Or because the driver was looking for somewhere to hide?

Jacquot decided to find out.

Letting off the hand brake, he let the Renault roll forward and turned into the single street that led through St-Beyelle. It was cobbled and the tyres bubbled over the stones, the car picking up a little speed as the slope steepened, fast enough for Jacquot to touch the footbrake as he coasted through the tiny settlement, eyes flicking to left and right, looking for a car, for figures.

But there was nothing.

The village, apart from a few lights and the smell of burning charcoal – a back-garden barbecue – seemed deserted.

A minute later he was out of St-Beyelle, could feel a roughening in the road surface and up ahead could see where the village's cobbles ran out and farm track took over. Before he reached it, he pulled in to a gateway where the road surface was not too bad and opened the glove compartment to retrieve his gun. Sliding it into his pocket, he got out of the car, leaving the driver's door open.

It was a gorgeous evening now, warm and soft, the sun lost behind the slopes of the Vaucluse hills, a deep blue sky banded with tapered layers of low cloud, their bellies stained a dusky pink that somehow made the blue backdrop a deeper, darker shade. Now some distance from the village, the sharp if beckoning smell of burning charcoal had been replaced by an altogether more natural scent – of rich red earth dampened by evening sprinklers, wet lush greenery, and fresh-cut grass. He could smell the dry stones in the low wall along one side of the track, the recent passage of goats, and a hot pulse of heat from the fields either side – vine and melon and maize, a browning stand of it shifting and shuffling with a breeze he couldn't feel. Somewhere to the right a dog barked, and Jacquot tensed. But it was a distant and solitary call, one of those country mutts chained to a post or a tree, left out in the yard, its long lonesome bark one of boredom not warning. Nothing better to do.

With the comforting weight of the Beretta in his jacket pocket, bumping against his hip with every step, Jacquot walked on – alert to each sound, each movement around him. He was about a hundred metres from the Renault, now out of sight behind him, and about fifty metres from a stand of broken down old barns and drying sheds when suddenly the chirrupping sounds of insects and the soft *whoosh* of a passing bat were drowned out by the grinding start of an engine, a clash of gears and the spitting angry rasp of tyres on dusty grit as a car swung out from the barnyard and set off down the lane, heading away from him in a lurching, jouncing race, back the way it had come.

It was impossible to get a registration number thanks to the fading light, the swirling dust, and the jolting speed of the car, and no way could he catch up with it. But there was now no doubt in his mind – given this evasionary tactic – that this was the same car that had been following him, its wheezing, asthmatic whine as it careered away along the track bearing the umistakable signature of an old VW Beetle.

In less than twenty seconds the car was well ahead of Jacquot who had started into a jog, holding his gun now rather than let it bang against his hip. A few seconds more and it was lost round a bend and powering back down towards the main road. For a second or two longer Jacquot wondered whether to keep after them or go back to his car and try for a chase. But it didn't take him long to realise that neither was a practical option. They were too far ahead of him now, they had got the better of him, and as he came to a halt in the lane he saw brakelights flash once, way down the slope, and a set of headlights swing onto the main road, turning towards Apt.

They'd known he'd spotted them, known he'd be waiting for them at St-Beyelle – if they'd scouted out for the Gilbert murder they'd be familiar with this terrain – and had done the only thing they could do. And it had worked for them.

It was the killers – the sisters – in an old VW.

He was certain of it.

49

THERE HAD BEEN A HEART-HAMMERING moment of panic as the two sisters swung out of the barnyard, followed by a rush of elation as they hit the main road and accelerated away in the direction of Apt. Behind them, Chief Inspector Daniel Jacquot had been left standing in the middle of a country lane, too far from his own car – which they had seen him park – and too far from theirs to do anything other than watch them drive away.

But it had been close.

If the engine hadn't caught first time . . .

If they'd flooded it . . .

Of course, they should never have switched off the ignition. That's what younger sister had done before elder sister had time to suggest they keep the engine ticking over.

The two sisters had been watching Jacquot for a little over two weeks now, sometimes staying in the area, camped out in the VW, or returning to the house near Pélissanne, twenty minutes south on the autoroute.

Like their other targets, photos of Jacquot had been supplied and rough personal details provided, and the two women had taken it in turns to keep a watch on police headquarters in Cavaillon until they made contact and found their mark. Marina had been the first to spot him, walking across the car park at police headquarters and out on to the street. She'd been sitting on a bench in the garden of Église St-Jean just across the road from the building and he'd passed close enough for her to make the match, noting the jeans and slip-on loafers, the linen jacket catching in the breeze, and the brilliant white T-shirt. As in the photos, there was that strong, well-shaped face and those broad shoulders, but the once close-cropped hair had grown out and he was taller than she'd expected.

But the photos, Marina decided, did not do the man justice, did not adequately convey the real sense of him. Crossing the road, he had come straight towards her, as though he intended having a word, only to pass on his way – had he actually smiled a greeting at her? – close enough for her to see the dark shading of stubble on his jaw, the green of his eyes, a wave of dark hair curling over his collar, and the bare feet slipped into loafers. Close enough even to catch the scent of him: soap, tobacco, leather. It was tobacco he was after; twenty metres past the church he went into a *tabac* and a few minutes later came out unwrapping a pack of cigarettes.

This time he crossed the road before reaching the church and from a distance Marina had watched the man's long, easy stride as he made his way back to headquarters. In the next two hours she'd established which floor his office was on, which window was his, and what car he drove: a battered old Renault with dusty windows and two hub caps missing. He liked his music, too. One afternoon, as the car swung out of the car park, he had his window down, elbow out, with Eric Clapton's *461 Ocean Boulevard* playing loud enough for her to catch and recognise the tune. Her brother used to listen to it all the time.

That first evening, after making him, as she drove back to Pélissanne, Marina had found herself thinking of Chief Inspector Daniel Jacquot in a less than professional manner. It was the bare feet that had done it, something oddly and uncomfortably arousing about that glimpse of skin around his ankles, the intimacy of the observation, its easy physicality, and for the last ten kilometres of the drive home she'd stayed in the slow lane on the autoroute, with only one hand on the wheel.

With their target confirmed, it hadn't taken the sisters long to establish the pattern in the man's day. How he lived. Where he lived. And who he lived with. But if police headquarters had been easy to watch – and Jacquot's movements around Cavaillon and the surrounding countryside tracked easily enough without the two women being noticed – the millhouse was an altogether different proposition. After seeing Jacquot turn left those first few evenings, driving up a marked *impasse* towards a distant flickering of lights through the trees, they might have found out where he lived, but it was another matter seeing what went on there.

As far as they had been able to establish, there was only that single access road to the millhouse, a long sloping lane that ended just a few hundred metres past the property, petering out into lightly wooded hillsides and open pasture higher up. They did this by locating a vantage point across the narrow guttering of the Colavon valley on the slope of the Grand Luberon and finding an isolated spot from which to spy on the property through binoculars. From here, shifting their vantage point around the slope, they had familiarised themselves with the size and shape and lay-out of the house, counting two cars and three people: Jacquot and two women. One of them was the woman he lived with – the target they'd selected – but the other had remained unknown until one afternoon in Déscharme's art supplies shop on place Lombard when elder sister, browsing along the shelves, had heard Claudine introduce her daughter to a friend she'd bumped into.

At first the daughter's presence had seemed a complication they could have done without. Mother and daughter never seemed to stray far from the house, or each other, but gradually the idea had lodged in their minds that targeting both women – getting rid of the daughter too – was easily manageable and would greatly increase their final victim's sense of loss and grief. And, as elder sister said, a satisfactory way to combine the last two injuries for their final victim – a suitable double climax. But for the purposes of their research, to do their job properly, they needed a closer, more detailed sense of the property.

Since they couldn't easily drive past it as they had done with their other targets they decided to walk past the house. Kitting themselves out in boots and rucksacks from a camping store in Salon they'd hiked up the *impasse* as though on a cross-country route to St Pantagruel, and passed close enough to hear the sound of music, a phone ringing and a woman's voice call out. Once past the millhouse they had carried on up to the first ridge and then doubled back down through the pine and holm oak, taking up position some twenty metres beyond the old millrace, at the back of the house, with a view of the courtyard, terrace, kitchen and studio. Pulling binoculars from their rucksacks the sisters had settled down to wait and watch.

In the days that followed, they'd stayed in close contact with Claudine and her daughter, and it didn't take long for the sisters to see what a handsome woman the mother was. There was something about the way she strolled down the aisles in the town's *super-marché*, tall, slender and somehow effortlessly elegant in her short denim skirt, T-shirt and espadrilles, leaning forward over the delicatessen counter to examine more closely a fish or a cut of meat, the way she touched a finger to her lips, the way she slid the notes from her wallet at the check-out. And nice too, *très agréable*, *très sympa*, greeting the check-out girl with a smile and a few words as she might an old friend – *bonjour*, *ça va*, and then *merci bien*, *à bientôt* – her voice husky and honeyed, her laugh, when her daughter said something funny, clear as crystal ringing across the car park as she pushed their trolley to the car.

But while Marita had remarked on this, Marina had stayed quiet, eyeing Claudine with a stern and savage jealousy. The looks, the easy style, everything about the woman set her teeth on edge, made her want to smash her down, get rid of her. Here was the woman who held that man in her arms, the woman who lived with him, cooked for him, cleaned for him – and loved him. And was loved back. And younger sister thought, too, of the life this woman lived, as well as the man she lived with, and she knew she'd been short-changed. This was how you should live your life, with a good-looking guy in a beautiful house, not in a shared family farmhouse on some bleak Corsican hillside where the only men you met had hands like sandpaper and hot breath that stank of bad teeth, stale beer and garlic. If you were lucky, they chewed parsley before they plunged their tongues into your mouth. The kind of man her elder sister had ended up with, and look what had happened to her.

As usual, Marina had been busy daydreaming as they followed Jacquot's car out of town – imagining his grief at the loss of Claudine, and how she would effect a meeting, how she would soothe him, make him well again, without his ever realising it was she who had killed Claudine – when her sister had tapped her leg and nodded ahead. He was slowing down, pulling in to the kerb and the emergency lights were blinking on.

Marina had only seconds to react: either carry on past him and risk being followed if he had made them, or get off the road.

'Take a right,' Marita had said, pointing to a narrow opening no more than twenty metres ahead. And with a stamp on the brakes, she'd made the turn and powered away down the lane.

Beside her, Marita looked back towards the road.

'He's turning round,' she said. 'He's coming back. He's spotted us.' She glanced at the track ahead. 'See that barnyard up ahead? We'll pull in there and wait.'

And that's what they'd done, under cover of the dust cloud they'd stirred up, watching him pass the entrance to their track but take the Brieuc turn, for all the world as though he'd missed it in the first place and was just doubling back. But Marita knew that wasn't the case. Somewhere along the line, this Jacquot had found a link, connected the killings – she was sure of it now. And he'd been on the look-out.

But was he looking for a black VW Beetle? And two women?

Certainly she and Marina had been in the frame – it was only to be expected. The last time they'd called home one of the cousins had told them that a detective from Ajaccio had paid a call at the gendarmerie in Scarpetta and had the local man come out with him to Tassafaduca, knocking on the farm door, asking to see them.

The deception had gone well enough and the *flic* from Ajaccio had left Tassafaduca none the wiser.

But now . . . ?

'He knows,' said Marina, settling herself behind the wheel on the road to Apt, foot hard down on the pedal and feeling a thumping in her chest.

'I think he has known for a long time,' replied Marita.

'Do you think we should let it rest for a while?'

'I don't think it makes any difference. Whether he knows or not. There's nothing he can do now.'

They drove on for a while in silence, towards a darkening sky, Marina thinking about Jacquot, Marita going through their plans for the days to come. So much to do, so much to arrange. And so little time. At Apt they turned off the main road, switched on their headlights and headed south over the Luberon heights to Lourmarin and then Cadenet, weaving their way back to Pélissanne.

Outside Lambesc, Marita turned to her sister.

'Did you get the scissors? The dye?'

'Yes,' replied Marina.

'And the kit?'

'It's on the way.'

Marita nodded.

Beside her, Marina licked two fingertips, pulled a pellet of gum from her mouth and tossed it out of the window.

'I could eat a horse,' she said.

'A pizza will have to do,' replied Marita.

50

THE SUN MIGHT HAVE GONE, a few brave stars starting to glitter in a darkening sky, but it was still warm when Jacquot arrived at the millhouse, wondering if the Manichella sisters had already discovered where he lived, and deciding they probably had. There were no lights on inside, but a glow came from the rear terrace. Crunching over the gravel of the driveway, turning down the side of the house, he found Midou swinging lazily in a hammock, a tangle of logs crackling in the fire pit, and a bottle of white wine open on the table. There was also the unmistakable scent of marijuana hanging in the still air.

'*Maman*'s having a rest. She's pooped.'

'She okay? I'll go up . . .'

'No, no, she's fine, just a little peaky . . . out of sorts,' said Midou, swinging her legs out of the hammock and sitting astride it. 'And you'll wake her. Best leave her.'

'How long has she been sleeping?'

'A couple of hours,' said the girl, glancing at her watch. 'After she finished work in the studio. Said she was going to lie down for a bit.'

Jacquot felt a flutter of unease.

'Maybe I'd better go and check . . .'

'You sit there, I'll go and check,' said Midou, unsaddling herself from the hammock. 'I know you. You'll just go and wake her, to make sure she's still breathing.'

Five minutes later Midou was back.

'Out like a light,' she said, refilling her glass. 'But it'll do her good. She's been looking a little tired.' It was said with no intent to criticise, but Jacquot found himself on the defensive.

'It's the exhibition,' he said, maybe too quickly. 'Always the same. A month before the opening she gets the jitters, thinks she can't paint, and tries to do too much.'

'You think it's just that?' asked Midou. 'Or this Blanchard thing?'

'Well, that certainly doesn't help, but I don't think we're seriously at risk.'

After his close encounter an hour earlier, Jacquot knew he wasn't being entirely honest with Claudine's daughter, but he judged it better to downplay the threat rather than amplify it.

That evening Claudine did not make an appearance. After a pleasant evening together during which he and Midou had grilled some steaks on the fire-pit, tossed up a salad, and finished a further bottle of wine, she took her leave, leaning down to kiss his cheek.

'Don't worry,' she said, patting his shoulder. 'It'll be fine. And so will *Maman*.'

Half an hour later, finishing off the last of Midou's spliff, Jacquot took a torch from the kitchen and wandered around the house, out to the driveway and back to the terrace, flashing the beam between the trees, pausing to listen out for any suspicious sounds above the gentle trickling of the mill stream and the low static beat of insects.

But there was nothing. Just a deepening darkness sliding like oil through the trees, a pleasing, comforting sprinkle of stars through the branches, and a gentle, swaying contentment in his head.

Too much wine, he thought, too much grass. But still . . .

Back in the house, he locked and bolted all the doors, made sure the windows were secured and, leaving the hall light on, climbed the stairs to bed.

Part Three

51

ON THE LAST FRIDAY OF the month, a little before lunchtime, a convoy of lorries came off the A7 autoroute, pounded across the Durance bridge and pulled up one behind the other, hydraulic brakes wheezing, on the corner of Cours Bournissac and rue Dumas. All four were painted in black livery, the carrier's name – France Auto Logistiques – printed in shadowed silver across the lorries' sides. A few moments later the police tape that had been put up the night before to seal off place du Tourel from all approach roads was lowered and the lorries moved forward and parked. Within thirty minutes their crews were hard at work – all dressed in black T-shirts, hard hats, big-soled climbing boots and gunslinger tool belts – hauling out scaffolding from the back of the lorries to start rigging the stage for the appearance of Monsieur George Benson the following evening. A holiday feeling gripped the residents of Cavaillon and it wasn't long before word spread through the bars on Cours Bournissac and along the pastry counter at Auzet's that there was almost certainly going to be a surprise guest appearance from George Benson's sometime playing partner, Monsieur Al Jarreau.

Jacquot watched these preparations from his table outside Fin de Siècle. It was late afternoon and the construction crews had pretty much completed the public seating areas and were now working on the stage scaffolding around the town's Roman arches. It was through these that Monsieur George Benson would make his entrance, playing on two fronts – to the street crowds milling along Bournissac and to the paying audience in seats and side bleachers in place du Tourel.

'You going to be there?' asked Guy Fourcade, tipping more pastis into his glass and shovelling around in the bucket for fresh ice.

'Wouldn't miss it.'

'Professional or social?' asked the town's examining magistrate, dropping ice into his glass.

'Both I should think. On hand, of course, but sitting with Claudine and Midou and praying no one needs me. What about you?'

'Row four, behind the Mayor. You?'

'Bleachers, in front of the tourist office.'

'You hear the rumour about Jarreau?'

Jacquot nodded, smiled.

'Who told you?'

'Patric at Le Tilleul. He had some press boys up from Nice, and they said it was as pretty damn near certain as it got.'

'It would be a treat. Let's hope.'

The two men fell silent, and watched the first spotlights being swung into place on scaffolding gantries set behind the back row of bleachers. All around was the ring and clang of scaffolding, and the tap-tapping of hammers.

'I was talking to Rochet the other day,' Fourcade continued. 'He said there might be leads on the Blanchard case. That it's part of a bigger operation, like you said.'

Jacquot had been waiting for this ever since Fourcade had strolled past the bar, seen him and joined him for a drink. It might have seemed like an accidental meeting, but Jacquot knew better. Even so, Fourcade had finished his first pastis before he started in.

'Six murders so far, in a little under five months. Different jurisdictions so they won't have been flagged. Three in Marseilles, and two outside Forcalquier since the Blanchard killing.'

Fourcade nodded, took it in. Gave it a minute or so's careful consideration.

'Suspects? Leads?' he asked.

'Two sisters. Corsican. Marita Albertacce and Marina Manichella. We're keeping a low profile on the investigation so we don't spook them. Right now we need to draw them out.'

'They're here? Around Cavaillon?'

'That's a distinct possibility,' said Jacquot, recalling the close encounter in St-Beyelle the previous evening.

'You're laying bait?'

Jacquot finished his Calva.

'You could say.'

'What? Who?'

'Claudine and Midou.'

Fourcade gave a start.

'Claudine? You're not serious?'

'I wish I wasn't. But that's where the action seems to be pointing. Two sisters getting even for the deaths of their brothers. Targeting anyone who was involved, but taking it out on their families, lovers . . .'

'Is there anything you need? Any help?'

Jacquot was surprised to hear what sounded like genuine concern from the town's prosecutor.

'Just keep an eye out for a dark-coloured VW and two women, one tall, one short. If you spot them call me.'

Over on place du Tourel a bank of lights blinked on, bathing the stage in a bright glare that seemed to make the dusk grow darker. In seconds, it seemed, a host of moths and other insects swarmed in the beams of light.

'If I were looking to get even, it seems to me tomorrow evening would be a good time to do it,' said Fourcade.

'Exactly what I was thinking,' replied Jacquot.

52

'A FIFTY SAY YOU'LL NEVER guess who just flew into Le Mas Bleu.' Jean Brunet looked particularly pleased with himself.

It was Saturday morning and Jacquot had come to the office early to catch up on some paperwork. He had left Claudine and Midou, still asleep, at the millhouse, and locked the front door behind him.

'Put me out of my misery.'

'Well, I'll give you a clue,' Brunet began.

'And I'll give your bony, biking arse a kicking if you don't tell me *de suite*,' replied Jacquot with a dangerous smile.

Even under the threat of assault, Brunet managed to stretch it out a few more moments.

'Mademoiselle . . . Virginie Cabrille.'

Jacquot, with his feet up on his desk and his ankles crossed, sat up at that.

'You are joking?'

'She's booked the whole place. *Le tout*. A private party for the George Benson concert.'

'And how . . . ?'

'I bumped into Gunnar Larsson, Valbois' boyfriend, remember? He was picking up supplies at Artagnan's – the most beautiful melons. Their chef is thinking of . . .'

'Cabrille. Cabrille,' Jacquot interrupted. 'I want to hear about Mademoiselle Virgine Cabrille, not Larsson's blessed chef.'

'Ah, the Mademoiselle, *mais bien sûr*. She came in last night, by helicopter, with a couple of friends. And apparently there are more joining her today.'

'How long are they staying?'

'Just a couple of nights. Larsson told me the place had been booked solid, but Mademoiselle made it worth their while to cancel all reservations. They made up a story about a fire in the kitchen. So sorry. Hotel closed. With – get this – Mademoiselle offering to cover the cost of complimentary accommodation at some future date for all those guests whose rooms she'd taken.'

Jacquot got to his feet and reached for his jacket.

'I think we should pay her a call, don't you?'

'She sounds like the kind of woman I'd like to meet.'

Half-an-hour later, Jacquot and Brunet turned down the drive of Le Mas Bleu, passed between the second set of pillars and parked in its gravelled forecourt. They were hardly out of their seats before Valbois came down the steps to greet them.

'She is playing tennis, Chief Inspector,' he told them, when Jacquot asked where he could find Mademoiselle Cabrille. At the mention of her name, a stricken expression had settled on Valbois' face, as though Jacquot's presence there could only mean that something was about to go horribly wrong, and that the lucrative deal he and Gunnar had negotiated might somehow be at risk. Jacquot reassured him that it was just a personal call and that there was nothing to be alarmed about, taking the path to the tennis courts that Valbois had pointed out.

The sound of play soon reached them – the pock-pock-pock of a rally, followed by a shout of glee and howl of protest.

'It was out! Over the line.'

'You need glasses, *chérie* . . .'

Coming through an arch of drooping scarlet bougainvillaea Jacquot and Brunet stepped out onto a decked terrace beside the court. There was a small wood-built changing room, a bamboo-fronted bar beneath a split cane canopy and a number of tables, chairs and benches set out in its shade. Jacquot and Brunet ordered coffees and took a table.

On court two women were about to play a point. One was blonde, with a ponytail sprouting through the back of her baseball cap, bending forward, racket in hand, waiting for the delivery. Across the net, unmistakable with her slicked back black hair, was Virginie Cabrille, arms and legs tanned a warm caramel, their toned length emphasised by a tight, short-sleeved tennis shirt and pleated skirt. She wore a white sun visor, long white socks and trainers, and had a sweatband round each wrist.

'It's Cabrille serving, right?' asked Brunet, as the lady in question tossed the ball in the air, rose on her toes, and smashed it hard and square across the net. It sliced past her opponent before the other woman had a chance to move.

'And what makes you think that?' asked Jacquot, clapping lightly at the ace. Down on the court, farthest away from the terrace, Virginie Cabrille glanced up at them before pulling a ball from the band of her under-shorts and setting up another serve. If she recognised Jacquot she gave no sign of it, bouncing the ball before tossing it high.

'Because she's a hard one,' said Brunet, as racket connected with ball. 'No way blondie's going to win. It's black-top in charge.'

Another ace whipped down the court and Brunet nodded.

'See what I mean?'

The two women played on for another ten minutes with Virginie Cabrille finally taking both game and set. Picking up towels and wiping themselves down, they opened the wire door, closed it behind them and came over to the terrace. As they approached, Jacquot got to his feet and gave Mademoiselle Cabrille a smile and nod of greeting.

It was not returned. Although she had met him on two separate occasions, the last time only two months earlier, Virginie Cabrille conjured up an expert look of confusion, of possible embarrassment, a lost, do-I-know-you sort of expression.

'Daniel Jacquot, Mademoiselle. We met a couple of months ago at your house in Roucas Blanc.'

She gave him another closer look, as though maybe, vaguely, she remembered.

'I was with Chief Inspector Muzon, from police headquarters on rue de l'Evêché.'

'*Mais bien sûr*. I remember now.' And she stepped towards him – just one step – and held out her hand. So that he had to reach forward. She gave a sharp little smile. 'Yes, of course. That's right. Your wife is an artist. And don't you live around here somewhere?' She turned to her friend, held up a finger. 'Why don't you go ahead? I'll come up to your room in a minute.'

'That's right,' said Jacquot, gesturing to their table, that she should join them there. 'Can I offer you a drink, Mademoiselle? Some water? Coffee?'

She shook her head. 'That's very kind, Chief Inspector, but I really must be getting on. It was good to . . .'

'Tell me,' he continued, not giving her time to cut the conversation short, 'did you know that a murder was committed here, at Le Mas Bleu, just a few months ago?'

Virginie Cabrille frowned.

'A murder? Really? No. How could I know such a thing?'

'A young woman,' said Jacquot. 'A bride, on her wedding night. She'd married one of the policemen at the shoot-out in your house in Roucas Blanc. I told you about it when we met there. With Chief Inspector Muzon?'

She shook her head.

'I'm afraid I don't recall . . . And I certainly didn't know that there'd been a murder committed here. Now, if you'll please excuse me, I really . . .'

'You are here for the concert? For Monsieur Benson?'

'That's right, yes. A small party of friends.' She gave another short, brisk smile, as if to enquire whether it was any business of his.

'They say Monsieur Al Jarreau might be making a guest appearance.' Jacquot turned to Brunet, who nodded in agreement.

237

'Well, that would be nice,' she said. 'Will you be going?'

'I wouldn't miss it,' said Jacquot, smiling broadly. 'Maybe I'll see you there?'

She gave another short little smile, a maybe smile, as though it was no great matter to her whether he did or did not, then nodded to Brunet, turned on her toes and went after her friend.

Both men watched her go, racket and hips swinging, skirt swirling.

Brunet gave a soft approving whistle.

'Like I said, a hard one.'

Jacquot nodded.

'Did you see her eyes?' his assistant continued. 'Colder than a crocodile's. I don't think she blinked, just set them on you and looked. A kind of lazy, hungry look, if you know what I mean. Like she was sizing you up for a bite. And not a friendly bite . . .'

53

THERE WAS NO DOUBT IN Jacquot's mind that Virginie Cabrille had recognised him the moment he'd stepped through the arch of bougainvillaea, found a table and ordered coffee. Maybe she even knew their paths would cross on this trip to Cavaillon, had planned it deliberately. The way she glanced over at him, then turned her attention back to the game, pulled the ball from her shorts and served her ace . . . as if he didn't exist. Or, if he did, that he was of absolutely no interest to her. And she had behaved in exactly the same manner off-court, with a remarkably assured performance of failing to recognise him until prompted, when all the time she knew very well who he was, and why he was there.

Brunet was right. A hard one, through and through. What Jacquot couldn't work out was why she should bother with the subterfuge, pretending not to know him.

Of course she knew him.

And he knew her.

It was a ridiculous game to play.

But she had played it very well indeed, immediately distancing herself from him, in front of Brunet and her friend, and distancing herself, too, from anything the Manichella sisters might have planned. As Brunet drove them back to Cavaillon, Jacquot wondered why she should choose to be so closely involved. The two brothers – Taddeus and Tomas Manichella – were hardly family, and in personal terms all she had lost was a few days' freedom while her smart Paris lawyer found whatever loopholes he could to effect her release, with all charges dropped. Hardly enough to warrant involvement in a killing spree, carried out by two sisters whose thirst for revenge – an old and well-established Corsican tradition – was driving the action. That she was funding the two sisters, supporting them, he was in no doubt, but whether for kicks, for a laugh, or for some deeper, more complex reason, Jacquot was still unable to say.

He was equally in no doubt that her presence, that particular weekend, at Le Mas Bleu, was no coincidence, and as he and Brunet arrived back at headquarters in Cavaillon, Jacquot had a sudden and discomforting thought, which he couldn't shift, that while he and Virginie Cabrille played their game of cat and mouse, something had happened at the millhouse. Back in his office, he called Claudine. The phone rang six times, Jacquot holding his breath, his heart rate beginning to pick up. When the ansaphone connected, he jammed down the receiver and hurried from his office.

With the concert preparations closing so many of the access streets in Cavaillon, it was an agonisingly slow journey out of town. Once again he wished he'd taken a squad car, or had the emergency blue light he could fix to his roof, to get everyone out of his way. But he wasn't driving a squad car, and he didn't have his emergency light, and every snail's pace metre, every hold-up and red light was a torture, stop-starting all the way along a crowded Cours Leon Gambetta, the midday sun scorching down, pulsing off the road and beating against the Renault's dusty bodywork.

And then a 'beep-beep' and a flash of lights from a car coming towards him. A very familiar car. With two very welcome, familiar faces visible behind the windscreen.

'We were just going to call by your office,' Claudine called out as their progress was halted almost parallel to Jacquot's car. Midou leant across her mother and blew him a kiss. 'There's some shopping we need to do. We thought we'd take you to lunch first. Maybe Gaillard's?'

'We'll take you, but you're paying,' shouted Midou.

Jacquot took a deep breath, heart somersaulting with relief, almost angry with them for causing him such concern. But he held it in, drowned it with relief.

'Good idea. Just what I was thinking. Park at headquarters. I'll meet you there.'

There was a beep from the car behind and Jacquot drove on, down under the railway bridge, around the roundabout and back into town, seeking out Claudine's Renault just a few hundred metres ahead in the slow-moving line of traffic.

From now on, he determined, he wasn't going to let them out of his sight. Even if it meant an afternoon trailing round the shops.

54

BY THE TIME THEY ARRIVED back at the millhouse, with Jacquot never more than two cars behind them, Claudine pleaded fatigue and said she was going upstairs to rest. She was tired, she explained, after the wine at lunch and from their shopping, and she wanted to get a couple of hours' sleep before the concert. It was going to be a long evening. The information, given to him by the stairs, was accompanied by the merest peck of a kiss and a wagging of the finger whose meaning Jacquot recognised. She was not to be disturbed. An hour later, closing her books at the kitchen table, Midou too said she was going for a rest.

'Got to be fighting fit for George,' she told Jacquot, also pecking his cheek before disappearing upstairs. Standing in the kitchen, warm sunshine slanting through the blinds, Jacquot heard her bedroom door close, and the house, as he finished his coffee, settled into a peaceful, slumbering silence, broken only by the low *chirk-chirk, chirk-chirk* of insects from the garden.

Jacquot washed up his cup and laid it on the draining-board. Then he leant against the sink and looked around the empty kitchen. It was the heart of the house, where everything happened, and now it was quiet, empty. He looked at the beams in the ceiling, through the half-open door leading to Claudine's studio. Three years ago he'd come here for the first time, staying overnight, followed by

242

a weekend here and there when work allowed, when he'd cut her some wood or fix some faulty window latch; when she'd watch him, take the measure of him. But most of the time – because it was short, stolen time – they spent in her bedroom, warm and soft and prettily scented, muslin drapes shifting in the breeze, a bee buzzing in their folds; brief, afternoon encounters (when she called him or he just dropped by), encounters that ended with a coffee here in the kitchen, or a glass of wine out there on the terrace, or Claudine still asleep in her bed as he stole from the house. Until, finally, she'd slipped him a key and then helped him move his stuff from the loft apartment on Cours Bournissac.

And now someone was putting all that at risk, someone intent on bringing their happiness and love and comfort to an end. Striking at him, through Claudine. Or Midou. Or both of them.

Now, in this still afternoon heat, after losing the sisters in their car just a couple of evenings back and meeting up with Virginie Cabrille that morning at Le Mas Bleu, Jacquot wondered how he could have been quite so sanguine when he spoke with Georges Rochet and Solange Bonnefoy and Guy Fourcade about using Claudine and Midou for bait. He'd felt such confidence about it initially: that they'd find the sisters, that something would happen, that the threat would be removed. A hotel or *chambre d'hôte* would call in to say that two women matching the photos they'd all been given, had just checked in, and by the way they were driving a VW. And then it would all be over, the threat gone, the two sisters somehow apprehended before any attempt could be made on one or both of those women asleep in the rooms above.

Jacquot thought of the sense of loss and sorrow he'd felt when he'd heard of Marie-Ange's murder – a woman he'd hardly known, but one who had . . . occupied his thoughts in a way he might not have anticipated – and he suddenly understood just how much worse it would be to lose Claudine. Or Midou. The thought of it – just the merest possibility of it . . .

Gritting his teeth, stunned now by his own over-confidence and underestimation of the opposition – the true threat the sisters posed

– Jacquot opened the fridge, found the Beretta in the salad drawer and slipped it into the back of his jeans. Pushing open the back door he went down the steps to the yard and, standing on the stone slabs and old grinding wheels that made up this tree-shaded terrace, he looked around, from the back corner of the house where the old mill-wheel had once stood, and up the slope of lawn to where the millrace came out of the trees. On one side of this stone channel the trees began almost immediately, in a border extending up the slope, but directly in front of him and to his right, past Claudine's studio, the terrace gave way to an expanse of lawn, a small swimming pool and the kitchen garden where Claudine grew all her own produce – and often sat at her easel to paint. Even in the heat of summer this garden flourished, some hidden, underground spring keeping the vegetables and herbs and flowers in a rich profusion; and the grass he walked over, soft and springy underfoot, was always green, never needed watering.

Without thinking, Jacquot set off up the slope, feeling the sun beat down as he stepped out into the open, the barrel of his Beretta pressing against the small of his back as he strolled up to the line of trees: a cluster of olive, some holm oak and further up a spread of thin pine. The closer he got to the trees, the noisier the electric *tzzzz-tzzzz-tzzzz* of insects became, his eye caught by the flick of a lizard's tail and the rustle of leaves as it scampered away. At the edge of the lawn the ground became rougher, and as he pushed aside an olive branch he cursed his espadrilles. For a moment he thought about going back to the house, finding something more suitable to wear, but he decided to go on; he didn't intend to go far; he'd manage with the espadrilles, he thought, even as a twig scraped against his bare ankle. Just a brief scout around.

Despite the espadrilles, the scrapes and scratches, the heels sometimes falling loose, even having one of them snatched clean off as he stepped through the undergrowth, Jacquot made his way through the woods, keeping the house on his left, ranging from a few metres inside the treeline to some twenty metres beyond it. It was not a journey he made often, maybe once every few weeks to clear the undergrowth or load up with kindling for the fire-pit, but it was familiar ground. Normally, he'd be looking at his feet, stooping over for firewood, but this time he kept looking back at the house, now spread below him, his eyes on a level with its first-floor windows – Midou's bedroom, and the landing corridor, their own bathroom and Claudine's dressing room at the far corner – searching for the best angle, the clearest view.

And then he found it, a small hollow where the slope of the hill dipped into a narrow ledge of almost flat ground and the back of the millhouse presented itself almost unobstructed– from the swimming pool and long windows of Claudine's studio on the left, past the terrace and fire-pit, the back door and kitchen, to the dining room and *salon*, with the upper windows ranged above.

Jacquot paused for a moment, looked ahead. Ten metres away the stone channel of the old millrace showed through the trees and the woods on the other side began to thicken. Another ten paces and his view of the house would be compromised as the angle sharpened and the perspective changed. Here, he decided, was the best view of the house, and above its pantiled roof he could see, across the valley, the rising green slopes of the distant Grand Luberon.

Sitting himself down, Jacquot pulled a crumpled pack of cigarettes from his pocket and lit up the last one, the click-click-click of his lighter adding another layer of sound to the surrounding buzz of insects. Drawing in the first smoke, he let it out in a plume, tapping the ash into the now empty packet. The last thing he wanted to do was start a fire, but the spot was perfect for a quiet, contemplative smoke – the sun dappling through the trees, the ground warm and soft, the air sharp with the smell of pine from the conifers behind him. Here, he thought, would be a fine place to build a small pergola, somewhere for him and Claudine to sit as the days ended and shadows lengthened. No need for a roof, just a section of decking, a couple of canvas chairs they could stow away beneath the planking . . .

He was working out the logistics – they'd have to lose a tree or two to maximise the view and provide proper access, maybe using the tree stumps as support for the deck – when his eye was caught by a glint of silver amongst the leaf litter just a couple of metres to his right. For a moment he just looked at it, his attention held, wondering what it was – a coin, a piece of jewellery – as he finished his cigarette. Putting out the hot tip in the empty cigarette pack and folding it tightly, he slipped it into his pocket and got to his feet. A couple of steps and he was there, closer now to that silver flash that had caught his eye. He reached down, fingers pushing between the twigs and leaves . . . And it was paper, a piece of silvered paper, a sweet wrapper . . . He opened it up and sniffed it a couple of times. A sweet, minty scent still strong enough to make out . . . chewing gum.

Putting it in a shirt pocket he looked around and realised, by a combination of broken twigs and a squashed scooped-out hollow, that he was standing in what looked like a kind of long nest. Whether he was imagining it or not, whether anyone else would have been able to see it, he was certain now that he could make out the shape of a body – elbows there, the chest, the narrower tapering of legs behind him – with his own espadrilles firmly planted at waist-level. He knelt down for a closer look.

At first it was a question of focus, trying to read the leaf litter, no longer a rough carpet of browned leaves and acorn husks and pine needles at his feet but, close to, a more intimate weave of twigs and knotted stems . . . And there, hardly able to believe that he had seen it, found it . . . a single curl among all the stiffened angles. A twist of colour that shouldn't have been there. He leant forward, just a few centimetres, and squinted. A strand of material. Blue. Snatched from someone's coat, a sleeve maybe, and caught there.

And then something truly startling.

At the top of the outline. Where the head would have been.

If he hadn't been focusing, squinting, looking so carefully, he might never have seen it.

A hair. What looked like a single hair, also caught on a twig.

Adding the strand of blue cotton to the gum wrapper that he'd found a moment earlier, he reached forward for the twig with the hair, lifting it away from its companions, the hair shivering, catching, unfolding, as long as his hand.

A dark colour, blackening towards one end.

It had to be from a woman.

Jacquot got carefully to his feet, feeling an angry tightness in his chest.

There was no doubt about it.

They had been here.

Right here. This close.

And he hadn't heard or seen a thing.

55

LIKE CLAUDINE AND MIDOU, JACQUOT had had every intention of taking a nap before the evening's entertainment. But by the
time he'd found separate envelopes for the gum wrapper (its silvered
exterior a perfect surface for prints), the twist of blue material, and
for the dark strands of hair (he'd found three more in quick succes-
sion), he could hear movement above – a door closing, water
running. Going through to the *salon*, he poured himself a drink and
settled in front of the TV news. He'd wait till the girls had finished,
then quickly go up and get himself changed and ready.

'Wake up, *Gran'père*!' It was Midou, shaking his shoulder. 'Too
much wine at lunch, if you ask me.'

As well as the shock of being so suddenly woken, and the shame
of dozing off like an old man in front of the TV, was his surprise
at seeing Midou. She looked exactly like her mother – a younger,
shorter, thinner version – and she was beaming with excitement.
A night out at a concert after weeks poring over her books and,
more recently, being kept at home by Jacquot, and Midou Bécard
was clearly ready to rock, in a pair of rhinestoned white jeans,
white T-shirt and black rhinestoned waistcoat. Her hair was styl-
ishly ruffled and gelled, and her face delicately made up to bring
out the elfin, gamine quality of her character.

'You like?' she asked, slipping her thumbs into the waistcoat pockets and giving him a twirl as he straightened himself up. 'I got it this afternoon while you were loitering outside Pascal's, looking grumpy.'

'I was not grumpy . . .' he began, clearing his throat, knowing he had been, but then Claudine came into the *salon*, and he felt his heart quicken and his breath catch.

If Midou looked good, Claudine was a dream. She was wearing a cream silk *ao dai* which her friend Gilles Gavan had brought back after a recent trip to Cambodia. Jacquot might occasionally have found the voluble little art historian and lecturer and some-time painter a bore, but he was entertaining enough in short bursts and Claudine's best friend, and that was good enough for Jacquot. Gilles also had impeccable taste. On the other side of the world, he had seen the traditional Khymer *ao dai*, thought of Claudine, and had the best tailor in Phnom Penh run off half-a-dozen outfits – for summer and winter, in silk and cotton, in blues and reds and emerald greens. He'd also bought slippers to go with them, daintily embroidered in gold thread and each with a curled toe. The *ao dai*'s long light shirt and full trousers suited Claudine's tall rangey frame and, with a silken length of scarf wrapped around her neck, she looked simply ravishing. He, by contrast, was still in his jeans, espadrilles and Levi shirt and looked drab and dishevelled.

'You both look – magnificent,' he said, struggling off the sofa.

Claudine gave him an arch look.

'Which is more than I can say for you. So get a move on or we'll be late.'

Thirty minutes later, showered and changed, the millhouse secured, Jacquot drove them down the *impasse* and out on to the main road. It was still early, a little after seven, but Claudine had decided to make a night of it, arranging to meet up with friends for drinks in town before George Benson took to the stage at ten o'clock. Beeping their way through the crowds heading for place du Tourel and the supporting acts, they parked once again at police headquarters and set off for their pre-concert drinks party.

While Claudine and Midou mixed with their friends on a roof-top terrace in the old town, Jacquot took the opportunity to call Brunet to make sure that everything he'd asked for had been put in place: two reserve *képis* with binoculars on the flat roof of the tourist centre, and two more on the roof of La Poste, to keep an eye on the crowds; photos of the Manichella sisters handed out to every patrol, along with details of their car; and everyone equipped with two-way radios.

'Where are you?' asked Jacquot, after Brunet had confirmed that everything had been done according to plan.

'Corner of Sadi Carnot and du Tourel,' Brunet told him. 'In Bertrand's bookshop doorway, at the back of the stage.'

'How does it look?'

'Mayhem, but fun. A good crowd, that's for sure.'

They signed off, Brunet promising to get in touch if anything turned up. Pocketing his radio, Jacquot joined Claudine and Midou, took a drink and decided he might as well start enjoying himself.

Safety in numbers, he thought, safety in numbers.

56

JACQUOT MIGHT HAVE BEEN OFF duty, as excited as anyone in the audience as the moment for George Benson's appearance drew nearer, but he was still very much alert. Within minutes of taking his seat beside Claudine and Midou he had scanned and discounted their near neighbours – certainly no pair of women sitting together – and he could see no one who looked to be in any way a potential threat. Also, because their side seats were at an angle to the stage there seemed little possibility of the sisters having any kind of opportunity to take sniper-style pot shots at them, unless they were on stage themselves or had climbed one of the trees on Bournissac – and it was no easy matter to unpack a rifle and scope, take aim and fire, with crowds of people all around them. Nor were there any windows that he could see that would provide the killers with any kind of vantage point.

Their banked seats were also high enough, Jacquot now realised, to provide an excellent view not only of the stage and the bleachers opposite, but of the audience below, tidily seated in rows. Claudine had brought a small pair of binoculars with her, which Jacquot asked for, and he swept them over the crowd, picking out familiar faces: Guy Fourcade, just as he'd said, in the fourth row behind the Mayor; Dominique Crystal who owned Restaurant Scaramouche, and her family; the Préfet and his new, much younger wife; Michelot, their over-enthusiastic director of tourism; as well as a number of others whose backs and shoulders and profiles Jacquot could make out in the growing darkness.

But no sign, so far as he could see, of Mademoiselle Virginie Cabrille. He was wondering whether, for some reason, she'd decided not to come when his eye was caught by a movement in the central aisle.

And there she was, sashaying towards the front rows with a group of her friends, ten or twelve of them at least. Jacquot was close enough for his view of her to fill the lenses: slicked-back black hair, bare shoulders, a black basque-style top over skinny jeans, a glittering necklace, bracelet, earrings, watch, her scarlet lips moving as she said something to the girl on her arm, the girl she'd played tennis with that morning. She looked young and glamorous, carefree and excited, and as she found their row, five back from the stage and just behind Guy Fourcade, and ushered her friends into their seats, she cast her eyes over the crowds as though searching for someone.

Jacquot wondered if it was him she was looking for, and the very next second, just as the thought lodged in his head, she lifted her eyes – deeply mascara-ed – and looked at the bleachers to her left and right. As she did so, for a split second, their eyes met, so close through the binoculars that Jacquot felt a jolt, as though she could actually see him, as though she'd caught him watching her. For a wild, idiotic moment he expected her to smile or wave at him, but he knew there was no way she could have made him out in a crowd like this, in the gathering darkness. And then her eyes were past him, and she was turning back to her friends, finding her seat and making herself comfortable, just the back of her head and bare shoulders visible.

But there was no time left for him to watch her. Up on the ridge of St-Jacques rockets sailed up into the darkening night sky and exploded, one after another – golden palm trees and extravagant blooms of sparkling colour, followed by the time-lapse bop-bop of the explosions. As the twinkling embers fell back to earth a disembodied, amplified voice came from a dozen speakers set around the stage in the centre of Cavaillon.

'*Mesdames, Messieurs . . . Je vous présente . . . Des États Unis . . . Monsieur . . . George . . . Benson . . .*'

57

EVERY LIGHT WENT OUT AND a wave of cheering and clapping and whistling rippled across place du Tourel and Cours Bournissac. In the darkness, shadowy figures could be seen crossing the stage – the supporting musicians and backing singers, Jacquot supposed, taking their positions. And then, when everything had settled – breathless, excited seconds when the crowd seemed to freeze with anticipation – a single spotlight speared through the night sky and illuminated the Roman arch.

And stepping into the light came George Benson.

White tuxedo, black T-shirt, black trousers. Immaculate.

A roar of approval and welcome swept through the heart of Cavaillon. Waving to the crowds, Benson walked to a stand of guitars, selected a cream-coloured Gibson archtop and lifted the wide leather strap over his head, settling it onto his shoulder. Stepping forward to the microphone, he bowed to the audience in front of him and to the crowds on Cours Bournissac, and smiled that George Benson smile.

'*Bonsoir*, Cavaillon. It's good to be here.'

Another rolling roar of delight from the crowd.

Without further delay, he turned to his backing group, nodded three times and then swung round into the opening bars of 'Breezin''. In an instant, the audience was on its feet and the game was on.

Up in the bleachers, Jacquot, Claudine and Midou did the same as everyone else, if only to see what was going on down on stage, and very soon there wasn't a body in the crowd not swaying to the Benson beat, as endless classics, with only the briefest interruptions for guitar changes or adjustments to the equipment, beat through that hot balmy night in Cavaillon. 'Love Times Love', 'On Broadway', 'Turn Your Love Around', 'Never Give Up On A Good Thing'.

When Benson broke into 'Feel Like Makin' Love', Jacquot slipped an arm round Claudine's waist from behind and nuzzled her ear.

'You are so, so beautiful, I just want to eat you up,' he whispered.

'If I don't get to you first, *chéri*,' she whispered back, over her shoulder, pressing her body against his. The sliding silk skin of her *ao dai* was so light and thin as she moved against him that it felt as though she were naked. She smelled of flowers and fruit, and her neck, where he brushed his lips, was warm and smooth.

That was when the radio clipped to his belt gave its signature bleat.

It was Brunet back-stage at the Sadi Carnot end.

'Boss, there's a security guard looking for you. She's got a note for you, something from the man we're all watching . . . She's up in the bleachers but can't find you.'

'What's she look like?'

'Short blonde hair. Pretty. In the black France Auto Logistiques kit. The name tag says Julie.'

Jacquot looked around, straining to see over the heads of the audience. And then he spotted her, coming down the stepped aisle, a clipboard carried in the crook of her elbow and with a small torch which she flashed from side to side, like a cinema usherette checking row numbers, standing up on tiptoes to see over the crowd.

'Got her,' said Jacquot, waving to her, and broke the connection.

Just as Brunet said, the security guard was wearing the FAL logo on her black shirt, with a security shield below it and a clip-on photo-pass. After making her way along the row, she asked if he was Daniel Jacquot, requested identification (fortunately he had his badge), and then handed him an envelope stamped with the France Auto Logistiques logo. Inside was a folded hand-written note from a Pierre Gingelle inviting him to the singer's back-stage suite during the short intermission. Daniel's name had been given to the event organisers by Georges Rochet who, in his absence that evening at the *opéra* in Orange, had designated Jacquot his official representative. According to Gingelle's note, Monsieur Benson simply wanted to extend his thanks for such a pleasant evening. Although it was official, a professional courtesy call, Jacquot felt a surprising thrill and blessed Georges Rochet for this unexpected kindness, knowing how much Jacquot liked the singer and how much he'd been looking forward to the concert.

'Can you wait here, please, with my wife and her daughter, while I'm away?' he asked.

The young woman called Julie shook her head. '*Je regrette*, Monsieur, I'm afraid I can't do that. *C'est pas possible*.'

'Then can I bring them with me?'

'If you wish, Monsieur, but the invitation is for you alone. I have no instructions for your family.'

Jacquot knew that that wouldn't go down well; neither Claudine nor Midou would be too entertained at being left outside the door while he had a chat with the singer. Maybe there was an after-show party, he thought. Maybe he could somehow wangle an invitation . . .

He spotted the two-way radio clipped to Julie's belt.

'Can you call your boss and have him let you stay here while I'm away? Tell him it's an official police request.'

'If you want, I'll try.' She pulled the radio from its holder on her belt and flicked it on. She hunched over to keep out the sound of the music on-stage, but Jacquot could just about make out what she was saying and heard the crackle of a reply. At first, it didn't sound too good; there was a sense that his simple request would cause unnecessary problems, that it couldn't be accommodated.

There was further explanation from Julie – she was with the town's Chief of Police, she said; it was he who had made the request – followed by another crackle of instructions. She looked up at Jacquot and smiled, held up her thumb. She'd got the okay.

'But you must be back before the start of the second half,' she warned him. 'Ten minutes only, Monsieur, then I have to go.'

'I understand,' said Jacquot. '*Merci bien.*' Then he tapped Claudine on the shoulder and, leaning close to her ear, told her what was happening, that Julie would be staying to keep an eye on them while he was away.

'Just so long as you understand that if you don't get us a pass for the party afterwards, you'll be sleeping in the guest room. For a week.' Claudine drew back from him with a stern, disapproving expression, but he could see that she was pleased, that at least one of them would be meeting Benson.

'And don't worry,' Midou chipped in. 'In case someone tries to kidnap us, I came prepared.' She opened her beaded tote bag and, making sure that no one could see, she flashed the inside at him. Jacquot caught a glimpse of a service Beretta, one of the guns from the millhouse. He was about to say something when she snatched the bag back and closed it. 'Don't ask. You're not taking it off us. And *Maman*'s got hers, too.'

Jacquot looked stunned.

'You didn't say not to, and we always keep one in the car,' said Claudine.

He was about to say something when Julie tapped his arm.

'The break's at the end of this song, Monsieur. You must hurry Just go down to the back of the bleachers where you came in and wait for Sylvie. She's coming over from back stage and will show you where to go.'

Up on stage, a spotlight settled on the keyboard player and the first tinkling notes of 'The Greatest Love Of All' brought another rising roar of approval from the crowd when they recognised the intro.

'I'll be back before the second half,' shouted Jacquot into Claudine's ear, and then kissed her neck. 'I'll give George your love.'

Smiling his thanks at Julie, who took his place beside Claudine, Jacquot made his way to the aisle with many *s'il vous plaît*s, and *je m'excuse*s. Even the aisle was crowded with people, dancing and swaying to the beat, but he made it to the top of the stand and then took the stairway down to ground level. When he reached the last two steps, he saw another woman, also in the FAL security strip, heading in his direction. She looked more senior, more authoritative than Julie, with the name Sylvie printed on her photo-pass.

'Chief Inspector Jacquot? Would you follow me please?'

'*Bien sûr, oui*,' he replied and kept close as she led him from the bleachers to the far end of the stage. They stopped by a wired gate closing off the pavement leading to the Roman arch. On the other side was a sound-recording truck, its tailgate open and steps leading up to a mini-recording studio where three sound engineers were poring over their consoles. Jacquot couldn't help but feel the quickening of his heartbeat. This was just amazing.

Beside him, Sylvie's radio came on. She reached for it, switched to receive and listened. Away from the bleachers, here behind the stage, he could hear more clearly: a request for her to report to G Section where there'd been an incident.

'*Oui, oui. J'arrive*, I'm coming.'

She switched off her radio and turned to Jacquot with an apologetic smile.

'Can you wait here a moment, please?'

'Sure, of course. Is there anything the matter? You need any help?'

Please, thought Jacquot, please don't let anything get in the way of my meeting George Benson.

'Nothing at all,' she assured him. 'There are always problems at these kind of things – probably some kid trying to get on-stage, or drugs maybe.' Sylvie shrugged, managed a short smile. 'You never know what's going to happen. But in case I get held up, do you have the letter with you . . . the invitation my colleague gave you? And your ID?'

Jacquot patted his pockets and nodded.

Sylvie looked relieved.

'*Parfait, parfait.* In a minute Monsieur Gingelle's assistant will come for you, to let you in,' she explained, gesturing at the padlock. 'Her name is Claire. Tall, red hair.'

'No problem,' said Jacquot, giving her a smile.

She returned the smile and then headed back the way they had come, reaching for her radio as she walked.

Out of Jacquot's line of sight, Benson was coming to the end of 'Greatest Love', and Jacquot tapped his foot to the beat, pulled out his cigarettes and lit up. Up on the bleachers, he'd never have been able to manage it; this was a perfect opportunity. In the recording van on the other side of the fence, one of the engineers caught his eye and gave him a strange look – as though he shouldn't be smoking there either – but Jacquot paid no attention.

Up on-stage, Benson brought the ballad to a close and the audience erupted. Any moment now, the lights would dim, Benson would leave the stage for his break, and Jacquot would have his moment.

But the lights didn't dim. Instead, he heard George Benson's voice ring out over the *place*, deep and rich and hugely amplified.

'I hear there's a rumour y'all thinking here that my old friend Al is gonna be joining me tonight. Well, I sure am sorry to disappoint you folks.'

There was a wafting sigh of disappointment from the crowd, and a whispered '*merde*' from Jacquot who'd hoped, along with everyone else, that the legendary jazz man would be making an appearance, and that he, Jacquot, might even get to meet him as well. But Benson was speaking again. 'Which means, my friends, you're just gonna have to make do with another good old friend of mine . . . Monsieur Carlos Santana.'

Whoops, whistles, the place went wild. Jacquot, too, was stunned to think that Carlos Santana would be appearing. And then the roar of the crowd increased even more. It was suddenly clear that Carlos Santana was coming on-stage. Right now, when there was supposed to be a break and Jacquot was about to meet George Benson. In the recording van, one of the engineers pushed back from his console and Jacquot caught sight of a small monitor showing Benson and Santana at the mic together, and out on stage he could hear the first twanging, sinuous notes of 'Lately' as the two guitarists started up.

'Help you?' On the other side of the gate a security guard had appeared from nowhere. Behind him, the sound engineer looked on from his console.

Jacquot wondered if the engineer had called the man in. He pulled out his letter.

'I'm Daniel Jacquot. Chief Inspector Jacquot. Sylvie from FAL told me to wait here for Pierre Gingelle's assistant, Claire.'

'Who?'

'Claire. I don't know her surname. She's . . .'

But the guard was frowning, looking at him oddly, and Jacquot felt a sudden wash of doubt flood through him. His stomach turned and his blood ran chill.

Something wasn't right.

'Claire. She's Pierre Gingelle's assistant. The event organiser,' he insisted, flicking away his cigarette.

Every word he spoke sounded hollow, wrong . . .

The guard started shaking his head, just as Jacquot had known he would.

'No Pierre Gingelle that I know of,' he said, shifting his beefy shoulders, settling his jowls into his collar and hooking his thumbs into his belt. 'And no Claire, neither.' He had the look of a man getting ready to use some muscle. 'You got any ID?' he asked.

But Jacquot didn't bother to reply.

Instead, he spun round and raced back to the bleachers.

As fast as he could.

And as he ran he prayed he was wrong, prayed he was mistaken. But as he started up the steps he knew he'd been had, knew he'd been fooled – Sylvie, Julie, Claire, Pierre Gingelle. It was all a set-up. But they'd been so convincing, the two women. All the FAL kit, the clipboards, the torches, the security passes, the two-way radios. The note mentioning Rochet. The intro call from Brunet. Even Julie saying she couldn't stay with Claudine and Midou and having to make a call to her supervisor to get it okayed. Whoever they were they had done their homework and left nothing to chance, even taken some risks – relying on his own gullibility.

And then he remembered Julie's stubby little fingers, working the channels on her radio.

The dirty fingernails.

He was at the top of the stairs when he remembered that, and with an icy stab at his heart, already knowing what he would find, he pushed through the dancers on the stepped aisle as Benson and Santana worked their strings on stage.

Pausing two steps above their row Jacquot looked down across the swaying heads.

No Julie.

No Midou.

No Claudine.

58

'JEAN! *C'EST MOI.*'

Jacquot was trembling, breathless, the police radio slippery in his sweaty hand. He was on the top level of the bleachers, scanning the crowd below, oblivious to the performance on stage. Another huge roar had greeted the opening chords of 'Give Me The Night', but Jacquot heard nothing beyond his own thumping heart and the crackling of his radio.

'You sound like you've been doing some dancing, Boss,' said Brunet. 'You getting ready to meet the man?'

'There is no man. No nothing. It's all a con, Jean. They conned us. Where are you?'

Brunet snapped to.

'Same place. Corner of Carnot and Bournissac.'

'Stay there. I'll find you. And put out an all-points alert for four women, two in FAL kit. Maybe a VW too. Our boys here, and all the centres – Apt, Manosque, Pertuis – and the autoroute, north and south. *Tout le monde.*'

'*T'as pigé.*' You got it.

By the time Jacquot reached Brunet – after scrambling down from the bleachers and through the gate where only moments before he'd waited for Pierre Gingelle, flashing his badge at anyone who stood in his way on his dash round the back of the stage – the initial onslaught of loss and fear and anger had been replaced by a more focussed, analytical frame of mind, everything switching to automatic.

Where could they be?

Where were they being taken?

And what could he do about it?

He didn't let himself stop to think how much time he had to do it.

'All points alerted,' said Brunet, steering his boss into the bookshop doorway, just a few steps away from the loose, swaying crowd on Sadi Carnot, effectively at the back of the stage. 'But there's going to be a lot of traffic pretty soon.' He nodded towards the stage where George Benson, with his back to them, was starting the windup. On this side of the *place* the acoustics were different from the seated area and bleachers, the music batting down from the steep sides of the St-Jacques hill with a tinny, out of synch echo.

'It'll be just as difficult for them,' said Jacquot, looking round.

Brunet's radio crackled

Both men heard the message. From a squad car on the outskirts of Cavaillon to Headquarters Despatch. A shooting on Avenue Dupont. A car off the road. Another car stolen. A single casualty. Male.

'They're heading for the autoroute,' said Jacquot, almost to himself. Gesturing at Brunet's radio with his own, he asked, 'Any details?'

Brunet raised the radio and passed on the question.

'Vehicle off the road is a black VW,' came the response. 'Rear tyre shot out. Witnesses heard muffled gunshots prior to crash. Owner of a stolen taxi says a woman flagged him down, ordered him out at gunpoint.'

'Just the one woman?' asked Brunet.

The radio crackled again. 'That's all,' came the reply. 'Says she floored him. Doesn't remember anything else.'

'When was this?'

'A few minutes ago. We were filling up with gas just down the road. Heard the commotion and got down here *tout de suite*.'

'*Allons-y*,' said Jacquot, grabbing Brunet's sleeve.

At close to midnight on a Saturday and with the concert only just concluding – now a rackety, distant soundtrack beyond the rooftops – the road out of town was busier than normal, traffic already starting to back up on Verdun, slowed down by the obstruction up ahead on Dupont. With lights flashing and siren wailing the squad car he and Brunet had commandeered on the corner of Sadi Carnot and Demille overtook the single line of stalled outbound traffic. It wasn't long before they saw other flashing lights up ahead, two police units and an ambulance already on the scene, traffic cones put round the rear end of a black VW Beetle jutting out of a tree-lined ditch.

Pulling up beside the cones Jacquot leapt out and hurried over to the VW, following the silvery scar along Dupont where the wheel rim had scraped and gouged a swerving path across the road surface. Clambering down the side of the ditch, noting the FAL decals plastered onto the VW's back windscreen and bodywork, Jacquot reached the open driver's door. The car was a mess inside, the seats clear but the back and front footwells a jumble of clothing and rubbish thrown forward when the VW had ploughed down into the ditch. The back of the driver's seat had also been tipped forward, but not, Jacquot suspected, from the impact since the passenger seat remained in an upright position. Given the VW's limited space, Jacquot guessed that Claudine and Midou had been dumped on the back seat, out of sight, maybe covered in a blanket, while the two sisters took the front seats, and that the driver's seat had been locked forward to more easily get them out after the crash.

Thanks to the reek of burnt rubber from the shredded tyre, the steely scent of scorched metal from the buckled wheel rim, and the sharp, dusty smell of cordite in the VW's tumbled interior, Jacquot knew that there was little chance of his identifying any remaining trace of Dyethelaspurane. But he had no doubt that that was what the sisters had used to put Claudine and Midou out of action, showing them to the 'official' car beneath the bleachers, for whatever reason, before subduing the pair of them with drug-drenched cloths. Except that one of them – Midou or Claudine – had not been put down as effectively as planned, but had managed to find a gun and shoot out the tyre.

Jacquot wondered what the cost of that action had been – in terms of injury from the subsequent crash, or reprisal from the sisters. It was not something he wanted to dwell on. Pushing away from the car, he climbed back out of the ditch and found a sergeant of gendarmes waiting for him.

'There was an injury?' he asked.

'The taxi driver,' the sergeant replied. 'You'll find him in the ambulance, getting stitched up.'

'And witnesses?'

'The woman over there, with her dog. She saw it all.'

Jacquot thanked him and hurried over to the ambulance to find a large man in a plaid shirt and baggy jeans being attended to by a medic. There was a nasty gash across the top of his forehead, just below the hairline and raised up on a sizeable bump.

'I was slowing down on Boulevard Sebastiani, coming out on to Dupont,' he told Jacquot, 'when this woman just stepped in front of me – out of nowhere. For a second I thought she might be a fare, flagging me down. But then I saw the gun. Waving it, she was. If I hadn't been slowing for Dupont, I'd have hit her sure as shit.'

'Description?'

'Tall, kind of stooping, and thin. With a hard face on her. Short blonde hair – ouch!' The man winced as the medic worked on his cut. 'Careful, *copain*, that hurt.'

'Clothing? How was she dressed?' prompted Jacquot.

'Black shirt, black trousers. Looked like a uniform. Security badge with a name tag . . . Simone . . . ? Something like that.'

'Sylvie?'

The taxi driver shrugged. 'Could have been. I don't know. It was all over so quick.'

'So she got you out of the car . . . ?'

'With a gun in my face, I moved fast I can tell you. Left the keys in the ignition and was about to make a run for it when she gave me this.' He pointed to his wound with a nicotine-stained finger. 'A woman. How do you like that? I'll never live it down.'

'So she took the car and then what?'

'Don't ask me. I was out good and proper. But I'll tell you one thing – they won't get far. I was about to fill the tank at the Total garage on Verdun. Pretty near empty, I was.'

'How far could you have driven?'

The driver lifted his hands from his lap, spread them, shrugged. 'Twenty, maybe thirty kilometres if I watched my speed. *Pas plus*. No more.'

Thanking him for his time, Jacquot crossed over to the woman with the dog. She was in her fifties, wearing carpet slippers and a housecoat, arms wrapped tightly around herself. Jacquot showed her his badge and asked what she had seen while her dog sniffed at his mocassins.

'I was on the corner of Allée Guende when that car came racing past.' She pointed to the VW. 'I heard a bang. Lots of bangs. Two, three, maybe more, and then I saw it swerving around the road like the driver was drunk. There were sparks coming from underneath it. The next thing I know it's up over the pavement and into the ditch.'

High above, a helicopter roared past, the sound of its rotors batting down on them. George Benson or Virginie Cabrille? Jacquot wondered, watching its flashing lights disappear over the rooftops.

He turned back to the woman in the housecoat.

'There much traffic about?' he asked.

'Not too much then. Not like now,' she added, nodding at the cars filing past, curious faces bathed in blue and red light staring through the windows.

'So what happened then?'

'*Alors*, for a moment I did nothing. I was just shocked, you know. It happened so quick, so close. But then this figure scrambles up from the ditch and looks around. She's wearing trousers but it's a woman. No question. She sees the taxi coming out of

Sebastiani and makes a beeline for it. Next thing I know, she's behind the wheel and driving it back to the car. By this time there's another figure got out of the VW. It looked like she was hefting something up onto the pavement. Like a sack of something. The first one parks and I don't get to see much of what happens after that. Next thing I know they're in the car, doing a U-turn and heading off down to the bridge.'

Jacquot thanked her and walked back to the VW.

'What next, Boss?' asked Brunet, coming up behind him.

'I want this car out of the ditch, put on a flat-bed and taken to headquarters. And get the boys to go over it with a fine tooth-comb.'

'It's Saturday night, Boss.'

'Tell them it's me. And I'll owe them.'

'Anything else?'

Jacquot nodded.

'Time to pay a call. Le Mas Bleu,'

59

WITH TWO *KÉPIS* TAKEN ALONG for good measure, Jacquot and Jean Brunet arrived at Le Mas Bleu at a little after one o'clock in the morning. If they had expected the place to be bedded down for the night, they were wrong. The drive was lit – an uplighter between each cypress – and every window blazed, the gravelled forecourt ringed with flambeaux. The previous morning they'd been directed by Valbois to the tennis courts, but it was clear from the sound of music and laughter that the action had now moved to the swimming pool. Since the entire hotel had been booked by Mademoiselle Virginie Cabrille, they didn't bother to ask for her at reception, but simply followed the music, led on by a shifting blue light splashed across the side of Le Mas Bleu. The party in progress could only be hers.

There were maybe thirty people at the pool, sitting at tables around a tented bar, dancing under the trees or playing in the blue lapping water. They were young, in their twenties and thirties, a smart set in easy, elegant evening clothes or swimsuits and wraps, relaxed, having fun. A mixed jazz and samba soundtrack played in the background, no louder than the chatter and laughter of the party. It fell away as Jacquot, Brunet and the two *képis* made their approach, one head after another turning in their direction.

As he walked down the side of the pool, Jacquot searched for

Mademoiselle Cabrille but couldn't see her. Making his way to the bar where a dreadlocked barman was mixing Mojitos, he asked where he could find her.

'Right here, Chief Inspector,' came a voice.

He turned.

Virginie Cabrille had appeared from nowhere, arm in arm with her tennis partner. Her hair was still slicked back though two oiled wisps hung like black tails either side of her forehead. She still wore the black basque top she had worn at the concert, but had exchanged the jeans for a pair of voluminous pasha trousers. It was clear she'd been dancing, her throat and the skin between her breasts shiny with sweat. She flicked back one of the black tails from her forehead, and licked her lips as though she'd justed tasted something warm and luscious.

'Twice in one day,' she continued. 'What a treat. So how was the concert, Chief Inspector? Do tell me you enjoyed it?' She gave him a mirthless but teasing look, her eyes, black as tapenade, piercing into him.

It was the smile that did it.

Jacquot felt a hot, coiling anger, felt his guts twist and harden into a steely knot. He did not waste any time. Staying at the bar, and loud enough to be heard, he said, 'Mademoiselle Virginie Cabrille, I am arresting you on a charge of conspiracy to murder.'

For a few seconds, the only sound save the soft samba backbeat was the gentle slap of water against the sides of the pool. Even the barman stopped working his cocktail shaker.

Virginie Cabrille frowned, but a frown that did little to ease the smile from her lips.

'I'm sorry. What did you say?'

'Arrest. Conspiracy. Murder.' Jacquot gave each word its own weighty importance. 'Your arrest, Mademoiselle.'

'And when exactly was this murder?'

'*En effet*, murders, Mademoiselle.'

She took a sharp breath.

'A serial killer, no less. How exciting.'

269

She cast around her friends, all now watching this exchange with interest. There was a ripple of nervous laughter. Either her friends were in on the set-up, or they weren't quite sure what to think. Jacquot favoured the latter view.

'Don't forget to tell him about that bank job, 'Ginie,' quipped one of the party, a handsome young man with a glass of champagne in one hand, the other gently stroking his companion's thigh.

Jacquot nodded to one of the *képis*. A set of handcuffs was taken from his belt and he moved forward to put them on Virginie Cabrille.

While Jacquot reeled off her rights, short, sharp and brief, she held out her hands, wrists uppermost, for the handcuffs. As the *képi* snapped them on she never took her eyes off Jacquot. A cool, calculating look, the same amused smile, as though she knew something that he didn't.

When the cuffs were secured, the *képi* stepped back. Virginie Cabrille looked down at them, shook the links as though getting the feel of a piece of jewellery, and raised them so her friends could see.

'Most elegant, Chief Inspector. And, as you may know, an item of restraint with which I am not unfamiliar. Normally I use two pairs, or four. Or rope, or tape . . .' She turned to her companion and the girl leant in and gave her a light kiss. Virginie whispered something in her ear.

'We have a car in the drive, Mademoiselle.'

'Chauffeur service. How splendid. Lead me to it, Chief Inspector. I have a feeling that our evening is just beginning.' She turned to the rest of the party. '*Mes amis*, *bonsoir*, enjoy yourselves. I'll be back in a little while.'

'I wouldn't bank on that Mademoiselle,' advised Jacquot, his voice chill and low.

'Oh, really? Well, we'll just have to see, won't we?'

60

WEDGED BETWEEN THE TWO *KÉPIS* in the back seat of the squad car Virginie Cabrille remained silent as Brunet drove into town from Le Mas Bleu. In the close confines of the car, Jacquot could smell her. Warm and exotic, rich and close, a musky, leathery scent that filled the car's interior with an oddly masculine aroma, like the sinuous smoky trail of a good cigar. In the passenger seat, watching the starlit countryside slip by and the lights of the town draw closer, Jacquot shook a cigarette from his pack and lit up, as much for the pleasure of the smoke as a way to cover the smell of her. And as he smoked, he stayed silent. He'd said enough already; and he knew, too, that silence had a way of unnerving even the strongest, most determined suspect.

At police headquarters, Brunet swung down into the basement car park and came to a stop by the lift doors. Even here there was no need to speak, the two *képis* helping Cabrille from the back seat and escorting her to the lift, just as they'd been briefed to do on the way to Le Mas Bleu. As the doors opened, Virginie Cabrille stepped in between her guards, turned and gave Jacquot another smile. Not even the lift's panelled neon lights could pale her deep tan, her glamour, the shift of her breasts in the low-cut black basque. On either side of her, the two uniformed *képis* kept their eyes to floor and ceiling.

'Chancing it, aren't you, Boss?' asked Brunet, as the lift doors slid closed.

'She's guilty. We just have to prove it. Simple as that.'

'Simple as that.' Brunet nodded.

'At least while she's here, the sisters are on their own,' said Jacquot, dropping his cigarette and grinding it out.

Up in his office he pulled out his chair and slumped down into it. The last time he'd been here, Saturday morning, Claudine and Midou had been safe at the millhouse; then there'd been lunch together at Brasserie Gaillard; shopping in the afternoon; the drinks party in the old town, and then the concert. Claudine in her *ao dai*, Midou in her sparkling rhinestones. Now they were gone, out of reach, out of touch, and, Jacquot knew, in deadly danger. As he sat there, not quite sure what to do next, he realised that his heart was beating fast, his mouth dry, and his stomach clenched with fear. Not good, he thought, not good at all. Pulling himself together he reached for the phone and made two calls.

By the sound of it, Jacquot decided that Solange Bonnefoy had not been in bed and asleep. She had been drinking, her voice slurred and furry and hoarse. But she was not so drunk that she didn't snap to when Jacquot told her what had happened and what he wanted.

Bernie Muzon, on the other hand, must have been dead to the world, dragged painfully awake from his dreams.

'Daniel? What the fuck . . . ? Do you know . . .' Jacquot could see him reaching for his watch or the alarm clock '. . . what the fucking time is?'

Like Solange, however, he came to when Jacquot told him what had happened.

'Call Solange Bonnefoy. She's expecting you. Pick up the warrants and get right out to Roucas Blanc. Break down the doors if you have to.'

Jacquot had just put the receiver down when the phone started to ring. He snatched it up again.

'Chief Inspector Jacquot, this is Maître Simon Paul, in Paris, at the offices of Belmond Frères. I believe you have taken a client of mine into custody. *Garde à vue.*'

Normally Jacquot loved nothing more than a little light legal jousting, particularly with slick Parisian lawyers who thought they knew it all. He might, for instance, have asked for the name of the client, knowing full well who it was; or how Maître Paul had got his direct line number; or how and when he had heard about the arrest; or requested more detailed information with regard to the professional legitimacy of Belmond Frères before confirming any arrest over the phone. There were any number of responses he could have come up with, most of them based on playing the dull provincial policeman, all of which he knew would exercise any lawyer and give him an edge. But this was not the moment for such games; these were not normal circumstances.

'If you are calling on behalf of Mademoiselle Virginie Cabrille,' said Jacquot, as Brunet came into his office and took a chair, 'then you are correct. She is indeed in custody.'

A sigh came down the line, followed by a gentle tut-tutting.

'A great shame – in terms of your career, Chief Inspector. A great shame.' The voice was low, amused, in control. 'However, to limit any further, more grievous, damage might I suggest you release her immediately. And without charge.'

'That's a suggestion then, not a threat?' Jacquot tried to picture his adversary. Thin, he decided, judging by the voice; maybe bald. A bowtie? Spectacles? Possibly.

'Please accept it as my best professional advice,' crooned Paul down the line. 'Let me put it like that.'

'And let me put it like this, Maître Paul. Mademoiselle Cabrille is not setting foot out of this building. Not only is she under arrest for conspiracy to murder . . .'

There was an indulgent '*poufff*' of disbelief at the end of the line.
'*Vraiment*, this is a joke, surely . . .'

'. . . but she will be helping with an ongoing investigation.'
'Oh I don't think so, Chief Inspector.'

'In which case I suggest you get yourself down here, *cher* Maître, and persuade me otherwise. Until such time, we will continue with our enquiries. I will have you put through to the switchboard, so that your call can be transferred to your client in the holding cells.'

And with that Jacquot broke the connection.

'You didn't put him through to the switchboard,' said Brunet with a smile.

'Oh, didn't I?'

61

AT A LITTLE BEFORE THREE in the morning, Virginie Cabrille was taken from her holding cell on the first floor and brought to an interview room on the second. There were no windows in this room, and just a single neon panel in the ceiling. There was a table, chairs, a tape-recording unit, two doors and a long mirror-like observation panel.

Brunet and Jacquot stood behind the glass and watched their suspect settle herself. When the duty sergeant left, by the door leading down to the holding area, Virginie Cabrille arranged herself sideways on to the table, crossed her legs and inspected her fingernails, idly swinging her foot as if to some unheard rhythm in her head. Though her jewellery had now been removed, bagged and tagged during the form-filling and photo session in the receiving hall, she still looked as tanned and as glamorous as she had in the lift, quite content, it seemed, to spend whatever time it took in that room. There was a confidence, an assurance, a certainty about her. That within just a short few hours, even less, she would be released.

Jacquot had other plans.

'You first, or me?' asked Brunet, relishing the prospect of taking her on.

'*Après toi*,' said Jacquot with a grim smile. He knew there was nothing his assistant liked more than a challenge in the interview room, and this looked like it might turn out to be one of Brunet's more memorable encounters. There was no need to brief him. He knew the way to go.

Virginie Cabrille did not look up when Brunet entered the room and took the chair across the table from her. It seemed that her nails were a more pressing concern. Despite the hour – despite her game of tennis, the concert, the party – she looked not the least bit weary. Other prisoners, sitting at that table, would have pleaded tiredness, talked about human rights, demanded that a lawyer be present. Mademoiselle Cabrille had done none of these things.

Jacquot drew out a chair and settled himself down to watch.

The interview began in the usual manner, and with the usual Brunet flourishes. Jacquot had seen the act a number of times and was still fascinated by it. It was like watching a particularly wily old mongoose circle a cobra. A masterclass. Every detail precisely calculated to unsettle the suspect.

A pen was taken from his breast pocket, ballpoint clicked down with the thumb. A spectacle case was brought out from an inside pocket, opened, glasses unfolded, put on. A file was opened, the contents flicked through. A new tape was taken from his pocket, unwrapped and slid into the recorder. Throat cleared, with a fist to the mouth.

The *fonctionnaire* in every detail.

But a deadly *fonctionnaire*.

And, after testing the tape, off he went.

'*Alors*, Inspector Jean Brunet with suspect Virginie Cabrille.'

Jacquot saw her smile at the word 'suspect'.

'Time 3.09 Sunday, July twenty-fifth 1999.'

He looked up at Mademoiselle Cabrille for the first time.

'Your address, *s'il vous plaît*, Mademoiselle?'

'I have already supplied those details,' she began, 'but if you need them repeated . . . Maison Cabrille, Roucas Blanc, Marseilles.' The voice was low, bored.

The information was laboriously copied down. Without raising his eyes, Brunet asked: 'Is that "Roucas" with a "c" or a "q"?'

'Guess,' said Virgine Cabrille, with an easy, if venomous, smile, now tapping her nails on the tabletop.

There had always been the possibility, of course, that Mademoiselle Cabrille would not say a word. It was a difficult trick, Jacquot knew, to pull off in a police interview room. Every suspect, every villain who sat there, thought that they could do it, but very few succeeded. Anxious, uncomfortable, isolated, the temptation to speak out – to complain, to threaten, to deny – was hard to resist.

But it was clear that Virginie Cabrille appeared to feel no such constraint. She seemed quite content to answer any question she was asked, without any conditions or any lawyer present, as though she had nothing in the world to fear. It was increasingly clear, however, that she resented the interview being carried out by a subordinate like Brunet when she had been relishing the prospect of a set to with the man who had arrested her in front of all her friends.

Jacquot wondered, as he sat there in the gloom of the observation room, whether she knew he was watching.

He was certain she did.

Her performance, he knew, was for him.

He was equally certain that Brunet was beginning to annoy her; the formal, functional questionning; the endless repetition; the laboured note-taking – as though writing was a skill with which Brunet was not yet entirely comfortable. If the Biro had been a pencil, Jacquot was in no doubt that at some stage Brunet would have licked its tip.

The foot swinging faster, the nails tapping harder, the replies more clipped, more bored, Virginie Cabrille was starting to grow impatient.

Another fifteen minutes and Jacquot would take over.

In the meantime there were other things to do.

62

'IT'S GOOD OF YOU TO come in, Vincent. I appreciate it.'

'One of our own, Daniel. It goes without saying. And you've got pretty much the whole squad working on it. The rest of us are out on Dupont going over the crash site.'

Vincent Pilger was head of Cavaillon's scene-of-crime unit, a quietly spoken man with a broad beak of a nose, thinning brown hair and sad, sloping blue eyes. Like the rest of his team he wore rubber gloves, plastic bootees and a white Nyrex one-piece suit that swished softly as he moved. He and Jacquot were standing in front of the black VW Beetle that had been dragged from the ditch on avenue Dupont and brought to the basement parking lot. It had been driven onto a sheet of thick white plastic and items taken from its interior were already piling up on a line of trestle tables also standing on the plastic sheet. Both passenger and driver doors were open, bonnet and engine cover too. It looked like the beetle it was nicknamed after, wings spread, ready to take flight. It was dusty, dirty and tipped to one side where the tyre had been blown out. One of the headlights had been smashed and snatches of grass from the ditch were caught in the front bumper and front nearside wheel arch.

'What have you got so far?'

'Not an accidental blow, *c'est certain*,' said Pilger. 'Rear offside tyre shredded with bullets. Four shots, given the holes we've found in the wheel arch and the shell casings in the back footwell. I'd say someone in the back seat deliberately blew out the tyre.'

Jacquot thought of the guns that Claudine and Midou had brought with them to the concert. Which of them had done it? he wondered. Which of them had blown out that tyre? Which of them had decided on the tyre rather than their kidnappers? If they had a gun, they could have shot through the front seats as easily as the wheel arch. But he knew that neither Claudine nor Midou would have been able to do that. They'd have gone for the softer option.

But how, Jacquot wondered, had the two sisters overlooked their bags, failed to search them? It was a mistake that had cost them dear. And with Vincent Pilger on the case it would continue to do so.

But at least Claudine and Midou were still alive. One of them certainly. Or had been. Say twenty minutes after being taken. And conscious too. But that had been hours ago. What had happened since then? And where were they now? Somewhere within a thirty kilometre radius according to the cab-driver – unless, of course, the sisters had stopped at a petrol station and filled the tank. If, that is, they had bothered to check the gauge. And if they were heading for the autoroute, which way had they turned? North or south? How many exits? How many possible destinations? Jacquot knew the answer, and drew a deep breath, trying not to lose hope.

'Paris plates, as you can see. And looks like they did some camping too,' Pilger continued, nodding at the tables. 'Rolled up ground mats, sleeping bags, a tent, basic cooking equipment in the boot. As for the interior, the usual mess; sandwich wrappers, pizza crusts, crisps, nuts, bits of paper, a few gas and *Péage* receipts, duct tape, road maps. You know the kind of thing. But there's no blood we can find.'

'Mind if I take a look at the tables?' asked Jacquot, relieved to hear that no blood had been found, either from the gunshots or the subsequent crash.

'It's all yours. Like I said. One of our own.' Pilger gave him a consoling pat on the arm. 'So it'll be large ones all round.'

'Let's hope so,' said Jacquot with a grim, but grateful smile. 'And thanks again.'

Over at the tables he snapped on a pair of powdered latex gloves and sorted through the larger items – the ground mats, sleeping bags and camping equipment. Rolled up with one of the sleeping bags was a dark blue mohair jumper with shiny brass buttons. He picked it up and held it to his nose. A strange mixed scent of flowers and sweat and the farmyard reached him. He guessed the jumper hadn't been washed for some time, and guessed, too, that the strands of material he'd found in the linen room at Le Mas Bleu and in the woods behind the millhouse would match it perfectly.

Putting down the jumper, he turned to the next table and the smaller items: a lipstick, a hair clip, sweet wrappings, pens, pencils, coins, a dented can of Diet Coke and an empty bottle of Orangina. The first thing he picked up was a chewing gum wrapper. Silver foil exactly the same as the wrapper he'd found the previous afternoon at the millhouse. And an open packet of mint chewing gum. He could almost smell her breath. There was also a crumpled pizza napkin with a lipstick stain on it, a pair of brand new pliers (for the car, or removing teeth? Jacquot wondered idly), some scissors, a roll of thick silver duct tape that might well match the tape used on Berri and Chabran, and various scraps of paper.

He was opening up the first of these scraps when one of Pilger's team came to the table with a bag in each hand. Jacquot recognised them immediately – Claudine's cream silk clutch and Midou's tote. He picked them up, one by one, sorted through the contents – tissues, lipsticks, perfumes, a set of house keys, a fold of notes pressed into the back of a cigarette packet, and a couple of ready-rolled spliffs in a side pocket of Midou's tote. But no guns. If Marie-Ange Buhl had still been alive, and working on the case with him, he'd have handed the bags to her. Chances were, she'd have got something from them – like a bloodhound taking a scent. She'd have known where to look, where to go. But she wasn't with him; he was on his own. All he got from the two bags was a wave of loss and fear and longing.

Jacquot put down the bags, and turned back to the scraps of paper, opening them up one after another: autoroute *Péage* receipts, parking tickets, chits for petrol, a flyer for an oriental rug sale. Tipping them closer to the light, he looked for the locations. And there they were: Cavaillon, Forcalquier, Manosque, Marseilles and Salon, the last two pointing south, Salon just down the road, no more than thirty kilometres away.

It was on one of these pieces of paper – a car park ticket taken out in Forcalquier just a few weeks before he went there with Brunet – that Jacquot found something else: two sets of hand-written numbers.

Phone numbers.

And two sets of initials. MV and PB.

He held the piece of paper up to Pilger.

'Mind if I take this?'

'Help yourself,' replied Pilger.

63

BACK IN HIS OFFICE JACQUOT picked up the phone and tried the two numbers from the scrap of paper. The first number, beside 'MV', answered after four rings with an automated recorded message. He left his name and number, but not his rank. The second number, beside the letters PB, rang and rang until eventually Jacquot broke the connection. After stopping to collect incoming documents from the fax machine he went downstairs and took over from Brunet in the interview room. As his assistant picked up his things – pen, spectacles case, file – and left the room, Jacquot saw Virginie Cabrille's eyes follow him. Jacquot had a good idea what she was thinking. Virginie Cabrille and Jean Brunet would not have been a partnership made in heaven.

'And now the big guns,' said Virginie, eyes settling on Jacquot as he took Brunet's seat.

He didn't waste any time.

'Where are they?'

'Where are who, Chief Inspector?' She worked her neck, as though her time with Brunet had taken its toll, rolled her shoulders, her breasts shifting in the basque.

'You know very well who, Mademoiselle. The sisters. Marita Albertacce and Marina Manichella.'

'Now, I know that name . . .' she began.

'Mademoiselle Cabrille . . .'

'Virginie, please.'

'Let me make myself absolutely clear, Mademoiselle. Last night my wife and her daughter were abducted by the Manichella sisters . . .'

'Your wife? *Mais ça c'est affreux*,' said Virginie Cabrille. Then she frowned. 'But . . . but you're not married, Chief Inspector. I'm right, aren't I?'

Jacquot kept his voice low.

'I would advise maximum cooperation if I were you, Mademoiselle. Because this time you will not be leaving police custody quite so smoothly or as swiftly as you have in the past. It's now just a question of how long you spend with us. And I am talking years, not hours or days.'

Jacquot took a sheaf of faxed papers from an inside pocket, unfolded them one by one and slid them across the table.

'Copies of search warrants, Mademoiselle. Taken out for your property in Marseilles, for your cars, and for your bank and phone accounts. 43 67 33 58. That's one of yours, isn't it?'

'The lodge, not the house,' she replied, drawing the documents towards her and casting an eye over them, before pushing them back as though they were of no interest.

Jacquot nodded. Just as he'd guessed. The number with the automated message under MV. Mademoiselle Virginie. Suitably feudal, and a crucial link between the woman sitting opposite him and the sisters. That confirmation gave his confidence a solid lift. Now he wouldn't need to call Muzon to check the number. Now he knew. He was in control. He was getting there. All that was left was that other number preceded by the letters PB.

Virginie Cabrille raised her chin, indicating the last piece of paper he'd put onto the table.

'And that?'

'Another warrant. For the Druot Clinic in Marseilles.'

'Very efficient, very imaginative, Chief Inspector.' She drew the warrant towards her. 'And who, I wonder, issued these warrants?'

'The Marseilles *Judiciaire*. Maître Bonnefoy.'

'Aaahh! My old friend Solange Bonnefoy.'

Jacquot reached forward, and drew back the Druot warrant.

'And how is the dear lady? Such a horrible thing to happen,' continued Virginie Cabrille. 'Poor, poor woman.'

'So you know about the bomb that killed her friend?'

'Doesn't everyone, Chief Inspector? It was on the news,' she replied, her eyes on his. 'TV and radio. How could I not know about it? And so close to my own home. *Quelle tristesse.*'

Jacquot held her gaze, and felt a hot, almost irresistible violence rise up in him. He wanted to reach across the table and throttle her, put his hands around her callous, complacent little neck and squeeze as tightly as he could . . . squeeze the life out of her. Instead, he cleared his throat, and dropped his voice to a low, persuasive note.

'I will ask you once again, Mademoiselle. Where are the Manichella sisters, and where are they holding my family?'

'I can't think what you're talking about, Chief Inspector,' she said, putting her hands together, lining up the fingertips then sliding them between the folds of her pasha trousers.

Brave words, thought Jacquot, and wondered if she'd be quite so relaxed if she knew that they had the Manichella sisters' black VW down in the basement. For now, he would keep that to himself.

Squaring off the warrants and rolling them into a tube, Jacquot got to his feet.

'Thank you for your time, Mademoiselle. I'll have someone show you back to your quarters.'

He'd reached the door when he heard her voice behind him.

'So you're keeping me here?'

He didn't bother to turn.

'Oh, yes, I'm keeping you here,' he said, and the door closed behind him with a satisfying click.

64

AT CLOSE TO FOUR IN the morning, there wasn't much that Jacquot could do. It was, he reflected, like standing under the posts back in his rugby days, waiting for a penalty kick or conversion to be taken by the opposition. The kicker placing the ball, lining it up then stepping back, pacing it out, reaching where he wanted to be and then gathering himself. The hush of the crowd. And that long, silent moment when time stands still. Will he slice it, or make it sail between the posts?

And all the time there is nothing you can do but wait and pray.

'I'll come get you if anything turns up,' Brunet had told him, and now Jacquot lay in the dark of the bunk room where officers could catch up on some sleep if there was no time to get home. Streetlights angled up against the ceiling, split by a set of blinds that didn't quite close, the mattress was thin, the pillow hard and the blankets rough but serviceable. Jacquot had taken off his shoes and jacket, curled up on his side and pulled the blanket to his ears. Somewhere in the old town a drunk shouted, a car droned past, and Église St-Jean chimed the quarter then the half. He closed his eyes and thought of Claudine and Midou.

Where were they?

How were they doing?

He was certain they were still alive, a sure and vivid certainty. Not happy, not comfortable, frightened certainly, but alive.

In his mind he went back to the concert, their row in the bleachers, the three of them standing there, watching the show. And that security guard, Julie, coming to get him. And he hadn't recognised her, or suspected a thing, not for a moment, nor her sister, Sylvie, waiting for him at the bottom of the steps, in that shadowy, empty, echoing place beneath the bleachers.

Maybe if he'd seen them together, side by side . . .

But in that place, at that time . . .

So convincing. So utterly compelling.

The short blonde hair, the clipboard, the uniform, the two-way radio, the call ahead from Brunet.

And he'd left the Manichella woman there with Claudine and Midou, left them in her care, even requested that she stay with them – to keep an eye on them, for God's sake. And at first she'd refused, goddammit. How convincing was that? Finally being persuaded by him to contact her supervisor – her sister, of course – for permission to stay.

It didn't take much thought to work out what had probably happened after that. Starting with the call that Sylvie had made when she left him at the security gates, letting her sister know the coast was clear, Jacquot out of the frame.

And what would Julie have said when she received that message? He could easily imagine it. Claudine and Midou had been asked to join Jacquot, to meet George Benson. Julie could show them where to go. She would accompany them, if they liked?

And they'd have been as taken in by the uniform as he had been until, somewhere behind the bleachers, in those empty echoing shadows, while he had waited in vain for Pierre Gingelle, the two sisters had drugged them, bundled them into the car and headed out of town, using the back streets behind the bleachers to make good their escape.

Except one of them, Claudine or Midou, not as sedated as the sisters had intended, had found her gun and, not willing to shoot her captives – it took a great deal to pull a trigger when the gun was pointing at someone – had aimed instead at one of those humps of the wheel arch either side of the back seat, blowing out a tyre. Plucky girl, whichever one it was, thought Jacquot. Just what he'd have expected.

Yet despite this unforseen development, the rest of the operation, from start to finish, from the first introduction in the bleachers to the kidnap itself, had been seamlessly executed, nothing less than a scrupulously planned operation. Finding out about the concert, finding out that Jacquot and Claudine and Midou were attending, that Brunet was Jacquot's assistant, that Rochet would be away at Orange for an evening of opera, and that Jacquot would be head of service in Rochet's absence.

Then there were the uniforms. The kit. The FAL logos. The identity tags and passes. This was no take a-chance, put-together job. This was professional. This was more, far more, than two sisters from the hills of Corsica could possibly have hoped to arrange unaided. Which was why he was glad that Mademoiselle Virginie Cabrille was currently behind bars. Because she was the brains behind all this, Jacquot was sure of it, the sisters just the hired hands.

But luck had been on the sisters' side, too. They might not have had the expertise to put the whole thing together by themselves, but they certainly had the gumption to get themselves out of a tight corner – finding another car and making good their escape, driving off to wherever it was they had holed up. Somewhere between here and Marseilles, within a thirty kilometre range if the taxi driver was right about the petrol in his tank and how far it would get them. Of course, they could always have pulled into a filling station – in which case they'd be caught on the security video of a local garage fore-court. Brunet was on that now – calling gas stations to check their video loops and putting out the stolen Citroën's registration number. If the sisters planned on driving any distance, they'd be picked up soon enough. If they didn't, it was because they were off the road, out of the car, back where they wanted – and needed – to be.

But where? How far away?

In the country, Jacquot decided.

A farmhouse, a country *mas* . . .

Somewhere isolated. Standing alone . . .

Somewhere . . .

'Boss! Boss!' Brunet was shaking his shoulder.

Jacquot sat up, startled awake, heart suddenly hammering. He knew immediately where he was but he couldn't for the life of him remember how long he'd been sleeping. The last time he'd been woken so abruptly had been the evening before, by Midou, before leaving for the concert. A lot had happened since then, and in his waking, for just the shortest moment, he'd thought he was back there, in the *salon* at the millhouse, sprawled on the sofa.

But it was just for that small, precious moment.

'What? Tell me,' he said, struggling off the bunk, looking at his watch. He rubbed the sleep from his face, reached for his shoes and pulled them on while Brunet brought him up to date: no sign of any Citroëns driven by women on forecourt footage from autoroute garages and 24-hour filling stations within a fifty-kilometre range; the France Auto Logistiques security uniforms the sisters had worn easy to source from two separate suppliers; and their black VW down in the basement traced to a Monsieur Georges Roland Gauthier at an address in Melun, just south of Paris.

'So what did he have to say for himself?'

'Not a great deal. On account of his recently beginning a four-year sentence in La Santé for receiving stolen goods. I've spoken to the prison authorities and they woke him up, had a word. According to Monsieur Gauthier, the last time he saw his VW was last December, parked in his garage. He assumed it was still there. I'd say he's lying – took a wedge for the car and his silence. Money for nothing.'

Jacquot raked his hands through his hair and thought about it.

It made perfect sense. You need a car that can't be traced back to you and whose registration is in order. What better than to 'borrow' it, sourcing what you need from someone serving time?

And then, when you're finished with it, you return it. It was certainly the kind of thing that Virginie Cabrille could easily have set up, given her father's known connections. Maybe she'd even provided the sisters with a safe house in the same way, something belonging to a prison inmate, another Monsieur Gauthier, where they could stay while they planned their strikes, somewhere they couldn't be traced.

A house, in the country. Not a town apartment.

Somewhere quiet, out of the way.

And somewhere close.

'Good,' said Jacquot. 'Good work.' He got to his feet and stretched, reached for his jacket. 'Anything else?'

'It may be nothing . . .' Brunet began.

Jacquot gave him a look. 'Jean, *s'il te plaît*, this is not the time to start . . .'

'The napkin.'

'The napkin?'

'The one in the VW. All scrunched up it was, smeared with lipstick. With all the rest of the stuff. I went down, took a look at the tables.'

'A napkin?'

Brunet smiled, leaning against the doorway, hands tucked in his pockets.

'The kind you get with a takeaway. And there it was. That other telephone number. On the bit of paper you had? PB? The same number's printed on the napkin. Address too.'

65

THE OWNER OF PIZZERIA BLAZOTS had opened up early and was reading a Sunday newspaper at the bar when Jacquot and Brunet swung into the car park. The sun was up, still hidden somewhere behind the hills, but lances of lemon light speared into a thin, blue, cloudless sky, letting everyone know it wasn't far off making an appearance.

Pizzeria Blazots was a twenty-five kilometre drive from Cavaillon, just outside Salon, on the town's southern flanks, one of a dozen businesses on a small trading square close to the river and the autoroute. Set between a hardware store and serviced laundromat, its double picture windows were plastered with hand-painted posters proclaiming the best *feu de bois* pizzas in the region – *Rien Plus Meilleur.* As Brunet and Jacquot pushed open the door, the scent of burnt wood from two massive brick stoves behind the serving counter suggested that, despite appearances and surroundings, the boast might not be without foundation.

You find the real jewels where you least expect them, Jacquot always said.

Blazots' owner, Gino Condotti, was a slim, wiry fellow in his early forties, a dash of silver hair at his temples and a dark stubble reaching high up on his cheeks. When Jacquot apologised for the early call, Condotti waved it aside.

'This is my time,' he explained. 'The ovens cool overnight and someone has to be in early to feed them up. No gas here. Wood only. It takes time, sure, but it's worth it. Coffee?'

With large espressos served, and a dish of pizza romana *biscotti* set between them – miniature pizzas crusted with sun-dried tomato, studded with garlic and dusted with oregano – Condotti took the photos of the two sisters that Brunet handed him, looked at them one after the other, then held them out side by side as though to compare them. He shook his head.

'This one I don' know,' he said, dropping one of the photos on to the counter. 'But this one . . .' He pursed his lips then nodded his head, still holding the picture of the smaller, younger sister. Marina Manichella. He slid it onto the counter and tapped it with a finger. 'This one I do know.'

'She a regular cusomer?' asked Brunet, reaching for a *biscotto* and dipping it into his espresso.

'Once, maybe twice, a week, enough for me to recognise her.' Condotti pushed the photo back to Brunet.

'How long has she been coming in?'

Condotti gave it some thought.

'Maybe three or four months. Something like that.'

'You ever talk to her?'

'Sure. We friendly people here. Over the counter, you know? Or clearing tables. Word here, word there. But she not a local, I can tell you that for certain. Never seen her round town. I got the feeling . . . she just dropped by . . . driving past on the autoroute, maybe. We're close, and the pizzas here are better than anywhere else.'

'And she never came in with anyone? She was always alone?'

'*Si, tutto solo.*'

'She ever order a takeaway?' asked Jacquot, taking over from Brunet.

'Now and then.'

'Did she phone in the order, or just drop by and wait?'

'Most times she call before – real sexy voice. Then come by and pick up.'

'How long between making the order on the phone and coming by to pick it up?'

'The usual . . . the time it takes to bake the pizza. People, they don' like to have the pizza stay too long in the box. They want it straight from the oven, so it's crisp and hot, and get it home and eat it quick. And she never come by in our busy time, you know? So there's no rush, no delay.'

'So you never delivered?'

Condotti shook his head.

'How far do you deliver?' asked Brunet, as Jacquot considered this.

'Depends. Normally it's just around town. Say five or six kilometres range. We just got a few scooters, so country lanes are out. But a big order – like twenty pizzas, a party somewhere – then, sure, I drive it out myself in the van. Got a warming oven in there, see? But for one pizza . . . ?' he smiled, shook his head. 'It'd have to be close.'

'And it was only ever one pizza? She didn't order any more than the one?'

'So far as I recall, just for her. Regular, sometimes medium, but never the *grande*.'

'You recall the last time she was in?' asked Jacquot again.

'Couple of days ago. Phoned, picked up, left.'

'You see what car she drove?'

'Black, for certain.' Condotti shrugged. 'Cars, you know . . . I maybe am Italian, but cars . . . *pouf*!' He spat on his fingertips and waved his hand dismissively. 'Pizza? Yes. Women? Yes. Wine? Yes. But cars . . . *No, molto grazie*.' He nodded to the empty coffee cups. 'You wanna 'nother?'

Jacquot shook his head, but Brunet said that he'd take a refill, clearly hoping that more of Condotti's *biscotti* would also be served. He'd polished off the first dish in a matter of minutes.

'I tell you what,' Condotti said, working the Gaggia, the black coffee spurting into the cup. 'She don' like cars too much neither. Never clean it. Dirty, you know. Always dirty.'

292

'Was she ever with anyone? In the car, I mean, travelling with her?' Brunet took his cup with a nod of thanks.

Condotti shook his head. 'Like I say. Always alone.' He seemed to consider this for a moment, then he ducked beneath the bar and came out with a large cake tin. He pushed it under one arm, levered off the lid and spilled some more *biscotti* onto the empty dish.

'Tell you something, though,' he continued, shoving the cake tin back under the counter. 'You ask me, she didn' just come for my pizza. A real flirt. Sometimes she used to sit there in the window and chat up the boys working here. And customers too. She liked the young ones. Up there in her late thirties, I guess, but she always hits on the kids.'

'Any of them do anything about it?'

'Took a couple of them round the back, so I heard. One of the customers, one time. A waiter.'

'Any names?'

Condotti turned down his mouth, shook his head.

'Just kids. Could have come from anywhere,' he said.

'You recall anything else?'

Condotti looked at the two men. Let a slow smile slide across his lips.

'She built, you know what I'm saying? Big tits. And this tight little blue jumper she wear, buttons open halfway down. You couldn't help but look, you know what I'm sayin'? Like a TV set, it take your eye, you can' look away. Good legs, too. She may be on the short side, but the undercarriage . . . it look pretty neat.'

And with that, Jacquot and Brunet slipped off their stools. They might not have got a delivery address, but they'd learnt more than they'd bargained for.

'Hey, you don' finish my *biscotti*,' said Condotti, when he saw they were getting ready to leave. There were maybe six of the pizza biscuits left. 'Here,' he said, reaching for a Pizzeria Blazots napkin and tipping them into it, twisting the top.

In exchange for the napkin wrap, Brunet passed over his card.

'If she comes in again, be sure to call us. Like the moment she

293

steps through the door. And when she does, take your time getting her pizza baked.'

'Sure, no problem,' Condotti replied. 'So, you mind me askin'? What she done?'

'Won the *Loto*,' said Brunet.

66

JACQUOT AND BRUNET DID NOT return immediately to Cavaillon. Once back in the car, Jacquot drove south out of Salon heading towards Lançon past the town's small airstrip, then west to Cornillon and Miramas, before turning north towards Eyguières. He drove slowly, an elbow poking out of the side window, looking to left and right across fields of maize and droop-headed sunflowers, to distant wooded slopes and rocky hilltops, his eye holding on any building – barns, farms, drying sheds, and huddled pantiled roofs. At Eyguières, he turned right and followed a narrower road whose surface sent up a thin stream of rust-coloured dust behind them. From here he joined the Chemin de la Liberté before finally crossing the concrete levees of the Durance and slipping beneath the autoroute. Rather than join it and head for home, Jacquot continued on his cross-country route, gear changing up into the foothills of Roque Rousse, before starting down towards Pélissanne, keeping, as far as he could, within a ten-kilometre radius of Salon. The time it might take to bake a pizza.

By now the sun was up and casting long shadows, the car's interior filled with the warm gusting scent of the countryside, occasional stands of roadside cypress flicking fingers of shadow across its bonnet. Somewhere along this route, thought Jacquot, somewhere within this rough circle that he had marked out, or just outside it, were Claudine and Midou. Within, say, twenty minutes' drive of Pizzeria Blazots. Maybe, right this minute, actually within sight. In one of those farm buildings down there on the valley floor, or somewhere amongst that scattering of terracotta roofs. The thought was tantalising – so close, so near.

Yet all it did was fill Jacquot with a gut-knotting sense of frustration, a sense of powerlessness that made him grip the wheel, clamp his teeth and badly misjudge a turn, clashing his gears on a particularly sharp right-hand bend as he dropped down towards Aurons and Vernegues.

Because this was about as far as the Cavaillon taxi that the sisters had hijacked had been able to reach. Of course they could have refilled, but as Brunet had established no Citroën had been reported on the security videos of any garage forecourt within a fifty kilometre range of Cavaillon. And so early on a Sunday morning, all the smaller filling stations in-country would have been closed for the night.

He wondered how they were fixed for transport, wherever they were, now that they had lost the VW. They might have made it back to base last night but they'd never be able to use the Citroën now, not a stolen car, with the registration number so widely spread.

Or did they have some other means of transport, a back-up to the VW?

Not for the first time in this investigation, Jacquot wished he'd had Marie-Ange sitting beside him. In Marseilles, while they'd worked on the Lafour case together, she had had an uncanny ability to zero in on a house – to know that it was somehow significant. And as far as Jacquot could recall, she was usually right. If she'd been sitting here now instead of Brunet she could probably have directed him to the very door.

But Marie-Ange was gone. This time he was following his own hunches. Which, at this moment, were thin on the ground.

'We've probably just driven right past them,' said Brunet, giving voice to what Jacquot was thinking. 'This house, that house – down that driveway, through the trees over there. You want to stop at every house and knock on the door and see who answers.'

'Tell me about it,' said Jacquot, levelling out on to the flatlands west of Lambesc. 'But we don't have the time and, as usual, we don't have the resources either. We're just going to have to wait for a break. And hope it comes soon.'

'Maybe la Mademoiselle back at headquarters has decided to come clean, admit everything, and take us to the sisters.'

Jacquot grunted.

'You know something? I just can't see that happening.'

Five minutes later, with a lazy swing of the wheel, he turned on to the autoroute slip road and pressed his foot to the floor for the drive back to Cavaillon.

'You want a *biscotto*?' asked Brunet, indicating the napkin in his lap. Of the half-dozen that Condotti had given them, there were now just two remaining.

Jacquot's eyes were fixed on the road ahead. For a moment it seemed as though he hadn't heard what Brunet had said.

'I said, do you want a *biscotto*?'

This time Jacquot glanced down at the napkin, then back at the road.

A moment later he shook his head.

'All yours,' he said.

67

IT WAS EARLY MORNING AND Marina Manichella was still asleep in her bed. But her elder sister, Marita, had managed no more than a couple of hours, woken by a hot, gritty anger that had gripped her since leaving Cavaillon.

Everything had gone so well at first, better than they could have dreamt of in what was by far the most ambitious of their exploits. The way their uniforms had worked, gaining them access to restricted areas with just a flash of their badges . . . simple laminate badges put together at their kitchen table. So easy. And the way the cop's assistant, Brunet, had fallen for that line about Jacquot meeting the singer, even giving them directions as to where to find him. And how easy it had been to persuade the man to leave his women in Marina's care. How easy to have him wait by the gate while they lured the two women down to the car, put the pads over their faces, and bundled them into the back seat. And all those people so close.

But then, on the way out of town, it had all fallen to pieces.

The ringing clamour of gunshots, that wrenching, screaming skid, bouncing over the pavement and tipping into that ditch.

And all this . . . mess-up, because Marina had failed to put the girl down properly in the first place, failed to properly search their bags and, as a result, failed to find the guns. With Marina, you just

298

couldn't take anything for granted, thought Marita bitterly. Of course, she could understand her younger sister not thinking that the women might be armed and, given the time constraints, not being too thorough in her search. But still . . .

Yet somehow Marita had kept her temper, all the way back to Pélissanne, saying not a word, eyes on the rear-view mirror for any flashing blue lights coming up behind them, or casting ahead for patrol cars and road blocks. Inside lane, 110 km/h, and not a fraction over. But as soon as they were back at the house, hiding the car in the barn and toting the two bodies – armpits and ankles – into the basement, she'd laid into Marina. Just like they did at home, just as they'd always done. There had been a slap, recriminations, tears, with Marina stamping up the stairs and locking her bedroom door. The same as it always was.

But it could have been worse, Marita reflected now, watching from the kitchen window as the sun broke cover over a distant wooded hilltop. Another kilometre or two and they'd have been on the autoroute where those gunshots would have finished everything. The autoroute was no place for bullets and shredded tyres. Too fast, too busy, and too many cops. But on avenue Dupont they'd recovered, saved themselves. Flagging down the Citroën, transferring the women from one car to the other, and getting out of there as the first sirens started wailing.

At least, thought Marita, the girl had shot at the tyres and not through the front seats. Which was what she would have done, if the positions had been reversed. Same result but shredding the driver and passenger, not the tyre. Knock out the opposition first. Then take your chances. She wondered if the woman's daughter had considered that. Must have done, Marita decided. But then, the girl wasn't used to killing. Would have gone for the softer option.

Turning away from the kitchen window, she poured herself more coffee, listening out for movement from above and below. But there was no sound. The women in the basement still not stirring, and her sister still asleep. Just like every morning. The last up. The last to help with breakfast, or cleaning, or prepping.

This was the first time since arriving on the mainland that they'd had a real set-to, but it had been brewing since they'd stepped off the ferry. Marina was just so selfish, always so self-absorbed. She needed to be married, that's what . . . have children, and a man to keep her in line.

Not that her younger sister lacked resolve, Marita acknowledged. Marina was as eager to settle scores as she was. When they'd plugged those wounds together all those months ago, Marita could feel the anger, the hatred, radiating off her. Marina had taken Taddeus, her favourite brother, and by the time she was finished and the coffin lids had been nailed back in place, her teeth were set and her eyes sharp and hard. She wanted blood. Lots of it. A just accounting. And when the call had come, when the arrangements had been made, she'd been impatient for the off.

But all that had changed when they reached the mainland. The freedom, Marita supposed; the being away from home. The big city. The bright lights. All the shops, and the cars, and the people. And the men, of course. Always on the look-out, was her younger sister. Always drawing attention to herself, never one to keep a low profile. Always the devil between her legs. The barman and fisherman in Marseilles before they even moved up here, that kid in Forcalquier, the pizza house waiter, and God knows who else. Anything in trousers. Even the cop Jacquot. After that first sighting, Marina couldn't stop talking about him: taller than in the photos, better-looking, neatly dressed, cool, the kind of man . . . On and on she went. Marita knew that tone of voice, recognised that dreamy look, and had a fair idea what was going on in her sister's tiny little mind.

Of course, Marina still delivered when she had to. She was the one who had put the gun to Sleeping Beauty's eye and pulled the trigger, she was the one who'd pressed down the cushion over that old girl's face, and steered the carpenter's arm towards the spinning blade and held it there. When it mattered, her sister remembered why they were there, who they were doing this for.

But now, thanks to her, they had no car. Or rather, no car that they could safely use, every *flic* in the country on the look-out for a red Citroën taxi. The original plan had been that they'd return the VW to the house in Melun where they'd picked it up, dumping the two bodies en route, and then catch a train back from there, board a ferry home. But that was no longer an option. Now they'd have to find some other means of transport, some other way to shift the bodies from the house, leaving the Citroën hidden in the barn until arrangements could be made to have it moved when the heat was off, to be dumped in a wood somewhere, wiped down, no prints, nothing for the authorities to work on.

No traces. That's what they'd been told.

Except now, thanks to Marina, the *flics* had their VW, and everything in it. Whatever they'd left in it, no time to clear it, strip it, wipe it down.

Above her head, Marita heard floorboards creak, a door open and footsteps pad across the landing and down the stairs. Through the arch between the kitchen and *salon*, she saw Marina swing round off the banister and head towards her.

Still in pyjamas, an open towelling gown loosely tied, the indolent slap-slap of her slippers on the tile floor.

Sitting at the kitchen table, cradling her mug of coffee, Marita kept a stern expression on her face, unflinching, following Marina with her eyes every step of the way.

'*Bonjour, bonjour, ça va,*' her younger sister sang out, as though nothing had happened the night before. Just another morning, another lazy start.

Marita didn't waste a moment before starting in.

'What was in the car? What did we leave?'

Marina helped herself to the freshly brewed coffee and dragged out a chair from the table.

'Nothing,' she replied, lips bunching, blowing across the top of the mug. 'Camping stuff, sleeping bags, a couple of maps, magazines, a few coins . . . that sort of stuff. Nothing we need.'

'Garage receipts? *Péage* slips?'

Marina shrugged, made a moue. Maybe. She wasn't going to say.

'I told you to clear it out a hundred times.'

'There's nothing. It's fine. A few things, that's all.'

'We shouldn't have left anything.'

'There wasn't time. If you hadn't been in such a hurry . . .'

'Hurry? Didn't you hear the sirens?'

Marina fell silent, sipped her coffee.

Marita could see the jaw setting, could see that her younger sister was getting cross. She took a deep breath, tried to calm herself. Now was not the time. There were still things to do. It wasn't over yet. They needed to stay focused.

Somewhere beyond the border of trees that concealed the property from the road a car drove past. A distant sound, at the end of their unmarked turning, a harsh grating of gears as that tricky bend for Aurons came into play.

'When are we going to do it?' asked Marina, keen now to change the subject, as the sound of the car died away.

Marita gave it some thought.

'Tonight,' she said.

68

MAÎTRE SIMON PAUL WAS WAITING in Jacquot's office at police headquarters when he and Brunet arrived back in Cavaillon, the bells of Église St-Jean ringing out over the town, calling the faithful to mass. He was a dapper, sleekly suited man in his early forties. He had quick, sharp eyes behind heavily framed round tortoiseshell spectacles, and had arranged a thin spread of fair hair to cover as much pink scalp as possible. His back was straight, his knees pressed together, his hands held clasped in his lap. There was a very expensive-looking briefcase beside his highly polished black lace-ups. When Jacquot came in he didn't move from his seat or extend a hand in greeting.

'Maître Paul,' said Jacquot, who'd been warned by the duty sergeant that the lawyer was waiting for him in his office. 'I wasn't expecting to see you so soon.'

Jacquot supposed the man could conceivably have driven from Paris, or caught a train, but he had the rested, pampered look of someone who'd been taken to Le Bourget, put on a private jet and shuttled down to Marignane, most likely the Cabrille jet.

'And I had not expected to wait quite so long before seeing my client,' replied Paul in a reedy little voice that seemed somehow to match the thin hair.

Jacquot went behind his desk, shrugged off his jacket and settled in his chair. He suddenly felt tired and rumpled, unlike his visitor.

'Please accept my apologies, Monsieur,' he began. 'I was busy with a case of kidnap and multiple murder. Had I known you were waiting here, why, I would have dropped everything and come running.'

Maître Paul gave a tight little smile, dimpling his shiny, well-shaven cheeks, and was about to bat the sarcasm back when Jacquot's phone rang. He held up a finger and took the call, grateful for the interruption. It gave him time to gather himself. His case was not strong and he knew that if he wasn't careful this shifty little lawyer from Paris would have his client out of custody.

'*Oui, allo*?' he said, settling an accommodating smile on his visitor. Muzon was calling in with an update on his search of the suspect's property in Roucas Blanc.

'You should see the house, Danny. Last time we were there, it was a building site. Now it looks like a spread in *Elle Decoration*.'

'You find anything?'

'Nothing of any consequence in the house. Nor the lodge. We're still waiting on phone and banking records, but should have something later today. No one's very happy at having to move on a Sunday, but we're putting on the pressure.'

'What about the cars?'

'Nice collection. A Porsche Speedster . . . one of the old ones, you know? A new Jeep, and a rather fine limo. English. Daimler Jaguar. Long wheelbase. All the extras.'

'And? Any fibres. Blue . . . like I asked?'

Across the desk, Paul glanced at his watch and harrumphed.

'No fibres – all the cars have leather trim so not great for picking up fabrics. Fingerprints sure, but there's only a couple of sets the forensic boys have been able to lift. Oh, and a tin button, brassy colour, squeezed down the back seat of the limo. Stamped with a hunting horn. You know, one of those curling ones?'

Jacquot felt a stir of excitement. The blue mohair jumper they'd retrieved from the VW had brass buttons. But he couldn't remember if they had a hunting horn motif or if there was a button missing.

'Anything else?'

'Got a call from Laganne. He's been out at the Druot Clinic off Prado going through their dispensary records. It looks like there might be a shortfall on their Dyethelaspurane, just like you said, but they're still checking. Of course, the clinic's playing safe, saying that if there is anything missing, then the mistake will be at source with the maker and distributor, and we'll have to take it up with them – in Switzerland.'

'Thanks Bernie, I appreciate it,' said Jacquot, feeling another shiver of excitement. It was all starting to come together.

'Anything we can do, *copain*. We'll get her yet.'

Jacquot put down the phone. Across the desk, Paul reached for his briefcase.

'And now, Chief Inspector, if you wouldn't mind . . .'

'Of course, of course,' said Jacquot, and getting to his feet he ushered the lawyer out of his office. 'I'll have my assistant show you to an interview room.'

After Brunet had taken Paul off to see his client, Jacquot pulled on his jacket and took the lift to the basement where the VW stood alone in an echoing garage. He went over to the evidence tables and found the blue mohair jumper.

He turned the buttons to the light.

Eight of them. Each with a curled hunting horn stamped into the metal.

Then he matched the buttons to the buttonholes.

Nine of them.

One button was missing.

69

VIRGINIE CABRILLE LOOKED REMARKABLY FRESH for a woman who'd spent the night in a police cell. According to Mugeon, the duty sergeant, one of her friends from Le Mas Bleu had brought in a change of clothes and various toiletries while Jacquot and Brunet were down in Salon. Now the black basque and pasha pants had been replaced with a more business-like outfit – trousers, court shoes, and a blue check shirt with pockets and epaulettes. She sat straight-backed with her legs crossed and arms folded. There was the woody scent of a man's cologne, but Jacquot knew it wasn't the lawyer wearing it.

The two of them were seated side by side, holding a whispered conversation, Maître Paul's briefcase open on the table. When Jacquot entered they carried on whispering with nothing more than a glance in his direction, as though Room Service had just arrived to deliver an order.

Jacquot pulled out a chair, made himself comfortable. He leant over to the recording machine, slipped in a tape and tested it.

'If you don't mind, Maître, I have a few questions for your client . . .'

Across the table, Paul turned towards him. His smile was beatific, the blue wash of neon light flashing off the lenses of his glasses.

'And if you don't mind, Chief Inspector, I have a few questions . . .'

'Another time maybe, but right now I have a murder investigation on my hands . . .'

'Which my client is in no position to help you with,' Paul replied, raising his voice to interrupt, the smile fading fast. 'Mademoiselle Cabrille,' he continued in a lower, softer tone, 'has no information on these spurious claims of conspiracy and kidnapping and murder, and I demand her immediate release.'

Jacquot spread his hands, gave Mademoiselle Cabrille a tight little smile.

The smile was not returned. It was perfectly clear that what had started out as a joke, an amusement, was now beginning to wear thin.

Jacquot turned back to her lawyer.

'And that, I am afraid, is something I cannot possibly allow. There is mounting evidence . . .'

'Evidence?' enquired Paul smoothly. 'Exactly what evidence? "Mounting" or otherwise?' A grin slid across his lips but his eyes stayed hard and flinty behind his glasses.

'Enough to see your client in a very great deal of trouble.'

Jacquot made it sound as strong, conclusive and as threatening as he could, but he was also vividly aware that the woman across the table had been cleared of all charges the previous November, with a great deal more 'evidence' ranged against her than he currently had. Jacquot knew that his position was weak and that with Maître Paul's deft legal finessing Virginie Cabrille would likely have the upper hand in any hearing. What was it that Noël Gilbert had said at the wedding . . . how had he described this man all those weeks back? 'Slippery as a peeled grape,' that was it. And 'snappy', too, according to Claude Peluze.

Across the table Maître Paul started to shake his head. He waved his hand dismissively as though there was nothing he had yet heard that came anywhere near to being 'evidence'. He then changed tack, pulled a notepad from his case and started flicking through the pages.

'I believe . . . I believe you have issued certain warrants, Chief Inspector?'

'For your client's home and cars, phone and bank records. That's correct.'

Jacquot noticed that the lawyer wore a wedding ring. It was loose on his finger but a pink bony knuckle kept it in place. For a brief moment Jacquot wondered what the man's wife was like. Probably as thin and knuckly as her husband's finger, he decided.

But Maître Paul was hurrying on.

'And where were these warrants sourced?' he asked, his voice low and smooth and level. 'At such short notice? On a Sunday?'

Jacquot guessed that the lawyer already knew the answer but had asked the question to gain some leverage, in a further attempt to discredit Jacquot's case against his client.

'The Marseilles *Judiciaire*. Maître Bonnefoy,' Jacquot replied, knowing what Maître Paul would make of that particular name. This was the woman Paul had trodden all over when Virginie Cabrille had been held in Marseilles on suspicion of involvement in the Lafour case. Jacquot wasn't wrong.

'Hah, my learned friend Madame Bonnefoy,' cried Paul with barely suppressed glee. 'I might have known. She loses in one case against my client and is determined now to stir up fresh trouble. To level the score. A clear case of judicial harrassment, pure and simple, if she signed those warrants on the basis of what you have laughably described as "evidence".'

'And those searches are currently being carried out,' replied Jacquot, coolly, refusing to be drawn.

'To what possible end?' sneered Paul.

'Why, the successful prosecution of your client, *cher* Maître. What else?'

There was a moment's pause. Paul idly fingered his wedding ring, then pulled back his cuff to check the time as though he were in a hurry to be out of there. Along with his client.

'But right now,' continued Jacquot, 'there are just a couple of questions I would like to ask.'

'As I said, Mademoiselle Cabrille has nothing to say. No comment to make.'

'Then she will certainly be spending a little more time . . .'

'What do you want to know, Chief Inspector?' It was Virginie Cabrille, the first time she had spoken.

'Ah, Mademoiselle, I had almost forgotten you were here.'

Jacquot gave her another smile, a smile he found difficult to hold. Once again, all he really wanted to do was put his gun to her head and demand she tell him where Claudine and Midou had been taken, or face the consequences. For a few satisfying moments he imagined the muzzle of his Beretta pressed against her forehead, the skin sliding beneath it, his finger on the curve of the trigger.

Shaking away the image he asked, in as calm a voice as he could muster, 'Do you happen to know Marina Manichella and Marita Albertacce?'

'I have told you. Yes, I do.'

'You have met them?'

'No, I have not. But I know who they are. As I have told you.'

'So you haven't met them? Not in Marseilles? Not in Corsica? Not here in the Luberon?'

She shook her head.

'I told you, we have not met.'

'And you're sure of that?'

'Absolutely sure.'

Jacquot nodded.

'So . . . never?'

'I think my client has made it eminently clear . . .'

But Jacquot paid no attention to the lawyer, moving on quickly.

'Tell me about your cars, Mademoiselle. At home in Marseilles. I gather you have a fine collection?'

Cabrille gave him a frosty little look.

'A Jeep, a Porsche, a Daimler. Hardly a collection, Chief Inspector.'

'*Dites-moi, s'il vous plaît.* Is there any possibility that the Manichella sisters might have ridden in your Porsche, as drivers or as passengers?'

'It's a Speedster. A classic. No one drives it except me, and there's not enough room for two passengers. Anyway, if I haven't met them, how could they . . .'

'That's a no then?'

'It's a no.'

'And the Jeep?'

'No.'

'And the Daimler?'

She shook her head impatiently.

'That's a no as well?' Jacquot nodded at the tape recorder.

'You are correct. Quite correct. It's a no.'

'Not the faintest possibility . . . ?'

'Chief Inspector, I really . . .' began Paul.

But Jacquot wasn't listening to the lawyer, all his attention focused instead on the woman sitting beside him.

'And you can also confirm, here, in front of your counsel, that the telephone number, the one I mentioned earlier – 43 67 33 58 – is yours. For the lodge, I believe you said?'

'Correct.'

'The number is not listed. Am I right?'

'You are.'

'And it was recently changed?'

'Yes, it was. But not at my request. SudTelecom made the changes when the renovation work began at Roucas Blanc. New lines had to be installed.'

'So can you think of any reason why the Manichella sisters might have that new number?'

The question caught Virginie Cabrille by surprise. She stiffened just a fraction, then her shoulders straightened.

'I can think of no reason.'

'No explanation?'

'None that I can think of, Chief Inspector.'

Sitting beside her, Maître Paul was following the exchange but Jacquot could sense a certain discomfort creeping in. He glanced at the lawyer. He was right. There was a tension in the man's shoulders, a frown forming above his spectacles. Too much was going on here that he didn't know about, hadn't prepared for, too much of an edge in the slant of Jacquot's questions, which suggested that he was squaring up the nail before the hammer came crashing down. It was exactly the impression that Jacquot had wanted to convey. That of an iron-clad case. Except he knew it wasn't.

'And would I also be correct in assuming that you do not know the current whereabouts of Madame Claudine Eddé and her daughter, Midou Bécard?'

Maître Paul's frown deepened.

Virginie Cabrille put a hand on her lawyer's arm.

'The Chief Inspector's lover,' she explained. 'And her daughter. Apparently they're missing. Which is what all this bother is about. As I told you, the police seem to think that I have something to do with it. Isn't that so, Chief Inspector?'

'I don't think, Mademoiselle. I know.'

Then Jacquot turned to Maitre Paul.

'Which is why, Monsieur, your client will remain here at police headquarters until arrangements can be made to have her transferred to more suitable lodgings.'

Jacquot leaned across the table, switched off the tape recorder and retrieved the tape. He got to his feet, slid the tape into his pocket and then looked hard at Virginie Cabrille.

There was one more card to play, the only one left, and he played it.

'Unless, of course, you choose to help the authorities with their investigation, with any information you may have in your posses sion.'

There. He had said it. Nothing less than the offer of a deal, a way out for Virginie Cabrille, a chance for her to avoid prosecution. He hated doing it, hated every word, but time was short and he knew now that he had no option. Not with the clock ticking and Claudine's and Midou's safety at stake.

'As I say, it could all be very different, Mademoiselle,' he continued, less hostile now, desperate to get something from their encounter, even if it meant hand-feeding her the lines. 'Given your late father's professional activities, his . . . associations . . . Maybe you heard something? Perhaps a rumour in Marseilles?'

Jacquot could see that Virginie Cabrille knew exactly what he was doing, what he was offering.

'Nothing to do with you, of course. But useful, possibly valuable information to pass on to the authorities,' Jacquot said. 'Now that you come to think of it . . . ? Maybe some connection? Why, you could be out of here . . .'

As he spoke Virginie Cabrille smiled, a shrewd, calculating smile, as though they were sharing a private joke. The smile unnerved him. But then, the smile slid away and she started to shake her head.

'I regret not, Chief Inspector. Otherwise, of course, I would be only too happy to help.'

70

IT WAS LATE AFTERNOON AND the house in the hills above
Pélissanne was silent, with just an occasional stop-start shivering
and cranking from the old fridge in the kitchen, and the slow ticking
hum of a ceiling fan. Out on the back porch, where Marina nursed
a rum and Coke and smoked her last cigarette, it was a different
story. The sun might have slipped behind the ridge, leaving the
house and garden in shadow, but the heat stayed on, still and heavy,
the slope of garden and surrounding trees alive with the insistent
drilling buzz of insects.

It had been a long day, spent clearing the house, packing
suitcases, and burning anything that could be burnt in the
salon's open fireplace. Nothing to be forgotten, her sister had
said, nothing to be overlooked. The house to be left as clean as
they'd found it. And all the time, whenever an opportunity
presented itself, Marita had grumbled on about the car. In police
custody. With whatever they'd left inside. And their fingerprints
all over it.

'Just as well they dabbed the cousins then,' Marina had told her,
'and not us.'

But Marita would have none of it. They'd made a mistake, and it
was Marina's fault, and she knew that her elder sister would hold
it against her for as long as she could. One more thing to blame

on her. It had only stopped when Marita went upstairs for a rest, and Marina was left to supervise the fire in the hearth.

Now, sitting on the terrace, she was hungry and bored. And down to her last cigarette. There wasn't much left to drink either – just a splash of rum, no Coke, no wine, no coffee, no milk. And the fridge and cupboards as good as empty. Which made the drifting scent of a neighbourhood barbecue all the sharper.

As well as the hunger and boredom, Marina also had to acknowledge a growing sense of dissatisfaction; the thought of leaving the mainland for the family farm in the hills above Corte was not one that filled her with any great delight. When they'd first arrived on the mainland, the end of their adventure had seemed just a vague and distant prospect. But now that it was so close – a day or two away at the most – Marina felt a strange and unexpected sense of loss.

The truth was, she didn't really want to go home. She was enjoying it here, and there was nothing much for her in Tassafaduca. It was different for Marita, of course; she had the children, her husband (soon to be released from prison), and the farm to run. But for Marina there was nothing more to look forward to than the full-time care of their increasingly frail but demanding parents, playing second fiddle to her elder sister, and a weekly visit to Corte for the market. Hardly the kind of future to set her pulse racing.

As she sat there on the porch, Marina wondered whether Mademoiselle Virginie might set something up for her. Some kind of job at the house in Marseilles, like Tomas and Taddeus. A housekeeper perhaps, someone to keep the place in order. Or maybe she'd just split. Go her own way. Find a new life. As she stubbed out her cigarette, she decided she wouldn't be taking the ferry home. Somehow she'd give Marita the slip and . . .

'I've had an idea.' It was Marita.

Marina's heart leapt. Her sister had come down from her room, out onto the porch, and she hadn't heard a sound.

'*Merde alors*! You scared the life out of me . . .'

Marita chuckled, and pulled up a chair.

'You should be on your guard, *petite*.'

Marina always hated that diminutive '*petite*', but she knew that when her sister used it, it meant she was in a good mood. Their earlier contretemps appeared to have been forgotten.

'Idea?' Marina asked, noting that Marita had re-dyed her hair, back to its original dull black.

'How to dump the bodies. And get out of here. Get home.'

The first two propositions were of interest. The third was not.

'How?'

'We hire a taxi. Tonight. For a trip to Marseilles.'

'And the women?'

'In the boot.'

Marina considered this.

'What about the driver?' she asked. 'Won't he have something to say about it?'

'That's the beauty of the plan. We kill him too, soon as he gets here. Put him in the boot with the women. Then we drive to Marseilles, dump the car and walk away. By the time they're found, we'll be back on the farm.'

Oh, no, I won't, thought Marina.

Instead she said, 'We'll need to find the right kind of taxi.'

Marita frowned.

'The right kind of taxi?'

'Driver, I mean. The right kind of driver. A weed . . . a twig of a man. Not like that carpenter guy in Marseilles. Getting him up on that saw table, remember? Someone we can lift easily, toss in the boot. And we don't want some muscle bound *gorilla* to deal with either.'

Marita started to nod.

'Makes sense,' she said. 'And better make sure it's not a Citroën either.'

'Which means,' replied Marina, 'that we'd better check them out. Take one in to town, another back. Choose the most suitable. Which is just as well. I need to get some cigarettes. And whisky, too, if you want a drink. You finished your last bottle.'

'A drink would be good,' said Marita. 'You got a number?'

'In the kitchen drawer. Loads of cards.'

'Okay. But no hanging around. There and back. And Pélissanne, not Salon.'

71

THE CALL CAME THROUGH ON Brunet's phone at a little after seven o'clock. Jacquot, who was standing by his assistant's desk, picked it up.

'She here. Now.' The caller didn't bother to identify himself, his voice low and urgent. Jacquot could almost see the hand cupping the mouthpiece. The voice was also vaguely familiar.

'Who is this, please?'

'Gino Condotti. Pizzeria Blazots.'

Jacquot stiffened.

'The woman in the photo?'

'That's the one. Sitting right here. A table in the window.'

'Is she alone?'

'Not alone, no. She with a man, a young man. The taxi driver, I think.'

'Taxi driver?'

'There's an empty taxi in the car park.'

'Did they come in together?'

'I don' know. I arrive just a few minutes ago and they already here. Half their pizzas are gone, so maybe thirty, forty minutes.'

'Gino, try to keep them there as long as possible. Offer them coffees, some of those *biscotti* of yours. A drink on the house, okay?'

'*Si, si*. I unnerstand. But come quick, eh?'

Jacquot didn't waste a moment. He ordered up two squad cars, four *képis* and, on his way down to the underground car park, hauled Brunet out of the bunk room where he'd spent the last couple of hours. Ten minutes later they were thundering across the Durance bridge and looping round on to the autoroute, blasting through the *Péage* gate with sirens wailing and lights flashing. It took a further fourteen minutes to reach Salon, Jacquot briefing his team by radio as their convoy howled along the fast lane, sirens and lights doused as they neared their slip road exit.

Sunday evening traffic was light after the autoroute and it didn't take long for them to reach the Blazots trading estate. As instructed, the two marked squad cars took up positions off the main road, hidden down side streets and ready to give chase if the need arose, while Jacquot and Brunet coasted into the car park and came round the back of the block as though they were making a delivery at the trade entrance. Condotti was waiting for them, as agreed, and came hurrying over. His face said it all.

'They gone. They don' wan' coffee, or *biscotti*, or drinks. Just each other is what I'm sayin'. They out of here like their pants on fire.'

'*Merde*,' said Jacquot. 'How long?'

'Just a few minutes. Maybe five, six . . .'

'What kind of car?'

'A blue Mercedes. With a PelléCab light on the roof and the company name on the door panels. They a local firm, over in Pélissanne.'

'Any idea where they were going?'

'Somewhere private, I guess.'

'I mean which direction.'

'Back across the autoroute, that was the way they were headed.'

'You know where the office is, for Pellécab?'

'We got their card, all taxi cards – for customers who want a lift home. I bring it for you, here.' He pulled a business card from his shirt pocket and handed it to Jacquot through the driver's window. 'The cab number is eleven. I write it on the back.'

'Gino, *merci bien*,' said Jacquot, passing the card to Brunet.

'Tell her when she get her Loto winnings she come here and spend it, okay?'

Condotti gave Jacquot a wink, and then stood back as he swung back out into the car park and on to the road. Up ahead, the two squad cars pulled out to follow, keeping a hundred metres back as instructed.

It didn't take long to locate the PelléCab office, a whitewashed, single floor property on the corner of Gambetta and Charles de Gaulle in central Pélissanne. It wasn't much larger than a domestic garage, two of their cabs drawn up to the kerb, drivers sitting outside on an old sofa, smoking and chatting, waiting for calls.

Once again the two squad cars held back, pulling into a Post Office car-park near by to await instructions while Jacquot parked beside the cabs and went straight into the office. Its front door and every window stood wide open, to bring in some evening cool after the heat of the day which had left the small room stuffy and smelling of plastic, bad coffee and cigarette smoke.

The dispatcher, a worn-looking woman in her fifties, hair dyed red, face puffy and punctured like an old balloon, sat behind a wire-glass window and gave Jacquot a squinting look through a curl of cigarette smoke.

'I'm looking for a cab.'

'Then you come to the right place, Monsieur,' she said, with a look on her face. She'd just seen him get out of a car. What did he need a cab for?

'And a driver,' continued Jacquot. 'Number eleven.'

The woman sighed, rolled her shoulders, as though she'd known this wasn't a routine call, preparing herself for bad news.

'And you are?'

Jacquot showed his badge.

'What's he done now, then?'

'He's not in any trouble. It's the fare he picked up we want a word with. A young woman. It wouldn't have been more than an hour ago? I just need the pick-up address.'

'Well, he didn't get anything booked through here. And he's off tonight anyway.' The woman finished her cigarette and mashed it out in a tin ashtray.

'He moonlight?'

'They all moonlight, *chéri*. Scribble their own numbers on the back of our cards. Special rates. Not much we can do about it. Just so long as they turn up for their shifts when they're meant to.' She nodded past Jacquot at the drivers outside on the bench. 'The older ones are always the best, the most reliable. It's the young ones like Albert take advantage.'

'Albert?'

'Albert Garbachon. Al.'

'Can you call him in?'

'If he's in the car and got his radio on, sure. You want me to try?'

'Just say you got a fare for Aix and no one to take it.'

'Like that happens,' grunted the woman, picking up a desk mic and putting the call through.

'Al . . . Albert, you there? Got a fare for Aix, you interested? Everyone else is out.'

There was a crackle of static. She repeated the call, but there was no response.

'Either he's in it and switched off,' said the woman, 'or he's out playing.'

'You got a home address?'

'Sure,' she replied. 'Lives out on St-Cannat, with his mother. Can't remember the number but the house is painted pink and there's a palm tree out front. You can't miss it.'

72

THE PALM TREE WAS A sorry sight, set out on the pavement in a panelled wooden container that looked like it doubled as a waste bin, any sign of soil hidden beneath a layer of accumulated rubbish. The palm stood no more than two metres high, webbed with hairy bark, its thick collar of brown leaves drooping beneath a dozen dusty spears. The house behind it looked equally unloved, a single-storey rose-coloured villa surrounded by a green metal fence, the paint blistered and stained, the metal fence panels rusted and warped. A pair of gateless brick pillars framed the entrance to a short drive which led to a plastic, corrugated lean-to on the side of the building. Even without getting out of the car Jacquot could see there was no sign of a blue Mercedes.

Reaching for the radio mic, he issued his instructions to the squad cars that had pulled up behind him. One car to go back and stake out the taxi office, the other to drive round town. If either team saw the Mercedes, they were to make no move, just call it in. As for Jacquot and Brunet, they stayed where they were, a few metres back from the palm tree, and settled down to watch and wait.

Taking advantage of the stop, Brunet flicked back his seat and closed his eyes while Jacquot smoked three Gitanes on the trot, tapping their unfiltered ends against the driver's door panel before lighting up. It was an agonising delay and he found it hard to contain his impatience and anxiety, asking himself the same questions over and over again, and always persuading himself he was giving truthful answers.

Were they still alive? Yes.

Were they close? Yes.

Was he going to find them? Yes

And save them? Yes, yes, yes.

It all seemed so unlikely, sitting there in a squad car on a Sunday evening, on the broad, empty expanse of boulevard St-Cannat, watching an occasional car slide past, not a single pedestrian, the only sounds a whistle of breath from Brunet, a lazy chatter of cicadas and the distant sound of a television. Yet somewhere close by, not too far from here, Claudine and Midou were being held by two cold, callous killers who'd already murdered six people in the space of a few months.

Claudine and Midou.

Soon, God; let him get to them soon, he prayed.

Before it was too late.

He was reaching for his fourth cigarette when he saw the Mercedes in his rear-view mirror. It cruised past them and lurched up over the curb to park in the driveway of the rose-coloured villa. Brakelights went out, the car shuddered as the engine was switched off. But only one person got out – the driver, Albert Garbachon. He wore jeans, sneakers and a tucked-in green polo shirt with the collar up. A hefty gold chain swung from his wrist.

He was locking the car when Jacquot came up to him. He turned with a startled, apprehensive look, as though Jacquot were some loan shark's heavy come to collect a debt, or, more likely, an aggrieved husband dropping by for a chat.

'Albert Garbachon? Al?'

'*Oui, c'est moi. Et vous?*'

Jacquot flashed his badge, looked the man over. Late twenties, tall and lanky, with narrow shoulders, thin arms and a solid tyre of fat over the top of his jeans. He looked like an athlete out of training, gone to seed. His hair was black and hung over his eyes in a curling fringe, and on one side of his neck, in the open collar of his polo shirt, was a slanting oval bruise – you could almost see the teeth marks.

'Been in the wars?' asked Jacquot, nodding at the bruise as Brunet joined them.

'So? What's it to you?' Garbachon replied, rubbing the side of his neck against the collar of his shirt, as though the movement might somehow remove the blemish.

'The person you were with. This her?' cut in Brunet, showing him the photo.

Garbachon gave it a look, nodded.

From the house came a woman's voice.

'Albert, *c'est toi?*'

'*Oui, Maman, j'arrive. Un moment.*' He turned back to them.

'We've been waiting for you,' said Jacquot.

'Been out. Up in the hills,' he said, and a slow smile curled over his lips.

Jacquot glanced into the Mercedes. A travel rug lay crumpled on the back seat. With his mother at home, and his passenger unlikely to invite him into her house, it wasn't difficult to work out what Albert Garbachon had been up to in there.

'You ever pick her up before?' he asked.

Garbachon gave another smirk and shook his head.

'First time,' he replied, hard pressed to keep the swagger out of his voice. First time and he scores. Dinner to boot. 'But she's booked me for later. A round-trip to Marseilles.'

'You got an address? Where you picked her up, dropped her off?'

'Up near Aurons. On the St-Croix road.'

'House name? Number?'

'She was waiting for me at the side of the road.'

'Any houses close by?'

'A few. Up there it's hard to tell.' Garbachon gave a shrug. 'You just glimpse the odd roof, back off the road, that's it. Probably one of those.'

'Sounds like you're going to have to come with us then,' said Jacquot, glancing at his watch. 'Better tell your mother.'

73

WITH AL GARBACHON IN THE back seat providing directions, and the two squad cars a safe distance behind them, Jacquot took the Aurons road and drove up into the Pélissanne hills, a series of limestone bluffs and craggy ridges rising above the treeline, the road a dusty single track winding through the woods. It was the same road that Jacquot and Brunet had taken that very morning, only this time they were taking it the other way.

Coming round a steep, sharp bend that had had Jacquot clashing the gears that morning, Garbachon pointed ahead.

'Up there, by those cypresses. That's where I picked her up. And dropped her too.'

Without stopping Jacquot drove past, glancing to his right. As far as he could see there was a slope beyond the trees, a hidden gully-like depression dropping away from the road. There could have been a dozen houses down there, and you'd never have known about it. Twenty metres further on they passed an opening to the right, just about wide enough to take a car, and then, on the other side of the road, a second opening on the left. Both clearly led to unseen houses, but in which one were the Manichella sisters living? And in which one would he find Claudine and Midou? If they were there at all.

'Any ideas?' asked Brunet, turning round to Garbachon. 'When you dropped her back here, did you see which direction she took?'

The cabbie shook his head.

'I just stopped by the cypresses, like she told me, and she got out. That's it. I drove off, checked the rear-view mirror, and there she was, right where I dropped her, watching me go. I didn't see where she went after that.'

'Then we'll have to check both sides,' replied Jacquot, waiting for the next bend before pulling in to what looked like the remains of an old quarry where all three cars could be easily parked. Five minutes later the two squad cars pulled in beside them and Jacquot told them what they were going to do.

'The house on the right first. If it's clear we'll head down to the cypresses. It'll be one or the other. You,' he said, turning to Garbachon. 'You stay here and watch the cars, *compris*?'

Checking their guns and lowering the volume on their radios, Jacquot, Brunet and the four *képis* set off down the road, slipping under the cover of the trees at the first opportunity. Thanks to the loud buzzing of insects their progress through the sloping woods and tinder dry leaf litter was less noisy than it might have been, and pretty soon they were huddled behind some rocks on the edge of the first property. It was an old country *mas* with ivy spreading across the walls, blue shutters and a solid wood door. There was no car visible in the driveway and no sign of life save for the warm scent of a barbecue.

'Spread out through the trees and keep me covered,' said Jacquot, drawing his gun from its holster and checking the breech. He flicked off the safety and, stepping from the trees, he made for the nearest part of the building, moving quickly, keeping low in case anyone was watching. Slowly, carefully, he made his way round the side of the house, peeping through the windows, hoping to see the sisters before they saw him. He was close to the back of the house when a man's voice rang out.

'Here! What are you up to? What do you think you're doing?'

Even if he hadn't been speaking it, Jacquot would have known that the man coming out of the undergrowth buttoning the flies of his shorts was English. He wore a blue Chelsea football shirt, short socks and sandals, his face and arms and legs as red as a plum tomato. The house was clearly a holiday rental and the man coming towards him, wiping the fingers of one hand on his shirt and brandishing a set of barbecue tongs in the other, was well within his rights to ask who the hell Jacquot was. When he saw the gun, however, he faltered, started to back away, but Jacquot slipped it into its belt holster and, straightening up from a crouch, pulled his police badge from his pocket.

'Chief Inspector Daniel Jacquot, Cavaillon Regional Crime Squad,' he said, in English. 'And you are?'

'Bill Somers,' said the man. 'And that's my wife, Pauline, and the kids.'

Jacquot turned to see a woman in her mid-forties, more browned by the sun than reddened like her husband. She was dressed in a blue swimsuit and matching sarong, straw hat and plastic flip-flops, and had appeared from round the back of the house. She was carrying a breadboard, a carving knife and baguette. Two young boys, seven or eight, also dressed in blue Chelsea strip, peeped out from behind her, eyes wide. Jacquot wondered whether they'd seen the gun.

'Monsieur Somers, I am so sorry for this . . . intrusion.' He looked back to the trees where he had left Brunet and the *képis* and waved them out. Somers, his wife and kids watched in astonishment as the five men appeared from the trees and came towards them.

'What's going on then?'

Taking Somers' arm, Jacquot led him over to his wife, introduced himself once again, apologised for any inconvenience and said that he was looking for two women, one tall, one short, mid forties, late thirties, called Manichella.

'Don't know their names, but that'll likely be them across the road,' said Mrs Somers. 'Keep to themselves, they do. And no one else up here.'

'Boot-face and Gina, we call them,' said Somers. 'That's Gina

Lollobrigida, see? Looks just like her, she does. When she was younger, of course.'

'How long have they been there?' asked Jacquot.

'Here when we arrived,' said Mrs Somers. 'We thought they lived there. Locals. Being French and all. Went round at the start of the holiday, just to say "*bonjour*", but it was clear they didn't appreciate the friendly visit.'

'Never been back,' said her husband. 'See them every now and again, driving past, but that's it.'

'You happen to recall the car they drive?'

'Black VW. Beat-up old thing,' replied Somers, looking past Jacquot at Brunet and the uniformed *képis*. 'So what they been up to then? Something big, by the look of you lot hiding in the trees.'

'Drugs,' said Jacquot. 'We had a report that they were selling drugs.'

'Oh, drugs, is it?' said Somers, clearly disappointed. 'Like being back in London, eh, Paulie?' He chuckled. 'Place is heaving with them back there. Here too, by the sound of it. You can't go anywhere . . .'

'And have you see them recently, Monsieur Somers? Madame?'

'Last night. Late. We was out on the porch, Paulie and me, and we heard their car pull in, doors slamming. Wasn't a VW, though. Different engine sound. You can tell those old VWs. Wheezy, aren't they?'

'Around midnight?'

'Thereabouts. Bit later maybe. You're on holiday, you don't check your watch too much.'

'And today?'

'This afternoon,' said Somers's wife, not wanting to be left out. 'I was coming back from town and there was this taxi pulled over. One of them getting in. Gina, I think it was. Couple of hours later the cab was back. Didn't see it, but heard it.'

Jacquot took this in, nodded.

'Well, thank you for your help, Monsieur, Madame. And I am so sorry for the mix up. It seems we have the wrong house.'

Pauline caught his eye and smiled coyly.

'Gave me quite a start, you did.'

'Again, I can only apologise, Madame. But for now, I would be most grateful if you would stay here, near the house. Please, under no circumstances, leave the property. Just . . . stay in your garden and enjoy your barbecue. Either I or one of my men will drop by later, so that you'll know it's safe.'

And with that, he gave Mrs Somers a small bow, smiled at her husband and followed Brunet and the *képis* round to the front of the house.

74

'IT'S TIME TO MARK THEM,' said Marita to her sister.

They were sitting at the terrace table, cases packed and left by the front door. Marita had a glass of whisky, Marina a rum and Coke. She had just mashed out a cigarette and was blowing a cone of grey smoke into the sky. Her hair was still wet from dying it back to black.

For the two sisters there was just one final job to do. And then it was over.

'What time is the driver coming back?' asked Marita, finishing the last of her whisky.

'I told him midnight,' replied Marina.

Marita glanced at the clock in the kitchen. A little after nine. She nodded.

'Plenty of time,' she said. 'Are you ready?'

'Ready,' replied Marina.

Getting up from the table, they reached for their Berettas and fixed silencers to the muzzles. Marita did the job swiftly, but Marina was not so slick.

'It looks so easy in the films,' she said, trying to line up the correct end of the silencer with the tip of the muzzle. Two steady hands just didn't seem to be enough.

Marita sighed. She was about to take the gun and do it for her when the join and twist action was successfully negotiated.

'Don't forget the marker pen,' she said, and led the way back through the kitchen.

Though it was still light outside, just a few pin-prick stars starting to show, the interior of the house was dark and gloomy, the door leading to the basement lost in shadow beneath the staircase. Marita unlocked it, reached for the light switch and started down the stairs, Marina closing the door behind her, juggling gun and marker pen.

The basement occupied just half of the ground floor area, where the slope of the land allowed sufficient headroom to make it habitable. In years gone by, livestock had been accommodated there – goats, a cow or two, and horses for the plough. Now its floor had been levelled and a thin concrete skin laid over bare earth, the low-ceilinged space divided into three rooms leading off a short passage. On the left side of this passage were two doors – to a boiler and utility room, and to a smaller space almost completely filled by a large deep-freeze cabinet. The third door, standing on the right of the passageway, was the one that Marita now opened, stooping just a little so she didn't bang her head on the doorframe, and reaching for the light switch. Marina had no such trouble.

The room was long and narrow and lit by a single neon tube. An old kitchen dresser had been placed along one wall and a workbench on the other. The shelves of the dresser were packed with glass jars filled with nails, screws, all sorts of rusting bits and pieces, old tin boxes and tilting flowerpot towers. On the workbench was a clamp-vice, a blade grinder and a small rotary saw, the wall above it a pinboard panel racked with tools. Although the basement had a concrete floor the smell of damp earth was still strong, the cellar's stone walls flaking with old distemper, its ceiling hung with dust-thickened hammocked spider webs.

At the far end of the room, past the dresser and the workbench, were the two women, Claudine and Midou. They were bound by duct tape to two kitchen chairs, facing away from each other, arms

331

secured behind their backs, wrists heavily taped. As a precaution, to prevent them working on their bindings, their fingertips had also been taped. It looked as though they were wearing silver gloves.

As the door opened and the light flickered on, both women turned their heads to watch Marita and Marina come in. It was only the second time the sisters had come down to see them. On the first occasion, Marita had brought some buttered bread and water. She'd removed the tape from their mouths and fed them herself, one after the other, allowing them choking gulps of water from a tipped jug. Then she'd re-taped their mouths, switched off the light and locked the door. The second time the two sisters had come down together, with a slop bucket. While Marina held a gun on Midou, Claudine was cut loose and encouraged to take advantage of this, with a single warning that if she did anything foolish her daughter would be shot.

Stiff from being bound in a chair for so long, with headaches from the Dyethelaspurane still gently thumping, and certain in the knowledge that these two women would do exactly what they said without the least scruple or delay, neither Claudine nor Midou had done anything to annoy their captors. Meekly they had used the bucket, been given more water, then been re-tied and left alone in the darkness again.

In much the same way that they had accomplished the slop bucket visit, Marina now held a gun to Midou's head while her sister cut away the tape holding Claudine's arms and ankles to the chair, helped her to her feet and led her to the far wall. Turning her back to this so that she was facing down the length of the room, Marita then tied her hands in front of her with the end of a length of rope hanging down from a metal hook. Taking the other end of the rope, Marita hauled in the slack through the hook until Claudine's arms were raised straight above her head, the silken sleeves of her *ao dai* falling past her elbows. As her weight tautened the rope, Marita tied it off on a bracket fixed to the wall, leaving Claudine with two options: she could either keep her feet flat on the floor leaving her arms stretched painfully above her head, or stand on tiptoes to ease

332

the weight from her elbows, wrists and shoulders. Whichever option she chose, she remained powerless to do anything more, like a writhing snake held by the tail, a wild, panicked expression in her eyes as she watched Marita repeat the operation with her daughter – another hook, another length of rope, hauling the arms upwards – trying to speak through the duct tape but managing only tearful whimpers of protest.

'You mark for Taddeus,' said Marita, when the two women were secured, side by side. 'And I'll do Tomas.'

Pulling the cap off the marker pen, Marina knelt in front of Claudine and, licking her lips in concentration, drew a single cross on her crumpled, dirty *ao dai*, just above the left knee, adding two more crosses to her arm and shoulder, a final cross drawn just a few centimetres above Claudine's right eyebrow.

When she had finished she handed the pen to Marita and watched as her sister marked out the corresponding wounds on Midou that had brought down their brother Tomas.

Four crosses on one of the women, three on the other.

And then it was done.

The two sisters stepped away, Marina going back to the workbench and picking up her gun. Checking the mechanism with a gentle but business-like snick-snick she waited for Marita to join her.

In a minute there would be blood. Marina could feel the excitement, almost shivering with the pulse of power.

'Are you ready?' asked Marita, coming to stand beside her.

Marina took a deep, steadying breath.

'Oh, yes,' she replied, and raised the gun in both hands to take aim.

75

JACQUOT WAS RATTLED. HE WAS also tired, more than a little frightened and, for the first time he could remember, running short on confidence. What made it worse was not that they'd targeted the wrong house, but the way the Englishman, Somers, had come from nowhere, taken him so completely by surprise. If it had been the right house and those barbecue tongs had been a knife, an axe, a gun, the game would have been over. That basic mistake, that moment of carelessness, had really thrown him.

But he was angry too, a low, simmering agitation that made him grit his teeth and narrow his eyes, and try hard not to acknowledge his beating heart but think instead of all the things he might do to the Manichella sisters and Virginie Cabrille if anything – anything at all – happened to Claudine and Midou. He was certain they were there, in the second house, and that closeness, coupled with his inability to break down the door immediately, right now, without any further delay, and free them, fed his anger. Equally nourishing was the horrible possibility that they might not be there, might have been hidden elsewhere, and were even now dead or dying.

The sisters' last laugh.

Virginie Cabrille's final bravo.

In the next few moments he would know.

At the top of the Somers' drive, the six men gathered in the shadows and looked down the road towards the line of cypresses and, beyond it, the next turning. Jacquot wasn't taking any chances. Singling out one of the older *képis*, he told him to get back to the cars and radio Cavaillon for back-up, as well as all available squads from Salon and an ambulance.

'The *képi* gave a swift and, Jacquot suspected, relieved salute and set off down the road at an energetic jog, as though keen to be far enough away to be out of earshot if Jacquot changed his mind.

Jacquot looked at the remaining men.

'Everyone ready? So let's go.'

Crossing the road at a run they reached the trees and started forward down the slope, Jacquot and Brunet leading the way, the sky now starting to darken, the buzz of insects falling away. Half way down the incline the house finally came into view, its low pantiled roof cut by branches and framed by tree trunks. It looked like a distant swimming pool, rust-coloured not blue, set in shadow. And not a light showing. Something still, silent and . . . evil.

It was, Jacquot decided, a perfect hide-out. Far enough from the road and so thickly bordered by trees that you could walk or drive right past it and have no idea that it was there, a steep limestone bluff rising beyond. No lights would show through the trees or above the incline, no sound was likely to reach beyond its walls. Pausing on the slope, with maybe twenty metres of trees before the land levelled into the front yard, Jacquot briefed his team – two of the *képis* to go round to the back of the house and one to stay where he was and watch the drive – while he and Brunet carried on ahead.

With every crouching step, the sharper, more focussed, Jacquot became, listening out for any sound, watching for any movement, momentarily distracted by the flitting passage of a bat.

'Looks dead,' whispered Brunet, squatting down beside him, both men giving the two *képis* sufficient time to take up position at the back of the house. Away to their left, among the trees, could be heard a distant whisper of their progress, the shuffle of leaves, the occasional crack of a twig that made Jacquot wince. Finally it was silent again.

'How do you want to do it?' asked Brunet, scanning the darkened windows across the front yard.

'To tell the truth, I don't know. Maybe just . . . go up and ring the doorbell.'

'Good a way as any,' replied Brunet. 'Go for it. I'll keep you covered.'

Jacquot gripped his colleague's arm, gave it a squeeze.

'See you inside.'

'*Que oui.*' You bet.

As quietly as he could, Jacquot stepped forward, out of the trees, joining the narrow track that led down from the road and opened into the villa's sloping front yard. There was no car, and no garage that he could see, no sign of habitation. Glancing back, he tried to make out Brunet but the shadows were deepening and his assistant was lost in them.

Moving forward, out in the open, uncomfortably aware of every step, Jacquot slid his gun from its holster and took in the house. Whoever owned it, he thought, had taken little care of it. Snaking weedy tendrils had crawled forward into the gravel, the paint on the wooden shutters was peeling badly, and one of the two urns either side of the front door had cracked in half, spilling soil on to the step. There was a stale, sun-slaked smell to the place – of dry earth and abandonment. Maybe, thought Jacquot, like the owner of the VW, the person who lived here had been called away for a longer time than he or she had expected.

Just a few metres from the front door, he had a change of heart. Rather than ring the doorbell, he decided to skirt the property, take a look around it first. In an instant he was glad he had. Turning down the right hand side of the house he came to a kitchen door, a bulging black bin liner set on its step, knotted at the top. After the leafy scent of the woods and the sun-dried staleness of the front yard, the warm smell of rotting food was a sudden and forceful reminder that this house might look deserted, but it clearly wasn't.

He peered through the glass panel of the kitchen door but the room was too dark to make out anything. He tried the handle. The door opened. No lock. But he closed it again, unwilling to make his move, wondering, as he continued down the side of the house whether they were watching him, the sisters, like that Somers man, waiting for their moment.

He reached the back yard and, for the first time, felt a human presence, there on the decked terrace jutting out from the house. Two canvas-backed chairs set at a square wooden table. A magazine. Two glasses.

Keeping close to the back wall, he climbed the steps to the deck, placing his feet carefully, feeling for squeaks and creaks. As he drew closer he could see that the magazine was curled open at the horoscopes, that there were small cubes of ice still to melt in the glasses, and that the big square ashtray was filled with a jumble of lipstick-stained stubs, one of which smouldered gently.

They had been here, the sisters, just moments before, the glass terrace door pulled to one side, open, inviting.

This was the way they had gone.

And Jacquot followed, flicking off the safety on his Beretta.

76

'YOU MISSED. HOW COULD YOU miss?'

Marita started to chuckle. Shaking her head in disbelief, she stepped forward, crossing the room towards Claudine and pointing out a saucer-shaped chip of stone removed from the wall behind her.

'By a metre! A sitting target, right in front of you, and you miss.'

She walked back to the door, took up position beside Marina and, holding the gun in both hands, levelled it on Midou.

'My turn,' she said. 'For Tomas.'

The gun spat and jerked, the tip of the silencer snapping back and upwards.

But the aim was true.

At the far end of the room the two women let out muffled screams, and Midou seemed to quiver, then flung back her head, hopping on the spot, tiptoes scrabbling for purchase as a widening red stain spread down the leg of her jeans from just above the knee – the first of the wounds that Marita had plugged in her brother's naked body all those months ago in a farmhouse kitchen in Corsica.

'*Voilà*,' she said. 'That's how you do it.'

As Marita stood aside and Marina took her place, the two bound women at the other end of the room shrieked and squirmed.

'A moving target,' said Marita, as Claudine scrabbled this way and that, desperate to avoid the coming shot. 'Stay still, *chérie*, or it may be the worse for you,' she called out. 'Stay still and take it, like our brothers.'

'For Taddeus,' whispered Marina, levelling the gun, taking a bead on the marker-pen cross on the leg of Claudine's *ao dai*, the cross that she'd missed the first time.

With a slow hiss of released breath, Marina squeezed the trigger, and the gun leapt in her hands.

This time there was no mistake.

The impact of the bullet spun Claudine off her feet and left her twisting helplessly at the end of her rope, a line of blood trickling from beneath her silken trouser leg, down between her toes. A low, disbelieving whine rose from her throat and her leg trembled and jerked as though a jolt of electricity was passing through it.

'Two down, five to go,' said the elder sister, taking up position, legs apart, looking down the barrel of her Beretta for the next cross, higher up on Midou's arm.

'Wait,' said Marina, the shiver of excitement in her voice unmistakable. '*Un moment. Attend.* Candles. We need candles. Some atmosphere. Something festive.'

She crossed to the old kitchen dresser on the left-hand wall, sorted through the glass jars on the shelves, pulled open the two drawers, ran her fingers through the mess inside. But there were no candles.

'There are some upstairs. *Reste*, I'll get them,' she said, and was out of the room before Marita could stop her, footsteps sounding down the passage, up the wooden stairs.

'Kids,' said Marita to her targets at the end of the room. 'Always a game. Always drama,' she sighed. 'But sometimes the real drama doesn't need any props. Don't you agree?'

And she raised her gun, took careful aim on Midou's slender arm and squeezed the trigger.

'For Tomas,' she whispered.

77

JACQUOT HAD LEFT THE KITCHEN and was halfway across the *salon*, the tiled floor deadening his footfall, when, out of the corner of his eye, he spotted four suitcases standing by the front door. He'd been heading for the dining room, through an archway leading off the *salon*, but changed direction and crossed over to the suitcases. They looked new, their bulging blue fabric sides unmarked, the two smaller cases with extendable handles for wheeling along. There were no stickers and no labels, the zippered lids on all four bags secured with tiny padlocks. It was then that he heard a door creak open, somewhere below him, and the scuffle of shoes.

With nowhere to hide, Jacquot tucked himself in behind a closed door beneath the main staircase. He assumed it led to the basement, and he was right. On the other side of it, footsteps pounded up the wooden stairs and the door burst open so forcefully that it banged against the toe of his shoe, swinging back and slamming shut. As it did so Jacquot saw a short, dark-haired woman dressed in jeans, boots and jumper stop in her tracks and start to turn in his direction, as though suddenly, subliminally, aware that there was someone behind her.

And as she turned, bringing up a gun, Jacquot sprang from his hiding place and, judging himself close enough, swung out with his own gun hand. He didn't aim the strike, it was simply instinctive, a wild lunging swipe. And at first it seemed to be too low, glancing off the woman's shoulder, only for the pistol grip in his fist to connect with a mighty crack against her temple. Her head snapped sideways and she dropped on the spot, caught round the waist by Jacquot who could only watch in dismay as her gun spun from her grip, flew high into the air and came tumbling down, far out of reach. On the tiled floor it would have clattered dreadfully, might even have fired off a round, but instead it landed on the sofa, bounced a couple of times and then lay still.

Bundling the woman onto the same sofa, Jacquot knelt beside her and turned her face into what little light there was. Though the hair was now a different colour, he recognised the face immediately – Julie, the woman who, the evening before, had come to find him in the bleachers. In her black polo shirt and black trousers, with her name tag and security badge and business-like clipboard. He remembered, too, the newspaper picture that Brunet had sent from Ajaccio. Marina. The shorter and younger of the two Manichella sisters. Receiving first prize at an agricultural show for the best honey. But she didn't look so happy now. Her eyes were shut, her mouth open, and the side of her head was matted with blood, trickling down the hairline and pooling into her ear. Jacquot felt for a pulse in her neck, and found it. She was alive, but clearly out of the game.

It was in the heartbeat silence that followed their tussle, kneeling beside the sofa, that Jacquot heard a distant cry that seemed to rise up from behind the closed basement door. There was a pleading in the sound, a muffled note of despair and agony and terror. It was a frighteningly familiar sound, too, and Jacquot knew at once it was Claudine. Jumping up from the sofa, he raced to the basement door and turned the handle. The lock was new and oiled and it gave without a sound, the hinges opening without a squeak. The stairs, too, did not let him down – firm and thick and solid – and just a few silent seconds later he stepped from the last one and found himself in a long, neon-lit passageway. There were three doors, two closed on the left and one open on the right. It was from this door that the low, desperate moaning came. And the unmistakable 'click-click' sound of a gun's breech mechanism.

In an instant Jacquot was at the door – Claudine and Midou just two bloodied bodies twisting from a ceiling beam at the end of the room, and the elder Manichella sister standing with her back to him.

'*Vite, vite, chérie*, you are missing all the fun,' she said, and glanced over her shoulder.

'Police,' called Jacquot. 'Put your weapon down.'

She didn't, of course.

And Jacquot knew she wouldn't.

Which was why his Beretta stayed on her every centimetre of the way, as she dropped into a crouch, spun round and swept up her gun.

They squeezed their triggers just a fraction of a second apart – the crashing blast of Jacquot's Beretta filling the room, covering the no less lethal *phut* from Marita's silenced gun.

For a moment the two shooters looked at one another.

Then they crumpled to the floor.

78

JACQUOT SAW HIS SHOT HIT Marita a few centimetres below
her left collarbone, just off centre, and he watched her jerk backwards under the impact, gun skittering across the floor, her head
coming down with a mighty crack on the concrete.

But that same moment, still deafened by the blast of his own
gunshot, Jacquot felt a massive blow against his left hip. For a
moment he stood there in the doorway, like an old man steadying
himself againt the motion of a train, then tottered back a step and
fell.

The pain of his landing, in a sitting position against the open
door, was excruciating and, eyes wide with shock and disbelief, he
felt what he knew was a wet pulse of warm blood flow across his
skin and settle between his legs. Looking down at his lap he could
see the side and front of his linen trousers soaking up blood in a
widening scarlet stain and he wondered, sitting there blankly, if he
was going to die.

But the pain was too great for death, he decided. In death any
pain would be numbed, surely? And there was certainly no numb-
ness about the agony lancing like a dagger through his left hip. He
also knew for a fact that a coldness seeped through the body in
the moments before death. But he didn't feel cold, just that soaking
sticky warmth. Laying his gun aside, he raised his left arm and let

the fingers of his right hand explore the source of the blood and the pain, gently fumbling at the torn pocket of his trousers.

And there it was . . . a raw, delicate opening at the tips of his fingers.

But that wasn't all. Further back was another scorching fumarole of pain from the torn flesh of the exit wound, an open flapping hole far wider and more ragged than the entry wound.

Jacquot felt a rush of shock at the damage he had found. He really had been shot, and shot quite badly. But the next instant he was aware of something infinitely more harrowing, a growing wail from the other side of the room, its volume and insistence breaking into his dulled consciousness.

From where he sat he lifted his head to see Claudine struggling against her bonds and screaming at him through her silvery duct-tape gag – a repeated, two-syllable phrase that could as easily have been 'Daniel' as 'Midou' or 'Help us'. And then he saw Midou, beside her mother, her body hanging from its bindings, her head on her chest, her white T-shirt and white rhinestoned jeans stained a horrible scarlet.

It took only a minor attempt to get to his feet to persuade Jacquot that he'd never be able to manage it. The pain shafting through his pelvis like a thousand white hot steely speartips made it abundantly clear that such an attempt would be cruelly dealt with. The only thing he could manage was an elbowed haul across the floor, on his stomach, dragging his legs behind him.

'*J'arrive. J'arrive.*' I'm coming, I'm coming, he called out, surprised by how dry his mouth was, how constricted his throat, and with every push back with his elbows, propelling himself forward, he flicked out a tongue over lips that felt suddenly hot and parched. Finally, panting from the effort, the points of his elbows painfully skinned by the rough concrete, he reached Claudine, the side of his head brushing against her leg.

'It's okay, it's okay . . . soon have you down,' he managed to say, but he knew at a glance that that was easier said than done.

The only way he could release her was by reaching up to undo the rope knotted around its bracket. As gently as he could he rolled onto his back, sobbing with the pain, and pressed his palms to the floor, pushing himself up against the wall, centimetre by centimetre – the back of his head, his shoulders – until he could reach up with his hand, find the knot and start to untie it.

Twist and unwind, twist and unwind he went.

'Nearly there, nearly there,' he called out, his voice croaky and tight, while Claudine hopped round to face him, raising herself on tiptoes and stretching up her arms to provide some slack. 'Another twist and another . . .'

Then, suddenly, the knot was loose and the rope was pulled from his hand as Claudine tugged it clear of the hook and dropped down beside him, favouring her good leg and pulling the tape from her fingers and mouth.

'You're hurt . . . She shot you . . .' she said, now tearing at the rope around her wrists. When her hands were free, she lifted back the corner of his jacket and stared at the spread of blood.

'Oh, *mon Dieu!*' she cried.

'It's not as bad as it looks,' he said. 'And you? Your leg? You okay?'

'I'm fine, I'm fine. It kind of hurts but doesn't. Even when I move it. Just . . . hot.'

'Can you get to Midou? Can you get her . . . ?'

But before he could finish, Claudine was off, levering herself up against the wall and hopping over to her daughter, one leg bloodied, limp and useless.

In seconds she had the rope holding Midou off its bracket and, taking the weight with one hand, reached out her other to catch her daughter round the waist. Letting go the rope the two of them came to a slumped rest in a puddle of blood.

'She's not moving, Daniel. She's unconscious . . .' There was fear and panic in Claudine's voice.

'She'll be okay. It's just shock,' he croaked, praying it was true as he palmed himself over to them, hands sticky and slippery with blood, his and Claudine's. 'Which is good, it's good; it's blanked her out. No pain.'

When he reached them he took in Midou's wounds – the first on the side of her thigh a few centimetres above her knee, the second just below the elbow where it had clearly shattered one of the bones in her forearm. Both entry and exit wounds dripped with blood.

'Just two shots, right? Two shots? That's all?' he asked Claudine, looking to see if there were any other wounds on Midou.

'Just the two,' confirmed Claudine, cradling her daughter. '*Grâce à Dieu. Grâce à Dieu.* I thought we were dead. Finished. It was . . .' Tears streamed down her face; tears of joy, of fear, of pain, Jacquot couldn't tell. 'Thank God you got here, Daniel. Thank you, thank you . . . and thank you, God.'

'She'll be fine, she'll be fine,' he said, wrapping an arm round Claudine's shoulders, as much for his own comfort as hers, the relief that he had got to them in time, and that she and Midou were both safe, washing over him in waves. 'But we need to get her to a hospital before she loses too much blood,' he continued, starting to unbuckle his belt. 'Here, help me pull it through,' he said, handing the buckle to Claudine and angling his hips. 'We can use it as a tourniquet.'

As Claudine tugged the belt free, Jacquot grunted with pain at each jerk. He could feel sweat popping out of his brow, seeping through his hair and running down his chest. It felt as though his body was leaking, with sweat and with blood. But with one final, jarring tug the belt was free, and Claudine was looping it around Midou's thigh, slipping the leather tongue through the buckle and pulling it tight.

'Can you get upstairs?' he asked, wincing with the pain. 'I've got men out there, waiting. They may even have heard my shot. They'll help.'

'Of course, of course,' said Claudine, passing Midou into his arms and starting to lever herself up. 'Will you be okay?'

'I'll be fine. Don't worry. Just go to the front or back door and start shouting.'

But it wasn't to be.

Claudine wasn't going anywhere.

'I'm afraid, *mes chers*, that your men will be no help at all,' came a light, teasing voice.

Jacquot and Claudine spun round.

Standing in the doorway, a gun in her hand, was Virginie Cabrille.

79

'MY, MY, WHAT A MESS you've made, Chief Inspector.'

Virginie stepped into the room and pushed Marita's shoulder with the toe of her shoe. The crumpled body moved, but did not respond.

'How ever will I clear it all up?' she said, looking around the room, tut-tutting to herself. 'Then again,' she continued, her eyes finally settling on Jacquot, 'maybe I don't need to. *Enfin*, it rather speaks for itself, don't you think?' She waved the gun at the body on the floor, at Jacquot, Claudine and Midou. 'Two sisters, driven by revenge, and you, desperate to protect your family. A harrowing crime. A shoot-out. And not a single survivor, no witnesses . . . I'm sure we can make it look convincing enough, wouldn't you say?'

Through the pulsing fiery pain in his hip and thigh, Jacquot tried to take it in, make sense of what was happening. It didn't take him long. He might have got rid of the sisters, but with Virginie Cabrille taking their place he, Claudine and Midou were as good as dead.

And she was right, Jacquot realised. She wouldn't have to do a thing. Just shoot them all where they were. It might be difficult for a crime-scene team to accurately read the passage of play and come up with a plausible explanation – who, when, how? – but whatever their findings Jacquot knew it was unlikely that Mademoiselle Cabrille would ever be called on it.

'How did you get out?' he asked, wincing as he tried to straighten himself, turn and face her. The question was academic, almost laughably irrelevant, but he knew with a chill, terrible certainty that all he could do now was play for time. 'You were not to be released. I made that quite clear.'

'Not clear enough, it seems. At least, not to your local examining magistrate. A Monsieur Fourcade, I believe. Since he had been provided with no information from you, and no evidence, and since he was unable to contact you to confirm the charges laid against me, he had little option but to grant my lawyer's request for my release into his care. As a result, I am currently recovering from my ordeal at Le Mas Bleu, with my lover, who'll be only too happy to provide an alibi for this brief visit.'

Moving past Marita's sprawled body, Virginie Cabrille went to the kitchen dresser, wiped the edge of it with her fingers and leant against it, Marina's gun swinging idly from her fingers.

'Of course, I had to give a sworn undertaking to return to police headquarters tomorrow morning for further questioning from you. Which, naturally, I will do. Anything to help the authorities.' She gave an icy little chuckle, her black eyes twinkling with mischief. 'But since you won't be making that meeting, and since there really isn't any evidence to speak of – I'm right, arent I? – I'd say I'm free and clear. Wouldn't you?'

'What happened to my men?'

Virginie gave a brittle little laugh.

'Men? Really? But they went down like little puppy dogs. The two down the road I locked in the boot of a squad car. The others, I regret, were not so fortunate.'

Jacquot was stunned, couldn't believe it. She'd killed four men? Brunet and the three *képis*? It certainly didn't say much for their own chances of survival.

'I don't believe you,' he said, a sudden beat of confidence in his chest; just a metre or so from his left foot, his eye had been drawn to Marita's gun.

Virginie Cabrille rolled her shoulders in a lazy shrug.

'I am really not bothered, Chief Inspector, whether you believe me or not. Just please don't imagine that anyone's coming to help you.'

Beside him he could hear Claudine start to whimper softly, desperate to get her daughter out of there, away to safety, but unable to do anything about it, the blood still dripping from their wounds. He put his hand on her wrist and squeezed tightly. He heard her sniff and take a breath, trying to settle herself.

'Ah, Madame Eddé, I believe?' said Virginie Cabrille, turning her attention to Claudine. 'And your daughter, Midou, if I'm not mistaken. How nice to meet you at last. And so much prettier than those photos we have of you.' She lifted the gun and touched the end of its silencer to her lips, gave a little frown, as though of recognition. And then, 'You remind me . . . you remind me of that woman in the TV ad. You know, the one for that moisturiser . . .'

But Jacquot wasn't listening. Dropping his head to his chest so Virginie Cabrille wouldn't see what he was looking at, his eyes locked on to Marita's gun, gauging the distance, working out how to reach it, make a grab for it, aim and fire it . . .

He wondered if he could do it. The pain would be gigantic, of course, and Virginie Cabrille already had a gun in her hand, but there was nothing else for it.

Their only chance . . .

As unobtrusively as he could, he started to shift his position – as if he was uncomfortable, needed to accommodate his pain – pushing away a little from Claudine, and putting himself another few centimetres closer to the gun. He also needed to keep Virginie talking, distract her somehow.

'So I was right then,' he said, interrupting the TV ad talk, taking advantage of the moment to reposition himself once again. 'It *was* you? Behind all this?'

'Yes, you were right,' she replied, turning back to him. 'I could see it in your eyes when you came to Roucas Blanc, that you'd made me, knew it was me. I'm right, too, aren't I?'

Jacquot nodded, shifted position again, leaning over onto his right hip as though to ease the pain in his left. The movement put him another few centimetres closer to the gun.

'From that moment, yes. After we left, I just couldn't shake the idea that you had something to do with it. I didn't know how . . . didn't know about the sisters then. All I knew was that you were involved. Supplying the killers, supporting them.'

Virginie Cabrille sighed.

'They had a good run, didn't they? Absolutely ruthless, the pair of them. *Alors*, it hasn't quite worked out as we'd planned . . . You and that girl, that sidekick of yours. It was supposed to be different, you see. The two of you were meant to suffer, like all the others. Not die.'

'But why? Why involve yourself? Why take the risk?' asked Jacquot, desperate for more time, praying her attention would wander, that something would distract her.

'Why? Because Taddeus and Tomas were special,' she replied, her voice still low, but filled with menace, suddenly pushing herself away from the dresser, making the flowerpot towers on the topmost shelf wobble and grate. 'For twenty years they looked out for me . . . became closer to me than my own family. Taught me every-thing I know,' she continued, coming towards them, stooping now to pick up Marita's gun, smiling at Jacquot as she straightened up, shaking her head; she'd seen it too, seen what he'd been planning.

Jacquot sagged, closed his eyes and let his head fall forward as chill despair washed through him. She had won, snatched away his one chance of levelling the odds. They were surely dead now.

'When they died,' she continued, 'trying to protect me, I knew I had a score to settle. Just like their family.'

Swinging the two guns by their trigger guards, Virginie Cabrille stood in front of him, a couple of steps away, just out of reach.

Jacquot raised his head, looked up at her.

'They were hired guns,' he said. 'Nothing more. Killers. Just a pair of low-life hoodlum *gorilles*.'

'That's right. They were,' she said, her voice hardening, eyes narrowing. 'But they were *my* hoodlums, Chief Inspector. My

351

brothers too. Blood brothers. And I wanted someone to pay for what happened to them. Wanted it very much. And I mean, really pay. Pay dearly. And you know what? I knew I could do it. I knew I could get away with it. Which is what I'm doing now.'

The next instant she stopped swinging the guns and flipped them forward, into her grip, their long silenced muzzles ranging between Jacquot, Claudine and Midou.

'So who first, Chief Inspector?' She levelled one of the guns on Midou. 'Why don't we start with the girl? She won't feel a thing, I promise.'

'*Non, non, non*. You can't, you just can't,' Claudine cried out, harsh and then suddenly defiant. 'Don't you dare, don't you even think such a thing . . .' And she pulled Midou to her, tried to scrabble away, pushing out her shoulder and half turning her back to shield her daughter from the gun.

'For God's sake, wait, wait!' said Jacquot, desperate to stop what was happening, trying to lever himself towards Virginie Cabrille, holding up a blood-smeared hand as though to push her away, push the gun aside.

It was a hopeless effort, and he knew it.

She was going to shoot Midou.

And then Claudine.

And then him.

She'd leave him till last.

He could see it in her eyes.

She was going to make him watch.

Claudine had sensed it too, just as he had.

'Please, please. I beg you,' she called from behind him, her voice softening, pleading. 'She's my daughter. She's seen nothing. Me, Daniel, okay. But not my daughter. You can't . . . you just . . .'

'Oh, but I just can,' said Virginie Cabrille. 'Here, watch . . .'

And she thumbed back the hammer – a double click – and moved a little to one side, to see past Claudine's protective shoulder, to take proper aim on the bloodied girl.

'Ah, there she is, there she is. I can see her . . .'

352

And Jacquot watched in horror and disbelief as Virginie Cabrille's finger tightened on the trigger.

'No,' he cried out. 'No, no, no . . .' and flung himself towards her, reaching out for her legs, hoping somehow to throw her off balance, to bring her down.

But she stepped back, out of range, steadied the gun again, and . . .

In the confines of the basement the gun shot was deafening, a blast of sound loud enough to cover Claudine's shrill, piercing scream.

A blast.

A mighty, shattering blast.

For several seconds Jacquot tried to make sense of it.

A single blast. An echoing, terrible, clattering sound that bounced off the walls of the room and rang in his head.

A gunshot. A real gunshot.

But Virginie Cabrille was using one of the sisters' guns.

With a silencer, screwed into the muzzle.

There could be no blast.

There could be no gunshot. Just that low *phut*.

That's when Jacquot saw the figure in the doorway.

Brunet, lowering his gun.

And Virginie Cabrille – a wide-eyed look of shock on her face, her chest pushed out as though she was trying to straighten her shoulders, the guns dropping from her hands, her eyes closing with a flutter and her body toppling forward.

80

'I SAW HER COME THROUGH the trees at the back of the house,' said Brunet, kneeling beside Jacquot on the basement floor. The medics had him laid out, flat on his back, his left trouser leg scissored open from waistband to knee. Pressure pads had been applied to his hip and a saline drip attached to his arm.

Jacquot was the last to be treated. When the medics arrived he'd put them to work on Claudine and Midou first, watching as the two women were treated, their wounds attended to, the blood loss halted. As soon as they'd been stretchered from the basement, the medics had set to work on him.

'At first I couldn't think who it was . . .' continued Brunet. '. . . How she'd got through . . . Why the two *képis* back in the woods hadn't seen her.'

'Did she kill them?' asked Jacquot, trying to remember their faces, their names.

'Just the one,' said Brunet. 'Ferdi, the older of the two. My guess is he must have seen her. The other one doesn't remember a thing, just a major chop to the neck and a helluva headache. Garbachon, too, and the other *képi*, out cold and locked in the boot like you said.'

Jacquot winced as a needle was plunged into his thigh.

One of the medics gave him an apologetic look. Had to be done. Sorry.

'I waited till she was out of sight behind the house,' Brunet continued, 'and then came after her. By the time I got to the terrace, there was no sign of her. Then I saw the body in the salon and thought it must be her. I was checking her out when I heard Claudine start screaming. After that, it all happened so fast . . .'

But Jacquot was having trouble concentrating, a gentle, swaddling heaviness creeping over him. He tried to blink his eyes into focus, but he felt them drift away from Brunet's face to the ceiling above him.

'Won't be long now,' Jacquot heard one of the medics say.

The words had a strange, dipping texture to them, as though the medic was in a different room. Distant. A little tipsy, maybe.

'I think he's gone aready,' he heard Brunet reply. 'Eyes are closed . . . mouth open. Just like he is when he takes a nap after lunch . . .'

Jacquot tried to close his mouth and open his eyes, tried to say something, tried to think of something to say.

But it was suddenly beyond him.

Nothing was working . . .

81

IT SEEMED TO JACQUOT THAT he'd been trying to open his eyes for a long time. And now, at last, he had managed to do it. Squinting, blinking, trying to focus, a few cautious glances to left and right to establish where he was – not yet confident enough to move his head. A stretch of slatted blinds. A wall-mounted television on an extendable arm. A canula taped to the inside of his elbow with a plastic drip feed attached to it. Stiff sheets, and the smell of chemicals and polish. A bedside table with a water carafe and glass.

A private room. A hospital.

He was in a hospital and he was alive.

It took a few more minutes to check himself out, a kind of mental inventory, sending out messages to his arms and legs, fingers and toes, testing everything; finally lifting his head from the pillow, raising an arm, trying to bring saliva into his parched mouth. He looked back at the bedside table. The water carafe was a torment. And remained so. He might lift his head and raise an arm, but there was no way he was going to reach that carafe and pour himself something to drink. The great weight of bandaging that he could feel wadded around his hip, not to mention the possibility of pain, of doing further damage to himself, made that a reach too far.

He'd been shot in the hip. He remembered a jagged, splintery

356

entry wound on the jut of his pelvis, and a flapping exit wound at the back and top of his thigh . . .

But the next thing that came into his head – like beaming flashes of light – were the names Claudine and Midou.

Where were they? How were they? Were they close by?

In the same hospital? Beyond the blind, which he could tell from movements on the other side had been placed on an indoor window?

'Welcome back, Chief Inspector. You had us worried for a moment.'

For a moment . . . For a moment . . .

A woman drifted into view.

She hadn't been there a moment ago . . . He hadn't heard a door open or close . . .

He turned towards her and tried to focus on her. Her hair was dark and tied back and she wore black-framed glasses. She was dressed in a white lab coat unbuttoned over a grey shirt and jeans. There was no stethoscope around her neck, but Jacquot knew she was a doctor.

'I'm in a hospital . . .' he began. So stupid. Of course he was.

'Clinique Aix Pasteur. And I'm Doctor Parri. The one who stitched you up.'

Stitched you up . . . Stitched you up . . .

She gave him a smile that overlapped the last three words. When she spoke, it seemed that the words didn't quite match the movements of her mouth. A kind of time delay, as though his ears were learning how to hear again. It was the strangest sensation. He knew he was coming round from an anaesthetic, but . . .

But then he remembered something, something important:

'Claudine? Claudine Eddé?' The name came out with a croak. 'She came in with me. Is she here? Is she okay?'

Dr Parri moved to the bedside table, poured some water. His eyes tried to follow her but she was always just ahead of him. He felt a hand come behind his head . . . a glass tilted to his lips. A hard rim that caught his lips. And cool, fresh water. It seemed to sluice into his mouth, and he felt it spill down his chin before he worked out how to contain it, swallow it.

'One floor below,' the doctor was telling him, as she lowered his head to the pillow, returned the glass to the bedside table. 'She will be pleased to hear you are back with us,' she continued, taking a tissue to wipe away the spill of water on his chin.

Back with us . . . Back with us . . .

Another overlapping smile.

'And Midou? Midou Bécard, her daughter?'

'Also one floor below, and also on the mend. The baby too.'

Again the last three words seemed to come after the doctor had finished speaking.

The baby too . . . The baby too . . .

The words took a moment to register.

Baby? Baby?

Midou? Pregnant? It couldn't be.

Jacquot felt himself frowning, trying to work it out – the when, the where? The who?

It seemed the doctor sensed his uncertainty. She coloured slightly and faltered.

'Your wife Claudine is pregnant, Chief Inspector. Four months. Didn't you know?'

Didn't you know . . . ? Didn't you know . . . ?

Jacquot took a breath, was suddenly quite unable to order his thoughts.

Claudine, pregnant? She was pregnant?

Jacquot felt tears brim and his throat thicken.

'I . . .'

ALSO AVAILABLE IN ARROW

Confession

Martin O'Brien

'Tight plotting, excellent characterisation. Jacquot is here to stay'
Daily Mail

'Wonderfully inventive and involving . . . Jacquot is top of le cops'
Daily Express

Chief Inspector Daniel Jacquot knows the streets of Marseilles like
the back of his hand. He ought to – he was born there. And
Marseilles knows him, as the hero who once scored the winning try
against England at Twickenham. But now he is a cop, passionate,
incorruptible and often inspired.

When the niece of Marseilles' Chief Examining Magistrate vanishes
into thin air, and another girl is found dead, it is to Jacquot that the
authorities turn. Working undercover for the first time in his career,
he finds himself in the terrible underworld of his beloved city –
locked in a deadly battle of wits with a woman whose long and
unforgiving memory is matched only by her taste for pain.

'A sexually-charged atmosphere that is as chilling
as it is engaging' *Sydney Morning Herald*

'The Marseilles scene . . , seems to be written by a native.
O'Brien's ability to deliver a sense of place makes him
worth watching' *Washington Post*

arrow books

THE POWER OF READING

Visit the Random House website and get connected with information on all our books and authors

EXTRACTS from our recently published books and selected backlist titles

COMPETITIONS AND PRIZE DRAWS Win signed books, audiobooks and more

AUTHOR EVENTS Find out which of our authors are on tour and where you can meet them

LATEST NEWS on bestsellers, awards and new publications

MINISITES with exclusive special features dedicated to our authors and their titles

READING GROUPS Reading guides, special features and all the information you need for your reading group

LISTEN to extracts from the latest audiobook publications

WATCH video clips of interviews and readings with our authors

RANDOM HOUSE INFORMATION including advice for writers, job vacancies and all your general queries answered

Come home to Random House

www.rbooks.co.uk